I0699039

# Spilt Seed

## A Comedy cum Tragedy

All rights reserved
Published January 20th 2025 in the United States of America by Big Fun Words Inc.
LCCN: 2025900271
ISBN: 979-8-9865971-2-6
Kindle ISBN: 979-8-9865971-3-3

Cover Design by Spilt Seed LLC.
Cover Art is used under license from Png Kong
Typefaces used on Book Cover is Party Std
and Garamond, Copyrighted by Monotype Typography Ltd
Used under license

Typeface used in book is Garamond
Created by Claude Garamond. Copyrighted by Monotype Typography Ltd
Used under license

Printed in the United States of America

Big Fun Words Inc.
1309 Coffeen Ave
Suite 5626
Sheridan, Wyoming 82801
www.bigfunwords.com

This book is dedicated to the people of the United States of America
May we always be free and may we always aspire to be brave.

Table of contents


Chapter 0                                                                                          1
Snip, Snip, Accidents happen. Introduction to the Narrator.
Chapter 1                                                                                          4
Meeting some gods. Decisions.
Chapter 2                                                                                         10
Resurrection.  Awakening.
Chapter 3                                                                                         13
Waking up is hard to do. Is this sexual healing?
Chapter 4                                                                                         23
Welcome to the world. Kismet. Robots are everywhere.
Chapter 5                                                                                         31
A bad day for women's rights and the Tampa Bay Lighting.
Joyful new beginnings.
Chapter 6                                                                                         36
Holy shit, the robots are everywhere!
Chapter 7                                                                                         39
Dr. Conrad Petersen is Twitterpated.
Norma Leah falls in love. Weirdness is relative.
Chapter 8                                                                                         44
The food here sucks. A window to the world.
The view isn't pretty.
Chapter 9                                                                                         58
Conrad Peterson has a date. Fred is going out.
Chapter 10                                                                                        63
Introducing the real Millie.
Chapter 11                                                                                        68
Weird Shit happens everywhere. We are going back in time.
Chapter 12                                                                                        71
'Don't call me Kitty Katz' She hearts Yoda.
Robot Doctors get all up in your Netherlands now.
Sad news is a part of life.
Chapter 13                                                                                        77
Reality sucks.
Chapter 14                                                                                        88
Hole in One. Your electric transporter goes how far?
Chapter 15                                                                                       101
Some people whack off more than others.
Should we be eating beef? Shit happens.
Chapter 16                                                                                       117
It's hard for an OBGYN Doctor. Patient Thyme is Healed! Homeless. Shared Experiences.
Chapter 17                                                                                       124
A long ride. Alligators. Life's a beach.
Chapter 18                                                                                       135
Sometimes tidbits need to be inserted into a story, so it makes sense.

Table of Contents, Continued.
Chapter 19                                                              139
High school Graduation.
The parental unit is pleased. Young love.
Chapter 20                                                              147
Goodbye hospital. Taxi ride. Civil unrest.
Government Housing is for shit.
Chapter 21                                                              160
More Kismet. Don't call me Liz. Loving some eggplant.
Chapter 22                                                              165
America gets Foreign Humanitarian Aid.
Human Doctors. An Awakening.
Chapter 23                                                              170
Sookie needs help. It's all on film. Jesus had big feet?
Chapter 24                                                              181
Another Visit with the Cow and the Grasshopper.
A directive. Dreams.
Chapter 25                                                              187
Stand back, I don't know how this is going to work!
Lube is nice.
Chapter 26                                                              191
We are lawyers now! You are not gay, are you?
Chapter 27                                                              198
A brand-new husband. What's a klaxon?
Chapter 28                                                              203
Whip cream tastes good. Wendy Williams reaches out.
Chapter 29                                                              206
The Texas Militia finds its Captain. Torpedoes away!
Chapter 30                                                              216
There is a hole in the ship, dear Kitty, dear Kitty.
Chapter 31                                                              218
Tension. What are we?
Chapter 32                                                              222
Meeting the friends. Willem is not well.
Chapter 33                                                              227
Is that a shark? Rescue at sea.
Chapter 34                                                              231
It's been a long time.  We aren't all that close.
Willem is really in bad shape. A surprise phone call.
Chapter 35                                                              242
Yoda meets the Robot god.
Wendy and Willem get a surprise.
Chapter 36                                                              250
Let's talk about what happened over the past twenty years. Surely, we all agree?
Chapter 37                                                              255
Robots can have sex and kill people.
Chapter 38                                                              258
Now we know. Millie gets outed. Big Prayers. Bigger Plans.

Table of Contents, Continued.
Chapter 39                                                    265
Judge this. Not rosy in Texas
Chapter 40                                                    269
Debating with the Priest.
The Government would like your sperm.
Chapter 41                                                    282
Swoop in and pick the boy up. Those are some nice tits.
Chapter 42                                                    288
Court is in session. Texas Criminal Justice Hospital Facility
Chapter 43                                                    291
The Calvary arrives. Prayers. Delivering the goods.
Chapter 44                                                    302
Let our people go.
Chapter 45                                                    306
Nothing is easy.
Chapter 46                                                    308
Hard time. The Rock. An idea.
Chapter 47                                                    314
Cozbi, on the scene. Texas Militia In Action.
Chapter 48                                                    318
Flying on another Jet Plane.
Marmalade's Church. Business issues.
Chapter 49                                                    325
Bob beats the bishop while a queen makes her move.
Chapter 50                                                    330
Leaving the yellow rose behind.
Introduction to the Bible, Juice style. That Church is Wack!
Chapter 51                                                    343
This is what being is poor is like now.
Stupid Wagers. Bad Proposal.
Chapter 52                                                    348
Driving. Meet my wife.
Making A New Friend. Information controls the world.
Chapter 53                                                    363
Bob is in a bad place. His parents, worse.
Chapter 54                                                    371
Planned Parenthood calling. This happened fast. Too Fast.
Chapter 55                                                    380
Nice to meet you, officers.
Throwing rocks in glass houses is not productive.
Chapter 56                                                    386
Getting people riled up is profitable. Texas Legislature.
A bad day, indeed.
Chapter 57                                                    395
You knew about this?!?
This is how democracy works.

Table of Contents, Continued.

Chapter 58    399  
Dinner. New bed to sleep in. Conrad says.  
How it was. How it is.

Chapter 59    425  
The Police are here to talk to you.  
What is that thing and how do I put it on?

Chapter 60    433  
Working it out.

Chapter 61    438  
Call a lawyer! Household appliance fun.

Chapter 62    445  
Passing out. Another visit to the great beyond.  
Breaking rocks and ribs.

Chapter 63    452  
Everyone gets his day in court. No one wants this.

Chapter 64    460  
Hoover's aim is true. Setting Mitch Free. Rescue.

Chapter 65    472  
Public reactions. Wedding bells.

Chapter 66    477  
A better day in court. Less than brief.  
Not Guilty, Guilty. Your name is, *what?*

Chapter 67    486  
The Priest has arrived. Moral Quandary. A plan is hatched.

Chapter 68    497  
Kismet. Keys to happiness.

Chapter 69    503  
RickRolled. A children's play.  
Sermon in the Lion's den. Shots are fired.

Chapter 70    514  
Old school chums. My ego is hungry.

Chapter 71    520  
An audience with the gods.  
Darkness

Chapter 72    527  
Resurrection. Rickrolled, again.

Chapter 73    533  
Unfinished Business. Now we know.

Chapter 74    538  
Where this story ends.  
Five Years Later

Notes from the Authors    542

**Spilt Seed.  Some things to know before reading.**

Real court cases – meaning the ones that really happened and have some effect on our lives, look like this:
*Price Waterhouse vs Hopkins (1989)*

Imaginary Court Cases - meaning the ones we executed literary license and created, look like this:
Union of Gerbil Services vs Feline Protective Patrol (2045)

This book contains references, veiled and direct, to companies and persons that exist or existed in the real world.  Neither the authors nor the publisher has any association with named companies or public personas of real people mentioned or referenced.  Thoughts and opinions expressed in *Spilt Seed* are those of the authors and do not reflect the opinions, actions or future actions of the publisher or any named entities.

Spilt Seed is a work of fiction. The authors are not responsible for bunched underwear, flaming hair, emotional outbursts or any one of dozens of personal reactions that may occur when reading Spilt Seed.  It's just words, organized in a specific order for the reader's entertainment.

There are fucking swear words in this goddamn book. A lot of them.   If readers are offended by swear words, the rest of the subject matter is likely to be a goddamn freak out.  Readers have been fucking warned.

Comments, positive and negative are welcome.  Death threats, threats to our safety or the safety of our loved ones is not welcomed at all.  Such things will be turned over to the non-fictional authorities.
Comments can be sent to:

LoveFreedom@SpiltSeed.com

Chapter 0
Snip, Snip, Accidents happen. Introduction to the Narrator.
Someplace in the United States of America
Land of the Free(ish) Home of the Brave(ish)


*K C A M. I see the letters clearly in my rear-view mirror, reflected off a big shiny grill on what, as I learned much, much later, was a fully loaded Mack dump truck.*

*I blame the accident that is about to happen on sex. Specifically, the relatively successful three way I had a week prior with the checkout nurse at the vasectomy clinic I had just come from, Veronica and her roommate whose name would escape me even if I had ever bothered to learn it when I was sandwiched in between the two of them a few weeks earlier. Had Veronica not been so familiar with me and the purpose for my visit to the vasectomy clinic where she happened to work, maybe she would have insisted that I have an actual driver to take me away from the flop and chop I had experienced not more than thirty minutes earlier.*

*"It will be nice to go bareback next time." She said to me with one of those grins that is usually reserved for when a person has just experienced mind blowing sex or is anticipating an extra-large chocolate ice cream cone.*

*Yes, I conflate sex and eating ice cream. Who doesn't?*

*I remember that Veronica patted the top of my head like a schoolboy and handed me the extra-large bag of frozen peas I had brought along to celebrate with. I can almost visualize the stupid grin I had on my face when she asked if I was sure the car could drive itself. "Of course it can!" I'm sure I rubbed the dashboard like an idiot. "This car is awesome! It came and got me, didn't it?" My Tesla Model S could be summoned from a parking space. It sure as shit was not able to safely drive me home or anywhere else. At least not without a sober, relatively competent human person behind the steering wheel. After I watched the very cute but obviously not very smart nurse walk her very tight ass back into the mirrored doors of the clinic, I got out of the front passenger seat of the car, walked around and got in the driver's side and told the car in only a slightly slurred voice to take me home.*

*Getting hit by a Mack truck wasn't the first accident or even the second. The first accident was the big bag of frozen peas breaking open. I remember looking down at the little green frozen orbs falling like a waterfall onto the floorboard of the car.*
*In my inebriated state, (to be perfectly clear, I was totally fucked up at the time. Mostly on the valium pills I took, but those were added to the drug store vodka I picked up and drank on the way to the snip joint. I am pretty sure that the relaxing effect of anesthesia probably helped things out some as well.)*

Pro hint: when they tell you not to drink before or after a surgery, listen.

*The alcohol induced haze likely contributed to the extended amount of time my head was down as my eyes were studying the marvelous pattern the frozen orbs of relief made on the floor mats of the Tesla. I might not have completely comprehended the car announcing that the self-driving capabilities of the automobile were being disabled. The second accident is when the front of the Tesla came to an abrupt halt against the big bumper on the back of a tractor trailer. I caught a glimpse of that big ol' K C A M just as the airbag in the steering wheel blew its load covering me with white dust. This is when the opening credits of the third accident begin. Things went dark for me in a hurry when the back window exploded. I'd like to think in those moments I was theorizing on the merits of the Irresistible Force Paradox. We've already established I can be a bit a goddamn moron. I was probably thinking about sex.*

*Yeah... That's how I got to this spot right now. Sex.*

*My name is Dr. Justin Thyme. I was a podiatrist in case you give a fuck, and you shouldn't because I don't give a damn about your feet and I'm not going to be your doctor in any case.*

*What you should know is this: The story I am about to take you through has absolutely nothing to do with me.*

*Well, most of it has nothing to do with me.*

*I am just a student of the bullshit that happened before my accident and witness to the malarky that I experienced after.*

# Chapter 1
## Meeting some gods. Decisions.

*"You paying attention to me?"*

*The darkness of my being remains. I know I am out of it. I may be dead. I may be alive. Maybe I am someplace in between. I don't know if I have been out for an hour or a few days. There has not been anything except a vast nothingness in my head for an indeterminant amount of time.*

*"Yoo Hoo. You with me?"*

*It's a female sounding voice. Normally, I would happily jump to attention at such a thing however, this female voice sounds like it is coming from someone's grandmother or a matronly radio announcer. I look in the darkness of my mind and watch, completely unconcerned as the black is broken by a white cow that walks towards me. A rather large grasshopper rides on its back.*

*"Is that you talking?" I ask the cow.*

*"Do you see someone else here that might be talking?"*

*"There is a grasshopper on your back." I observe. For some reason, the talking cow isn't what I cared about first.*

*"Do grasshoppers talk to you often? The grasshopper is my... Let's just say she is my good luck charm." The cow answers.*

*"Cows don't talk to me often." I say.*
*"Never, I would think." The cow scoffs.*

*There is silence that is neither uncomfortable nor particularly comfortable. Like the black that had been my existence for the foretold indeterminant amount of time, the silence just is. The grasshopper shifts on the cow's back.*

"We are waiting for Bruno." The cow explains patiently. She starts chewing on something. Cud, I suppose, although being a city dwelling sort of person, I don't really know what cud is.

I also don't know who Bruno is and it doesn't feel right to ask. For all I know, the cow is talking to the insect and not me. Like just about everything else, whom the cow is addressing and who or what Bruno is doesn't seem particularly important. A few minutes pass. Hell, it could be a few hours or days for all I know. Time has become a very nebulous thing in the workings of my brain. Commotion comes from some point I cannot see, but I can definitely sense something. The black seems to shake as a giant bear materializes from the darkness. For reasons only known by the bear, I suppose... he has a giant gold earring in his left ear.

"Hello, Bruno." The cow says politely. We were just sitting here with Justin.
"I was at the celebration of arrival service with Farrah Fawcett. She is still so sad about her death. Did you tell this dude why we are here?" The bear makes a motion with its paw. I assume the motion is at me, but who knows?

The cow shakes her head slowly. "Justin didn't ask."

The bear looks at me from the darkness with a curious expression. "Why didn't you ask what a cow is doing in your subconscious? Doesn't a talking cow seem fucking strange to you?"

"Farah Fawcett is dead?" I ask. "Am I dead? Also... a talking cow and a talking bear should seem odd to me, I would think. Because your presence here and your unusual ability to speak isn't seeming all that odd, makes me think that I am indeed, dead."

The bear looks at me with a bored expression. "Have you always been in the habit of answering your own questions?"

The cow moos softly. "He is a doctor, Bruno."

A piece of paper materializes in the bear's paw. I have no idea where it came from. The bear isn't wearing one of those cute vests that bears always seem to be wearing *in animated videos and in children's books. I realize that I am not inclined to ask the bear anything. A sure sign of death, not being interested in anything, I think to myself. At least I believe I am thinking it.*

*"Says here, he was a fucking podiatrist. Almost doesn't qualify as a doctor... probably had a foot fetish and got off on it." The bear growls. I think the bear might have a cockney accent. Am I making the accent up in my mind? I sigh. I don't know if I am thinking or even hearing things correctly.*

*"You doctors are predictably alike. You think you know everything! Farah has been dead for thirteen years, you fool. You didn't know that? She died the same day as Michael Jackson. We aren't celebrating him though. Not yet. He has work to do." The bear is jumping around in an animated fashion. What was that children's series of books called? With the bears? Did they have cockney accents? I can't remember... but that's how the bear named Bruno was jumping around. Like the bears in those children's books. It starts to bother me that I don't feel anything at all. This is what dead is. Talking animals that may have pet insects. The cow must be here to take me to whatever happens next. I am not sure what the bear means. Maybe the bear is the devil or some sort of god. Does the grasshopper mean something? I don't know and I realize, as much as I can realize anything, I don't feel enough to care.*

*"I think I was like seventeen in 2009. Farrah Fawcett wasn't in my spank bank if you know what I mean. To be honest, I didn't know much about Michael Jackson either. Except you know, the gross stuff."*

*The bear gives me a look and shakes his head. "Justin Thyme, you were in an accident. A car accident. Do you recall that in your spank bank?"*

*"You are using that colloquialism incorrectly." I say, rather bravely since I believe I am now dead and these two, make that, three animals... still don't know what the role of the grasshopper is... are here to escort me to the next life. "I do recall the accident. I hit a truck. Then another truck hit me."*

*"Totally your fault, you dumbass. You are a fucking doctor, and you drove after a goddamn vasectomy. It's as dumb as Jackson taking propofol to fall asleep. Dumber. At least he wasn't a danger to others." The bear growls. He turns to the cow. "You did tell me this one is a smart ass. You weren't wrong. He is also a moron."*

*"I am never wrong." The cow says calmly.*

*"I was thinking of blaming it on that nurse. Veronica. She put me in the car." I say with a defensive tone. I know if I could feel anything, I would be relieved that I could remember the woman's name. Remembering the names of the women I sleep with has always been tough.*

*"That girl is so dumb she almost drowned when she was ten and dropped her scratch and sniff book in a swimming pool." The bear scoffs.*

*"I don't think I understand what you are telling me." I say to the bear. I really don't. I see the cow roll its eyes.*

*"That girl is so dumb; she really thought your car would drive your sorry ass home." The bear's head seems to come close to mine. "Your fault. Not hers. We don't blame dumb animals when things go wrong for animals smart enough to know better."*

*Ah, Veronica wasn't that bright. That is probably a true statement that I cannot debate. I have never been in the habit of giving my potential sexual conquests IQ tests before I bed them.*

*"Careful, Bruno. We don't want him to know too much just yet." The cow says with a tone so like my grandmother that I swear it sounds exactly like her telling me not to tease her cat. She turns to me. "We are here to see if you want to stay."*

*"Stay?" I ask. Know too much? I think to myself. What am I not supposed to know?*

*The cow nods. I note that it appears the grasshopper has elected to take a nap. "Yes, stay. As a human, on earth."*

*"Is there an alternative?" I ask. I don't remember any talk of alternatives in Sunday school, but I also can't remember the Sunday school teacher's name who I was constantly trying to get a peak down her dress that was always favorably too loose around the neckline for a thirteen-year-old horny boy.*

*"Yes. The alternative is not being a human or alive on earth." The bear growls.*

*"Do I get to hang with Farah Fawcett if I stay here?" I ask.*

*"Did you hang with her a lot when you and she were both walking around on earth?" The bear asks.*

*I think I shrug.*

*I have no idea if I really pulled off a good fuck you kind of shrug. I know I can't wave my hands in front of where I can see so... maybe the whole sarcastic shrug thing is lost on these three. "I did not, of course. Maybe I saw the movie "10" once."*

*"That's Bo Derek, you moron." The bear sighs. "Unless Julie Andrews is in your spank bank."*

*"Hey! Now you got it right!" I exclaim. I sigh. I think I want to feel tired, but feeling anything really seems out of reach currently. "I guess I would like to stay among the living." It occurs to me to provide more clarity. "On earth."*

*"I am so glad to hear that." The cow says with a tone that sounds like a cross between a car salesman and a suicide hotline operator talking to her fifth customer of the day. "Justin Thyme, you are a very, very important person in the future. Times are becoming very dangerous. When you wake up, the world will be a very different place, but you will be rested and healed and able to help people in ways only you can."*

*"You done with the pep talk, Reverend Moo?" The Bear asks sarcastically.*

*"Reverend Moo. That is pretty fucking funny." I comment. The grasshopper wakes up and spits. A big blob of blackish brown goo flies towards me."*

*"Your good luck charm upchucked on me." I say.*

*"Now you will have luck." The cow replies.*

*"Luck is only beneficial if it is good luck. How long will I be out? I'd like to watch the NHL finals, if possible, I think the Avalanche have a chance." I say.*

*"Nighty night, you ignorant mother fucker." The bear growls. Without warning, a large paw swipes across my face and everything... the cow, the lucky grasshopper, the bear with the earring and the darkness... is all gone.*

Chapter 2
Resurrection.  Awakening.
Someplace in the United States of America
Land of the Free(ish) Home of the Brave(ish)


*I am aware that the darkness has returned. There is nothing else. I'm not sure what there was before there was darkness. More darkness I was unaware of? I can't feel anything more than what the darkness provides, which is nothing. I look into the abyss of my mind for the cow, its lucky charm or even the bear. I vaguely remember the earring wearing bear swiping at me with its massive paw.*

*The darkness breaks a little in the distance. I wait, feeling no anticipation or worry. The bear lumbers into sight, it is walking slowly. As Bruno's features become clearer, I see that the large golden earring has been swapped for a diamond. The bear gets close, or what I perceive as close and stands on its hind legs. "Justin Thyme?"*

*"Yeah." I answer. "That's me. The guy you knocked out yesterday. Or... the day before, I guess."*

*The bear lifts its head and laughs. It is a long and hearty laugh. I see the bear's teeth and tongue. I am telling you, what I see is exactly like what an animator would create if he drew a laughing cartoon bear. Only, no vest.*

*"Nice earring. You dig that up yourself or find it on the street on some dude's ear?" I ask.*

*"My status has changed from when we last visited. I am higher on the ladder now." Bruno says. "You have been remembered. You are lucky I am here. Sometimes you meat puppets just get forgotten."*
*"Am I?" I say with what I think is a sarcastic lilt in my voice. "Lucky? I am not sure lucky is how I feel." Even though, I feel nothing. Maybe that is lucky. The cow walks into the picture slowly. The grasshopper still on her back. "He is with us." The cow says softly. "Good... Good. It is his time."*

*"My time for what?" I ask. "Dinner? I suppose I could eat." I don't remember ever feeling hungry.*

*The cow shakes her head. "It is your time to pay back your debt of life. All living things owe a debt for the life they have been given no matter how short or long that life was."*

*"How much do I have to pay?" I ask. It occurs to me that I should be worried about the amount. Student loans, the payment on the condo, the lease payment on the Tesla. Things add up. I need to make sure I still have enough to keep up with my whoring lifestyle.*

*"All of you until time takes you." The cow says. The grasshopper jumps to the top of the cow's head. "As I told you before and I will tell you again, you are of great importance to the people you will soon serve. Do your best to make things better for all that you touch."*

*"I'm a podiatrist. I can help them not have sore feet." I offer. All of me? Until time takes me?  That sounds... terrible.*

*"You will be more than a doctor now." The cow says. She seems to gesture to the grasshopper who promptly coughs up another loogie of brown phlegm and spits it at me. "So long as the stain remains, you shall have the luck of the grasshopper."*

*"Grasshoppers are lucky? I thought they were locusts... like from the Bible."*
*"Grasshoppers and Locusts are two different beings." The cow says. "Don't believe everything... for that matter, anything... you read that was written when most of mankind was illiterate."*

*"Good advice, Reverend Moo." Bruno the bear growls. "I have to attend to the three United States President's annual memorial party. We need to get this going."*
*"The president died?" I ask, thinking about the guy that was President of the United States of America on the day of my accident. He was an old guy. People always joked about his age.*

*The bear shakes his head. "You will have some catching up to do when you get back. Monroe, Adams and Jefferson all died on this date."*

*"Do you celebrate everyone in heaven?" I ask. "Monroe, Adams and Jefferson died a long time ago. Where are you putting me?"*

*The grasshopper laughs first. It sounds like a little chuckle but continues in rapid fashion. The cow joins in, followed by the bear.*

*"What's so funny?" I ask.*

*"That you think we are from heaven!" The bear says as he comes close to me and looks back at the cow. "Any parting words?"*

*The cow shakes her head. It occurs to me that I do not know her name beyond the seemingly sarcastic Reverend Moo the bear had called her. "It's not going to be easy. Just do your best, Justin Thyme." She moos. "You will be fine. You have the luck of the grasshopper!"*

*The bear appears to look off in space before leaning forward. His snout seems millimeters from my face. "I have to tell you... you seem to attract spectacularly stupid people."*
*"Is that a warning?" I ask.*

*The bear shakes his head. "Just an observation about the confederacy of dunces that seem to constantly orbit you." From the darkness, Bruno's large paw comes swinging at my head and quite suddenly I am acutely aware of every possible nerve ending that exists in my body. As Bruno's image fades, I hear him growl, "Good luck on saving that twat waffle of a society you live in... you sarcastic bag of shit."*

*I'd try to take the time to explore the exact meaning of twat waffle with the bear if I weren't paralyzed with pain from the roots of my hair to bottoms of my feet.*

Chapter 3
Waking up is hard to do. Is this sexual healing?
Microsoft Hospital Powered by HoloLens Artificial Intelligence
Someplace in the United States of America
Land of the Free(ish) Home of the Brave(ish)


The pain. Oh, my lord, the pain. I can visualize it coursing through my body. It's like an enraged building fire that keeps finding new sources of fuel as it destroys the surrounding structure. I can't exactly move yet. Subconsciously, I think I need to try opening my eyes, but some part of my brain is screaming, *you will open the goddamn eyes when I tell you it is time to open the goddamn eyes!* I don't know where this asshole voice in my head came from. I suppose he has been there all along. Maybe I have never really needed a jack-booted thug based in my subconscious shouting at me until now. I have no idea how long this goes on, but eventually the neural forest fire on my face, torso and lower extremities starts to morph into that weird feeling when some limb or appendage falls asleep. That's when I become aware of a completely different sensation of movement across the entirety of my body with a pressure near my midsection.

I concentrate on taking a few breaths. In. Out. In. Out. I could use my hearing; I think to myself. As if a Willy Wonka is living in my head shouting orders to a flock of red blood cell sized Oompa Loompa's, that angry voice shouts out, *Open the goddamn ears, I guess we want to hear!*

My ears clear. The audible tones of a woman moaning with... *is that ecstasy?* The audible sounds of fucking, at least one side of it, fill my ear canals. Her moans are in sync with my movements back and forth. Well son of a bitch, I think, I'm getting laid. Picking right up where I left off. Must be Veronica. Hope she waited however long the snip snip doctor told me I needed to not stick my dick in something so not to explode my testicles or whatever hyperbolic threat the doctor mentioned after he finished cutting my plumbing and as such ending my ability to successfully fertilize any woman's egg.

Can I get some eyes on the action here? I ask the voices in my head. *Give me the mother fucking eyes!* The angry voice calls out with a resigned tone. I try and lift my eyelids. They are stuck in place. Not with sleepy crud or those annoying rocks that form in the corners of your eyes when you have a little cold or something. Stuck. Like taped shut. I can't see! I try and say. Nothing really comes out of my mouth. I'm not sure I can speak either. *Not my problem, Bro. I turned the eyes on. Some physical issue. Nerves are working fine!* The voice in my head calls out. *Try squinting. Maybe get some tears going!*

*Bro? My subconscious calls me Bro?* The back-and-forth motion on my middle slows a little as the audible sounds of pleasure grow louder. I take the advice of the voice in my head and squint my eyes as hard as I possibly can. I feel a few tears form and flow from my tear ducts. *It fucking hurts.* Working my eyelids up and down, I get what I now realize is tape covering my left, non-dominate eye to release. Nothing is budging on the right eye. I am rewarded for the effort by a stinging sensation as light crosses my retina for apparently the first time in a while. I squeeze my eyes back shut. The moans have turned to a steady stream of grunting and whoever is getting off on top of me is bearing down harder on my middle. I'd like to mention how awesome it feels, but honestly, I can't feel a damn thing down there other than the pressure. I take a deep breath and try and open that left eye again, working a little slower this time.

The tape pops from the skin on my cheek and flies out over my eyelashes. I try and move my head without much success. *Can I move a little here?* I ask the voice in my head.

*I'm giving it all I've got, Bro.* The voice in my head answers sarcastically.

I try raising my eyebrow a little as the motion picks back up. The woman on top of me comes into view. The first thing that catches my eye is the bright orange image of a swastika tattooed on the bottom of her chin, which is tilted back. We can eliminate Veronica as the jockey. *I am being railed by a damn Nazi. I think sourly.* The woman is wearing blue scrubs that button up. The top is open. A web of colorful tattoos covers her upper torso from her ears to what I can see of her midsection. She is grabbing and squeezing her left breast, which from what I can tell is tattooed with a very detailed image of the forty fifth president of the United States. The nipple appears to be the man's tongue sticking out. This cannot be real. I don't pick up tatted up women. Sure, there has been the odd heart or little animal inked here and discreetly there on a few. Full face tattoos? No. That would be a quick, *Nice to meet you, let me call you a ride share to a place called... somewhere else.* I must be back in some sort of not dead but not alive realm. What I am experiencing can't possibly be reality. I shift my left eye to the surrounding room. I find the clock on the wall. The little hand is almost on the five. The big one is pointing at the tattooed woman's boob. Maybe the eight or the nine. It's either four something in the morning or four something in the afternoon. My eye shifts to a digital board mounted in the center of the wall. I see my name, *Justin Thyme.* Under my name is some small writing. I think it says *GCS=1, 30 June 22.* Under that in bold letters is *CARE 04 JULY 42* followed by a list of more small writing.

*July fourth, two thousand and fucking forty-two?* My brain screams. The voice inside my head must be scared. He ain't making comment. I move my left eye around and return to the digital board. *GCS.* Glasgow Coma Scale. I may be a lowly podiatrist, but I did have to go to med school and learn all the clever acronyms not normally used in the pedestrian world of podiatry. The Glasgow Coma Scale... *GCS for short* is how hospitalist classify coma patients. There are different levels. Eyes open, eyes closed, responds to voices... or not. The number *1* designates a basic vegetable with remaining human characteristics, principally a pulse. Someone who is in medical storage, a person who is no longer a person. The hospital is waiting for GCS 1 patients to fully expire. Usually so organs can be harvested and the body replaced with another body in the same condition to follow through the same process.

I shift my attention back to the space in front of me and the movements that have changed. The woman grinding her loins into my unfeeling midsection must have finished. She is bent forward, breathing heavy, her hands planted on my chest. I can see now that the right boob has a detailed drawing of a blond-haired woman's face. Like the detailed drawing of Orange Jesus, the right nipple is centered where the lips would be on the drawing. A silver ring hangs from the end of the nipple, which seems to ruin the aesthetic of the drawing if I was being critical about a boob hanging in my face. Which I am because I have no idea how the boob has arrived in front of my face, who the boob belongs to and maybe most annoying, I have no idea who or what the picture covering the right boob depicts. The woman is still breathing heavy. I can't move my head to get a view of anything more than the swinging, drawn upon tits or the bright orange swastika inked on the bottom of the woman's chin.

I feel I need to say something clever to the woman and only one thing really comes to mind. With a tremendous amount of energy and effort, I say my first words in over twenty years. I am sure that the words come out more as an unintelligible mumble than a snappy remark.

"Was it as good for you as it was for me?"

The woman screams, reinforcing the fact that I can still hear a full range of octaves. Like a gymnast off a vault, she dismounts me, covering herself with the unbuttoned scrubs in the same movement. I am not sure I had ever seen anyone pull on a pair of pants that fast.

"You!" The midnight... or midday... rider says, breathing hard. "You are awake!"

I steal a glance at my uncovered middle. My erection is *magnificent!* I can't feel a damn thing down there, but, *my goodness,* is it... *large!* I look back at the woman who has buttoned her blue scrubs back up. I think I nod. "I am."
The woman turns and starts to leave.

"Wait!" I gasp. The words are hard. "Wait!"

She returns to the bedside, her tattooed face blushing. "Um, I was just checking on you. On a schedule. I check on you every night."

"I think you were raping me." I say, hoping that the cheeky tone I intended in my brain is making its way to my mouth.

She shakes her head quickly. "Was not." She pulls a blanket up over me. "The bot will be here in a minute to check your vitals."

"I think you did just check my vitals."

"Vitals are not my job. Bots do that."

"What do you do?" I ask as the door opens.

"Check the bots." The woman says. She backs against the wall as a silver phallic looking robot rolls into the room. "Human other than patient observed in room. Visiting hours are between seven am and five pm. Please exit the hospital immediately." A female voice announces.

I move my eye to look at the tattooed girl. She puts a finger up to her lips.

I watch the robot curiously with my one open eye. It has approached the left side of my hospital bed. A little door opens on the side of the robot's structure and a device juts out, grabbing my wrist. I feel pressure as my blood pressure is taken.

"Elevated blood pressure. Observation noted and reported. Heart rate within acceptable range." The female voice is soft and almost soothing. The blood pressure cuff is released and retracted. Another door opens and a small lance pokes my shoulder, followed by a swipe of a cold piece of metal.
"Analyzing blood sample. Sugar, Good. Essential electrolytes, Good. Cholesterol, Good." The Robot pulls the blanket from me, exposing the still hard erection. I'd will it to go down, but I'd only just mastered control over my left eye lid. Controlling the rest of my body is clearly going to take some time.

"Prescribed catheter not present. Condition reported. Priapism observed and reported." The blanket is replaced.

"Patient is resting comfortably in stable condition. Three anomalies observed and reported. Visiting guests asked to leave." Without another word the robot rolls out of the room, closing the door behind it.

"What the fuck?" I mumble.

My rapist moves closer to the bed, I can see through my one open eye that she appears bewildered. "You are not awake. This is not possible."

"And yet, here I am." I say. My voice is hoarse, and my throat is starting to hurt. By products of being asleep for twenty years, I suppose. My eye moves toward hers. "Can you take the tape off my other eye?"

Wordlessly, the woman quickly tears the surgical tape holding my right eyelid shut from my face. I feel bits of skin and eyebrow go with it. "Ouch." I moan, squeezing both eyes shut. She pulls the loose left tape off causing a small reverberation of the same pain.

"Coma." The woman points a tattooed arm and hand at the chart on the wall. "You are in coma. GCS One. Not conscious."

"That is typically a side effect of the medical condition known as a coma." I mumble, my eyes still shut. I open them slowly, mentally preparing myself for the dim lighting in my hospital room to stab my right retina. The sensation is just as bad as it was on my left eye when I was being ridden like a rocking horse.

"Is it really 2042?" I ask looking up at the woman. My vision is really fucked up. I think she has shiny blue hair. Must be the bad lighting in the room.

The woman shakes her head. "No. It's almost five in the morning."

"The year. Is the year 2042?" The bear had told me I was surrounded by a confederacy of dunces. I am starting to understand what he was referring to.
The woman nods.

"Am I paralyzed?" I ask. "I can't feel my legs." I put some serious thought to moving both my hands and am rewarded with the sensation of the blanket moving. "Hands work..." I look back to the woman who has a sheepish look on her well inked face.

"No. Not paralyzed." She dips her head and mumbles. "I gave you shot."

My mind races. "A shot?"

"Yeah. In your back."

Except for my conversations with the cow and the bear, my brain has not been especially active for twenty years. If I am being honest, I didn't really try hard in medical school to learn a ton. It wasn't a fetish that guided me toward podiatry. It was laziness. And... ok, *some* women's feet do turn me on a little, not that *those* women were regular patients of mine.

I think for a moment before it comes to me.

"You gave me a fucking spinal anesthesia?" I think I shake my head. The little voices in my head seem to have gone on lunch break.

The woman's eyes get big. "How do you know those words?"

"*Fucking* is big part of my vocabulary." I mutter. "How much did you give me?"

"This time, 25 mg bupivacaine."

"*This time?*" My voice, feeble as it is, seems to be in decline.

"I tried it a few times at 20 mg. You didn't last as long on that dose." She glances at my midsection. "25 mg did the trick."

Only little bits and pieces of my brain is online. I search for any memory of the different spinal anesthesia's and their half-life effectiveness on the body. Spinal injection of 25 mg of bupivacaine. I should regain feeling in my legs in a few hours. Maybe. If this woman knows what she is doing. "A few times? Why?" I ask. "Why would you do this?"

"Trying to get pregnant." The woman says. She takes some tape from the supply cabinet and tears off two strips. "I will tape you back up. You don't have long left."

I raise my right hand. It's a slow, sloth like movement. "Wait. What do you mean I don't have *long left?*"

"Six to nine months." The woman says. "The condition you have only last six to nine months. Then...." The woman makes a motion like she is being hung with a rope. "It's all over."

"How long have you been a nurse here?" I ask.

"Eight months now." The woman shrugs. "You only have a month left... maybe."

"How long have you been drugging me and riding me like American Pharoah?" I ask.

"Who is American Pharoah? Is he a patient here? Do coma patients communicate with each other? The other nurses must see to him." The woman shrugs. "Three months? I had to take a video course on how to do the spinal tap thing. That took a few days."

"You..." I am speechless. "You learned how to do a spinal tap on a video course? In a few days?" *I am doomed to a lifetime of scooting around in a wheelchair.*

"I did all my medical training on video. Spinal Taps are, like a whole hour! And the dude selling it was like Mexican or something. He had the towel on his head and everything. I could barely understand him cause' his American was so bad."

I take a deep breath in and exhale before saying what is likely the most medical thing I had ever said. "Bring me my charts."

The woman looks confused. She shakes her head from side to side. The hair isn't just blue. It has streaks of pink and yellow too. "You must mean your record."

"Charts. Record. List of what *the fuck* has been done to me while I have been laying in this bed." I narrow my eyes that are working a whole hell of a lot better now. "Yes, my record. Please get my record."

The tattooed arm juts out. "It is there." She drops the arm.

I don't look over at the electronic board on the wall before I say, "I don't see 25 mg of bupivacaine being administered through a spinal tap on that chart."

The woman snorts. "That's because I didn't put it in your record."

"What sort of hell have I woken up in?" I ask out loud.

"Microsoft Hospital Powered by HoloLens Artificial Intelligence." The woman answers. "That's where you are. We try to make people better." She shakes her head sadly. "But, not you. You won't be getting better. The record says that you will be gone in six to nine months probably. It's on your record. That's why I choose you."
"What's with the swastika." I ask. I don't expend the energy to point at her chin. "Are you a Nazi?"

"Nazis don't have hair." The woman says with a matter-of-fact tone, as if I asked her what day it is. She points at her multicolored hair. "I have hair, see. Can you see? You *are* in a coma." Her hand moves to the spot below the bottom of her chin, and she proudly pronounces, "If you mean my swastika, it means joy. Which is also my name, Joyfull. I am Joyfull."

"Your name is Joyful?"

"Joyfull. Full. Like Full of Joy." Joyfull the nurse bites her bottom lip before continuing. "But I want to be more full of joy and full of baby, which is why I make sex with you. I didn't think you would mind. Cause'. You know. You won't be here in a month or less."

I nod my head slowly. The woman's stupidity becoming clearer to me with each exchanged word. Hopefully the video on spinal taps was comprehensive and I will get to walk again. "Well, you should have read my *records* better before you chose me to rape in order to get a baby."

The woman wrinkles her forehead and stares at me. Minutes pass. It may be that I have just come out of a coma. This person's ability to communicate with me seems... I don't know, broken? Disjointed? Incomplete? It is almost like she is not a native... what did she call it? *American language speaker.*

"I can't rape *you*. *You* are a *man*. I am a *woman*. Besides... I want a baby. Not *you* I want. I mean... eww! You are like, gross old. And you are in a coma, and you are going to die soon." She holds the two pieces of tape up. "You go back to coma sleep now." Without asking... or waiting for me to close my eyes, Joyfull puts the tape back over my eyelids. I hear the door of my room open and close.

A couple of thoughts fill my mind as I look at the back of my taped shut eyelids. First, does the average nurse in 2042 think that the primary sign that a patient is in a coma is that the eyes are taped shut? Also... *Old?* I shake my head. I'm about her age! Slowly... everything seems to move very, very slowly at the moment, I raise my right hand to my face and take the tape off both eyes.

Chapter 4
Welcome to the world. Kismet. Robots are everywhere.
Microsoft Hospital  Powered by HoloLens Artificial Intelligence
Someplace in the United States of America
Land of the Free(ish) Home of the Brave(ish)


It is with a great deal of relief that I was able to move my legs at eight o'clock in the morning on July 4th, 2042.

Independence Day indeed!

The supersized erection went away shortly after that. I wasn't sure whether to be relieved or disappointed. I had discovered that I am strapped to the bed. Wherever the releases for the straps are located are not within my view or reach. My lips and mouth are so dry, I am pretty sure that a cat could use my mouth as a litter box. The taste in my mouth tells me that one might have. Joyfull never came back, and neither had anyone else. I looked for fifteen minutes for a button to push to summons a nurse. I am guessing that Microsoft Hospital such and such didn't see a need to give its coma patients a call button.

Shortly after 9:30am I hear the door open. I am sitting up as much as I am able and hoping to make the new nurse scream in surprise.

Instead, it is me that has to suppress a scream as a six-foot-tall robot that looks like a cross between the gold robot from the movie Star Wars and the Terminator enters the room. "8:00am wellness check, Patient Thyme, Justin GCS 1." The raspy voice sounds like it might be male. Or a woman that smoked five packs of cigarettes a day starting when she was thirteen.

"You are late." I say. My voice is still weak. The robot turns and looks at me.

"Patient is alert. Condition noted and reported." The thing comes to the side of my bed. It appears to be processing something. A gold-colored metal robot hand grabs my wrist and squeezes. "Blood Pressure, Elevated. Report generated. Heart Rate, Elevated. Report, Generated." The robot roughly pulls the blanket back. "Earlier reported priapism not present. Prescribed Catheter, not present. Report Generated."

"About that, can I get up? I really need to take a leak. It's been about twenty years." I ask.

"Negative. Patient Thyme, Justin GCS 1 is immobile. Installing directive for catheter from main database, please hold." The robot stands still for a few minutes while I process what it is saying.

"No! No catheter! Send in a nurse!" I rap on the robot's chest with my left hand. "Nurse! Send in a nurse!"

The robot seems to come back to life. "Catheter directive installed." It reaches out and grabs my wrist. "Assault on hospital staff is not permitted. Patient's actions have been reported."

"Get me a nurse!" I try to say it with my most menacing voice which I assume probably sounds like a mouse that has just seen the cat that shit in my mouth.

"I am programmed as a medical professional and can give you the health care you deserve." The robot says in its matter-of-fact raspy voice. From someplace, I have no idea where, the robot has produced a catheter.
"No!" I swipe unsuccessfully at the plastic tube. "You are *not* putting that in me! Nurse! Help!" I yell as loud as I can.

I am sure my blood pressure and heart rate is unacceptably high now. I hear the door open and for a short moment, I fearfully think maybe the robot has called for robot reinforcements. Both my heart rate and blood pressure drop a dozen points when I hear a female voice say, "There you are Maude. Off schedule again, aren't we?"

A blond woman about my mom's age walks into the room. She is wearing a creepy white nurses uniform complete with the little hat. Fucking diabolical this Microsoft hospital is.

"I do not need a catheter!" I announce. "Call your robot off me! Please!"

The nurse doesn't scream. She does take on a wide-eyed surprised look and does several double takes between the electronic board on the wall and me, sitting up in the bed. "Justin Thyme, GCS 1?"

"Just Justin Thyme. Previously GCS 1. Now perfectly able bodied." I say. That last part is not true at all. I am far from able bodied, and I know it.

"You are awake." She says. The robot pulls the blanket off me and grabs a hold of my flaccid member.

"Please make it stop." I cry out as I again unsuccessfully try to grab the catheter. Instead, I grab the robot's arm.

"Assault on hospital staff is not permitted. Report generated." The Robot says.
"I have never seen a catheter installed in a male patient that was conscious and without anesthesia." The nurse says with an oddly curious tone.

Wild eyed, I glare at the woman and see her smirking.

"Maude, dormant." The nurse walks over and removes the catheter from the now still robot's grip. She stands over me. "Well, this is a pleasant surprise, Justin Thyme. Do you know where you are?"

I nod my head. "Microsoft Hospital, something or another. Can you help me up? I need to take a leak."

"You are tied down to the bed. There is a tool to release you." The nurse says. I see her looking at my nakedness.

"Can you get the tool you speak of and let me up?"

The nurse shakes her head. "Coma patients must be released by doctors. Usually, it's done by the doctor in the morgue that signs the death certificate."

"Ok. How about a bedpan?"

The nurse looks at me surprised. "How do you know what a bedpan is?"

How do I know what a bedpan is? How does anyone *not* know what a bedpan is. "Not important." I say shaking my head. "Do you have one?" "Not on this floor." The nurse scoffs. "I doubt we have one in this whole facility. Body fluids are treated like toxic waste... only the Robots are allowed to deal with such things. and in any case, Coma patients usually have no need for a bed pan. If it isn't needed, it isn't here." She points at my crotch. "Just go. I will find a tool to release you, and we will change the bedding."

"This is humiliating." I moan.

"Not as humiliating as it will be if I let Maude put the catheter in you while I watch." The nurse grins. She pats my bare stomach and adds with a reassuring tone. "Just go. It's natural and I am a... nurse. Body fluids never bother me."

I sigh. "Ok." I close my eyes and am about ready to tell the little voices in my head to turn on the faucet when she interrupts me.

"Wait!" She says sharply. My eyes fly open. She grabs my cock and points it down between my legs with a wink. "Better this way. I would hate for you to drown." She grins. "Then Maude here would have to give you mouth to mouth resuscitation."

I sigh sharply with an impatient nod and let go. The comforting flow of urine starts. At first it is little painful. Then it just flows out of my body, emptying my bladder and relieving what I foolishly assess to be twenty years of pressure.

"I need to wash my hands." The nurse says softly. I will be right back.

"You weren't wearing gloves?" I ask with as incredulous as a tone as I can muster as she leaves the room.

"Coma patients rarely require us to touch them. Not many gloves on this floor. Frankly, I am surprised you have any ability to control your bladder at all. I have no idea why you weren't fitted with a catheter!" She calls back from outside the room. I look warily at Maude. The gold and silver hulk of metal seems to look down upon me with distain. Thankfully, it remains still. A few minutes later the human nurse is back. The smell of my urine is filling the room. She has a silver tool in her hand. "The doctor leaves it in her desk." She winks at me.

"It might have been nice for you to have found that before I pissed the bed."

"Eh..." The nurse stoops down and does something with the tool under the hospital bed. "It is just a little pee. It was fun for me. Pretty boring working here in the coma ward."

"Yeah. I met Joyfull earlier. You all seem to find ways to amuse yourselves." I mutter.

The nurse pops back up. Joyfull was in this room with you?" Her face is serious. I'd even categorize the expression as angry. "What was *she* doing in this room."

"Me." I say as plainly as I can.

The nurse shakes her head and kneels back down. "Ick. That's why the catheter isn't installed. I'm gonna need to wash my hands again. Now I wish I had gloves on." In another moment, I feel the belt around my middle release.

"Ahh." I say softly as the belt falls away. I start to shift my hips to get out of the bed.

The nurse springs up and puts her hand on my bare leg. "What are you doing? You can't just get up!"

"Why not?"

"Because you have been laying in a hospital bed for a few decades, that's why!" The nurse admonishes me.

I wave at her dismissively and slowly move my hips to the edge of the bed, my legs dangling over the side. "I'm fine. Just taking it slow." I look over at the nurse who is now leaning against the plastic footer on the bed, arms crossed, and lips pursed. "What's your name?" I ask.

"Millie. Millie Ratchet." She replies.

"You are Nurse Ratchet? Nurse *Millie* Ratchet?" I ask. I am trying to put more of my trademark sarcasm into my tone. I don't think it's coming out the way I want it to.

"It's my married name. I took the name of my ex-husband. And you are thinking of Nurse Ratched from that old movie." Nurse Ratchet says with a frown.

I look down at the floor, studying exactly where I want to stand, as if it matters. "Hell of a name for a nurse. What was your maiden name? Poison? Hitler?"

"Cockburn, actually."

I look over with a smirk. "Is that the old British spelling or the redneck south spelling?"

I see Nurse Millie Ratchet smile. It is a nice smile. A really nice smile. "Same spelling. Same people."

"Here I go." I push myself forward. I feel the bottoms of my bare feet hit the tile floor. Just as I feel the sensation of the cool tile on the tips of my toes, one of the angry voices erupts in my head. *Bro! What the fuck are you doing? We got nothing here! No retained memory of a system of balance, no muscle strength... did you look at your legs? They look like toothpicks with marshmallow bits attached. Jesus H. We are going down. Protect the head if you can....*

"Oh, no." I cry out as I fall to the floor.

Nurse Ratchet stands above me with a grin. She bends at the knees, so she is near my crumpled body. "What did you do for work... you know, before you got yourself put into a coma?"

I groan as I look down at my legs. They do look like toothpicks. My skin has old man crepe wrinkles. There is absolutely no muscle tone. I look up at the nurse. "I was a medical doctor. Podiatry."

"Ah. You were a *doctor.*" She nods. "That explains it." She pats on the robot. "Maude. Pick the patient up."

The robot comes to life and picks my askew body off the floor. Another robot comes in the room. Nurse Ratchet calls it Gloria and tells it to refresh the bed. I watch in some amazement from my perch in Maude's arms. In a matter of seconds the hospital bed is stripped, sanitized and remade. Maude the robot lifts me gently onto the fresh bed. "Thank you, Maude." I mumble as Gloria the robot takes the dirty linen and leaves the room.

Nurse Ratchet sits on the right side of the bed near my shoulder. She smells nice. Maybe it's just nice to smell something. I mean other than my own piss and Joyfull... I haven't smelled much for a while. "Did you let me do that for your entertainment?" I ask.

She pats me on the shoulder. "These days, I do everything for my own entertainment." She lets out a long sigh. "You have been gone for over twenty years."

"I know. I am trying to come to grips with that." I mumble, not *really* thinking that I should be coming to grips with the fact that I have been out of touch with the world for over 7200 days.

"A lot has changed." She says.

"Do we have flying cars yet?" I ask sourly.

"No." The nurse says. I am waiting for to tell me what *has* changed, but she just pats my shoulder again.

"You won't get to stay in this bed. Microsoft Med is very keen on charging for everything and there is no solid food on this floor. They will certainly want to charge you for solid food. You will be moved to a different room on a different floor." Ratchet pats my shoulder again. "I have a good feeling about you Justin Thyme. I think you might be something special."

"I bet you say that to all boys you meet that come out of comas." I say. I'm still not getting the right sarcastic tones to accompany my words.

"So far, I do." Nurse Millie Ratchet replies with a nod.

Chapter 5
A bad day for women's rights and the Tampa Bay Lighting.
Joyful new beginnings.
Someplace in the United States America,
Home of the Free(ish) Land of the Brave(ish)


As it happened, June 23rd, 2022, was a momentous day for many reasons. Not only was the Colorado Avalanche on the verge of an NHL title when they would triumph over the Tampa Bay Lightning, not only was the Supreme Court of the United States of America on the precipice of stripping constitutional rights from half of the citizens of the country, but also Norma Leah Isrow was preparing start a family.

Norma Leah had long known that her prospects for finding the man of her dreams was likely going to conflict with her professional aspirations. Norma, single except for a cat and a Ficus tree excused herself from her work as a managing partner at the World Wide Bank and went to the women's health clinic in a dilapidated strip mall that also housed a cash checking place and an auto parts store. Even then, the clinic had attracted the ire of Americans unsettled with the simple idea that a woman should have the right to maintain sovereignty and control over her personal health decisions, Norma Leah was greeted with a cadre of (mostly middle aged white men) protestors holding up homemade signs featuring dead babies and clever slogans like, *The right to control should not include the right to terminate a life* and *A Child is NOT a CHOICE!*. Norma Leah took the only parking spot available, a space between a rusted-out KIA featuring a bumper sticker that read *ABORTION, THE AMERICAN HOLOCAUST* and a jacked up 4x4 pickup equipped with an American flag waving in the breeze from its bed. A dour woman carrying a white cross ran up to the driver's door on Norma's Subaru shouting something unintelligible. Following the directions of the clinic, Norma pulled out her cell phone and after snapping a photo of the protester, called the clinic. After a few moments, a heavily armed security guard arrived wearing a plastic face shield over his balaclava covered face. After shooing off the cross carrying protestor, he helped Norma Leah from her car and placed a plastic face shield on her. Before setting off for the front door of the he pulled a lightweight hood over Norma Leah's head to shroud her identity.  Carefully, he started the process of guiding her through the two dozen or so protestors who shouted a string of rehearsed chants and epitaphs at the guard and his charge. Norma Leah heard herself called a baby killer, a slut and most mystifying, *a slave to the mistress of the devil.*

"Slave to the Mistress of the Devil?" Norma Leah muttered under her cloth hood. "What does that even mean?"

The guard grunted. "Yesterday, they called one of our patients a 'Slut worshiping whore for Jesus.'" He shakes his head. "One doesn't end up protesting on the sidewalk in the heat of the summer with a high IQ."

They approached the fortified building. The security guard manipulated the bio security locks on the solid steel front door of the clinic. With a whoosh, the door opened. Cool air from the interior of the building radiated over Norma Leah. She can hear light classical music playing inside. The guard gently presses her on the back. "Go on inside now. I must stand guard until you are through the security airlock."

Norma Leah turns and nods. Her eyes widen at the sight of an incoming projectile. The guard doesn't move as a water bottle full of a yellow liquid wizzes up and hits the side of his plastic face shield. Norma's mouth drops open. She is speechless at the sight of the assault of a man who is doing nothing more than making sure that she got from her car to the front door of the women's clinic. Her dismay heightens when the guard doesn't react, even as someone else's bodily fluid dribbles down the side of his tactical uniform.

"Happens all the time. Frankly, I'm glad it is piss today. Last week, one of those dudes was shitting in his hand and throwing it at me while reciting bible verses." The guard explains the event in an even voice before sighing. "The goddamn monkeys at the zoo act better than these idiots do." He points into the building. "Go. I will be here to take you back to your car when you are ready. It's getting late in the afternoon. Maybe the protesters will all go home before you finish."

Norma Leah Isrow steels herself for what is to come and walks inside the women's health center. She hears a whoosh as the heavy glass doors close behind her. A group of people are huddled around a flat television, built into a wall in the comfortably appointed waiting room.

"Fuuuckkk." Norma Leah hears a male voice say in a low groan. "I cannot believe this is actually happening."

Norma clears her throat. A younger woman forces a rehearsed smile onto her face as she turns. Norma sees that the woman's arms and neck are covered in tattoos. She raises her left hand in greeting. The word "YOU" is tattooed in bold black ink on her palm. "Hello! Can we help you?" The entire staff of the clinic turns and looks at Norma Leah.

"I am here for my appointment. My IVF appointment?" Norma Leah says with her firm boss voice, belaying the nervousness and apprehension she truly feels about the journey she is embarking on.

The woman looks surprised. "We didn't think that you would come."
Norma Leah wrinkles her face up. "Why would you think that?"
The woman gestures at the television with her right hand. Norma Leah sees that the word 'FUCK' is tattooed on the palm in a nearly unreadable scroll. "The Supreme Court is about to announce that they have upheld *Dobbs v. Jackson Women's Health Organization*. They are going to overturn *Roe vs Wade* and end the federal protections for women to obtain abortions. It will be big trouble for our clinic. This state has trigger laws that go into effect when... you know, when something like this happens."

"I'm here to get pregnant. Not end a pregnancy." Norma Leah says softly. She looks at the television. A blond woman on Fox News is questioning someone. The announcer wears a stern expression. Norma sees the line at the bottom of the screen introducing the person being interviewed as a spokesperson for Planned Parenthood. She hears the Fox announcer ask the spokesperson something about why the state of California allows women to obtain abortions right up until the baby is born.

A tall Asian man that Norma Leah remembers as the clinic's owner Dr. Wong, stands up. He points the remote at the television and turns the volume down. He walks over to Norma Leah Isrow. "Ms. Isrow." His voice has a tired tone to it. "I collected your eggs. It must be what, fifteen years ago?"

The woman nods. "Sixteen, actually. I was thirty years old."

The doctor nods. "Well, today is the day. Things are not looking up for my business. Today they have basically put women's health rights in the hands of state legislators." He shrugs. "Tomorrow... or someday, we may be looking at a ban on IVF treatments." He looks at her sadly before turning to the rest of the staff. It consists of the black nurse, the tattooed woman that Norma assumes is a nurse and a young man not more than thirty years old. Norma studies him. He has an earnest face, a strong jaw line and is well muscled. Norma wonders if he was one of the security staff. The doctor clears his throat. "Ladies and gentlemen, this is Norma Leah. We are going to get her pregnant. Let's get it done!"

Norma's eyes are on the younger man. He moves like an athlete. Something about him seems to intoxicate her. The black nurse grabs her hand and looks into her face with a smile. "Norma, I am so excited for you... Your baby is going to be beautiful!"

Norma Leah smiles weakly. "It sounds so weird to hear that sentence." She says in a soft voice. The nurse guides her to the centers operating room. She is handed a gown and after disrobing except for her socks, she puts it on and hops up on the examination table.

The young man comes in. He pushes a stainless-steel cart. Dr. Wong follows him. "Norma, this young man is Dr. Conrad Peterson. Up until about an hour ago, I had thought that Dr. Peterson would be taking over this practice." The older man smiles sadly. "Conrad may have to find another specialty. I'm not sure women's health clinics are going to be able to survive in this state."

Norma Leah Isrow feels butterflies in her stomach as she looks at the young doctor preparing items on the cart. Muscles are evident under his doctor's smock. Dr. Peterson looks at some paperwork. "Huh. How about that?" He says almost under his breath.

"How about what?" Norma Leah asks.

Dr. Conrad Peterson flashes a grin full of bright white teeth and shakes his head. "Nothing. Nothing at all. Just marveling at the coincidences of life." He moves to where she sits and pulls the stirrups from the end of the table. "Let's get you in position." Norma Leah can smell his scent as he gently lies her back onto the table and fits her feet into the cold metal stirrups. The young doctor smiles down at her before nodding at the older man. "Just like the real thing, this will be done in an instant and you won't feel much."

Norma Leah looks up at the young doctor dreamily. "Does it have to be that way?" She feels the coldness of lubrication between her legs. "All done." The Asian doctor announces.

Dr. Peterson softly pats her shoulder, his hand inadvertently lightly brushing across a stiff nipple. "That's it. You've a bun in the oven, Norma Leah."

Chapter 6
Holy shit, the robots are everywhere!
Microsoft Hospital Powered by HoloLens Artificial Intelligence
Someplace in the United States of America
Land of the Free(ish) Home of the Brave(ish)


*I am sitting up in a hospital bed in my new, new room. I have been moved twice. First it was some sort of robot hell emergency room where a silver penis shaped robot named Grady stood over me twenty-four hours a day measuring vitals. That was a couple of weeks of no sleep that made me consider that being in a coma isn't such a bad thing. After Microsoft Hospital Powered by HoloLens Artificial Intelligence figured out that I wasn't a liability, I was moved to my current room which is very much like the room I woke up from the coma in... only there is a window that I spend a lot of time looking out of and a video monitor on the wall that I have no idea how to operate. I'm just happy that GCS 1 doesn't follow Justin Thyme on the digital board hanging on the wall.*

*I can walk now with the aid of an aluminum walker. Physical therapy is six times a day with the help of one of those silver and gold robots. This one is oddly named Meathead. He isn't very nice, and he doesn't laugh at my jokes. There is a private bathroom in my room that I get to use... Shitting and pissing on your own is highly underrated! On the bathroom wall is a mirror. Let me tell you, it was quite a shock when I saw my reflection the first few hundred times. Let's just say I spent a lot of time crying on Nurse Ratchet's shoulder after the first time. Maybe the second... and fourth too. In my mind, I am like twenty-nine years old. The calendar says I am coming up on fifty and that goddamn mirror says seventy.*

*Nurse Millie Ratchet keeps coming to see me, even though she has nothing to do with my medical care. On the level I have been assigned to, no human has much to do with my care. There is a robot doctor named Tootie that comes and assesses me every day. That's in addition to the half dozen different robots that come in and out of the room doing this or that. Millie brought me some baked goods, but the Microsoft security robots won't let her give them to me. She says it is easier to sneak food into the coma ward. Probably because Microsoft Hospital Powered by HoloLens Artificial Intelligence isn't at risk for losing any money because of it. I haven't gotten around to asking why there needs to be so many robots. I would assume that one robot could be programmed to do all the shit that this cadre of machines is doing.*

*As it turns out, Millie Ratchet is about my age. A little older, actually. She is now how old my mother was the day I got my vasectomy and the start on my twenty-year nap. Millie has been very good about gently (and slowly) bringing me up to date about all the shit that has happened in the world over the last twenty years.*

*I haven't told Millie about the Bear, the Cow and the Grasshopper. I figure I need to keep her around as long as I can. As weird as that shit seemed to me, I assume it's still not cool to admit to talking imaginary animals in your head and I don't need the one bit of human interaction I have, to get scared off. For all I know, those three animals and my conversations with two of them were products of being pumped full of bupivacaine multiple times so Joyfull could ride me like a carousel pony.*

*I did tell Millie all about the memory of my experience with Joyfull. Apparently, I'm not the first and Millie is sure I won't be last nearly dead man that Joyfull takes advantage of. Millie told me that hospitals using robots (apparently all medical facilities use robots) are required by law to maintain human supervision over the robots. Human help is hard to find these days as a living wage was instituted a decade or so ago and few people want to work. Joyfull can't be easily replaced, so she can fuck up on the job (pun completely intended) and not be fired.*

*Millie has had to deliver some bad news. It is in my medical records that my parents passed on ten years ago or so. I was an only child. I had a cousin and some distant relatives I can reach out to, but I haven't yet. I have memories of friends. I asked if Millie is on Facebook. She laughed at me. Apparently, the Chinese bought Facebook on a Monday afternoon like eight years ago and shut the whole thing down overnight. Millie says they did it in the name of saving humanity. Based on my memory of Facebook, if that's the case, the Chinese were probably right. We are waiting to see if I live before trying to contact my old friends.*

*Millie says the world order is in disarray. The United States of America is no longer the world leader in much except producing firearms and military weaponry. The current President of the United States is a guy that was a reality show actor who ate ten live centipedes or something on some television show. I told Millie that the guy sounds like the forty fifth president, only without the centipedes. The forty fifth president did some weird shit, but I can't recall him eating live arthropods. Whenever I mention politics from twenty years ago, Millie changes the subject. I asked Millie about the monitor and watching television. She said I need an implant to control the monitor and there is nothing on to watch anyway. I guess most television shows now are only a few minutes long as that is the attention span of the average citizen. Millie almost always has that terrific smile on her face and a pleasant attitude. We tell jokes and talk about growing up. Like me, her parents are also dead, and she was an only child.*

*Millie tells me that cars mostly all drive themselves now and are electric. I tell her about my Tesla S that I had. She tells me that the founder of Tesla caught syphilis and went crazy before he died. Apparently, he bought Twitter and got into politics or something, but his business empire crumbled after people figured out, he was going bat shit crazy. Millie really doesn't like to talk about politics, how people act or what has caused the decline of the United States. I am excited to see what has happened in the world. It's like climbing into a time machine and going into the future twenty years.*

*I can't wait to get out of the hospital and live in the future.*

Chapter 7
Dr. Conrad Petersen is Twitterpated.
Norma Leah falls in love. Weirdness is relative.
Someplace in the United States America,
Land of the Free(ish) Home of the Brave(ish)


Norma Leah's cell phone chimes twice. She picks it up. "Hello?"

"Norma Leah?" A smooth male voice says.

"Yes?"

"This is... Umm... this Dr. Conrad Peterson." The voice says nervously. "From the women's clinic?"

Norma Leah catches her breath as she simultaneously becomes nervous and excited. "Is there a problem, Doctor?"

"Well, yes. No. Maybe. I hope there is no problem!" The Doctor laughs nervously. "Oh... Your pregnancy! There is no problem with your pregnancy! None at all. That went well!"

"Oh." Norma Leah says. "Well, what can I do for you?"

"Have dinner with me!" The doctor's voice almost squeaks with nervousness.

Norma Leah's stomach does a somersault. "Are you asking me out on a date, doctor?"

"Y..Yes?" Conrad Peterson stammers. "It's not totally inappropriate. I was fired yesterday by Dr. Wong. After your procedure. He thinks I need to go out on my own. He doesn't think there will clinics like his soon. Anyway, technically, I am no longer one of your doctors."

"         You want to ask me out?" Norma Leah asks. "I am almost old enough to be your mother, Dr. Peterson."

"Um, Well... I... You... Why don't you call me Conrad?" Peterson stutters.

"Conrad, I would very much like to have dinner with you." Norma Leah sighs, thinking about the young man's muscles. "Come by and pick me up anytime tonight after five."

*Two months later*

Conrad Peterson strokes the bare breast of Norma Leah Isrow. He lays naked beside her on the bed in his condominium. Their lovemaking had been especially energetic that morning. "I need to tell you something, Norma."

"Oh no. Is this where you tell me that you are gay?" Norma Leah exclaims with mock seriousness.

Peterson chuckles. "No. It's... well, it's just... You should know something."

"I know plenty of things." Norma Leah props herself up on one arm and looks into his eyes. "Knowledges comes to some of us as we age. What is it that you think I should know that I don't, young man?"

Peterson blushes. "I'm not that young."

"You are that young. What do you want to tell me?" Norma Leah steels herself for the breakup she is sure is about to come. Conrad had been lots of fun. Her belly is starting to get bigger, her breasts heavier. She is certain the young man is about to tell her that he is moving on to younger and firmer pastures.

"I know who the sperm donor is." Conrad blurts out.

Norma Leah scrunches up her forehead. She absently rubs her naked belly. "Don't tell me I am having an Asian baby." Her eyes go wide. "Not that there is anything wrong with that! It's just, I always suspected that Dr. Wong might have been a little on the cheap side."

Conrad shakes his head. "No... No..." He tweaks her nipple prompting a swift slap to his hand. "But your baby will be related to me."

Norma Leah sits up in the bed. The sheets fall off her naked body. "What did you just say?"

"It's not what you are thinking." Conrad rolls over and pulls some papers from the nightstand. "The sperm donor that you selected is my grandfather... or rather was my grandfather, Dr. Malcom Peterson. I recognized his donor number the day we did your procedure."

Norma Leah grabs the papers and looks at them. "This was supposed to be confidential. His identity. My use of his... seed."
The young man laughs. "It's so cute that people your age think that anything is confidential. Yes. There are references to the process being totally anonymous. That's bullshit. More than half of the world's living population has had a genome sequence publicized. Finding that random guy that hasn't at the least had a relative run a genetic panel is unlikely. In this case, I think your child will have lots of brothers and sisters. Grandpa Malcom was prolific with the sperm donor thing. It's like he needed reason to whack off." He touches the papers. "I don't think anyone ever seriously thought that women's reproductive rights would be at risk. I figure it is best if you have all the information about your baby to keep safe. I took the paperwork having to do with your procedure so you would know the details without having to do the research."

"So, what does that make you to my son?" Norma Leah had specifically asked for a male baby when she had signed up for the IVF procedure. "And is your grandfather still around to know about this? Is he creepy or is he a nice guy?"

"Heavens no. My grandfather died seven or eight years ago. Maybe before you even selected him as the donor. He and my grandmother basically raised me. My parents traveled a lot. He was a great guy to me and my friends. Not creepy... to any of us, anyway. He was a podiatrist. Had a thing for feet, apparently." Conrad pauses. "One of my buddies became a podiatrist. Maybe Grandpa Malcom had something to do with that." Conrad looks wistfully at the bed sheets.

"What?" Norma Leah asks. "Is there more to this story?"

Conrad sighs, "Grandpa may have been creepy. He succumbed to a stroke while he was massaging a patient's feet."

"That wouldn't make him creepy." Norma Leah answers. "He was a podiatrist. Strokes happen. Especially to older people."

"Well, they were in a janitor's closet at my high school." Conrad sighs. "It was at parent teacher conferences and the feet belonged to my algebra teacher."

Norma smiles. "Well, she must have had nice feet."

"The teacher was a dude." Conrad deadpans.

"Let's consider that there is a chance that your grandfather was a little on the eccentric side." Norma Leah pats him on the shoulder reassuringly. "If your grandpa looked like you, my son will be handsome."

"I would be his nephew, technically." Conrad offers.

Norma Leah frowns. "What do you mean?"

"If my grandfather knocked you up, the baby would be my father's half-brother, or my uncle. I would be the baby's nephew." Conrad explains. Norma Leah grins. "I am carrying your uncle?"

"You are. My half uncle, I think. Maybe that's an uncle once removed. If such a thing is possible." Conrad shakes his head. "I never really figured out the removed relative thing."

Norma Leah flops down on the bed beside him with sigh. "Well, that is some news."

"I have something else." Conrad says solemnly.
The woman rolls her eyes. "Are you going to tell me your grandfather was a politically active Republican?"

A fully nude Conrad quickly gets to his knees in front of Norma on the bed. "No, that's not what I want to..." Conrad stops and considers what Norma has asked. "Well, Grandpa Malcom probably was a Republican. My family has had a steadfast aversion to paying any sort of taxes." His right hand reaches behind his naked form and comes back with a glittering diamond ring. "Norma Leah, mother of my uncle, will you marry me?" Norma Leah Isrow pauses. Her eyes narrow and her face darkens before breaking into a big smile.
"Sure. But only if you tell me where you were keeping that ring."

Chapter 8
The food here sucks. A window to the world.
The view isn't pretty.
Microsoft Hospital Powered by HoloLens Artificial Intelligence
Someplace in America
Land of the Free(ish) Home of the Brave(ish)


*I am running everyday now. Ok. Maybe not running. Jogging fast. One of the droids must run with me. Meathead doesn't run apparently, but I have been informed by it that Microsoft Hospital rules demand a babysitter. A smaller silver and gold robot named JJ runs with me while Meathead watches. I try to outrun JJ. I can't, which makes me think that I may not even be jogging. Maybe walking fast is a better description. Millie is still coming to see me. I like it. I really look forward to seeing her and not just because I am confined to a small room with only a window to look out of and robots to talk to.*

*I am realizing that pre-coma Dr. Justin Thyme wasn't a very nice person. I definitely danced past 'jerk' during my days of being Dr. Thyme. I certainly associated myself with the path to 'bastard' and most likely I even reached the level of asshole on several occasions.*

*Millie has become my friend. Maybe the best one I have ever had, and she is certainly the only woman I have spent time with that I wasn't trying to bone and escape with some flimsy excuse. (It's a different book, but I had a whole system of excuses that rhymed in some fashion with the woman's name... Barb - I have to shop for some new garb. Molly - I need to meet up with my volleyball team. Cindy - I must take my sister Mindy shopping. I had a great excuse for the name Delores dreamed up, but never met the right girl.)*
*I have told Millie about all this. In fact, I have opened up to her about most everything in my past... The stupid shit I did in high school and college, How I decided on medicine because of the money.*

Pro Tip: Don't mention money on your med school application letter.

*I described how I selected podiatry because my pal Conrad Peterson, who also went to medical school had a grandfather named Malcom who was a podiatrist. He was a pretty cool dude and didn't seem to work very hard. I told her about the events leading up to my accident after my vasectomy, complete with the pre-event boozing, the trick with the Tesla, the dumb ass nurse I was fucking, (Veronica... Actual excuse used once; I had to chronicle a variety of foot funguses) the bag of frozen peas incident and finally the accident.*
*At first, Millie told me little about herself. She talked about her ex-husband. She told me that he is really religious. There is something there that she doesn't want to talk about. I never got married, so I don't have any idea what pain might be involved with getting a divorce. Probably more than messing up a girl's name you are fucking because you can't remember what excuse you used to avoid cuddle time. I don't pry on her personal life. I ask about her nursing career. She doesn't say much, except to say that working with the near dead has a therapeutic effect for her.*

*One day, we are eating some contraband chocolate chip cookies that Millie successfully smuggled into the hospital, and I asked about Joyfull, the midnight rider. (In my spare time, I had tried and failed to come up with a rhyming excuse to escape Joyfull.) Joyfull had apparently figured out a way to get herself knocked up and had quit the robot minder/ nursing gig.*

"What was up with that broad?" I ask Millie.

Millie's face sours. It's the most unhappy expression I have ever seen on Millie's face. "Did you hit a sour chocolate chip, or did I say something to piss you off?"
Millie shakes her head. "It's not you. And the cookies are terrific. I made them in the hospital kitchen a few minutes before I came up here."

"The cookies are definitely awesome!" I say. My words do not seem to lighten the mood.  "If it matters, I couldn't feel anything when she was riding me like circus clown on a stolen elephant." I smile, trying to force some light into the conversation.

"Joyfull is completely misguided, but she had good reasons for doing what she was doing. In fact, I would go so far as to say, Joyfull... as dumb as she appears to be... she was pretty goddamn innovative doing what she was doing." Millie says.

I shake my head. "I don't understand."

Millie sighs. "Joyfull is a lesbian. She and her partner want a child. You are a good-looking guy and by any professional medical opinion, you were not coming out of your coma. She saw an opportunity to get something she wanted."

"Fucking a guy in a coma is damn desperate. Has Intro Vitro Fertilization gotten to be that expensive?" I ask.

Millie cocks her head and looks at me in the most adorable way. She smiles, but it is not the *make Justin's heart flutter* smile... more a *you poor dumb bastard smile*. "Justin... IVF is illegal in the United States. It has been for about twelve years."

"I don't understand." I say. "What do you mean IVF is illegal?" Millie shrugs. "Women's health policy took quite a beating after your accident. The Supreme Court upheld *Dobbs* and decreed abortion to be something the states had control over. Immediately, some states outlawed it... but some had citizens vote to put the right to an abortion in the state constitution. Then there was a political... *shift* and the Republican Party had the house, the senate and the presidency. They voted to outlaw all forms of abortion, including IVF... which of course wastes female eggs."

My eyes are wide. "Holy shit."

Millie nods. "Yeah... well, a few years later, there is this case in south... all these miserable cases come from the southern states; The State of Mississippi vs. Steptoe, the plaintiff, was a Doctor named Steptoe. Mississippi arrested him for doing IVF at his fertility clinic. The premise was that in doing IVF, several of the woman's eggs would be disposed of, which constituted multiple abortions. Soon after the ruling, A Republican congress acted and made IVF illegal in the United States of America."

"What happened to the doctor?" I ask.

"He's still in jail in Mississippi." Millie answers.

"Jesus." I mumble.

"I am certain that Jesus has nothing to do with it." Millie says.

"Say…" I start to ask and stop.

"What?" Millie says.

"Joyfull had a tattoo of the forty fifth president on one of her boobs. There was a woman on the other boob… What's up with that? Do you know about this? Is it a thing?" I hold my breath and study Millie's face to see if I have gone too far asking about Joyfull.
I exhale when she shakes her head with that awesome smile. "I never saw much of Joyfull. I did know what her game was, obviously. Joyfull came to work after I left and got off before I arrived at work." I cock an eyebrow at the comment.

"You are such a dog, Justin Thyme." Millie slaps my knee. "She got off work… maybe the words *should* have been an intended pun." She sits back on my hospital bed. "Anyway, *I* never had any reason to see her naked, thankfully… The tattoos also could be a church thing." She sighs. *I feel a subject change coming up.* "Anyway… it's just a weird church. Fundamentalist group that has some strange practices. They worship the forty fifth president… literally they refer to him as the *Orange Jesus*. The other picture was probably a conservative justice on the court that became a stalwart against women's reproductive health care. Amy Coney Barrett. Retired just recently in fact."

I nod. I remember when Amy Coney Barrett was appointed to the court.

"There was probably a big cross tattooed on Joyfull's back." Millie adds with a sigh.

"I only had one eye open." I say with a smirk. And she never showed me her backside.

"At least you got to see her boobs." Millie says with a crooked smile as she stands. "I got to get bustin'... but, I brought you a little somethin'." She reaches into a bag and pulls out a small silver laptop embossed with a familiar piece of fruit. "I don't want to recap the last twenty years with you... it's too depressing. I brought you this old laptop. You can go through things yourself. You can get it hooked up to the hospital internet. We can talk about whatever you want about the past after you go looking."

I take the thing like it is the holy grail, which... to me right now, it is. "This is awesome. Thank you." I say. I look up at Millie. She looks apprehensive. My face must look confused.

"Hold still." She commands. "It's been a while since I have done this. I want to get it right."

"Holding still. I have gotten good at that. Did I leave some lunch on my face?" I answer with a genuinely confused tone as she grabs both sides of my head and pulls me to hers, locking onto my lips. We might have kissed for a few seconds or ten years. I could go back into a coma with that kiss and be just fine. She releases me and sits back. The smile is back. That radiant, life sustaining smile is back on Millie's face, and everything seems like it's going to be ok.

After pointing out a slip of paper taped to the laptop that had log in information for the internet, she leans in and kisses me on the forehead. "I need to go see some cousins. But, I will be back tomorrow. Don't make yourself sick with that computer." I watch her walk out of my hospital room.
The door closes before I realize that the goodbye had multiple rhymes. Not great ones, but... she is trying to connect with me! *Bustin'. Somethin'. Cousins.* And I got a kiss! Sometime I will tell Millie that the reason I did the rhyming thing was so I could remember the lies I told the women I was trying to escape spending more time with.

I open the laptop, type in the log in information and begin a twenty- four-hour marathon of hell.

*A lot has happened over the past twenty years. As is probably always the case with history, it started before you think it did and had ramifications far outside of whatever the objective was. The first thing I did was look up old friends. No Facebook, but there are other systems in place now to find people. Conrad Peterson became a doctor. He has a company called PPP that appears to make female sexual aid devices. That sounds like Conrad. He married a woman named Norma Leah Peterson. They have a son named Fredrick Ashley Peterson. Sadly, it appears that Norma Leah passed away in some sort of rock-climbing accident. I type in the name Marmalade Julius. Marmalade, Conrad and I played football together in high school. I am happy to see that he started a business called "Juice's Jyms". Its website claims to have the best e-gymnasiums in the country. I have no idea what that is. He also has a business called "Salt Juice" which is apparently some sort of salt bath. Marmalade was a running back at a big-name college football factory. He tore an ACL on the second play of his junior season. He got to play in the pros, but not for long before he had another knee blowout. I knew he had been a musician in high school and had gone off to LA or somewhere to be in a band. I did not know that he was such a successful businessman or that he had created three top ten R&B hits. Everything I read about Marmalade Julius online appears to be curated. Willem Williams was another buddy I had in high school. I knew he went to law school someplace. Michigan, I think. I type his name into the search bar and a lot of information comes up. Willem and his wife Wendy are both attorneys. They do product liability lawsuits. On his website, Willem looks exactly like I remember him. A tall, good looking black man with a strong jaw and intense eyes. His wife Wendy, who was also in our high school class is his female equivalent. I am a little jealous of their youthful and attractive appearances. They have a daughter named Katherine who also went to Michigan Law. There is photo of her with a guy I assume is her husband on the website. All these photos of the Williams family look super good, like they are pictures of what you should aspire to be if you a human.*
*I type in the name of the only cousin I ever knew; my father's brother's son, Hank Thyme, who played football with all of us. I almost burst out laughing when I see that Hank is now Henry, Father Henry Thyme. He is a Catholic Priest. There isn't much about Hank online.*

"Son of a bitch! Who would have thought that Hammering Hank... who wouldn't pass up pussy if it was dead... would become a priest?" I say out loud. I try and remember if I even knew that my uncle's family was Catholic.

*It occurs to me that I should look up some of the women I knew or the doctors that I worked with. Millie had shown me what few records there were on my visitors over the years. Conrad and Hank, (never Henry and certainly never 'Father Thyme') had been up many times, especially in the beginning. Marmalade and Willem (with Wendy, three times) fewer times and none the past ten years. Obviously, my parents had stopped coming up when they died. Other than that, there was no one visiting me. I suppose the number of people who come to see you when you are in a coma and presumed well on your way to the pearly gates - or in my case, the barn yard - is a commentary on how you were living your life. None of the women I was fucking and none of my business partners were ever on a list of my visitors.*

*I had found all the people I wanted to find.*

*The door opens and Lamont the robot comes in carrying a tray full of food. Robots never knock here. I look at the food. It all tastes the same, but it is called different things, and it usually looks a little different from day to day. If I am being honest, I call it food only because I eat it. Here is thing about food in the future. It only looks like food you want to recognize. Today is cheeseburgers and fries. The "cheeseburger" is some sort of vegetable like patty topped with a yellow substance roughly the same color as those little cheese singles wrapped in plastic. No dairy products were harmed in its production. The "fries" are a soy product of some sort. The ketchup is still ketchup. Only made with no salt and no sugar.*

"Thank you, Lamont. Can I get some salt and chocolate milkshake?" I ask the robot as the tray is set beside me.

*Lamont the robot is a silver android. It has a red kerchief inexplicably tied around its neck. I watch as it tilts its head at me in response to the request. It's the same request I make every time food is placed in front of me. I have learned from Millie that the head tilt is a sign that the robots are processing an irregular request.*

"Sodium consumption is bad for your health, Patient Thyme. Excessive Sodium leads to poor cardiovascular results, increased thirst and more frequent urination. Furthermore, it may be against state and federal laws for Microsoft Medical facilities to addition salt or sugar to any of our chef observed, scientifically developed meals." The Robot's head returns to center. "I will pass the request for a... Chocolate Milkshake... on to the kitchen staff." Without waiting for me to respond, the robot turns and leaves the room.

*This is the same response I get every day. I've yet to get a chocolate milkshake. Lamont the robot only responds to food centric commentary. If I were to ask it about the weather, I would receive no response. Likewise, if I ask the physical therapist robot Meathead about food, I get no response. I eat the 'cheeseburger' and 'fries' and keep browsing the internet for information.*

*The more I read, the more I understand why Millie would want to talk about anything other than the current social or political state of the United States of America. The political environment of the United States wasn't in good shape when I became the meat part of a truck sandwich. At that time, there was nothing but political derision. Everyone seemed to be on one side or the other. Somehow, things have deteriorated significantly. Over eighty percent of population of the country disapproves of the country's government. In particular, the people outright loathe congress where nothing productive ever seems to get done and what does get done is usually completely contrary to public opinion.*

*Here are a few of the things that shocked me as I browsed through the World Wide Web... Public schools start the day with a prayer - usually a Christian based prayer. (Despite most Americans proclaiming to be unchurched.) Mass shootings have not decreased, even though it is now apparently common for people to carry sidearms. Marijuana remains illegal federally, although it is legal for recreational use in forty six of the fifty states. The state of Texas, already an important standard in the creation of high school and college education material in 2022 has become something of a de-facto federal authority for a consortium of states that have signed on to the 'Alamo Compact'. Basically, whenever Texas signs a law into effect, the same law instantly goes into effect in twenty-seven or so other states.*

*The education system is in compete disarray. Public Schools are known as 'Gathering Centers for the Young.' Attendance is optional. Classes are mostly taught by Robots. A student can take lessons on-line. Texas sets up most of the learning curriculums for the entire country. It appears to me - at least based on reading public forums - that proper English is not one of the subjects' students are required to take.*

*History and Sociology also seem to have been forgotten. The public has stopped participating in elections. One reference mentioned a turnout of less than ten percent in an election with federal positions on the ballot. There seems to be no understanding that the founding fathers specifically noted in the constitution that America's government was supposed be "of the people, by the people". The population doesn't trust the United States Supreme Court any more than it does congress. Indeed, it seems that The Supreme Court has become just as, if not more political than the legislative bodies of congress and the senate. Unsurprising, half of the pubic continues to show favor to the whatever President it elects, albeit the favoritism is usually tempered by the prices of economic items presidential administrations have little control over.*

*I ask for more information about the Supreme Court. The court is collectively taking advantage of lifetime appointments and the disfunction of Congress to become quite active. In the last twenty years, the conservative majority court has gutted the Environmental Protection Agency, abolished the Internal Revenue Service (Texas et al vs Revenue Act 1862) and upheld a Montana law requiring general firearm studies in public grade schools. That's the small stuff. The same conservative majority court has upheld state laws banning all forms of birth control.*

*I put the computer down and look out the window. I can't see much. There is another Microsoft Medical building across from me. The sun is setting. Lamont the Robot will be around with dinner shortly. If I had the cheeseburger thing for lunch, dinner will be a bowl of chili made with the same 'meat' as the cheeseburger and a salad of greens unrecognizable by me. My stomach is churning as I am still thinking about the Supreme Court banning all forms of birth control when my supper arrives. I don't plan on bothering to ask Lamont for salt or a milkshake.*

"Lamont, can you get me a condom?" I ask the robot after it puts the tray down.

I expect the robot to ignore me and leave the room. Instead, it tilts its head, processes the question and after straightening its head back up, replies; "Microsoft Medical Systems does not make commentary on political or social positions. Birth Control of any kind has been deemed illegal by state and or federal law. Because of this, Microsoft Medical cannot comply with your request."

I study the tin man food deliverer. The response was obviously programmed. "How about a chocolate milkshake?" I ask. "Can I get a chocolate milkshake?"

The robot responds quickly. "I will pass the request for a... Chocolate Milkshake... on to the kitchen staff."

I eat the chili and the salad and return to the computer.

*The current Chief Justice of the United States Supreme Court is a woman named May Cornwall Bhutthert.*

"Justice Butt Hurt." I giggle like a sixth-grade boy. "Butt Hurt."

*As I continue watching videos and looking stuff up, I come to understand that the pronunciation of Bhutthert is not Butt Hurt, but Boo-thert. Still, hilarious last name to me. In one of the videos, Bhutthert justifies the court upholding* Tennessee v. Church & Dwight, *the seminal case on birth control access on the grounds that; There is nothing in the constitution regarding access to birth control. 'The founding fathers simply did not think that women needed to have access to birth control. If they had wanted such a thing, they would have put it in the constitution!' Bhutthert seem to gloat in the video. She goes on to reference some complicated saying from an eighth century Chinese philosopher as the proof for the self-created theorem.*

*It appears that congress thought the action of the Supreme Court as populous opinion instead of faulty legal logic it was and promptly passed federal prohibitions against all forms of birth control and the prescription of any substance for the purpose of birth control. I type 'what has been public reaction of no birth control' into the search bar. A dialog box pops up on the screen. At first, I think maybe there are censors... but the dialog box merely says this: Device is equipped with a EUROAI compatible search system with software updated to August 1st, 2042. Users can ask questions verbally for more accurate and smoother browsing. If users do not feel safe utilizing verbal commands, privacy screen should be used to protect search histories. EuroAI never retains user histories.*

That's weird, I think. Was I typing too slowly? Was what I typed not making sense? I clear my throat. "Ah... What has the public reaction been to the bans on birth control in the United States of America."

A long passage quickly appears on the screen.

*People assigned female at birth, in the United States of America, unable to legally make decisions regarding their reproductive status have largely stopped having sex with men. This has caused a steep decline in the national birth rate and as of this update, the population of the United States of America is dropping. Economists report that the collective spending power of the United States is receding at a rate equal or greater to minus 6.7% a year or a little over minus .5% per month. Leading Sociologists and Criminologists have issued reports that mid-level and violent crime is on the rise at 12.2% per year and will continue to increase over the next twenty-five years. This is directly attributed to the decrease in population in addition to an observed lack of human interaction between citizens of the United States. The effects of these elements are being experienced in other third world countries that adapted United States based laws and regulations on Women's health, firearm control and financial tools. The Gross Domestic Product of the United States hit an all-time low in July 2038 and continues to decrease month over month at a rate of negative .03%.*

"Jesus Christ." I say aloud.

A passage appears on the screen.

*Jesus Christ, also referred to as Jesus, Christ, Jesus of Nazareth and many other names and titles lived from circa 06 BC to AD 33. He was a first-century Jewish preacher and religious leader. He was the central figure of Christianity, at one time, the world's largest religion. In earlier times, Most Christians believed Jesus was the incarnation of God the Son and the awaited Jewish messiah, the Christ that is prophesied in the Hebrew Bible.*

"No, I didn't want the definition..." I read the passage. "Huh. Christianity is not the world's largest religion anymore. That's something." "Briefly tell me about religion in today's world." I say.

Over the past fifty years, participation in organized religion has decreased dramatically with only 48% of populations stating participation in any particular religion. Secularism, fundamentalism and participation in fringe societies and the occult have been on the rise. In the United States, Christianity, Catholicism, Judaism and Islamic congregations have largely shrunk to single digit participation figures in comparison with the population. Fringe fundamentalism based on any single religion is on the rise as is participation in the occult.

I ask some more questions about current pop culture and learn that the most popular video entertainment of the day is a lewd show called 'I Got Off on That'. It features women and sometimes men finding new ways to achieve orgasm. The most popular episode features a larger woman from the state of Arkansas riding astride a lawn mower pushed by her husband, a naked man whose genitals are clearly ensconced in some sort of cage. In the throes of supposed ecstasy, the woman's foot gets caught under the running mover and is badly mangled. I am a little surprised to learn that 'I Got Off on That' is very popular with men and women alike. The passage mentioned that up to sixty percent of the population watches multiple episodes of the ten-minute program daily. Labor unions went on strike to make sure members had a break in work at 8:00pm every night so union members wouldn't miss whatever episode of self-masturbation makes it on the air.

Social media apparently hasn't died but it has changed. It's all completely based on medically installed mobile technology now. Facebook was indeed destroyed, quite literally, when a company sponsored by the Chinese Communist Party purchased it and erased it after Meta would no longer willingly allow artificial influence from bots have any influence on elections in the US and European countries. It appears that Meta also would not let Chinese tech companies manipulate what the average American was seeing from day to day on Facebook feeds. One day the behemoth tech company was there. The next day it was gone... a company worth billions of dollars seemingly disappeared without a trace and the Chinese Government sold the American population that the reason it was done was to "Save Humanity".

I ask a few more questions and become informed that telecommunication devices are now mostly implanted in the user's body. These implants control most electronic appliances in the home. Everything from the monitors to coffee makers and toasters. There are very few networks available for a person to utilize an old fashion handheld style cell phone. I have no idea how this works, but apparently internal cellular phone users can elect to have their entire life posted on blog like websites. These minute-by-minute *accountings are scanned and rebroadcast on a popular internet-based program called "Shit Happens". The show runs twenty-four hours a day, three hundred and sixty-five days a year with the best happenings curated and shown every night at 6pm. Many people feel a sense of pride when something from their day shows up on "Shit Happens". Because of this, the citizenry is constantly doing to stupid things on purpose to get themselves a modicum of fame.*

*There apparently are no longer any independent news sources in the United States. Liberal news outlets are few, but rabid in nature, openly calling conservative politicians 'Nazi's'. Conservative news talking heads uses terms like "Fake News" and "Boring" constantly. They speak with a slang that I do not understand. I think back to my broken conversation with Joyfull that I blamed on me just coming out of a coma. She is just a product of her environment. Conservatives and Liberal news outlets alike seem to attack anything that appears to come from the Intelligentsia as something that must be evil as anyone who has dedicated their life to knowledge must be deficient in some manner. When ratings lag, the conservative stations up the game by asking people on the street to name things more "Boring" than the liberals. "That's Boring" has become a catch phrase of the right. Not to be outdone, Liberal news outlets constantly cast conservative voters as low intelligence and when there are the rare ratings grab by Liberal News sources, they make fun of fundamentalist religion participants. None of this seems particularly productive to me. When did people stop thinking for themselves?*

I look up at the clock. It is almost three in the morning. I have been browsing the internet and watching videos for like fourteen hours. I look at the computer. There is one person I didn't look up that I think I might want some more information about. I pull the computer close to me and type, "Millie Ratchet" into the search bar. A passage quickly appears.

*Millie Ratchet is a nurse for Microsoft Medical Systems. She is currently assigned to the HoloLens Artificial Intelligence division.*

There were pages of information available on my friends. It seems weird that Millie gets less than twenty words.

I squint at the screen and slowly type "Mildred Cockburn" before pressing enter.

A picture on the top of the screen shows a younger Millie Ratchet. She is wearing a big smile and a white lab coat. The name under the picture identifies her as *Doctor Mildred Cockburn*. Pages and pages of information follows.

Chapter 9
Conrad Peterson has a date. Fred is going out.
Somewhere in the United States of America
Home of the Free(ish) Land of the Brave(ish)

*Conrad Peterson was never the best student in his youth... or a particularly attentive participant in medical school. His father, also a doctor in addition to being a lawyer, an international best-selling self-help author and a lobbyist had picked out universities for young Conrad where it was accepted to pay for a degree rather than earning one the old-fashioned way. Conrad had picked Obstetrics and Fertility as a practice simply because he liked women's vaginas.*

Pro tip: Don't put any attractions to certain body parts on your Med School application.

*After getting fired by Dr. Wong because the older doctor correctly assessed that the vagina business was going to dry up, Conrad left the medical profession to follow what was probably his true interest, mechanical design. Combining one fascination with the other, Conrad started P.P.P. Inc. While some may think that the company was named after the wasteful government loan program that funded its creation, P.P.P actually stands for Peterson Prosthetic Pussies.*

*The first sex toy Conrad made was not a prosthetic pussy, but a supersized vibrator built to specifications requested by Norma Leah. Called the Malcom in honor of Conrad's paternal Grandfather and young Fredrick's sperm donor father, the device was powered by a battery like that in a cell phone and was a little over a foot long and weighed about a pound. It sold well, but not as well as the device called the 'Norma Leah', a life size interactive device based on the shape and dimensions of the lower half of Norma Leah Peterson. Fueled by a lack of sexual interaction with real women, men from all over the United States bought the Norma Leah two devices at a time. One for at work, one for at home, as advertisements for the product encouraged. Conrad quickly realized that he didn't need to engineer the device to wear out. Users quickly wore the quality-built appliances out, leading to more sales. Over Norma Leah Peterson's stern objections, the updated version of the device could be turned over and the back used as one might use the front.*

*Despite losing his mother at a young age, Norma and Conrad's son Fredrick "Fred" Peterson has made it through most of his primary education without significant drama. During these advanced times in an era where people demand personal space and almost everyone has an overwhelming desire to do as little as possible, "in person" classes are usually taught by Robot teachers. Robots never leave the job, never go on strike and don't get sick. School districts large and small eagerly adopted Robot teachers. No one really wants to learn much more than the basics, much less train to be a teacher. The results of students being taught by robots, predictable as they may be, are largely ignored: Good students don't excel the way that they should. Poor students don't get any attention at all and students with special needs are greatly harmed by inadequate attention from the education system.*

*Fred's best friend since grade school is T. Bob Good. "T" for Trump, a name given to him at birth by parents wanting to honor the forty fifth president by naming their firstborn son after him. When Bob and Fred started school, classes were still largely taught by human teachers. Bob was originally introduced to the school as Trump B. Good. After the kindergarten teacher refused to teach young Bob because of his first name, the Good family quickly changed young Trump's middle name from the letter B to Bob and told the school to call their child 'Bob'.*

*Bob did not do as well in school as his friend Fred. Bob's ability to pay attention to the fast-speaking mechanical teachers was as limited as his attention span. Mr. and Mrs. Good, loyal church goers and longtime supporters of conservative politics did little to help young Bob succeed as education wasn't as valued in their home and their own social standing seemed to be tied to constant participation in a video series called "Shit Happens". As he aged though the education process, Bob fell further and further behind from where he should have been. School Districts are judged on nothing other than graduation rates. Proficient or not, students are moved along. After one particularly poor semester resulting in a bad report card, the school system suggested that it may place the now teenaged T. Bob Good in remedial classes where a few human teachers could work with slower students. Never particularly active in their child's education, the Good parents rushed to the school and demanded that they be allowed to talk to these real humans about the school system's liberal politics and its insistence on negatively labeling students from God Fearing Conservative Households. T. Bob Good was allowed to remain in the mainstream classes where he continued to struggle.*

*What Mr. and Mrs. Good never caught onto; self-absorbed as they are, is that their pride and joy, young Trump Bob Good lives on what would have been called 'the spectrum of autism' less than a decade earlier. The self-absorbed parents missed another much more serious feature of Bob's personality. The young man has a passionate infatuation with masturbation.*

Fred sees his father as he comes down the stairs. Conrad Petersen is busy putting a Windsor knot in a necktie.

"Someone die, Dad?" Fred asks on his way to the kitchen.

"No? Why do you ask?" Conrad finishes tying the knot and turns to his adopted son. The man looks striking with his salt and pepper hair, his impressive muscle tone and a tan that mysteriously never seems to fade. "You mean the tie? I have a date. Her profile says that she likes her men dressed to the nines. I looked the expression up. It is code for *wear a tie.*"

"It's two in the afternoon. What time is your date?" Fred asks between bites of crispy dried carrots.

"Be careful. Those things will make your skin turn orange." Conrad comments. "My date is with a little lady who lives over at the Winchester Arms Retirement home. Dinner is served at 4:30. It's a first date. I figured we could get to know each other before dinner. That way she's already for the main event. Bedtime at those places sometimes happens before eight."

Fred yawns. After his mother passed away, his father dedicated himself to be of sexual service to older women. It had been going on for so long, Fred had never thought to question the attraction to women significantly older than even his mother would have been. He has little memory of his own mother. She died when Fred was five. Occasionally, Fred wonders what it would have been like to have grown up with his mom around. "Do I get to meet this one, Dad or she going to kick the bucket before date number two?"

Conrad smirks. "I doubt you meet this one. She doesn't even know my last name. Based on my messages back and forth with her, there is a chance that she may not know her last name." He points at the teenager. "What are you doing tonight?"

"Bob and I are hanging out. Maybe catch a little video action. He thinks his parents might be on *Shit Happens* tonight." Fred eats the last of the carrots and taps the crumbs from the bag into his mouth.

"Going to see any girls, son?" Conrad asks, finishing the knot in the tie.

"I don't think so." Fred answers. "Maybe, if we go to Mickey D's. It's real beef night. That always gets a good crowd. I am sure there will be girls there."

*Long ago, the largest hamburger chain in the world changed its name after purchasing the assets of its nearest competitor out of bankruptcy court. Federal law and it was assumed, consumer preferences had shifted away from beef. Most of the burgers served at the Golden M, as it was occasionally referred to, became made with a fabricated beef product or mushrooms. On an irregular basis, the chain would sell real beef burgers.*

"Don't you be eating any of those burgers, Freddy. Stick with the plant-based meats. Those meat patties...."

"I know.... I know.... We don't know who butchered the meat, where it came from, how it was killed... I know the drill dad." Fred smiles. "Have a good time with Mrs. Right Now."

Conrad frowns. "I think she goes by Ms." He points at Fred. "I need to check that out. No need to offend the woman."

"Better check the equipment before you go too far with her. Wouldn't want another Alex situation." Fred smirks. Alex Wynot was another *old lady* hook up that Conrad courted for several days before finding out that the *lady* was an eighty-five-year-old transgendered man who never had the guts to go all the way with the transformation. Conrad made the most of the situation. He sold Wynot a Norma Leah device.

"You know, son... some of the nurses over at the Remington are in their fifties. They might be interested in a guy like you."

Fred wrinkles his face in disgust. "That would be like being with my mom."

"Exactly." His father beams. "You let me know when you want your own Norma Leah. It would be free to you... because, you know, you are family."

"Gross Dad. Just Gross." Fred answers with an involuntary shake of his head.

Chapter 10
Introducing the real Millie.
Microsoft Hospital Powered by HoloLens Artificial Intelligence
Somewhere in the United States of America
Home of the Free(ish) Land of the Brave(ish)


*I lay in the hospital bed looking at the ceiling.*

Lamont the Robot brings in lunch. The Robot sets the tray next to the untouched tray of breakfast. After pausing while appearing to inventory the food on both trays, Lamont the Robot announces. "Patient not eating. Report Generated."

After reading all that I could stand about Dr. Mildred Cockburn, I had crawled into the bed and not slept. My mind raced most of the morning. How could she have been put into such a situation? Maybe I am thinking about it wrong. Maybe she attacked the situation exactly like she thought she needed too. What has the world come to where doctors are jailed for treating patients?

Lamont makes the beeping noise that I have come to recognize as a plea for my attention. I lift my head. "What?"

"Are you going to eat your breakfast?" Lamont asks.

I shake my head. "No. That shit is disgusting." I look at the cold soy-based eggs and pretend bacon on the plate. The sight of the food nauseated me when the little tin can rolled it in at six this morning just as it does now. I declined to go to physical therapy with Meathead. I'm sure that was a generated report too. "Take the breakfast tray with you. I will see if I can choke down lunch." The rubber eggs are usually followed by a lunch of vegetable based hot dogs on a gluten free buns, which, if eaten with enough mustard are palatable.

Lamont the robot picks up the uneaten breakfast and wheels out of the room.  A few minutes later the door opens. I sit up, anticipating Millie. It's a robot I do not recognize.

The little silver tube rolls over to the bed. "I am Dr. Lionel. I am here to do a wellness check on Patient Justin Thyme."

"Does this wellness check involve shoving a probe up my ass?" I ask sourly. One of the robot doctors seem to have an unexplained predilection for such things.

"No. Blood and vitals." The robot replies mechanically. I hold my hand out. My index finger is pricked and a blood sample taken. "Blood sugar, Normal. Electrolytes, Normal. PSA, Normal. No signs of terminal disease." The robot extends an arm from a little silver door. My blood pressure is taken. "Blood Pressure Normal. Pulse, Normal. Report Generated." The robot releases me and rolls backwards.

"You appear melancholy, Patient Justin Thyme. Are you feeling well?" Dr. Lionel the Robot asks.

"I'm fine." I say as I lay back on the pillow.

"Do you have any questions?" The Robot asks.
"Why do human beings suck?" I ask. I roll over and look at the robot, expecting a pause before it processes that it has no answer for my question and rolls out of the room.

Little lights blink on the top of Lionel the Robot before the reply is delivered. "Humans are conditioned to love. They need each other. It is important for humans to find other humans that they can find safe conditions to express themselves with. Humans depend on connections and compassion to be happy. Soon, you will be released from Microsoft Medical Systems. It is important that you find a human or humans that you can share connections and compassions with. I see that you are sad. Do you need me to prescribe medication to help you not feel while you are under the care of Microsoft Medical Systems?"

I study Lionel the Robot and think for a minute before answering. "No."

"Is there anything I can do for you Patient Justin Thyme?"

" You can tell me why society in the United States seems so fucked up." I answer.

Now I really expect the robot to silently roll out of the room. The little lights blink on top of the robot. "Microsoft Medical Systems does not comment on social or political issues." The robot rolls back and forth like it is going to add something before it simply repeats, "Microsoft Medical Systems does not comment of social or political issues." After a few more blinking lights it turns and rolls out of the room.

I lay back on the bed and stare at the ceiling, thinking about what Reverend Moo and now the Philosopher Robot, Lionel have told me. The cow had told me that things were in disarray, and I was being sent to help. Was I sent to help Millie? Society as a whole? I was in a goddamn coma for twenty years. What in the fuck does the cow and that goddamn bear want me to do? It appears the world needed significant help prior to my coma. What in the hell am I supposed to do now, twenty plus years on with little knowledge about how things work in the world today? Lionel's words keep running through my mind. *Humans depend on connections and compassion to be happy...* Millie hasn't had connections. I have no idea about compassion. She doesn't speak about her relationship with her ex-husband, and she hasn't mentioned anyone she is close to now. So far as I can tell, she has been completely separated from the humans she was connected with.

*Humans depend on connections and compassion to be happy...* I shake my head. I really want to see Millie.

A few hours go by. I hear the door open. It's Millie. I can *feel* it. I swing my hips over the side of the bed and jump up, almost knocking the open laptop off the bed. That damn laptop. I was so excited to learn about what the world was like after being Rip Van Winkle for twenty years. I glance at it as I rush towards Millie, it's still displaying the information I had spent the night reading about her. I meet her at the foot of the bed and grab her into a big hug. In seconds, both of us are crying our eyes out. I am crying because I see past that beautiful smile and I can feel part of her pain, now. It doesn't mix well with the pain I feel about missing out on the last twenty years, although I have little idea what might have happened if I had been a normal, functioning member of society over those twenty years. It's not as if I had exhibited any signs of traveling down the path of being an actual responsible adult prior to my accident. I guide Millie back to the bed. We sit on the mattress. I lift the computer. The screen comes on. We both look at the picture of Millie's smiling face.

"Hello, Dr. Cockburn." I say, My voice cracking. We both start crying again.

*Dr. Mildred Cockburn was a medical doctor in Dallas, Texas. In 2024, she was found to be in violation of the Texas anti-abortion law that prohibited any abortion after conception.*

*On November 21st of 2023, Focus Gluey Fork Paxton, a twenty-nine-year-old mother of two living in Dallas, Texas and her husband U.Ra Richard Paxton petitioned a Texas court to allow Mrs. Paxton to request an abortion from her medical provider as Mrs. Paxton's pregnancy, in its 20th week had been determined by Dr. Mildred Cockburn and other medical professionals to be non-viable. In one, unnamed medical professional's view, continuing to carry the baby would put Mrs. Paxton's life at risk.*

*On December 1st, 2023, a Texas district court judge ruled that Mrs. Paxton could proceed with an abortion stating that it would be a "miscarriage of justice" to force Paxton to continue the pregnancy. The State Attorney General of Texas disagreed and filed a petition against the decision with the State Supreme Court of Texas which immediately issued a halt in the ruling for Paxton.*

*Dr. Cockburn, who, at the time, owned the Pathway Women's Clinic ignored the order and on December 3rd, 2023, performed an abortion of Paxton's pregnancy at her clinic in Dallas. Cockburn was arrested on December 10th, 2023, by Texas Rangers acting under orders from the State of Texas Attorney General's office. Cockburn was sentenced to eighteen years in prison in an expedited trial on January 14th, 2024. She was released on parole on August 8th, 2033, on the condition that she no longer practice medicine.*

*Mildred Cockburn was married to Rexford Ratchet of Dallas, Texas who is the founder of the religious group, Christians in Pursuit of the Scoundrel Pontius Pilate. Ratchet filed for divorce on grounds of abandonment and unreconcilable differences in February of 2024. Texas courts granted rights and control of Cockburn's assets to Rexford Ratchet in a hearing on March 10th, 2024. In a separate hearing in April 2025, the state of Texas successfully petitioned the medical licensing board to strip Cockburn of her medical license. The State of Texas requested Baylor University Medical school to rescind Cockburn's Doctorate of Medicine. Baylor did not respond to the request from the State of Texas. Mildred Cockburn's whereabouts are unknown at the time of this query.*

Chapter 11
Weird Shit happens everywhere. We are going back in time.
Someplace in China.
At the time, neither Free(ish) or particularly Brave(ish)


*Robert and Thomas Katz were re-married in a fabulous ceremony on the island of Kauai in Hawaii. Gay marriage was made legal in 2015. The pair had run right down to the courthouse and gotten married in their suburban town on the very day it was legal to do so. The Katz's, both die hard Star Wars fans waited until 2018 to re-new their vows and make the union super official. The long wait for the fabulous occasion was only because the first May 4th time slot the Fern Grotto had was in the year 2018. After the fabulous event and following a night frolicking naked in the private pool at their seaside cottage Bob and Tom boarded an aircraft to China to collect their child that was born, as planned at the exact time on May 4th, 2018, that Bob and Tom recited their vows to each other.*
*Robert "Bob" Katz sells blood products. His company, HemoVerse buys and sells plasma and blood components to institutional buyers all over the world. With his jet-black hair, translucent complexion and naturally bright red lips, Bob bears an uncanny resemblance to a mythical creature that could be the mascot of his company. Thomas "Tom" Katz is tall and very skinny in a very terrific way. He is a jewelry manufacturer. He made the pair wedding bands the day after he and Bob met. Tom is every bit as feminine as any of the women he knows, and he strives to be more so in any way that he can.*

*During one of Bob's many professional visits to Mainland China, he built a relationship with MPM Genome, a company working on gene sequencing and, as it turns out, a process to choose the traits of a baby before it is born.*
*On August 4th, 2017, Bob and Tom Katz had sat down with the scientists at MPM Genome in China and selected what they wanted in a child.*

"White." Both Bob and Tom say in unison. The turn to each other and add in unison. "White-ish."

"Can he be sort of brown?" Bob asks.
"And tall. As tall as me, at least." Tom says. Bob nods in agreement.

"But muscular." Bob insisted. "Tom can't put muscles on his bean pole like frame to save his life."

"Certainly, he needs a dark complexion." Tom requested. "Not skin that is eggshell white like the love of my life, Bob."

"Six pack abs!" Both the men said at once. "And thick wavy hair." Tom added, pointing at Bob's head. "No widow's peak like Dracula here has."

*After the love birds had described the Adonis like creature they wanted for a child, the director of the lab asked who they wanted to use for an egg donor.*

"Egg Donor?" Tom Katz asked. "What do we need an egg donor for?"

"I thought MGM Genome had this all figured out!" Bob Katz exclaimed, worried about the wire transfer he had earlier completed to the Chinese lab.

The Lab Director of Mortal Physical Metaphysical Genome sighed politely in that way only Asians can when dealing with imbeciles. He folded his hands together and smiled gently. "Mr. Katz and... Mr. Katz, to reproduce human beings, we need an egg from a female and sperm from a male. MGM Genome will alter the DNAs of the sperm and egg to provide that the human you want will be born with the characteristics that you have described."

"Well, we are fresh out of female eggs!" Tom Katz exclaimed with a sarcastic tone, tears coming to his eyes. He turned to his partner in life. "Bobby, what ever will we do? I can make a nice diamond ring, but I can't make a goddamn egg! I know! I have tried!"

Bob so wants to make a comment about Tom's inability to cook anything past two hundred- and twelve-degree water, but refrains. Like nearly anything else in life, this is simply a transactional issue. He shakes his head slowly with a look of disappointment. Years of negotiating the cost of this body fluid and that body fluid had taught him that there is a sure way out of any misunderstanding or hiccup in the transactional process. "How much for an egg?"

The Chinese scientist smiles. Young healthy white women in China aren't available in high numbers, but they are available and almost everyone likes money, especially for something that was going to get tossed in a trash can wadded up in a pile of cotton anyway. "Another $100,000 should cover it, Mr. Katz."

Bob is about to call the whole deal off and ask for all his money back. Mentally he is accessing what sort of penalty he is willing to pay the Chinese customer to back out of the deal. (After all MGM is also a HemoVerse customer.) A hand grabs his arm. He turns and looks into Tom's pleading eyes. After a long sigh he pulls out his cellular phone and wires another $100,000 to MGM Genome.

On the 6th of May 2018 in Mainland China, after filling out the necessary Chinese adoption paperwork and making sure the United States State Department requirements were all met, Bob and Tom were handed a swaddled baby boy. They had already picked out the most fabulous name the two Star Wars fanatics could agree upon.
The young man would be called Yoda Storm Trooper Katz.

Chapter 12
'Don't call me Kitty Katz' She hearts Yoda.
Robot Doctors get all up in your Netherlands now.
Sad news is a part of life.
The Republic of Texas. Still, a part of the United States of America
The Home of the Free(ish) Land of the Brave(ish)


*It has been become clear that future medical care in the United States is… different than what had been considered the norm for much of the 20th and early 21st century. Gone are the days of a regular General Practitioner or regular Internist that you might see for a sinus infection or a broken bone. It was evolution that led to this. First, Insurance companies did joint ventures with the large pharmacy outlets. They didn't pay the Physicians Assistants and Nurse Practitioners enough and the product provided to patients suffered. Eventually Walgreens and CVS had to merge to stay afloat. Then 'Big Medical' was allowed to merge with 'Big Pharma' and the medical Robot concept came into play. Medical Schools around the United States closed. The ones that stayed open reduced the time one needed to spend in medical school and residency to become a doctor from the eight years Millie, Conrad Peterson and I put in to a little over two years, including six months of 'hands on robot care'. The results are mixed. My experience with Microsoft Medical Systems wasn't terrible. The Robots are pretty efficient, and it is not as if hospital food was gourmet and medical care was just dandy in 2022. After a while, I started to think of Meathead the Robot as my friend. I liked Lamont the Robot bringing me my food three times a day. Health Care is still very expensive for the average American. In 2022 when I was a doctor, the average American family spent around fifteen percent of its income on medical care. In 2042, the calculation is almost twenty two percent. In that regard, the United States of America leads the world in something besides weapon sales… Household Medical Costs. Most of the world outside of the United States was on a single payer health care system in 2022. Indeed, in what appears to be a rare instance of legislative efficiency, the concept was tried for exactly one presidential term between 2032 and 2036. And then a new presidential administration took office, more lobbyist were allowed to present Big Medical's case against the single payer health system and the Supreme Court stepped in and ruled that that medical care cannot be forced on anyone, let alone everyone and instructed congress to reverse the bill that had been loved by nearly every citizen of the country because it created an equitable system of health care.*

*CVS and Walgreens both filed bankruptcy after the real estate market crashed in 2035. A hedge fund created by Susan Icahn Buffett Milken, the great grandniece of Warren Buffett (mother's side) and Carl Icahn (Sperm Donor transvestite father) bought assets of the company out of bankruptcy and formed CV Greens. The real estate was quickly sold off and converted into transporter washes and apartment buildings. CV Greens is now a chain of small footprint store fronts where customers can find basic medical care, done by autonomous robots and drug distribution, done with ordinary vending machines.*

Kitty Williams had just finished her appointment with the Robodoctor at her local CV Greens. The anamorphic machine took her vitals, noted her pregnant condition, discovered the lack of any heartbeat in said pregnant condition and promptly provided Kitty a referral to an obstetrician on Kitty's health care insurance plan. Additionally, the Robodoctor sent referral information to a plastic surgeon who would certainly nip and tuck any unsightly loose skin on the woman back into place after the birth and a dermatologist to remove a small beauty mark that absolutely could maybe, possibly be cancerous on the left side of the woman's right breast. Kitty will be hounded relentlessly by both the plastic surgeon offices and the dermatologist's offices for months following the visit.

Yoda Storm Trooper Williams, he of novel genetic selection is Kitty's adoring husband. His two loving dads, Bob and Tom Katz, fans of the legendary, late filmmaker George Lucas and his memorialized creation, Star Wars, used a Chinese company to obtain their little Yoda. That company was investigated by the Chinese Government for fraudulent support of American Interests and was absorbed by a larger, Government controlled Chinese Genomics company soon after Yoda's birth.

Yoda's future physical traits had been carefully poured over. The smallest detail of their son's physical being was discussed, argued, and final agreed upon. Sadly, Bob and Tom forgot to inquire about two traits when they were thinking about what they wanted their son to become in life. First, Yoda was born straight as an arrow. (Gross, said Bob Katz when he realized who... or rather, what his son Yoda would be looking at when Tom and Bob took him cruising for young guys on the beach.) Second, Yoda seems to be as dumb as a bag of hair.

Katherine "Kitty" Williams was born in a fashion considered normal, even mundane. Her father, Willem Williams had sex with her mother, Wendy Williams. Lots of it. Neither Willem nor Wendy would really recall what sexual position Kitty was conceived in (It was missionary) but would both proudly proclaim that several positions would have been attempted during any singular sexual session. Kitty grew up in anyone's idea of a loving home. Her mother and father are both lawyers specializing in product liability lawsuits - normally representing the consumer because presenting cases *to twelve people too dumb to get out of civil jury duty* is just too good of a deal to pass up. Kitty was sent to all the right schools. She was introduced to all the right people. She was also educated about sex by her mother and father. Much of the William's legal business happened internationally. As the United States started to ban more and more forms of contraception, the Williams's would procure birth controls from exotic locations like Sweden and Norway for Kitty and her mother Wendy who had decided that bringing one child in the world *was quite enough work, thank you.*

Kitty knew how to take care of herself. Such things had to be done very quietly as even possession of birth control bills is considered a federal felony.

After primary school, Kitty took the six-month law program at the University of Michigan. Six months is one of the longest courses of legal study in the USA. Most colleges offer a six-week course that enables participants to begin their legal careers very quickly, albeit with very little actual legal knowledge. It was at the University of Michigan that she met Yoda, a star linebacker/running back for Michigan's virtual football team. Football, the physical sport involving grown ass men beating the hell out of each other on an artificial grass field was basically banned in 2032 for two reasons. First, a wide receiver (earning a little over one thousand dollars a month) playing for the Akron Zips was killed instantly when he was hit by a third string linebacker (who at the time was making close to a million dollars a year) from the Buckeyes of Ohio State. Ohio State was up 78 - 0 at the time. (The linebacker from Ohio State was quickly given a raise for his effort.) Second, women started to sue the NCAA *(Yes... sadly, this organization was still around.)* and the NFL for discrimination at not being given the chance to play football with either division. Seeing a likely loss at all levels of the judicial systems, a joint agreement between the NCAA and the NFL was made to make football (and later basketball with the NBA) both virtual and co-ed. Yoda Storm Trooper Williams was one of the star players for the Michigan Wolverines that took home the NCAA National Championship for four straight years, 2033 - 2036.

Kitty and Yoda met at a university mixer following the 2035 championship virtual football match over Quinnipiac University. The two made a beautiful, if intellectually ill-matched couple. She, a statuesque black woman of terrific genetic selection and Yoda, a gorgeously designed and built muscular jock with Northern European and African ancestry.

Bob and Tom had totally thought that their son would be a hit in all the fancy gay nightclubs with his imposing physical presence. When they were selecting the traits that would make their Yoda the most attractive man in the world, Tom suggested that the boy needed a closer. The "closer" hanging between Yoda's legs measured about the same length as his shoe size and when erect, a girth that would allow for a small swing to installed for a squirrel if such a thing was real or necessary. Needless to say, young Katherine found significant pleasure from the closer. It allowed her to both overlook Yoda's incredible stupidity and gift her Malcom vibrator to her law school partner, a petite Filipino man named Alejandro Cruz.

Kitty, as she likes to be called, proposed to Yoda while watching the northern lights on a virtual whale watching cruise in the Bahamas. After explaining to Yoda what marriage is (twice, before he said yes), Kitty told Yoda Storm Trooper Katz that she would not be sharing his last name. He would be welcome to become a Williams, but there was no fucking way she would go through life as Kitty Katz.

After clumsily explaining that he had no idea that women sometimes took the last names of their husbands as their own, Yoda said *Yes* to the marriage. After introductions to both sets of parents, a date was set. Willem Williams was not immediately impressed with his future son in law. After playing real contact football at a very high level in both high school and college, Willem had little interest in *virtual* sports and the object of his daughter's affection seemed stupid enough to drown in light rainstorm. Wendy Williams however understood completely what her daughter saw in Yoda and in fact, imagined the young man's magnificent body frequently when masturbating and only slightly less frequently during her and Willem's frequent marathon sex sessions. Bob and Tom Katz were privately disgusted that Yoda, their only son, a beautiful, fabulous boy, never decided that he was really a beautiful gay man. The couple, both whiter than rice, did appreciate Kitty Williams' statuesque beauty and of course, they wasted no time telling all their friends that Yoda was marrying a pretty *black* girl.

Kitty and Yoda were married at her parent's country club in an exclusive, non-religious wedding open to The William's clients, Bob Katz's clients and few of Kitty and Yoda's friends. Tom Katz made their wedding rings. A titanium band for Yoda inlaid with alternating dark blue sapphire and bright yellow citrine studs and for Kitty, a 2.5 carat diamond that made her hand nearly invisible. After the wedding, Kitty and Yoda moved to Dallas, Texas where she became head counsel for oil pipeline startup.

*A dead baby in utero is no joke in the modern world.*

*The laws prohibiting abortion were poorly written and as such doctors have become hesitant, even outright resistant to performing routine procedures, like delivering a still born baby before it's due date. The federal government adopted the Texas based law that allows anyone to turn anyone else in for suspected crimes against the state for financial reward. The reward to turn someone in who has performed an abortion, or a procedure that could be perceived as an abortion is now one million dollars. The offending physician would not only have to pay the million dollars but would have to spend 9 months in jail. (The penalty was arrived at because it represented the amount of time a human woman is pregnant.) Such accusations are most frequently made in secret. The accuser is kept confidential* (United States Supreme Court Case Bricks v Feathers, 2034.) *When the reward is enough to buy a new transporter, the physician performing the procedure must worry about everyone who might rat them out, from the attending nurses to the desk clerk to the janitors.*

Katherine "Kitty" Williams and her seemingly very stupid but good looking and well-endowed husband, Yoda Storm Trooper Williams are trying very hard to live as independent adults. They don't like calling their parents for things and as such, neither reached out to his or her parental unit despite the fact that either sets of monied parents... the Katz's or the Williams's would have had the power and financial ability to help Kitty and Yoda escape the mess that would threaten both of their lives.

Money: after all, solves lots of problems. It is but one reason that the rich get richer, and the poor get poorer.

Chapter 13
Reality sucks.
CV Greens Storefront, Dallas, Texas
Still a place in the United States of America
Home of the Free(ish) Land of the Brave(ish)


Yoda Storm Trooper Williams watches the reruns of *Shit Happens* on the monitor in the waiting room of the CV Greens. He smiles as a man dressed up like a big brown dog runs up a street chasing transporters. A young woman on a skateboard plows into the dog, sending everyone involved to the ground. "That's not as good as the woman whose dress got ripped off." Williams yells at the monitor. A new episode starts. Soon a bikini clad woman on a pogo stick hops into view. Yoda Storm Trooper Williams sits up straighter in his chair. "Yeah, this could beat the Dress woman..."
"The baby is dead." Cradling the bump in her middle, Kitty Williams, plops down in the chair beside her husband.

Yoda looks over at his wife and points at the monitor. "You think that woman has a bun in the oven? And... its dead?"

Kitty forces a smile on her face as she looks at the gorgeous face of her rather dense but well-endowed husband. "No, dear. The bun in my oven is dead. There is no heartbeat."

The wrinkles in Yoda's forehead crease and his brow furrows together. "That doesn't sound right. Maybe the baby is just sleeping."
With pursed lips, Kitty traces her husband's strong jawline. "Sweetie. Do you think that your heart stops beating when you sleep?" She watches her husband's hazel-colored eyes roll upward as if help was necessary to extract the answer from a dark closet in the corner of a relative empty mind.

"Umm...?" Refocused eyes alert her to the arrival of the delayed answer. "I don't know what happens when I am sleeping. I am asleep then. With my eyes closed."

"Our hearts are always beating dear. At least, when we are alive. When we are dead, our hearts stop beating." Kitty answers slowly.
"The Tin Man in Raiders of the Lost Death Star didn't have a heart. He was alive." Yoda says nodding his head while thinking about one of his favorite shows, a reboot of three franchises in one movie. "I think you might be wrong."

Kitty sighs and pats her husband's muscular leg. "Well, I might be wrong on the subject as it applies to the Tin Man... but the RoboDoctor in there says our baby is dead."

Yoda considers this information. "Robodoctors are pretty smart. They have to be programmed well." He lets out a defeated sigh. "So, we are not having a baby?"

Kitty wipes a tear from the corner of her eye. "We are not having a live baby." She puts her forehead on her husband's shoulder. "We need to find an obstetrician to deliver our daughter."

"And then she will be alive?" Yoda asks, his posture straightening. Kitty exhales and sadly shakes her head. "No." The woman pats the small volleyball shaped bump under her sweater. "We need to go now. I have an appointment with a live doctor across town."

Yoda looks at the monitor. "*Shit Happens* is on here." He says, pointing.
Kitty squints at the monitor. "*Shit Happens* is on everywhere. It's all anyone watches."

"We should submit this moment. This is Shit. Happening to us." Yoda says morosely.

His wife nods. "Indeed. But, if you send a recording of this moment to anyone, I will cut your dick off when you are sleeping."

"That would hurt." Yoda exclaims as he stands, having the good sense to extend a hand to his wife and helping her up. "Think I would wake up?"

"I wonder that every day, dear." Kitty Williams answers wryly as they leave CV Greens and get in their transporter.

Kitty Williams pilots the mobility device. She likes taking the controls from the vehicle. It feels good to have control of the machine, even though the transporter will grab the controls like a 1990's driver's ed instructor and take over at the slightest hint of speeding or swerving. Out of the corner of her eye, she sees her husband tapping on the entertainment screen in front of him. "It won't come back on." He complains.

Kitty smiles and reaches over to tap the power button. "It's the circle with the line through it, dear. It's always the circle with the line through it." The vehicle takes control from her with an audible tone and a disembodied voice calling out a warning. *Distracted driver. Taking the controls NOW. Let Geely get you there safely. Don't take control. Take a nap!* Rather than re-take the controls of the vehicle back, she turns in her seat and watches her husband start a game where it appears the object is to shoot clowns that pop up from the earth. Yoda is still very, very good at video games. He gets through several advanced levels very quickly.
"Let me do the talking when we see the doctor. Is that ok, Yoda." Kitty asks with her clear, firm lawyer voice.

"You got it, Kitty Katz." Yoda replies in a sing song voice as three clown heads disappear in a cloud of pink mist on the screen.

"Don't call me that." Katherine says in a whisper. She looks out the front window. The doctor's office is a large tower that goes up through the clouds. It is in view now. "We are almost there. Finish up your game."
"I can just pause it. What is the pause button? The circle with the line through it?" Yoda asks.

Kitty reaches over and pauses the screen as the transporter pulls up to the front door. "It is the two dots and the arrow."

"Seems weird. I always think that is the on and off button." Yoda comments as the transporter stops.

"Not for a hundred years or so." Kitty says. She is nervous. In her gut, she knows that this visit may not go well. While her specialty in Law School had been Moon and Ocean Real Estate issues, she had spent a week studying personal responsibility laws as they had become known as. Her future health is on a collision course with her current condition.

A robot clerk dressed in a lightweight spring print dress greets them at the door. "Hello, thank you for coming to One Health, Your Health, My Health. We are glad to see you, even if you are a little sick. Referral slip, please."

Kitty Williams hands up the piece of paper she had received at CV Greens. Why paper is still handed out in the year 2042 is anyone's guess. Kitty assumes it is because paper gets lost. Without the referral, she cannot see the specialist. She would have to pay CV Greens to do another referral. The robot clerk scans it with her right robot hand. Kitty notes that the ends of the fingers have been painted a bright pink. "K.K... Katherine W, W, W, Williams." The Robot Clerk Stutters. "I'm... I'm... I'mm... Sorry. My batteries are little l, l, l, low." The Robot Clerk's head bows forward and rests on the desk. Kitty looks at Yoda who shrugs.

"We can just go in?" He asks with a hopeful tone.

Kitty shakes her head. "I don't think so." She looks at the communicator on the desk, trying to decide who she would call if she could figure out how to use the apparatus. A door opens and a Robot dressed in a gray suit enters the area. "Can I help you?" The Robot asks in a voice that hints of anger, lack of patience and boredom. Management Robot. Kitty thinks to herself. Robots supervising robots were the newest way for corporations to save money. The medical business could utilize such things in the front of the house, but in the back, humans had to supervise the Robots. She holds up her referral slip. The Management Robot pushes the Robot Clerk out of the way. "Must be in position to scan." It offers in explanation for the action. Holding up a Robot hand, it scans the referral. "Twenty eighth floor, room 2...8...0...1. Your insurance has been billed for this visit." The Management Robot turns to Yoda. "You have a referral? Please show it to me."

Yoda gets down to the Management Robot's level. "I knew a guy like you once. Played for Ohio State. Those cheaters. Had a Robot on the team."
Kitty sighs. "He is with me. My husband."

"Proceed." The Management Robot says with a bored tone.
As the door starts to shut behind Kitty and Yoda, both hear, "Michigan Sucks. Buckeyes rule! Buckeyes rule!"

"Smart ass! I will show you who rules!" Yoda says loudly as he turns.

Kitty grabs his arm and yanks hard. "Let it go, Yoda. We don't care about sports right now." They step onto the elevator. A video monitor comes on as the elevator starts to rise. A blond woman appears on the screen. She has a deep tan and is wearing a red and white polka dot bikini and is clearly not pregnant. The scene behind her is an ocean beach. She sits down in a beach chair and starts talking about importance of a specific brand of pregnancy vitamins.

"We should stop and get some of those pills." Yoda points at the monitor. "That woman says they are good for babies."

"Our baby is dead. I don't need to take vitamins for the baby." Kitty remarks sadly. The elevator stops and the pair gets out. A RoboClerk greets them by name enthusiastically. "Katherine Williams! And... Yoda Storm Trooper Williams. It is nice to have you here as patients. May I see your referral?" The robot lifts an arm. Kitty holds the referral out and it is scanned.

"Your insurance has already been charged. The doctor will see you shortly. Please wait."

Kitty leads Yoda to a pair of chairs. They are the only two in the room. After a few minutes, a blond human woman opens the door. Kitty notes that the woman is far along in her pregnancy. She smiles at the person behind her, a human nurse with Kool Aid pink hair. Both laugh at some unheard joke. The blond woman nods at Kitty with a knowing smile as she makes her to the elevator bank.

"Cunt." Katherine Williams says under her breath.

Yoda sits up and looks around. "Where?"

"Hush." Kitty growls.

"Katherine Williams?" Kool Aid pink hair holds a handheld computer. She looks around the room before landing her eyes on Kitty. "Katherine Williams? Are you Katherine Williams?"

Kitty raises her eyebrows. "It appears that way, yes." She gets to her feet. "Come on Yoda. Let's go get this over with." Her husband stands and they walk through the door held open by the nurse.

"I see that you are here for a checkup? You were referred by CV Greens?" The nurse reads from a screen.

"I went for a checkup. There is no heartbeat." Kitty says in a flat tone.

The nurse smiles. "That's great! Let's get you weighed and then into a room. You are seeing a human doctor today! Dr. Worm will be right with you."

"Dr. Worm." Yoda remarks with a laugh.

The nurse leads Kitty to a scale. The digital readout indicates that she has lost weight since the last visit. "Keeping trim! Very nice! It will be easy to get back in shape after your baby is born!" The pink haired woman says with a tone indicating that the response is one of three or four she uses with every patient. She motions at the pair, leading them to a consultation room. "Please wait in here. Dr. Worm will be with you shortly."

"Dr. Worm." Yoda sniggers, shaking his head.
"Hush, Yoda." Kitty says through clenched teeth. She is nervous. She doesn't know this Dr. Worm. The doctor is simply assigned the referral.

*Patients don't have the luxury of picking their specialty doctors. The corporations that manage hospitals and medical groups had taken control of healthcare from the patient. Most care is provided by Robot doctors supervised by a human in some manner, Human doctors, for the most part, are paid performance bonuses based on the number of patients seen per day and on how many procedures the doctor can sell to patients. Bonuses are paid if the procedures can be performed completely by Robots. Several Supreme Court decisions led to this happening. It started with Dobbs v Jackson, which essentially laid the groundwork to strip the rights of individuals to make medical decisions. Later court decisions have upheld the decision in Dobbs. 'It is not in the constitution' has become the lead statement in many Supreme Court Rulings concerning the health and welfare of United States Citizens.*

The pair sits silently in the darkened room. "So, what happens next?" Yoda whispers.

"I don't know, Yoda." Kitty answers. She thinks about what will happen next. As a pregnant woman, she is no longer allowed to travel to foreign nations where an abortion might be possible. She harbors doubts that this Dr. Worm will be in any way helpful. She thinks that she should have called her parents, but they already have so much going on...

The white wall in front of them turns into a monitor. An advertisement featuring a perky blond woman who is impossibly fit starts. "Your baby is coming soon!" The woman bends forward in a seductive manner and waggles an index finger at the camera. "You need the latest in crib and transporter securement for your child. I chose Southwick Industries to keep my little Mushroom Burger safe while she sleeps. The camera pans to a toddler sized child seemingly asleep in a crib. As if on cue, the child wakes up and looks at the camera. "Thank you for keeping me safe in my Southwick crib, Mommy." The commercial fades out with the well-known Southwick Industries logo in a boldfaced font. A scroll at the bottom of the logo reads, "The standard for Cribs, Child Seats, Industrial Transportation Seating, Gas Chambers, Electric Chairs and More."

A commercial for PPP vibrators starts but stops when a woman wearing tie died scrubs walks into the room. A stethoscope hangs around her tattooed neck. "Hello Mrs. and Mr." The woman stops and looks at her electronic pad. "Mrs. and Mr. Williams. My name is Dr. Ivanna. You are here to talk about your pregnancy I see."

"We were expecting Dr. Worm. Are you in the right room? I don't want any trouble with the insurance company." Kitty Williams explains.

The woman gives a seemingly reluctant smile, the motion makes the mouse tattoo on the left side of her neck look like it waves a small mouse paw. "I am Dr. Worm. Dr. Ivanna Worm."

Yoda snorts. "Your name is Ivanna Worm? Ivanna... Worm... Like a little bird! I wanna worm!" He covers his mouth as he exaggerates the words. "That's hilarious."

Kitty Williams frowns. She notes the tattoo of a ring on the woman's left hand. "You took your husband's name?" She blows out a raspberry with her lips and gestures to Yoda. "His last name was Katz. We kept my last name."

The doctor's expression goes flat. "My husband's last name is Dick. Mike Dick. He didn't want to be Mike Worm. I have no idea why. Mike Worm is clearly better than Mike Dick. Anyway, It's cool. Not Boring. Not at all."

"Oh." Kitty says, unsure what to say next. She looks at her husband who has tears running out of his eyes.

"Her name could have been Ivanna Dick!" He says in a tone that suggests he isn't remembering that the doctor is standing in front of him. "Hush, Yoda. Please." Kitty says in a tired tone before turning back to the doctor. "Dr. Ivanna, you have my charts from the CV Greens Robodoctor. As you can see, my baby no longer has a heartbeat."

The woman taps on her pad. "Yes. You are correct. Do you want me to verify?"

Kitty shrugs and pulls her sweater up, revealing a swollen belly. "Have at it."

The doctor puts the stethoscope on her skin, the cold surface causes Kitty to jump. After tapping on the pad a few times and moving the stethoscope around some, the doctor takes a step back. "Your baby is dead."

Kitty's face remains expressionless. "Yes. I know. I knew before I went to the C.V. Greens Clinic. When are we taking it out?"

The doctor consults her electronic pad. "You are not due for another three months." She looks up and smiles. "So, three months from now."

Kitty regards the doctor cooly. "Lady... I have a dead baby inside me. I want it out of my body."

The doctor takes out a note pad and scribbles some notes on it before tearing the paper from the pad and folding it. "You might have noticed, all of our interactions here are recorded. You probably refer to this hospital as One Health. You may or may not be aware that the full name of this establishment is the First Assembly of Nazarene and Baptist One Health Care Center." She smiles weakly. "We simply are not in the position here to help you abort this pregnancy."

"It isn't a pregnancy. It's a miscarriage!" Kitty exclaims loudly. "At this moment, it is both a miscarriage of pregnancy and justice!" Yoda has become aware that his wife is losing her patience, her tone is very much like when he forgets to put the toilet seat down.

Dr. Ivanna Worm pats Kitty on the arm and hands her the slip of paper. "The management of this hospital says that you are pregnant and will be until you deliver the baby in three months." She nods at the paper. "You will be experiencing some cramping. It may be severe. I am referring you to a care giver that can help you with breathing exercises. He may also have some holistic treatments that may relieve pain, although, One Health does not recommend any sort of holistic treatments for pain... or for that matter, much of anything. We are very reliant on pharmaceuticals here."

"What if the dead baby inside me poisons my body?" Kitty yells at the woman as she rises from the chair. Yoda instinctively grabs her arm. "Let go of me, asshole!" She snarls. Something inside of Yoda's slow-moving brain encourages him to continue holding his wife back.

"The management of First Assembly of Nazarene and Baptist One Health Care strongly recommends... prayer." Dr. Ivanna Worm says in a tone suggesting that she has delivered the line countless times without ever believing the words spoken. "I personally recommend that you look into the breathing exercises from the provider that I wrote down for you." The doctor opens the door to the examination room and turns with a smile before leaving. "Please give me a positive rating on the way out. My compensation is affected by our patient's review of my services."
"Fuck you! And fuck your compensation!" Kitty shouts as the woman leaves. She is almost immediately replaced by the Kool Aid pink haired nurse. "I have some things to go over with you before you leave. First, on a scale of one to three with three being the best, how was your experience with Dr. Worm?"

Katherine Williams' eyes narrow. A low growl escapes from her lips. The piece of paper that Dr. Worm had handed her is crumpled. She throws it at the nurse. Yoda watches as it bounces off the forehead of the unblinking woman. "We are leaving! Let's go, Yoda."

Uncharacteristic to his normal aloof, unaware and self-centered personality, Yoda looks at the crumpled paper on the carpeted floor. Believing it might be important (After all, a human Doctor wrote it!) he reaches down and scoops it up, putting it in his hip pocket. Kitty is already out the door of the examination room when he hears the nurse say, "We have to go over your delivery room options. Do you want the real beef dinner or a modified protein dinner during your birth event?"

"I think she is leaving." Yoda says to the pink haired woman before hurrying to catch up with his wife.

Chapter 14
Hole in One. Your electric transporter goes how far?
Yoda and Kitty's place Dallas Texas
Still a place in the Land of the Free(ish) and Home of the Brave(ish)


"Aghhh." Yoda Storm Trooper Williams hears the cry in pain and looks closely at the monitor on the wall. *Indiana Skywalker and the Temple on Hoth* plays. Yoda has watched it so many times he has it memorized. "I don't remember Indiana Skywalker saying that in this part of the movie. The scene on the monitor changes. The movie is interrupted for a commercial break. A brief reminder runs promoting an upcoming episode of *I Got Off On That.* A short clip of a man using a biodegradable bag of mayonnaise in an unconventional way plays. "Ick." Yoda says to the monitor.

"Aghhh!" Yoda hears the cry again. "Kitty? Are you watching a movie without me?" He calls out.

"Get in here, you bastard!" Kitty Williams yells out.

Yoda pads towards the bathroom. "Bastard is not a good word anymore. It is offensive to people who don't know who their father is, so you aren't supposed to use it. Also, Bob and Tom are my fathers. I have two fathers... which I suppose could be considered a surplus of fathers." He opens the burnt orange bathroom door. His wife sits on the Texas Longhorn burnt orange toilet. Yoda had wanted to change the porcelain bowl to something more appropriate, like a Michigan Maize and Blue toilet... but the contract from the seller of the condominium demanded that the buyers keep the Texas Longhorn motif for at least ten years in exchange for being able to buy the residence. "Are you ok, Kitty?"
"What the fuck do you think? No! No, I am not OK. The Cramps!" Kitty doubles over. "Arghhghgh." She straightens. "Fuck! Fuck! Fuck! It hurts!"

Yoda stands dumbly in the bathroom door. "What do you want me to do?"

Kitty looks up, anger in her eyes. She sees genuine fear and worry in her husband's face and takes a deep breath. "I think I need a doctor."

"I think I can help!" Yoda announces, holding a finger up in the air to signal that he has an idea.

Kitty thinks he wants what he always wants... sex.  It was *so fun* at one time when Yoda wanted sex.  She grimaces and shakes her head. "No, Yoda... This isn't a thing that sex is..." Yoda has disappeared from the door. Kitty thinks briefly about calling her mother. Maybe she knows some off-the-books doctor. Her mother might also be more sympathetic than her nearly brain-dead husband who clearly isn't understanding the peril she is in. Kitty sighs. Her mother has her own issues to deal with. Kitty grits her teeth as another wave of pain rages through her midsection doubling her over. "I'm going to end up like Sammy Houston." She cries out.

*Texas has some of the most restrictive laws regarding pregnancy in the whole of the United States. In the 2030's, most of the states around Texas had adopted "trigger" laws. When Texas passed some new law, it "triggers" the states surrounding Texas to adopt the same law and enforcements. Called the "Alamo Compact" or the "Texas Agreement", the arrangement was affirmed by the Supreme Court (Estate of S. Houston v. Texas, et al) in 2039 when Sammie Houston, a fifteen-year-old Oklahoma resident died from sepsis after the baby she was carrying perished in-vitro. That the baby was conceived after being forcibly raped by a cousin was not a fact that was allowed to be brought into evidence because the court had already ruled that abortion for any reason was not a right under the constitution of the United States of America. The key matter at hand in front of the court had been the very law originating in Texas that had limited the care doctors could provide for young Sammy Houston. In the ruling, the court specifically upheld precedent before ruling that Sammie Houston et al, Oklahoma residents in fact, did not have standing to sue the state of Texas.*

"Sam Houston? The Texas Superhero?" Yoda asks. Disney had made several comic book movies based on a fictional account of the (male) historical figure. In the last movie, Sam Houston uses lightning bolts conjured from his hand to defeat an aggressive alien from outer space. The outer space alien looked suspiciously like a Latino earthling.

Yoda holds up the crumbled ball of paper that Kitty had thrown at the nurse with Kool Aid pink hair in the doctor's office. "This is the answer. I think. Maybe... I hope."

Kitty straightens herself up. She closes her eyes in disbelief. "God Bless you, Yoda. You poor, dumb thing." Yoda is un-balling the paper. "That Doctor. I Wanna Dick. Or Worm... Whatever she wanted to be called..." Yoda opens his communicator and dials the number on the paper. He patches Kitty's communicator in. "She said this guy can help. With the cramps."

A tone sounds in both their ears. "YoYoYo!" A rather energetic voice says. "This is Dr. Hole in One! Please leave a message at the sound of the tone." Yoda looks at his wife with confusion. Kitty rolls her eyes. Voice mail really isn't a thing anymore. It's only used by really old people and cable television companies, which are still around to the disbelief of just about everyone. People born after 2000 just can't be bothered to leave messages. Even if they are no longer receiving an internet signal from the cable company.

"This dude must be really old and using really old tech." Yoda says.

"Beep!" The voice says.

"Umm... Yeah... This is Yoda?" Yoda says, making the statement sound like a question.

"I am just joshing you! You got me. This is Hole in One." The voice says on the phone. "Joshing means kidding, by the way. You children don't know the old-time sayings."

"Your name is Dr. Hole in One?" Yoda asks. "That's a cool name. My name is Yoda Storm Trooper Katz Williams."

The voice laughs. It's a warm deep laugh. "Well, Yoda Storm Trooper Katz Williams, that is a pretty sweet name. My name used to be Smith... William Smith. People called me Bill. Except my mother, she called me son of a bitch or William. Anyway, I wanted to stand out. So, I changed my name."

"You changed it to Hole in One?" Kitty asks incredulously.

"First I changed it to Bear Skin Rug, cause what woman doesn't want to lay on a bear skin rug?" Dr. Hole in One says. "Turns out, not many do. But... lots of women want a hole in one! Also, it works well with my golf buddies."

Kitty rolls her eyes. "I don't have time for this." As if on cue, a wave of pain grips her, doubling her over. "Arghghgh!"

Yoda start speaking fast. "Dr. Hole in One, my wife Kitty, Katherine... she is pregnant, but the baby isn't breathing anymore. And she is in pain. Dr. Ivanna Dick... Worm... I can't get that name out of my head." He giggles before continuing. "She gave your number to my wife and said you can help. Can you? My wife is really in pain, and I love her very much and I can't stand seeing her like this! Can you help?"

There is silence on the other end of the call. "Give me your address." Dr. Hole In One finally says. "I have some holistic remedies to help."

"I don't need any goddamn holistic remedies, witchcraft or prayers to the fucking Flying Spaghetti Monster!" Kitty growls.

Wild eyed and knowing that Kitty doesn't approve, Yoda rattles off the address.

"I am close by. I will be right over." Dr. Hole in One says. "Flying Spaghetti Monster. Haven't heard that one in a while." The line goes dead.

"You fucking moron!" Kitty growls at her husband. "I need a real doctor that practices real medicine." Pain races through her, doubling her over again. It doesn't stop her from continuing to yell at Yoda. "You and your dumbass big dick. That's what did this to me. I should have listened to my mother and stuck with vibrators!"

Yoda shrugs. His fathers had told him to always meet Kitty's temper with love. "I love you, anyway." He says in a clear voice.

A few minutes later Yoda's communicator announces that someone is at his door. He leaves his wife in the bathroom and goes to the door. The tallest man he had ever seen hulks in the doorframe. Wild gray hair seems to sprout from the man's head like raspberry vines. An unruly, long beard streaked with black and gray is knotted with beads and unidentifiable jewels. Yoda looks up into the man's craggily face that is framed by one impossibly thick eyebrow. "You must be Yoda Storm Trooper Katz Williams."

Yoda nods. The man sticks out his hand. Like the rest of him, it's huge. Yoda hesitantly lifts his arm while looking at the giant hand. Hole in One pulls Yoda into a bear hug. "I'm a hugger. Good to meet you man. I am Dr. Hole in One."

"Nice to meet you, Doctor... One?" Yoda says with a voice muffled in the embrace.

"Where is the missus?" The giant man asks.

"The mess?" Yoda says, still in the man's embrace. "I don't know about any mess. Please don't tell Kitty. She hates messes."

The man lets out a big laugh. "Your wife Yoda! Where is your wife?"

"In the Longhorn bathroom." Yoda answers as he is released from the hug. "Come on, I will show you."

"Longhorns, Huh." The bear of a man says. "Hated that team growing up."

"Me too." Yoda says. "I played for Michigan!"

"Wolverines. That's a ferocious animal. Longhorn is something you eat. Like a bunny or a carrot. No one eats wolverine." Dr. Hole in One says.
"Do people eat buckeyes?" Yoda asks.

Hole in One shakes his head. "No, they are poison."
"I thought so!" Yoda says triumphantly as he opens the bathroom door. His wife is doubled over sitting on the orange toilet. "Honey! Dr. Hole in One is here. He says that buckeyes are poison!"

"Information I surely wanted right now." Kitty says through clenched teeth. Hole in One pushes past Yoda and clumsily moves to Kitty. "I need you to breath. Did you two do Lamaze classes?"

Kitty give him her best, *Are you fucking with me, right now,* glare. "No. I was opting for real medicine when I got pregnant."

The man places his large right hand on her back. "Sweetheart, breathing helps us control our body and mind. Let's start a set of fours. Inhale for four seconds. Hold it for four seconds. Exhale for four seconds." Hole in One starts. Yoda tries to follow.

"Come on, Katherine!" Yoda says. She would later note it was one of four times in their relationship together she had heard him use her full first name. "Breath with Dr. Hole in One!"

"Is this all you are going to do?" Kitty cries out. "I've got dead fucking baby inside me. Fucking breathing isn't going to help me."
The giant man lifts his head back and laughs. It comes out like thunder. "Oh... Oh, no. No, No, No. Breathing gets us to a couch or bed... someplace you can lie down. Then I am going to give you some morphine.

Breathing just gets things under control. Morphine... That is what is going to take away the pain."

A look of relief crosses Kitty Williams' face. She starts breathing with Yoda counting, albeit in a way that doesn't always get the four numbers in sequence. Soon, Kitty is able to straighten up.

"Alright, to the bed little girl." Hole in One assists her in standing while motioning to Yoda to help. Together the three get to the master bedroom.

"Nice, a real bedroom. None of that BDSM crap hanging about that all the kids seem to have these days. You two must not be into the religion too much." Hole in One comments. He guides Kitty to the bed. "You and your husband appear to be normal people. How did that happen?"

"I was created in a lab." Yoda says proudly. "My two dads built me."

Hole in One nods, contemplating what the man had just said. "Well... That's a nice story, Yoda. You appear normal, Kitty." He comments, grinning when he sees the woman smile at his statement through her pain. "Let's get you a little more comfortable."

"Where did you go to medical school?" Kitty asks, hoping the answer isn't also a well-known beach or tropical paradise.

Hole in One ignores the question as he helps her lay back on the bed. "I am going to put the medicine in your left arm, so lay on your side facing me. Keep breathing. Four in. Hold four. four out." The man commands. He pulls a small leather pouch from his pants pocket and extracts a hypodermic needle and a little glass vial. "Now a days, no one does it this way. A robot gives people shots. That's terrible. When there is no human involved, who is to know if it is done right?"

"How do I know if you do it right?" Kitty asks. Clenching her jaw as another wave of pain passes through her body. The breathing is helping, at least a little, she concedes to herself.

Hole in One loads the needle. After wrapping a band around her upper arm and finding the vein he smiles at the woman. Sweat beads on her forehead. "The breathing is helping? Yes?"

Kitty clenches her jaw. "Yeah. Sure."

Without taking his eyes off hers, Hole in One expertly slides the tip of the needle into her arm. "I bet this works better."

After a few moments, Yoda sees that his wife's body is relaxing. He allows his to relax as well. "How long will that medicine last?"

"An hour or so. I didn't give her much. Just enough to take the pain off so we can talk about what comes next." Hole in One says. "Yoda, go get a cool damp cloth and come wipe your wife's forehead."

Yoda leaves the room to get the washcloth. Hole in One sits on the floor next to the bed. His head still rises above Kitty who is laying on the bed. "Your husband, Yoda... he's a few sandwiches short of a picnic."

Kitty chuckles. "My dad says that too. Where did you go to medical school, Doctor?"

"We need to get you help. Your condition is very poor. I am guessing that Dr. Worm told you that you must carry the child to term. Is that correct?"

Kitty nods in a fast motion. A tear rolls down her cheek.

"That's crap and Worm knows it. That's why she sent you to me."

"You will remove the dead fetus?" Kitty asks. "Then do the dee and cee?"

Hole in One shakes his head and reaches up to hold Kitty's hand. Yoda comes back in the room and gently mops his wife's brow.

"Katherine Williams, I am not a doctor. The title is honorific. I bestowed it upon myself." Hole in One says, his deep voice melodic. And loud.

Yoda takes a step back and exclaims in a way that would make any soap opera star proud, "You aren't a doctor?"

"Of course I am not a doctor!" Hole in One exclaims. "These days, Doctors seem to live by the hypocritical oath. If they are human and not a Robot." He motions at Kitty. "Today, a doctor would not have given her relief... at least not before checking with his lawyer... or his hospital's lawyer."
Kitty giggles. "I think it is Hippocratic oath." She rolls on to her back. "I feel much better, Dr. Hole in One." She turns and looks at the giant of man who is leaning back against the wall by the bed. "What is next?"

"Well, now it gets complicated. Maybe Dr. Worm is a nice woman, but all the farther she is willing to go is to provide my number to people like you. I would not trust her in any case... but I trust no one. I had a woman doc up in Abilene that was willing to do these procedures, but the tattle tale laws got her." He chuckles. "You know who turned her in? The husband of one of the women she did a dilation and curettage for. Doctor saved his wife from terrible suffering, maybe death... and the husband turns the doc in and collects a big check." Hole in One sighs. "Such is the way our world has gone, I suppose."

*In 2021, the state of Texas, in a late attempt to ban abortion, created a law that allowed for suit to brought against the health services provider... not by the state, but by ordinary citizens. Most legal scholars saw this as an end run around the supremacy clause contained in the 14th amendment of the United States Constitution. In December of 2021, the United States Supreme Court effectively upheld the Texas law by dismissing the case brought against the State of Texas by the United States Department of Justice. Tattle tale laws - where the citizenry, not the state enforces a law - have become the norm in modern society. What better way to enforce ill-conceived and illegal laws than to put the enforcement of such laws in the hands of ordinary citizens - whose only incentive may be money?*

Hole in One stands, groaning and making old man noises as he moves. "I am nearly seventy-five years young. Never thought I would make it this far. My advice to you youngsters is to take care of your bodies. And stay short. Being this tall comes with challenges!" He straightens up. "You have a transporter?"

Yoda nods. Kitty has a goofy morphine induced grin on her face. "How far is the range?" Hole in One asks.

*Electric vehicles: once thought to be a panacea of solutions to the broad question of climate change, have become something of a set of leg irons on the American Public. Laws passed by a liberal congress prior to a disastrous midterm election in 2030 forced consumers to purchase electric cars by 2036. Several automotive manufacturers that had stuck with hybrid technology and internal combustion engines went bankrupt. Self-named Transporter companies - businesses that focus more on the interior of vehicles and passenger comforts rather than the efficiency of a powertrain filled the space.*

*Sadly, the people's government wasn't strong enough to consider all the ramifications of its actions, never mind the math involved with figuring out how much electricity was going to be needed to power such a venture. Electric vehicles never advanced much past 2025. Range was quickly limited to 100, 200 and 300 miles, by law. It's all the power grid can support as nuclear power is still, despite its promise of safe, clean, efficient electricity, considered to be a dangerous and expensive solution to power production.*

"We can go 100 miles!" Yoda says brightly.

Hole in One shakes his head. "That's not far enough. We need to get to the Bayou."

"The Bayou?" Kitty Williams asks.

"Like where LSU is? They are the Bayou Bengals. We beat them once. Regular season." Yoda opines.

Hole in One nods, raising his bush of an eyebrow at Yoda's comment. "Yes, we need to go to Louisiana. Specifically, we need to go to Holly Beach, Louisiana." He pats Kitty's shoulder. "And we need to go soon. Those cramps are bad now and they are going to get worse. There is of course, concern about bleeding and infection."

Kitty groans. "I hate long car rides. What's in Holly Beach, Louisiana?"

"Absolutely nothing." Hole in One grins big. "Well, that's not true. A couple hundred people live there. Probably just as many dogs and a big bacteria population in the water. It's not America's vacationland... but it is where we need to go." He pulls out an old-fashioned cell phone. "I have a transporter that will go three hundred miles. I will take you one hundred and fifty miles. Someone else from the resistance will take you from there." Resistance?" Kitty asks.

Hole in One harrumphs as he fiddles with the phone. "My term, I suppose. I don't use it around the others since one person got mad at me for calling them a bad name. We are a loosely tied together group of people who know that the current abortion laws were never necessary, are unconstitutional and unsafe for women."

"What is going to happen to me in Holly Beach?" Kitty looks at Yoda who appears to be staring at the white wall. "Can Yoda come?"

Hole in One considers her questions before answering. "If you want your husband to come, he is welcome. I will tell the drivers to expect two passengers."

Yoda comes in close to look at the phone, like a dog checking out a porterhouse steak that suddenly appeared on the living room carpet. "What IS that thing?"

Hole in One makes a noise that could be considered a *"Why-are- you-messing-with-me growl"* or a reaction to something he couldn't do on the phone. "It is a cell phone."

"That's old." Yoda exclaims. "And kind of Boring."

Hole in One laughs. "That thing you have implanted in your body is traceable, trackable and open to listening by anyone with a decoder which is every government agency, nearly any store you go into and almost every hacker."

"That's tin foil hat stuff." Kitty says with a grin. "The government isn't tracking us!"

Yoda has a frown on his face. "Wait, is that why I always see advertisements for the things I think about?"
Hole in One looks up from his phone call and points at Yoda. "You know it!" He says with a thumbs up.

Whoever Hole in One has called has picked up. The giant of a man mutters some words in the phone and ends the call with a shake of his head. "These old phones still work on a global 5G network set up a decade ago by the Chinese. These things are totally trackable too... but not as traceable as the 10G network you all have implanted in your bodies." He powers the phone down. "Let's go. My transporter is charged up. I will take you to Houston. It's farther than I wanted to go, but my contacts say we haven't time to set up a proper relay."

"What happens in Houston?" Yoda asks. Hole in One is helping Kitty up. He ignores the question.

"Do you have a 'go bag' ready?" Hole in One asks.

"A go bag?" Yoda asks. "No?"

Hole in One shakes his head. "Children, you have to be prepared. For anything." He shakes his head. "Let's get going. The resistance may have clothes, toiletries and such for you."

They get Kitty up. Yoda steadies her as they make their way to the door to the condo. Hole in one stops them just before opening the door. "If anyone asks, I am your uncle. It's really flimsy and it may not help... but if the authorities are watching, they won't let us do this."

"Do what?" Yoda asks.

"Exactly, Yoda. Exactly." Hole in One answers with a wink.

Chapter 15
Some people whack off more than others.
Should we be eating beef? Shit happens.
The Good Residence.
Someplace in the United States America
Home of the Free(ish) Land of the Brave(ish)


T. Bob Good opens the door as Fred Peterson approaches the townhome. The pair had sync'd the proximity meters on their internal communication devices. "About time. Where have you been?" Bob asks. He doesn't wait for answer as he turns, leaving the door open for Fred to walk through.

"Just talking to my dad." Fred answers.

Bob doesn't acknowledge the answer. "Today is all beef day at Mickey D's. We should go there. Want to ride the air boards or should we take the scooters? Wait, you can drive a transporter now! We should take a car to Mickey D's!"

Fred waits for his friend to turn around. Talking to Bob's back would be as useless as pissing into the wind. Better to just let him talk. Bob continues to rapidly suggest ways to get to the hamburger restaurant. After opining on how cool it might be to have a hovercraft the teenage boy turns. At 6' 2" tall, Bob stands about the same height as Fred. Unlike Fred, Bob's face is full of teenage acne and his eyes have a nervous darting quality about them. He and Fred have been friends since the third grade when Fred used a plastic knife to disable the teacher assistant robot that was shaking young Bob like a rag doll after the boy had refused to sit still in his seat.

"Whatdathink-Whatdathink, Freddy?" Bob rattles.
"I don't have a transporter, a helicopter or a hovercraft. You have two air boards. We can take those. Besides, the lines of transporters will be super long at Mickey D's for All Beef Night." Fred says calmly. "Should we go now or are we watching Shit Happens?"

Bob shakes his head. "My mom is up trying to get off on a crucifix from church. I guess it was the same thing that worked for a guy last week to get on the *I Got Off on That* broadcast. Also, she has a submission on *Shit Happens* she hasn't told us about. Dad says that he thinks that his video may get on the runner up category of *Shit Happens* tonight. I guess he fell out of a tree or something. I gotta stick around until then. The parental units would be soooo disappointed if I didn't see their big moment with them."

Fred nods. "That's great. We can eat dinner at Mickey D's later."

Bob nods energetically. "Real beef tonight. Gonna eat it? Gonna eat it? Gonna eat it? "You gotta try the beef, but if you ain't I'm a gonna eat yours!" The boy speaks rapidly as he turns and grabs a bag of potato crisps, opening it with a pop. "Want one?" He holds the bag out to Fred who shakes his head. Bob takes a handful and stuffs them in his mouth. "You ever wonder how many guys are jacking off at the same time in the world, Fred?" The words are mumbled as his mouth is full of crisps.

"No." Fred answers as he watches a few pieces of the chips fall from his friend's mouth. "I cannot say that is ever something I think about, Bobby."

"I think it might be ten percent of the world's population all at once!" Bob thinks and talks about masturbation constantly. "Shaking hands with themselves, you know?" He stuffs more chips in his mouth and talks while he chews. "You see.... It's dark over like half the world half the time, so that puts half the people in the right zone... right? And if eighty percent of those people are sleeping or working because some people have work all night, right? Anyway, that leaves twenty percent who are doing something else... I bet at least ten percent of those guys are spanking the monkey! And I bet that five percent of all the people in the light part of the world are getting a little love with themselves.... Why, that's...."

"Seven percent." Fred yawns. "Not ten percent."

"Yeah....seven percent." Bob whispers in awe, his eyes wide with amazement as he shoves another handful of chips in his mouth. "Seven percent of the world's population is whacking off at any given time. That's a lot of masturbation!"

"Are you counting women?" Fred asks. He doesn't mind allowing Bob to rattle off his factoids and wonderment about masturbation. Conrad had pointed out to Fred many years before that Bob might be a little on the spectrum of autism. Fred had read up on the condition. Public education (and surprisingly, even less so in private schools) no longer treats such students any differently than other students. As such, kids like Bob were free to experiment with social cues and other formative educative issues on their own with predictable results. Students with much more profound disabilities are often even more neglected.

Bob takes in a sharp breath. "Shit, Freddy... you think it is possible that almost fifteen percent of all the people on earth are masturbating at any one time?"

Fred smiles weakly. "Seems unlikely Bob, but you never know." "That would be a lot of cum, all at once." Bob says with a hint of awe under his breath.

"It's on! It's on! Say some prayers Bobby, *Shit Happens* is starting!" Bob's mother, Sookie Moonbeam Magi Good comes running into the living room. A robe is pulled tight around her waist, and she holds a large golden cross in one hand and some wet wipes in the other. "Monitor, ON!" Mrs. Good shouts. The wall of the living room changes from a white wall to a ninety-six-inch monitor. "*Shit Happens!*" Bob's mother shouts in a high-pitched voice ringed with excitement. The internet channel pops open. "Here it comes." Bob shouts out. "Think Dad made it?"

"Your old man just fell out of a damn tree. He ain't gonna make it. His shit is Boring, Boring, Boring and he knows it!" Mrs. Good shouts at the monitor. "Show me the money!"

The ten-minute program starts off with its usual introduction. A rapper and a country music star sing a short thirty second jingle. The narrator starts speaking quickly. He introduces the second runner up... or as the announcer calls it, *the second loser.* Fred watches with little interest as a woman is hit by a scooter driven by a person in a bear costume. Nonsensically, the bear stops the scooter and stands the woman up. A little unsteady, the woman groggily pats the bear on the shoulder and is promptly hit by another scooter this one driven by a person in a parrot costume. The bear and the parrot help the woman up and the trio bows.

"That one sucks. So staged." Mrs. Good proclaims. She points at the wall television. "You are Boring!" She shouts.

The next video is a man falling out of tree, but it isn't Mr. Good. Fred hears swearing from some other part of the house as he watches the screen. A man falls through the branches of a large cottonwood tree. As he lays bleeding at the bottom of the tree, he weakly raises a thumb in the air. "That's a lot better than you falling from a low branch into a mulch pit!" Mrs. Good screams to her unseen husband.
"Fuck me!" comes the reply from afar. "I'll come up with something better."

The announcer comes on. His face has a manicured, plastic look. His hair is puffed up on top and knotted into a long ponytail in the back. "The winner tonight just barely made it past the censors. Remember audience, all privates must be covered up to make it onto *Shit Happens!*"

"This is it! This is it! I made it!" Mrs. Good grabs her son and shakes his shoulders. "I made it Bobby! I made it! I am not BORING!"

Fred watches the video. The 24K high-definition liquid paint screen is clear as day. Fred sees Mrs. Good standing by a busy road. She is wearing a red dress and smiles for an unseen camera. Mr. Good perhaps? No... he would have acknowledged the video already, eager to voice his part in the production. Fred can't remember how these things work. There are rules as to where videos can come from, who can record them and what not. He isn't on the social media much.

On the second wave a car zips by. Fred can see the hem of the dress start to rise and almost instantly the entire dress is pulled from the Bob's mother's body. Her nipples are covered by little stars and there is triangle of material covering her crotch. On the screen Mrs. Good spins around, her naked buttocks on full display. Fred notes the detail of the tattooed crucifix on Bob's mother's back. All the members of the Good family's church have the same tattoo including Bob. The letters INRI stand out in block letters just above the crack in Mrs. Good's ass. On the screen, she shakes herself and smiles towards the camera. As the night's winner, the video is played again several times in slow motion.

"So awesome!" Mrs. Good exclaims. "So awesome! "I am going to be FAMOUS!" She smiles at Fred in a way that makes him feel uncomfortable. "I'm not Boring, am I, Freddy?"

Fred shakes his head slowly, avoiding verbalizing an answer. "That was great honey!" Cliffhanger "Cliff" Good comes into the room. Like his son Bob and Fred, Mr. Good is a tall man. Unlike his son who has a lot of acne on his face and Fred who is as pale as a piece of paper, Mr. Good is impossibly tan with equally impossibly white teeth. "Who's eyes were on that?"

"Reverend Savenutts." Mrs. Good replies, naming the minister their church, *Christians in Pursuit of the Scoundrel Pontius Pilate*. "I was at my private bible study session with him, and he suggested that my idea might make the show! He was right! Reverend Savenutts is very smart!"

Mr. Good embraces his wife and gives her a passionate kiss before exclaiming. "God is Good darling. God is Good!"

Fred had heard both Good parents tie the name of their deity with their own last name in the past. Fred hadn't been raised with any sort of religion. He was pretty sure that tying the last name of Good with any deity was probably blasphemous and offensive to the said deity. Sometimes, Fred privately wished he had religion in his life. It simply hadn't been a part of his upbringing. Conrad is a throwback to the 2010's. Like many in the modern population he didn't subscribe to any particular religion. He hadn't put his son through any religion classes either, opting his child out of the ones taught at the public schools. Fred had read up on the church of *Christians in Pursuit of the Scoundrel Pontius Pilate*. The tenements of the Protestant themed religion ran from permissive... (Fred was pretty sure that Mr. and Mrs. Good have an open marriage) ... to oppressive. No Alcohol. (Which was ok. Even the very stripped-down FDA is discouraging the use of any alcohol, a poison that tears bodies apart.) No smoking. (Unless the product smoked is Marijuana, hash or any one of several psychedelic drugs), all of which are still federally illegal but ok by most state laws for recreational or religious use. Specifically ok is all sorts of drugs meant to *get one closer to God*"). The church of *Christians in Pursuit of the Scoundrel Pontius Pilate* also forbids the practice or observation of any other religion and the one no-no that Fred found particularly revolting... The woman is always subservient to the man. The Goods had repeatedly tried to *save* Fred who had from an early age developed an ability to resist such overtures.

"Congratulations, Mrs. Good." Fred says noncommittally. He looks around for Bob who has disappeared. "Does this contest win money?" The woman shakes her head. "Just likes... Lots of likes on my profile. Maybe it will get a played a few more times. I am thinking of something grand for *I Got Off On That!* She puffs her chest out. *I Got Off On That...* it pays big! And… it is big time fame!"

Bob reappears in the kitchen and walks quickly past the three, avoiding even glancing in the direction of either of his parents. Fred notes that his friend's pants are unzipped. "Let's go Fred, before Mickey D's runs out of real beef!"

Fred follows him with a wave to Mr. And Mrs. Good. Once they are in the garage, Fred taps Bob on the shoulder. "Your fly is down Bobby. Zip up."

"Busted!" Bob announces. He turns to Fred with a guilty grin.

"You were jacking off?" Fred asks incredulously.

"Couldn't help it." Bob announces as he pulls two Air Boards off wall chargers. "Seeing that on the big screen got me a little excited."

"That was your *mom* on the screen." Fred says flatly.

"Boobs are boobs, Freddy. You think I care whose boobs they are? Samuel... the first one... said that *Our nakedness shall be uncovered, and we will be seen... We will take vengeance and spare no one!*" Bob pushes a button to open the garage door as he steps onto his Air Board. "Reverend Savenutts taught us that!" The board rises with an audible whoosh and Bob takes off down the driveway. He looks back and motions at Fred who hits the button to close the door before following out the closing door on his own air board.

After catching up to his friend, Fred shoves his shoulder. "That's just gross, Bob. Also, I am not sure you are using that bible verse in context."

Bob wrinkles his face up in disagreement. "I took vengeance on the situation by gripping my own tool. The issue was not spared!" He grins. "Besides, I was not whacking off to a video of my Mom's boobs." Bob regains his balance. "It was just a video. A video of boobs. Not my mom's boobs! It's OK."

Fred shakes his head. "You know, I can get you something from my Dad's business. I am sure Dad would just give you some of his products. Free."

"Then it would be your mom!" Bob bends over on the Air Board in laughter, almost completely losing his balance. "Nah, Nah... I like my left hand and when it's a little tired, I use my right." He turns to Fred. "Are you telling me that you weren't at least a little turned on by my mom's boobs? They are nice boobs!"

Fred shakes his head. He hadn't been turned on. Not in the least. He didn't think he needed therapy for the lack of such reaction... but maybe. It hadn't been the first time that he had seen Mrs. Good's... goods. She always seemed to be eager to show her privates to him. It was a subject he had decided never to bring up with his friend, Bob. As he had in the past, the thoughts are put in the back of his mind. The pair zips down a set of trails before catching the main road leading to Mickey D's. A long line of transporters sits in traffic waiting to turn into the restaurant's drive through lane. "People love them some real cow!" Bob cries out as he taps on the first transporter window he flies by. "Suckers... you should have gotten your fat asses onto a scooter or hoverboard! I'm gonna eat your burger before you pull into the parking lot!"

Fat hands with chubby fingers extend from windows, answering Bob's declarations with a display of obscene gestures as the pair moves past the long line. They slow at the front door of the restaurant. A group of their peers hang out around a pair of outdoor tables. Fred motions a greeting to the teens as he dismounts and hangs his and Bob's Air Boards on complimentary chargers. Bob walks over and starts talking to no one in particular. "Do they still have beef? We aren't too late, are we? I really want a real cow burger."

Fred sees a red-haired girl stand from the table. Anne Margret Eaton. She wears short cutoffs and a tight t-shirt that reads 'This Land was Their Land' across her ample chest. A sad looking American Indian in a full headdress is embossed under the words. "They still have beef; you blood thirsty vampire vulture." She points at Fred. "Better get one for him too, Freddy looks a little anemic. He's likely the only one here that could use a little iron."

Fred smiles. "Just a Shroom Burger, Bob. And Fries. No beef, please. You can have my ration of real beef if they are limiting it per person." He glances at the girl, hoping he isn't blushing. "Hello Anne. Nice to see you."

"I'm not fucking you, Fred. Get that image out of your head." The girl snaps. "Get me a coke, Bob."

"What flavor?" Bob calls out as he opens the door to the restaurant.

Anne Margret sneers at him. "Stop screwing with me Bob. Coke is the only flavor on the fountain. You know that. Can't even get plain water anymore." She sits down at the table. "I would love a *Dr. Pepper*... Shit is only sold in China and India now. They get *all* the good stuff."

*The EPA had been downsized to the point of irrelevance decades before by a ruling of the Supreme Court that declared among other things, that not only was such an agency redundant of the courts and congress (the majority opinion made it clear that the Justices thought that the EPA mostly made the courts redundant), but also there was no mention of the environment by the founding fathers in the constitution. As such, most accessible ground water and well water is unfit for human consumption. The Coca Cola company, now the sole provider of any packaged drink in the United States (after buying out all of its competitors) has reduced its offerings to Coke... albeit with alcohol added for those who still partake.*

Anne Margret turns her attention to Fred with narrowed eyes. "What have you boys been up to, beating each other's meat?"

Fred stammers.  He is definitely blushing now. "No... I... don't do that." Eager to change the subject and avoid talking about the methods of how Bob does do exactly that, regularly, he points at the girl's t-shirt. "Is that a slogan of a campaign you are working on?"

Anne Margret's eyes widen and her lips curl into a smile. "It is. I am writing my senior thesis on it. I think that we ought to pay reparations to the Native American people for taking their land. What do you think about that?"
Fred stays silent for a moment. His eyes find Anne Margret's. Shades of blue are gradient to a sparkling impossibly deep dark pool. "Well?" She snaps in a tone indicating she regards his hesitation in answering as derision from her deeply held belief.

"I was just thinking." Fred says. "If we pay reparations to the Native Americans, which I certainly think they deserve, who else..." His thought is interrupted by Bob.

"I got the burgers. BeefBeefBeefBeef for everyone! I got four delicious all beef Big Mac Whoppers!" He starts singing the jingle that

Mickey D's had adopted after they bought the assets of their biggest competitor, Burger King out of bankruptcy.

Fred looks at the hot pink tray in Bob's hand. "Bob, did you get my mushroom burger?"

"NahNah... You can eat the beef Freddy boy! Where's the beef? Here's the beef! Today is real beef day Freddy, we are eating like KINGS!" Bob starts in on the jingle again while dancing around with the tray of food. "All beef patty, special sauce lettuce cheese cooked on under a clean burning flame. Whopper, Whopper... who wants a whopper? We've got the real beef, trust no others.... All beef patty special sauce...."

Anne Margret leans into Fred. "He didn't get my Coke either. Or the fries. I will transfer some credits to you. Can you get me a Coke? The security guard inside grabbed my boobs the last time I went in there."

*Such displays are now common and no longer considered assault. Of course, such nonsense was challenged.* Jane Doe vs Gonzo Motors 2031. *A Secretary at the company made a legal complaint about a female supervisor who would grab the woman's crotch whenever she saw her. Gonzo, a company that specializes in electric mobility and transporter manufacturing said the supervisor was only doing so as an affectionate greeting. The case made it to the Supreme Court who collectively sent it back down to an appellate court for review. The appellate court re-ruled that grabbing someone else's body as a form of greeting was no more or less offensive than saying 'hello' and as such is protected as free speech. After the ruling, many women elected to accept the new federal living wage and just stay home and not work.*

Fred dismisses her offer of money with a wave and goes inside. The inside of the restaurant is packed with people, most severely obese, eating at hot pink tables. The clatter of automated restaurant equipment accentuates the audible noise of people chewing their food. He walks up to the computer and announces himself.

"Hello Fred Peterson. Are you paying with credit or government voucher today?"

"Credit." Fred pulls his charge card from his pocket and inserts it into the machine.

"Please confirm your identity with your chosen biometric." The machine says. Fred steps closer to the machine and opens his eyes wide. A short green light flashes. "Thank you, Fred your identity is confirmed. You can order ZERO Big Mac Whoppers."

The chain limits the number of its Big Mac Whoppers to two burgers per person so that supplies don't run out. "That's how he got four. He used my identification to get two extra orders." Fred mutters before placing his order. "I want to order a mushroom burger, loaded. Three Cokes and Three Fries."

The machine flashes a pleasing light blue color. "That is an excellent choice, Fred. You can save fifteen hundred calories by choosing fresh cut artificial apples or seven hundred and fifty calories by choosing cricket crisps instead of fries. Would you like to improve your health, Fred?"

"No, thank you. Place my order and charge my card." Fred says to the machine.

"Thank you for your continued patronage, Fred. Please watch this commercial while we prepare your order number." A video featuring an attractive woman and a visibly older man plays. The woman describes how she likes wearing her husband's disposable diapers when she goes out shopping because then she doesn't have to use *filthy* public restrooms. Fred waits patiently. The commercial ends and a receipt with a number on it is printed. A few minutes later a mechanical female voice announces the number from the receipt. Fred walks past a line of people waiting on their real beef orders. A man wearing full body armor stands at the counter. He puts his hand out. "I just saw you, over there... ordering. It ain't ready yet. Get to the back of the line."

Fred eyes the security guard. He has inked tattoos covering his entirely bald head. A large gun is strapped to each side of his rather large waist. Fred holds up his ticket. "Nope. They called my number. I didn't order the Big Mac Whopper."

The security guard eyes the receipt wearily. Fred thinks it takes the man too long to read the simple words on the little piece of paper. "You didn't order the beef? You Boring, man? I think you are Boring, fake news."

Fred smiles, not wishing to engage. He points at the counter behind the guard as a robot places a hot pink tray on the surface with three drinks, three fries and a foil wrapped item. "I think that is mine, sir."

The guard's face darkens. "What makes you think I am a sir? You have no right to assume such things."

Fred keeps a straight face. "My apologies." He points at the tray. "Can I have my food, please?"

The guard wordlessly steps to the side. Fred feels the security guard's hand grab his ass before he picks up the tray and walks back out to his friends.

"...I didn't consider women's orgasm because nothing comes out." Fred rolls his eyes as he hears Bob speak between bites of his all-beef hamburger. A chubby dark-haired girl has sat down beside Anne Margret. Fred has seen her around school. He thinks she might be named after a Chinese transporter company called Geely. Fred puts the tray on the table. Anne Margret grabs one of the drinks. The girl sitting beside her grabs another. Bob picks up the third. "Thank you for getting Geely a drink, Fred.  That was nice of you." Anne Margret says before turning back to the conversation. "So, Bob. Are you trying to figure out how many people might be masturbating at one time on the earth or how much ejaculate there might be from said masturbation."

"Both things, really." Bob says with his mouth full.

"It's not fair that you don't consider women in your calculations. Women masturbate too." Geely says as she drinks Fred's Coke.

"Yeah, but *nothing* comes out. My thoughts are on how much... you know, comes out." Bob wads up one foil wrapper and opens another Big Mac Whopper. He points at Fred. "One of those is yours."

Fred shakes his head. "I got Mushroom, Bob." He looks over at Anne Margret. "You want it?" She shakes her head with a look of disgust.

Geely sticks a chubby hand out and grabs it off the tray. "I'll take it." She quickly unwraps the burger and takes a bite of it. "Women do ejaculate, retard. It's called squirting. My brothers say that they see it all the time."

"It's pee." Anne Margret says before putting her lips around the star in her drink. Fred watches her freckled cheeks suck in.

Geely frowns and points at her. "It is not. It is not pee. It's just like the guys!"

Anne Margret shakes her head hard. Her long red hair covers and reveals her face like a peek show with a baby. "Guys spunk is sperm, goof. It's the little... sperm that fertilizes an egg. Girls... people who are a girl at birth, anyway... they don't make sperm. Girls make eggs."

"How do you know that?" Geely demands.

Anne Margret smiles as her lips wrap around the straw again. "My momma told me."

Geely grimaces. "You mom is wrong. It's just like the boys."

"Have you squirted?" Anne Margret asks Geely. She turns to Fred. "What about you Freddy? Have you squirted?"

Fred's jaw opens. "I... I..." He feels himself turning red.

Geely stands suddenly. "I have not! My brothers say that only special girl's squirt. The ones they see on the videos! I am not there yet! You guys are Boring!" She reaches down and grabs Fred's Coke before storming off.

"I guess she doesn't squirt." Bob says in a monotone voice.

"Or know where babies come from, how her body works or what she should and shouldn't be worried about." Anne Margret adds with a sigh.

"Do you squirt?" Bob asks the girl. Without hesitation, Anne Margret reaches across the table and slaps Fred on his right cheek.

"Why did you slap me?" Fred asks with an incredulous tone, rubbing the spot.

"You were within reach. Also, I suddenly had a strong urge to smack you." Anne Margret shifts her eyes towards Bob without really taking them off Fred. "Slug your buddy if you want to pass it on."

Undaunted, Bob leans across the table. "Well... do you?"

Ann Margret's right hand wings across the table, her palm catching the dead center of Fred's left cheek with an audible pop.

Fred's eyes widen. "What the hell, Anne Margret?"

She releases the straw clenched in her teeth with a grin. "Come on now, Freddy... You had to know that was coming."

Bob stands and points at the girl. "What's your customer ID number? I want another real beef burger." He motions at Fred. "I already used his number."

Anne Margret narrows her eyes and shakes her head. "You shouldn't eat *more* of those things. Three beef burgers are probably enough."

"ComeonAnneMargretIwantanotherRealBeefBigMacWhopper!" Bob says in a one breath, sing song voice before breaking into song. "All beef patty, special sauce lettuce cheese cooked on under a clean burning flame. Whopper, Whopper... who wants a whopper? We've got the real beef, trust no others! All beef patty special sauce lettuce cheese..."

"Give him your customer ID." Fred says under his breath. "Make it stop."

Anne Margret rattles off a series of numbers with a roll of her eyes. Bob walks quickly to the restaurant still singing the jingle. She leans into the center of the table. "So... you don't, really?"

"Don't what?" Fred asks, popping a cold fry into his mouth.

"Masturbate." Anne Margret sits back. "You said you don't do that. But you blushed, which makes me think that you do masturbate but maybe you don't want to talk about it or maybe it means that you really don't cause' you don't know how... which would be really weird." She motions to the inside of the restaurant. "We know that Bob masturbates. Any human that has met him even briefly knows that. The guy is going to write his senior thesis on masturbation."

"He is?" Fred asks incredulously.

The girl shakes her head. "I have no idea. It won't matter. The computer reads the subjects. I think that the entire grade is based on the subject. I suppose they could dock him for an inappropriate subject. I bet not though. A senior last year told me that she put fifteen hundred words into a document and sent it off. The words were in no certain order and the paper was senseless. In fact, that was the title of the paper. Senseless."

Fred furrows his brow. "What grade did she get."

"Success!!!" Anne Margret shrugs.

*The grading system had changed long ago as to not offend any student (or more important, any parent) or make any student feel bad. The grades now were, Success!!! Nice Job!! and Terrific! The exclamation points in place for those students (or parents) who can't read.*

"I am going to write my paper the correct way. On reparations. It's a subject I like. What are you doing yours on?"

Fred smiles and takes a drink of Bob's soda. "Now that I know I can put fifteen hundred words on a piece of paper and turn it in... That?"

"You are smarter than that." She nods at Bob's seat. "Random words on a page might not be a bad idea for Beating the Bishop Bobby."

"Beating the Bishop?" Fred asks.

"Beating the Bishop? Burping the Worm? Choking the Chicken? Painting the Pickle? Charming the Snake?" Anne Margret grins. "How old are you? Five? Aren't you the son of like the biggest sex toy maker in North America... probably the world? How is masturbation a foreign topic to you? There is no sex between actual people anymore. Self-Love, Procrasturbating and Menage a Moi is all we have. With or without your daddy's toys."

Fred feels his face turn red. "It's not foreign to me... I have to listen to Bob talk about it all the time. Maybe he's the guy you should be talking to about masturbating. He's all over it. Believe me."

Anne Margret sits back in her chair and grins big as Bob's voice is heard, still singing the Mickey D's jingle. "Freddy, I don't want to talk about masturbation. I just want to fuck... with you. It's fun!"

Chapter 16
It's hard for an OBGYN Doctor. Patient Thyme is Healed! Homeless.
Shared Experiences.
Microsoft Hospital Powered by HoloLens Artificial Intelligence
Someplace in the United States America
Home of the Free(ish) Land of the Brave(ish)

Millie lays beside me in my hospital bed. We had shared the lunch of cold vegetable hot dogs. After Lamont the robot brought dinner, we shared the meal of artificial chicken breast on a bed of synthetic rice. It wasn't too bad. I guess maybe because the right company at dinner makes shitty food taste alright.

Our time together today has been spent talking about the things that have happened over the past twenty years... mostly to Millie. She tells me about the court case and her time in a Texas women's prison (She helped a lot of women there. I am learning that Texas isn't so good about providing medical care in its prisons.) Our talks are interrupted and then punctuated with bouts of crying. From both her and me. We cry for each other. We cry for ourselves. We cry for the people of the United States.

Lamont the Robot comes into the room and reminds us that visiting hours end at 8:00pm. As Lamont is leaving, Dr. Lionel the Robot enters the room.

"Patient Justin Thyme, We have some great news!" The Robot says. The little lights on top it seem to blink happily if happiness is possible with Robots. "Microsoft Medical Systems has determined that it is no longer necessary to keep you here as a resident patient. You are healed!"
Millie scoffs and whispers. "It means that Microsoft Med has determined that it can no longer get paid to keep you here."

Lionel the Robot wheels back and forth. "You may spend the night, Patient Justin Thyme and tomorrow assistance will be provided to you.

Government has elected to provide you with living system arrangements for…" The little lights blink on and off for a long minute before the Robot continues. "Up to six months."

"Six months, huh." I say.

"That's a good deal." Millie whispers. "I thought you might get sixty days. I hardly ever hear of someone getting six months."

"You may not live that long." Lionel the Robot says. "If you expire prior to the end of Governments commitment to housing, your family may be due a tax credit from Government."

"Good to know." I respond with what I want to think is a sarcastic tone.

Lionel the Robot comes close to me. "We can still provide medication, so you do not care. Would you like to approve such treatment."
I look over at Millie. "I think Microsoft Medical Systems is also dealing drugs. Getting people hooked on something they must keep buying after they get out of here."

She smiles and touches her nose, silently.

"Seriously!" I exclaim. She nods.

"I don't want anything to make me not care. Please leave, Dr. Lionel." I say to the Robot.

"Response noted and recorded. Thank you for being a patient of Microsoft Medical Systems." The Robot rolls out of the room.

"I have a favor to ask." Millie says after the Robot has closed the door.

"Sure. What is it?" I turn to Millie and am shocked at what I see. Her face is red, her expression clearly embarrassed. "Can I stay with you?" She asks, her voice cracking.

"In my government housing? I am sure it isn't all that nice." I chuckle. "This is a private hospital and it's little more than concrete walls and a monitor that I can't get to work... and I bet it is nicer than where I am going."

Millie shakes her head. "Where you are going won't be nice at all. These walls are smooth. The government housing will either be built from cinder blocks or from old shipping containers. There might be a monitor, but it won't matter. You do not have a cellular phone installed in your body. Oh... and the room will be significantly smaller than this."

"Are you having problems with a boyfriend or something? I mean..." Millie is shaking. I put my hand on her arm. "Millie! Yes! Absolutely, you can stay with me." I take my hand off her. "What's up, Millie?"

She looks at the floor. I see tears starting to well up in her eyes. "I... I don't actually have a home to go to."

My eyes get wide. "You are homeless! How is that... You are a goddamn doctor! In the richest country on earth!"

Millie puts a finger to her lips to get me to lower my voice. She moves close to me and whispers. *"Formerly* the richest country on earth. I am sort of what they call a parole absconder. Because of that, I can't get a job under my real name, I can't rent an apartment. I barely make enough money as it is to live in my transporter."

"How did you get the job with Microsoft Med?" I ask in a soft voice.

"Friend that is high up in the company was in Medical school with me. *Millie Ratchet* is not a real person anywhere except at Microsoft Medical

Systems. My friend... she got me the job. The name Ratchet... well, *No one is going to look for me under that name.* Anyway, I may as well be one of the Robots." Millie smiles weakly. "Are you sure? You have been through so much and I don't want to impose, but..."

"You have been the light of my life since I got my life back, Millie Cockburn. I will help you however I can." I try my best to give her a reassuring smile. I am hoping the muscles in my face are working the way I want them too and she sees a smile and not a creepy clown face. "Besides, I am going to need a ride, and it sounds like you have wheels."

A tear rolls down Millie's face. "That silly dream came true." She sobs.

"Dream?" I ask.

Millie shakes her head. "It's... nothing. Stupid... really."

"I want to hear it." I say insistently. "Please?"
"A few days before you came out of your coma, I... I..." Millie stops and looks out the window, gathering her thoughts through several sobs. "I, ah... killed myself."

"You didn't do a very good job." I say with a deadpan tone. "Or, I am actually dead, which I think is a real possibility."

Millie nods. "You may have been a podiatrist... but you will understand this. I drank about a quart of grain alcohol that I dissolved twenty sublingual tablets of fentanyl in."

I raise an eyebrow and nod. "That's a no-take backs sort of action. If you did that, You really did kill yourself."

"Yeah. I'd had it. I'd had it with living this secret life. I'd had it with not having a family or friends of any sort. I'd had it with being alone." Millie gives me a hard look. "So, I decided to end it. Put on an adult diaper and wrote a note with instructions and everything. Drank the cocktail and drifted off."

"And then?" I ask. *I think I know what her answer is going to be.* "You are going to think that I am insane, and if you don't want me near you after this, I understand." Millie shakes her head and hugs herself. *"I had this dream.* A cow came walking through the darkness and started talking to me. She told me I had lived a good and honorable life. She asked me... well, I guess she asked me which way I wanted to go."

"What did you tell her?"

"I asked what my options were. She said I was still needed on earth, but if I didn't want to stay, I could come with her."

"Why did you elect to stay?" I ask.

Millie looks down and shakes her head. "I don't know. The cow was chewing something the whole time she was talking to me. Cud? Is that what cows chew? She kept saying something about being just in time... but, I think she was saying *find Justin Thyme*." Millie laughs. "I had never walked in your room prior to that morning, Justin. I sat fifty feet from your room for years and I didn't even know what your name was." She punches me in the arm, lightly. "So, are you still ok with a crazy defrocked ex con doctor living with you for a few months in a really small room?"

"Don't forget parole absconder." I grab her wrists and look into her eyes. "Millie, was there a large grasshopper riding on the back of that cow?" Millie's jaw drops and her eyes go wide. "No *fucking* way!" She looks at the closed door of the room and back at me. "You had the same dream? When?"

"Near as I can tell? When I went into the coma, the cow and the grasshopper came to me. Then there was a talking bear. The cow said the grasshopper was its good luck charm." I shrug and release Millie's wrists. "The grasshopper spit on me. Twice. Once after the accident and once before I woke up."

Millie stares at me wordlessly as she pulls down her scrub bottoms, exposing a pair of unsexy beige granny panties. I am about to make comment about the pass she obviously is making at me when I see her pointing. A brown splotch about the size of a fifty-cent piece is centered on her thigh just below the panty line. It looks like a birthmark.

"You didn't have that before?"

Millie shakes her head. "You have one too. About the same size."
"I don't think so. Not like that." I had checked myself over There were only a few fifty-year-old man liver spots that I had no recollection of as a 29-year-old man.

Millie leads me to the bathroom. "Drop your drawers, Justin Thyme."

I blush. "Years ago, you wouldn't have to ask twice... I am telling you; I don't have any spots on me."

Millie stoops and grabs my hospital bottoms, which aren't altogether different from her scrubs except they are prisoner gray and not pink. She pushes them down to my ankles and stands up. "I have already seen all of you, remember?"

"Ah, yes. The pee incident." I answer. "One of the seminal moments in my re-born life."

Millie uses a finger to turn my head to the left so I can see the reflection of myself in the mirror. On the center of my left butt cheek is a brown splotch about the size of a fifty-cent piece. "I thought it might have been a birthmark when I first saw it... but I think it is identical to one left on me."

"I guess we are tied together." I say. "With lucky grasshopper spit."

"We were both dead Justin. I read your report. You coded on the way to the hospital. You failed the caloric stimulation test three times before showing a reaction." She points to herself. "There is no way I should have woken up from what I did to myself. Absolutely no way."

"What do you think we are supposed to do?" I ask.

"I *think* we are supposed to make the world a better place. I am not at all clear how we are going to do that." Millie answers. "Visiting hours are over. They are going to kick me out soon. I will see you tomorrow. Sleep well." She gets up on her tip toes and kisses me on the lips before leaving me with my pants around my ankles in the hospital room bathroom. I look down at my limp member. It's sort of shriveled up like an old turtle not wanting to get any sun on its head. "A good-looking woman has her head inches from you and what respect do you show?" I hadn't had any sort of an erection since waking up from my near dirt nap with Joyfull bouncing on me like a five-year-old kid on a hopper ball. Apparently, I am unable to experience an erection without a fucking spinal tap. I pull up the loose-fitting pants. Happy anticipation and optimism fill my thoughts.

I have made a connection with a compassionate human being, and I am going to walk out of this hospital! Who gives a shit if my dick won't get hard?

Chapter 17
A long ride. Alligators. Life's a beach.
Somewhere in between south Texas and Southeast Louisiana.
Still a place in the
Land of the Free(ish) and Home of the Brave(ish)


Yoda looks out the window of the transporter. The darkness prevents him from seeing much. His sleeping wife snores softly beside him. Her reflection bounces off the darkened windows.

It was the middle of the night when Hole In One pulled into a parking lot in Houston. Yoda helped Kitty to the next transporter and Hole in One gave her another shot of something in the arm. The drivers of the new transporter communicated in grunts, giggles and hand motions. The woman's face is extra weathered. Greasy strands of blondish gray hair stick out from a Confederate flag handkerchief that is wrapped tight across her forehead. The man... Yoda assumes it is a man... is bald. He wears a leather vest with nothing under it. The transporter is clearly under his control because it weaves. Yoda wonders if it is possible to turn off the autopilot functions completely on a transporter.

The woman opens a bag and take out a vaporizing pen. Outlawed and reinstated several times over the years, the 'vapes' as they are called, allow one to smoke by inhaling steam produced when the lithium battery powered device heats up whatever substance the user has decided to inhale into their body. Yoda assumes the vapes contain some sort of drug. Each time the couple sucks on the little straw, they giggle for fifteen minutes or so.

After sucking on the pen and handing it off to her partner, the woman turns. "Weese bout der, Howda gurl doin?" The question is followed by a stifled giggle. "She no pop any ded kids out, dishee?

Yoda takes a moment to translate the pidgin English into something he can respond to. "Kitty is fine. She has been sleeping. Whatever Dr. Hole in One gave her is working pretty good."

The woman and driver giggle in unison. "She done got Roofied." More giggles. "Sleep damn nice on Roofy juice."

"I hope that doesn't hurt the baby." Yoda says with a concerned tone.
The woman shakes her head and sucks on the vape. "You puredumb man. Puredumb." She giggles more, tilting her head back and laughing loudly. "Puredumb!"

"I don't know what that is." Yoda answers morosely. He rubs his wife's arm. She shifts a little in her seat, making him happy.

The transporter makes an abrupt turn, throwing Yoda against his wife who mumbles in a drug induced stupor. The two in the front giggle. "Turn!" The driver shouts before erupting into more giggles.

The road is not paved and maybe isn't a road. Yoda thinks to himself as he bounces in his seat. He places his hands on Kitty to steady her.

"Wheeeee!" The woman in the passenger seat screams before erupting in a fit of laughter.

The transporter bounces hard. Yoda feels something grinding under him. The wheels maybe? He has never been interested in machinery in general. Transporters in particular. Kitty wakes up after one particularly harsh jolt.

"Where are we?" She asks groggily.

"In the transporter." Yoda says with as optimistic of a tone as he can muster.

"Thank you, Einstein." Kitty growls.

Yoda shakes his head. "I am Yoda. Who is Einstein? I don't know who Einstein is."

"Puredumb!" Comments the woman in the front seat. "Yoose in Lee-see-anna." She points out the dark windows. "Gator country!"

Reflexively, Yoda looks out the window for alligators. His own reflection stares back at him. "I don't see any gators." He mumbles.

"Da out der!" The woman exclaims. "In da swampy. Swimmin' round." She giggles. Her partner joins in.

"This was a bad idea, Yoda." Kitty whispers. "My communicator is not working. I didn't want to call my parents. They are going through so much, but we are in trouble. Call my father. Tell him to come get us." Yoda tries to use his communicator. Nothing happens. "I think they are broken."

"No service out 'ere." The woman cackles from the front seat. "Alls good. Yoose bout' der."

When Dr. Hole In One had dropped them at the pick-up point, he had pointedly told Kitty that the couple picking them up are a *bit off*. More couriers of illicit substances than active participants in any resistance, the couple had a vehicle that could get Kitty and Yoda to a rendezvous point on the Louisiana coast. The unseen resistance had apparently compensated the pair for their services.

The transporter comes to an abrupt halt. "Git down!" The woman hisses. She picks a fishing rod up from the floor of the transporter. "Git down!"

Yoda helps Kitty kneel on the floor of the transporter. He covers them both with a blanket. A bright light washes over the Transporter. Soon the whine of a surveillance drone is heard.

"Halt!" A loud voice calls out.

"Yeah, yeah, we stopped!" The woman calls out of her open window. She holds up a fishing rod. "We fishin'. Nothing wrong with fishing' is der?"

"Step out of the vehicle." The voice calls out.

"Mutherfuckers'! Da fuckin' Texas *Meeleetia* group." The driver says. The two front doors on the transporter open and The driver and passenger get out. Yoda hears Kitty whimper.

"There are two additional passengers in transport vehicle that must exit." The loud voice from the drone says.

"Da sleepin'". The woman says.

"All passengers must exit transport vehicle."
"Let's get out." Yoda says. "It says we have to."

"I don't want to!" Kitty cries. "We are in the middle of fucking nowhere. We don't have to get out! *They might kill us!*"

Yoda pulls her up. "I think we do. That voice said so. It will be ok, Kitty." He opens the sliding door and helps Kitty out.

"Just sleeping." He calls out to the flying drone that is hovering a few feet from the woman's head. It is silent for a few moments.

"Yoda Katz Williams, Male. Katherine Williams, Female. Two unidentified males." The arial machine zips around the transporter. "Transporter unregistered. Illegal operation noted. Report Generated."

"Fuck dis." The driver says. He pulls a shotgun from the transporter and fires at the drone.

"Incoming attack! Incoming attack. Report Generated! This is an unarmed surveillance drone. Halt your fire!"

Yoda looks at the passenger. "You don't look like a dude."

"Yoda. Hush." Kitty says with a tired tone.

"Dank ya." The transgendered woman says. "I been tryin' damn hard."

The driver fires again. Electrical sparks explode in the air with little pops and the drone drops to the ground. "Device incapacitated. Last location reported." The driver walks over and puts a third round into the top of the device.
"We out of here!" He announces. "Tell em' da on der own!"

The passenger turns to Yoda and hand him a flashlight. "Yoose on yer own from here. Git to da beach. Blue-Blue-Red is signal."

"Signal for what?" Yoda takes the flashlight.

"Purdumb." The transgendered woman shakes her head. "Da Pickup. Blue, Blue, Red. Git to da beach." She points to the south. "It da-ta way." The pair gets back in the transporter. The passenger leans out the window. "Yoose better git a move on. Dat der dead drone will send reinforcements." The rear wheels of the transporter spin as the driver swings the vehicle around and speeds off back up the rough trail.

"We are screwed Yoda." Kitty sobs.

"We need to get to the beach." Yoda grabs her hand. "Blue, Blue Red." Gripping the light in one hand, he pulls his wife along an animal trail with the other, guessing that he is headed south as the transgendered woman had directed. The ground is squishy and wet under their feet. Yoda can feel water getting in his shoes. "Sorry about your shoes Kitty." Yoda knows that Kitty really likes her shoes.

"It's ok, Yoda." Kitty says between sobs. "We should have just stayed in Dallas. I could have waited three months I suppose. Better to have died in bed than out in the middle of nowhere."

"We aren't going to die, Kitty." Yoda stops. He lets go of her hand and crouches down. "Get on my shoulders."

"What?" Kitty cries out.
"Get on my shoulders. We can move faster." Yoda says. "I saw it in *Revenge of the Jedi*. Fisto Mothma picked up Bossk Solo and carried her through a swamp like this one. Get on!"

When Kitty doesn't respond, Yoda gets down on his knees and forces his massive shoulders through her legs as he stands. "Yoda!" Kitty exclaims.

Undaunted, Yoda starts jogging down the animal path that is illuminated by the moon. He can hear the ocean crashing on the beach ahead of them. "We are going the right way! I hear the beach, Kitty!"

"Terrific." Kitty grabs a hold of her husband's hair and hangs on tight. "This is exactly how I thought my pregnancy might be."

"Really? I think this is pretty weird!" Yoda says.

"How are you not out of breath?" Kitty asks.

"I am strong." Yoda says.

"There is something behind us!" Kitty says. "I hear it!"

"I don't. I think something is blocking my ears." Yoda says. "Maybe that drone cast a spell on us!"

"I think it's my thighs, Yoda." Kitty's voice has a panicked tone. "Whatever is, it is running behind us!"

"Your thighs are following us?" Yoda effortlessly jumps over a log.

Kitty screams. "No, you idiot! There is an animal following us!" They break through the tall grass onto an expansive sandy beach. Yoda turns in a wide circle, conscious that a quick movement might throw Kitty off his shoulders and remove a significant portion of his wavy hair. A giant alligator comes out of the grass with a loud roar. Yoda rushes towards the reptile yelling at the top of his lungs. Kitty involuntarily adds a long high-pitched scream.

Yoda stops abruptly and lets out the biggest roar he can imagine himself making. The Alligator scratches in the sand before letting out another roar and turning back to the tall grass. Yoda roars again for good measure. He can feel his wife breathing heavy.

"You ok, Kitty Katz?" Yoda asks as he backs towards the beach, wisely keeping an eye on the tall grass.

"No. I am not. I am far from OK, Yoda."

"Want me to put you down? The sand is soft." Yoda says.

"I absolutely do not want you to put me down." Kitty replies. She tightens her grip on his hair.

"That was pretty cool Kitty Katz!" Yoda says happily. "We scared off an alligator!"

"That was the most frightening thing I have ever done." Kitty mumbles.

"That's what you said when we got married!" Yoda says happily. "That worked out ok too!"

"If you say so." Kitty grumbles. The sound of the ocean has gotten louder. Yoda turns around and pulls out the flashlight. He figures out how to operate it and points it towards the ocean. "Blue. Blue. Red." He says, repeating the effort several times. "Blue. Blue. Red."

Out in the ocean, a visual mirror of the pattern, Blue, Blue, Red reflects back at them. "They see us!" Kitty exclaims. "They see us!"

"I hope *they* is friendly." Yoda says. He hears a whine in the distance. "I think more drones is coming."

"Drones are coming." Kitty reflexively corrects him.

"That's what I said."

The shape of a small boat materializes in the ocean. It appears to be coming towards the shore at a high rate of speed. Yoda turns and sees several blinking lights in the air coming at them.

"Prepare to board, WET!" Comes a female voice from out in the water. "Get in the WATER NOW!" The voice says insistently. Yoda thinks that the woman's voice has an accent. It sounds like one of the voices he had heard when he and Kitty had experienced a virtual tour of London. He shrugs and starts walking into the water. Somehow Kitty finds more of his hair to hang onto. The boat must be electric. Yoda thinks. It makes no noise as it rushes to a halt thirty feet or so offshore.

A person leans over the side. "Let's go!" A female voice says, unaided by any loudspeaker. "Those drones are coming! Hurry! It's high tide. Not deep here. Get to the boat!"

Yoda high steps through the water as fast as he can. Once at the boat, the woman on board helps Kitty from his shoulders into the boat. "Get in!" The woman calls to Yoda. He hoists himself over the side as the front of the boat swings around and takes off into the Gulf of Mexico.

Yoda looks around. The woman with the accent that sounds suspiciously like the woman's voice telling London Tube passengers to 'Mind the Gap', *whatever the gap is,* she the only person on the boat other than he and Kitty. The woman wears all black. The boat is all black. She has a very serious look on her face under a pair of yellow tinted goggles as she looks between the front of the fast-moving boat and the digital gauges on the dash in front of her. Wind and mist from the sea blow Yoda's wavy hair into his eyes. "Where are we going?" He yells over the wind.

"Liberte'." She answers back. Yoda considers what she has said. He wants to ask if she said 'liberty' or 'liber ta' and decides that it doesn't matter. She points at Kitty who is shivering on a bench in front of the steering counsel on the boat. "There are blankets under each seat. Flotation vests too in case they are needed. Make your wife warm. We will arrive in twenty minutes."

Yoda lifts a seat not being sat on by his wife and silently congratulates himself for making the effort to not bother her. He tucks the heavy woolen blanket around the shaking Kitty and puts his arm around her. "The boat driver says we will be there in twenty minutes."

Kitty lifts her head. Her tear-streaked face is clenched in pain. "The cramps, Yoda. I hurt so much."

Yoda stands and yells at the woman controlling the boat. "She feels pain. Do you have medicine, Boat girl?"

"Yoda." Kitty groans.

"Sorry!" Yoda yells. "*Boat Lady,* do you have medicine for... dead baby pain?"

The woman holds a finger up in the air. She is looking off in the distance.

"She has one." Yoda says.

Kitty shakes her head as a wave of cramps doubles her over. The boat slows rapidly. The woman opens a compartment and pulls out a small paper wrapped package.

"We have company. You two need to stay under that blanket and keep very quiet." She hands the package to Yoda. "Unwrap this and inject the whole amount into your wife's arm. It will help with the pain, but she is going to be hard to move." The boat driver pulls out a pair of binoculars and looks at something in the distance. Yoda unwraps the hypodermic needle filled with 10mg of morphine. "I have never given anyone a shot before." He says to Kitty. Worry fills his voice.

"Just put it in me, Yoda. Please." Kitty pleads with clenched teeth. She pulls the collar of her sweater down so Yoda can get to her upper arm. Yoda closes his eyes and puts the needle close to his wife's bare skin. He is shaking with fear. "YODA!" Kitty shouts angrily.

Yoda gasps and opens his eyes in surprise. The needle is aimed at Kitty's face.

"Get that goddamn needle in my arm. NOW!" She growls.

Yoda takes a deep breath and pushes the pointy end of the needle into Kitty's arm and depresses the plunger.

"Thank you, dear." Kitty exhales and smiles. "Thank you. I know that was hard for you."

"Did you..." The boat lady mechanically crouches down. She grabs Yoda's hand and pulls the spent needle and his hand away from Kitty's arm. "OK. Good. She will feel better soon. I need you two to bundle up. There is a boat full of Texas Militiamen about two clicks from our location. I am not sure if they can see us or not; but I cannot have them follow us to the ship. I am going to cut in behind them and take another road to safety. It's going to add a bit of time to our journey, but we have more than enough battery to do it."

"There are roads in the water?" Yoda asks.

"It's a figure of speech." The woman says in her soft English accent.

"But we are going to be on a road? On a water road? Is that smoother than regular water?" Yoda inquires.

"It's..." The woman cocks her head and looks at the man like one might observe a neighbor who has just purchased a giant statue of the nude Marcellus to put in their front yard. "I'm going to take you where you need to go. Please sit tight and be quiet, OK?"

"OK, Boat Lady." Yoda replies. The woman goes back to the counsel and the boat starts moving, albeit at a slower pace. Yoda scoots close to Kitty and covers them both with the wool blanket, leaving just enough of his head uncovered so he can see where they are going. It is so exciting being on the water. It's the first time ever for Yoda being in a real boat! He asks Kitty if she has been on a real boat before, but she is already sound asleep.

Chapter 18
Sometimes tidbits need to be inserted into a story, so it makes sense.


*In 1891, the Shoshone National Forest was established. The Wrigley family incorporated their chewing gum company.*

*Also in 1891, Congress authorized the structure for the appellate court system. The reason that congress did this was because the Supreme Court of the United States of America was overwhelmed with cases and some of those cases had financial or social bearing on members of congress.*

*A Supreme Court Justice is appointed to the high court for a lifetime term. According to the Constitution, justices "shall hold their Offices during good Behavior." They cannot be removed from office unless they are impeached by the House of Representatives and removed after a trial in the Senate. To date, only one Supreme Court Justice, Samuel Chase, a man who was once described as 'a busy, reckless incendiary, a ringleader of mobs, a foul-mouthed and inflaming son of discord and faction and a common disturber of the public tranquility', has ever been impeached. That occurred in 1805, and he was acquitted by the Senate. The acquittal solidified the status of the men (no women on the court until Sandra Day O'Conner in 1981) and women appointed to the court. A lifetime appointment to the court comes with outsized power, and a terrific work/life balance. (The court is in recess 3 months out of the year,) All justices; men and women, get to wear a black dress to work every day. Justices are also still human. To date, no non-human form has ever been appointed to the court although many have questioned whether Clarence Thomas was or was not human. (Conclusive evidence either way has not been presented.) By nature of their humanity, Justices might appear to be self-serving and from time to time, they have been considered... lazy... and of course, arrogant. Over the course of its history, the court has continued to degrade the method and reasons that cases get picked. Frequently, the core issue of the case heard by the court is not the factor the court is actually casting judgement on.*
*In the early 2020's, a group of Texans, fond of beer, big diesel pickup trucks and guns decided that it was no goddamn good that Mexicans could just walk over the Texas-Mexico border and into a life of god given United States freedom any time one of the 'goddamn rapist/murders felt like it'. Over a spirited game of beer pong, these men (there were a few women present, but only the men voted) formed the New Texas Militia. In a*

*rare instance where the State of Texas used its laws to actually protect living human beings, members of the group were arrested during a counter protest at a Juneteenth festival. After explaining to the group that Juneteenth celebrates the end of slavery and not a mass immigration of Mexican people, a Texas District Judge found the men guilty of illegally possessing weapons for the purpose of forming and maintaining an unregulated militia. (United States v. Miller, (1939)).*

*The accused men of the New Texas Milita, mostly wealthy scions of oil barons and ranchers filed suit in Federal Court against the local judge and the State of Texas claiming that state violated the men's 14th amendment right to due process, asserting that Texas could not charge the men with creating a militia as the constitution only allowed such powers to the Federal Government. Additionally, The New Texas Militia filed suit to have their firearms returned to them as the seizure of the weapons violated both the 14th Amendment and the 2nd Amendment. A third suit alleged that the State of Texas had attempted to silence the men from speaking their mind about the 'goddamn rapists/murderers' constantly pouring over the southern border of the United States.*

*When the Supreme Court took the case, the public assumed that a decision would be rendered on the entirety of all the facts of the case. The New Texas Militia was basically hunting down Latino people, not only on the border between Texas and Mexico but all throughout Texas, Louisiana, Oklahoma and New Mexico, all members of the Alamo Compact. Chief Justice of the Court, May Cornwall Bhutthert led the questioning of the attorneys representing the New Texas Militia. Acting more like a prosecutor than a sitting judge, she asked a dozen questions about the activities of the Militia specific to how one might gain membership to the group, how many times a month the group might meet and what sort of activities the group did together. One of the questions improbably dove into what sorts of snacks the men in the Texas Militia favored during meetings (Answer: Pork Rinds and Frito Chips, marking the first time the words Pork and Rind was ever used in conjunction with one another in front of the highest court in the land.) A decision was rendered quickly. The only issue that the court chose to consider was whether the Texas Militia was an unregulated Militia or a regulated Militia. Bhutthert's rambling opinion for the majority claimed that any group could call themselves a militia but to be a Regulated militia, an oath must be taken, regular meetings must occur that included planned activities and snacks should definitely be served. In opinion of the United States Supreme Court, The New Texas Militia is a well-regulated Militia. Shortly after the successful court case, the men of the New Texas Militia renamed themselves the Regulated Texas Militia. Snacks were served at the meeting to celebrate.*

*In 2029, the Supreme Court of the United States of America decided that it was in the public interest to hear* Billy Dean's Gonzo Guns and Fun v The State of Illinois (2029). *Billy Ray Dean of Boggy Bottom, Illinois had imported a 2003 Type 90 Tank from the nation of Japan. Along with the Type 90 Tank, Billy Ray had also imported a Nissan Skyline, Three right hand drive Toyota Land Cruisers and a Honda Monkey. The Supreme Court, accustom to picking and choosing specific issues from appellate cases took the liberty to narrow the many undecided questions from Billy Dean's Gonzo Guns and Fun to one single issue: Is a 2003 Type 90 Tank considered a motor vehicle, and as such subject to current vehicle importation laws that require any vehicle not domesticated to National Highway Transportation Safety Board standards to be over twenty years old. The State of Illinois had strenuously objected to Billy Dean's Gonzo Guns and Fun taking possession of the said Japanese sourced Type 90 Tank on grounds that 1. A Type 90 Tank is not a motor vehicle as defined by the National Highway Transportation Safety Board. 2. The Type 90 Tank is an illegal firearm regardless of if it is considered a motor vehicle or not. 3. Billy Ray, separate from his business, Billy Dean's Gonzo Guns and Fun had used a specialized printer to create the parts necessary to make the armament systems on the Tank operational. 4. It's a fucking operational tank!*

*The Illinois Supreme Court had found against Billy Ray and his company on the issue of the Type 90 Tank being a considered a motor vehicle. In a narrow decision, the Illinois state court called the Type 90 Tank a legal firearm, citing District of Columbia v. Heller (2008) The Federal Seventh Circuit Court had affirmed all the issues pending against Billy Ray in Illinois on appeal. Citing his second amendment rights, Billy Ray Dean petitioned the United States Supreme Court to hear the issues regarding his claims against the State of Illinois. In an effort to conjoin issues, Dean claimed that; by continuing to prohibit him fair use of his motor vehicle, a Type 90 Tank, the State of Illinois violated his second amendment rights granted to him by the constitution. In a short-written opinion for the majority, Bhutthert explained that by denying Dean fair and ordinary usage of his Type 90 Tank, the state of Illinois violated Dean's second amendment rights to possess a legal firearm.*

*And so... in 2040 when the nation of India put a retired Kalvari class attack submarine up for sale, the Texas Militia was quick to purchase it, outbidding both North Korea and the small island nation of Nauru. The Regulated Texas Militia had already been declared to be "well regulated" and the decision in* Billy Dean's Gonzo Guns and Fun v The State of Illinois (2029) *paved the path for the Texas Militia to possess a fully armed diesel-powered attack submarine.*

Chapter 19
High school Graduation.
The parental unit is pleased. Young love.
The Eaton Residence
Someplace in the United States America.
Home of the Free(ish) Land of the Brave(ish)

Anne Margret finishes re-reading her thesis on reparations to Native American people. Fifteen hundred words on the nose. The longest thing she had ever written without the help of an Artificial Intelligence bot. She sighs and pushes the send button. She stares blankly at the screen and wonders if Freddy has even picked a subject for his thesis. He had told her that he wasn't going to use AI. Few people in the class would write their own thesis. Anne Margret thought that Fred certainly had the smarts to write a paper on his own. Little butterflies hop around in her stomach when she thinks about Fredrick A. Petersen. F.A.P. Funny initials for a guy who doesn't even think about masturbation. She thinks to herself, before calling up the command to ping Fred's communicator and then deciding against it.

"Anne Margret Eaton!" Her mother's voice calls up to her.

Anne Margret swishes her hair from side to side. "Yes, Mother?" There is no answer, which means the woman is coming up the stairs to Anne Margret's room. She pats the desk, counting to fifteen, the amount of time it *always* takes her mother to walk up the stairs and open her door. When she hits the number fourteen, a light tap is heard. "Come on in mother." Anne Margret says with a smile. On the count of fifteen, the door opens.

"Do we want to have a graduation party for you next week? Or are you satisfied with a little dinner, just you and me... maybe you can invite some of your friends." Elizabeth Wilma Eaton asks. Anne Margret looks up at her mother who has long red hair, just like her. She appears younger than her 70 years of age... plastic surgery in the modern age is top notch. Combined with stem cells, people don't have to look like they are aging unless they want to... looking old is an identity that a few people who can afford otherwise, choose.

"Think we should call my father?" Anne Margret plays with a strand of her hair.

Elizabeth Wilma Eaton gives her daughter her patented and often used, *WhyWouldWeWantToDoThat?* face. "I am sure he is very busy. When was the last time you spoke with him?"

Anne Margret thinks about it. "Two years ago. On my sixteenth birthday. He said to tell you hello. I think I forgot to tell you. So, *Big Hello* from the sperm donor who assisted in the manufacturing of me."

Elizabeth Eaton fashions herself the prototypical feminist. She hadn't actually had sex with her daughter's father. Or, really known him at all. The man was a serial technologist and inventor. He had owned companies that provided ways for people spread gossip about one another, pay for things and rockets for people to ride in, although interplanetary transportation had been banned after religious fundamentalist successfully lobbied congress to pass such a law, arguing that inviting people from other planets might decrease the relevance of a God if indeed one exists. Elizabeth Wilma Eaton hadn't actually had sex with anyone, ever. She is a 70-year-old virgin. At least, she is in her mind.

"Your father doesn't need to be included. It isn't like he was ever supposed to be included. I should have never agreed to let him contact you. He insisted on the contact, and I was weak." Elizabeth Eaton points at her daughters monitor. "You have a message."
Anne Margret turns and looks. Her thesis has been graded. "It isn't like my father would have had any problem finding me anyway. All our genetics are basically public information." She clicks on the message. An explosion of light flashes across the screen. A line of male cheerleaders, (Anne Margret's preference) jump up and down shouting her name as the word SUCCESS, followed by three exclamation points scroll across the screen. A dialog box appears asking if she would like to download her high school diploma.

"Looks like I graduated from High School, Mom." Anne Margret smiles briefly.

Her mother pats her on the head. "Good girl. I expected nothing less, of course. I did read your Senior Thesis. Good points made. I can't believe how brief your writing assignment is."

"How long was your thesis, Mother?" Anne Margret asks, already knowing the answer, as the subject had been brought up numerous times in the past. She knows her mother likes to tell her how hard things were when she was the same age as Anne Margret. Anne Margret can mouth her mother's response by memory as it is said.

The woman harrumphs. "My paper argued that the World Health Organization should campaign for all nations to stop the practice of genital mutilation. The paper was over sixteen thousand words. The minimum was fifteen thousand words. My paper was well received, and I got an A plus on it." She says with pride. "That was a long time ago. Eighty-Eight." She sighs. "After high school, I had to go to college for four years, grad school for another two years and later, law school for three years."

Elizabeth Wilma Eaton is a corporate attorney specializing in social services and product liability. (She is a partner at the firm Laston, Eaton, Isa, Litlcold.) A Conservative Supreme Court outlawed most forms of federally subsidized welfare for individuals after the recession of 2028. Since then, the Court made it a practice to grab cases challenging the lack of social safety nets for the sole purposes of squashing any such ideas early in the legal process. Barred to practice law in forty states plus the District of Columbia, E.W. Eaton had appeared (mostly unsuccessfully) in front of the Federal Courts countless times, arguing that states did have the right to protect citizens through financial aid. Except in cases where she could prove that the entirety of the aid was coming from state dollars and not federal dollars, the cases were usually lost causes.

Her daughter smiles. "We are encouraged to be brief, not be Boring and make fast, clear points."

"That you did dear." The mother nods at the still flashing screen. "And the computer gave you an A plus."

"It gave me a grade of Success!!!" Anne Margret smiles. "I don't need a graduation party. I just need to pick a college."

Elizabeth Eaton waves her hand dismissively. "Let's at least go out to dinner. Invite a friend or two. Are you still thinking of law school? I'd like it very much if you followed in my footsteps."

Anne Margret grins mischievously. "I thought I would follow in my father's footsteps and create things that destroy public trust in its government, unstitch the social fabric that unites us and gets our fellow citizens lost in space." She watches her mother frown in a very disapproving way. "Or I could go to law school and see what happens next.... Mom?"

"Yes dear?"
Anne Margret shifts her weight and looks at the floor uncomfortably. "I don't want to go to Michigan. I know you went there and it's a good law program and all... but it's six months, and I just don't want to do that sort of time when I can go elsewhere and get done quicker."

The older woman appears to mull the idea of her only daughter not attending the school that launched her law career. Michigan had long eschewed the other law schools race to the bottom, going from a three-year program to first a one-year program and then only six months. All the other schools had six to eight week law programs. In truth, E.W Eaton had not really wanted her daughter to be interested in Michigan. The school was highly ranked in the world of law, and because of that, students were expected to pay a high price for the education, brief as it may be. Foreign students pay even more, and as such, applications from students outside of the United States of America were given priority over domestic based applications. Favors would have to be called in for Anne Margret Eaton to be accepted into her mother's alma mater. One of the things that Elizabeth

Wilma Eaton hates is owing someone a favor which will certainly be called upon to be repaid at a most inopportune time.

"Wherever you go will be fine, Anne Margret." Elizabeth says with a clear voice. "Now, pick a friend and we shall have a nice dinner out. Try and avoid meat eaters. I simply can't stand the way such people smell."

Anne Margret smiles. An idea occurs to her. "Mom, you remember that boy, Freddy..." She clears her throat. "Fred Petersen? We were chemistry partners our junior year?"

"The boy whose father owns the sex toy business? Of course I remember him. Quiet kid. Nice. Do you think of him romantically?" Her mother asks.
"No Mom!" Anne Margret's face turns bright red, exposing both the fib and her feelings to her mother who had a knack of knowing exactly what people are thinking. "He's just a nice guy, you know. I think he might be homosexual, anyway."

"Gay, huh." Elizabeth sighs. "The nice ones always are... He hangs around with that Good kid. Trump B. Good? That name amused me when I saw it on your kindergarten roster. Took me back to the craziness of my younger days. Mr. Good won't be accompanying us on our celebratory dinner, will he?"

Anne Margret makes a face. "Absolutely not. The whole dinner conversation would be about masturbation. I might tell Freddy... Fred that he can being his father. Is that ok?"

"Conrad Peterson has done more for women with his silly toys than most men have. He is welcome to attend the celebratory dinner. I shall do my best to pretend to enjoy the conversation." Elizabeth Eaton replies. She walks towards the door, stops and turns. "Anne Margret... Just because I never found myself in a situation to accept a partner, doesn't mean you have to follow the same path. Just make sure that you can remain yourself in any sort of union, be it with a man or a woman... or you know, someone who is both."

"Yes, mother." Anne Margret rolls her eyes as her mother leaves the room. She mentally triggers the communicator to call Fred A. Peterson. The phone chimes lightly in her ear.

"Anne Margret?" An out of breath Fred Peterson answers.

"Freddy, you aren't supposed to pound yourself that hard." Anne Margret leans back on her bed. The beauty of an internal communicator is that it can be used at any time in nearly any position.

"I am out for a run." Fred answers, breathing heavy. "Almost done."

"What did you get on your term paper? You have turned it in, right?" Anne Margret asks.

"Success all the way." Fred pants.

Anne Margret sighs. "What was it on again?"

"The case against paying reparations to any group for past wrongs." Fred snaps back.

"What!" Anne Margret sits up straight. "What did you just say?"

Fred laughs. "I'm joking. The paper was on Entrepreneurship in the Modern Era."

"Kind of Boring."

"Says the girl who argued that the country should pay money back to Native tribes that no longer exist." Fred answers. "Look out your window."

Anne Margret smiles. The butterflies erupt in her middle. She pulls the blind on the window back. A sweaty Fred Petersen, wearing neon yellow shorts and a neon green shirt stands in the driveway. "Be right down." She disconnects the communicator and checks herself in the mirror. Satisfied, she takes the steps two at a time.

"What's with the noise?" Elizabeth Eaton calls out.

"Nothing Mother!" Her daughter answers as she opens the front door to the house.

"Nice outfit, sport. Want the girls on the space station to see you running?" Anne Margret asks sarcastically as she approaches Fred who rests with his hands on his knees.

"Are there girls on the space station? I thought we stopped allowing women to go to space." Fred says as he stands.

Anne Margret responds by punching him in the chest. "Maybe you want the guys on the space station to see you!"

"We need to talk about your propensity for violence." Fred comments as he rubs his ribs.

The front door of the house opens. Fred sees Anne Margret's mother and waves. "Hello Ms. Eaton." He calls out. The woman comes to the pair. "Look at you Fred Peterson! You are all grown up!"

"Happens, I guess." Fred answers, not sure how to respond to what can only be described as a clueless adult comment.

Anne Margret rolls her eyes. "Mom!"

Elizabeth Eaton seems not to notice her daughter's teenage exasperation. "Anne Margret tells me that you are graduating with her. What are your plans for the future, Fred?"

Fred's eyes shift back and forth between the two women as he shrugs. "I am not sure yet. Conrad, my dad... he wants me to work in the family business. I am not sure I want to do that." Fred smiles nervously. "Anne Margret wants to go to law school. I might investigate that. Maybe I can work for the government or something."

Elizabeth Wilma Eaton, hater of owing anyone a favor, finds almost little joy with the idea of anyone working for the government as most people who work in the modern government are brainless slaves to an ideal that isn't hers, have not worked to protect the people and in general represent the growing subset of population unable to carry on a proper conversation. She forces a smile on her face that would be construed as genuine to only the blind and says, "Government. Well. That is something. But most things are something." She nods at Anne Margret. "Has Annie invited you to dinner yet?"

"Thanks for ruining my moment, Mom." Anne Margret glowers. She turns to Fred with a red face. "I... umm... I... We would like to invite you and your father to dinner. Sometime. To celebrate our graduation."

Fred shrugs and smiles, happy to see that Anne Margret Eaton can be flustered. "Sure. I will ask Conrad... my dad. I need to give him a date. Do you have any ideas?"

Available dates are discussed. Fred does his best to remember the days that both women have openings in their schedule so he can relay the offer to Conrad. After ten minutes of back and forth, Fred excuses himself to finish his run and takes off.

Elizabeth Eaton puts her arm around her daughter. "Well, Fred seems to be a nice guy, if a little dim. Government lawyer." She shakes her head. "And most certainly, he is gay. You are right about that Annie. No doubt. *That outfit.*" Her mother shakes her head. "Whew! You could see him from the moon." She drops her arm and walks towards the house.

"I sure hope Freddy isn't gay." Anne Margret Eaton says with a sigh as she watches Fred A. Peterson run down the street.

Chapter 20
Goodbye hospital. Taxi ride. Civil unrest.
Government Housing is for shit.
Someplace in America.
Land of the Free(ish) Home of the Brave(ish)

*My expulsion from the hospital was about as exciting as a trip to the proctologist. First, there was an unimaginable number of forms that needed to be filled out on an electronic tablet that kept freezing up. I might have thought that such things would work better in 2043 than it did in 2022. Three Robots took me through the tasks. A real human - I think it was a middle-aged man, but something told me that might not be right — the, he could have really been a, she - came in and did something to one of the Robots. The person did not even acknowledge me, which was OK. I wasn't much in the mood for conversation.*

*I had to fill out a form for a new 'personal identification number'. The Robot assured me that my social security number was no longer valid. After filling out the form, a number was generated. 9362783204. The robot said it was a good number. I have no idea why. It looked random to me. I was given my belongings in a plastic bag from when I was checked in twenty years prior. I didn't bother taking anything from the bag. The iPhone and the Apple Watch were clearly broken. The wallet held nothing of any relevance or importance to me in the current day.*

*There was a form to fill out to have a communication device implanted in my person. I refused it. Not because I am especially opposed to the idea, I just had no idea how such a thing might be paid for. One form described the living wage I would receive and noted that the deliverance of any such thing could be delayed for six to twelve months.*

*Millie said that she knew where they would take me and that she would find me. For obvious reasons, Millie does not have an implanted communication device. Her legal status simply won't permit such luxury. She has told me that she would never get one even if she could.*

*Right before I might have gotten lunch (it happens to be artificial cod fish day. I can't say I am disappointed at not getting lunch) Meathead the Robot escorted me to the front door of the hospital where a driverless taxi waited for me.*

"Good Luck Patient Justin Thyme." Meathead said in his mechanical Robot voice. "I hope you do not return here, and you live a long time."
"Oh, Meathead." I tap the chest plate on the android. "You know that you will miss me. I only wish that we could have had more time together. Maybe we would have fallen in love."

Little lights blink on the Robot's head. "Microsoft Medical Systems do not allow me to express affection for patients, Patient Justin Thyme."
"That's a good policy, Meathead. You should not express affection for any patients here." I point in a random direction. "Now get up-stairs and Robot hump Lamont. I think he has a thing for you." Happily, I am getting my sarcastic sense of humor back. I am still working on material.

Meathead stands still. None of the lights flicker on his head.

The horn on the driverless taxi honks. "I think I need to go." I say to the stationary hulk of metal. "Meathead, Did I touch a Robot nerve with the Lamont comment?"

"Microsoft Medical Systems thanks you for choosing it." Meathead slurs. It looks down. A puddle of oily liquid has pooled at Meathead's feet. "I have malfunctioned. Report Generated."

"Gosh, I didn't mean to make you wet yourself, Meathead." I point at the puddle of oil. "Good luck with that, buddy." I walk out and get in the taxi. An Indian accented voice greets me.

"Hello Patient..." There is a pause. I realize suddenly that without a communication device or an RFID bracelet like I had in the hospital, the appliances that seem to run the world will not recognize me. The voice continues. "...of Microsoft Medical Systems. I am taking you to the Honorable Representative Nancy Pelosi Public Housing, Convalescence and Retirement Center. Please, sit back and relax. We will be at your destination in.... Sixty-Eight minutes.”

"Sixty-Eight minutes. It must be a long way.” I say. The taxi has started moving.

"The destination is only eight kilometers away.” The voice says. There is social unrest near the destination. We will avoid confrontation and take a different route. Please, sit back and relax. We will be at your destination in.... Sixty-Seven minutes.”

"Social unrest. Huh.” I sit back in the seat. A video monitor comes on in front of me. *A beautiful blond woman in a very small yellow bikini walks on a green grass lawn. 'Is your day going well? Let me tell you how it can be better.' Her hand goes behind her and reappears with a cylinder tube covered in colorful writing.*

"Where did you get that cylinder from?” I ask the monitor which thankfully does not answer. The woman on the screen continues her spiel; *'Angie's Amazake is a delicious way to get your tummy working again. Exclusive and unique malted real rice extracts are guaranteed to relieve users from painful constipation and irritation caused by eating synthetic foods. It is especially effective for people who have deficient motor skills or other difficulties caused by mental incapacitation.' The colorful canister of Angie's Amazake disappears, and the woman leans forward, exposing a full chest of cleavage. 'Someone you love is experiencing constipation right now. Won't you be a dear and fix them some Angie's Amazake?'* The woman blows a kiss at the screen and the video transitions to an episode of *Shit Happens.* For three minutes I watch shear theatrical stupidity played out on a video screen. The program breaks for a commercial. A buff and tanned suit wearing man dances out onto a screen to disco like music. He strips off his jacket and then his shirt. Standing topless, he continues gyrating before pointing at the screen. *Only you can insure your transporter against theft, fire and vandalism.* The commercial ends with the man hip thrusting - rather disturbingly - at the camera and shouting *Come and Get it, Baby!* While grabbing his crotch. A logo for 'Hathaway Auto Highway Authority Insurance fills the screen.

"Hey!” I call out, hoping the taxi is listening. “Can you turn the monitor off?”

"Passenger entertainment system suspended. Thank you for your request, Patient...." There is a pause. "Please sit back and enjoy the ride. We will arrive at your destination in... seventy-six minutes."

"That's longer!" I exclaim. "I can walk eight kilometers in less time than that!" I doubt that's true. I might not be able to walk eight hundred meters in an hour and sixteen minutes. It feels good to bitch though.

"There is continued social unrest near the destination. To avoid confrontation, I am rerouting us to your destination. Please sit back and relax. We will arrive at your destination in seventy-seven minutes."

The taxi winds through streets that are towered over by very tall buildings. I don't see a lot of people walking on the street. Several more turns are made and the landscape changes dramatically. The buildings get shorter. And everything is pretty run down. Windows are boarded up on buildings where it appears there is no business. There are more people on the street here. I see a man and woman fighting on a street corner. The woman rips off the sleeve of the man's shirt. "Where are we?" I exclaim more than ask.

"This is a neighborhood where people live." The voice in the taxi offers. "There are no more delays. Law Enforcement drones have quelled the civic unrest. We should arrive at our destination in.... three minutes. Thank you for your patronage."

The taxi slows to a crawl as other similar looking vehicles are ahead of us. I look behind us. A line of traffic has formed, blocking us in. After a few minutes, the Taxi voice makes an announcement. "Civil unrest ahead. This mobility device is out of service. Your destination, Honorable Representative Nancy Pelosi Public Housing, Convalescence and Retirement Center is ahead, two city blocks on the right. Please exit the cab and walk."

I look around. People are running now. I am wearing gray hospital issued scrubs. The paperwork I filled out suggested I shop at secondhand stores or ask for hand-outs from people for more clothes. My outfit isn't riot worthy, and it might attract unwanted attention. The doors of the taxi slide open. "Please exit the cab, immediately and thank you for your patronage. We hope to see you again soon."

Gingerly I get out of the taxi and hurry to the right side of the street. A man runs past me. "Get out of my way faggot!" He turns and yells at me as he runs by. "Boring fucking people shouldn't be out on the street."

I start walking. Two blocks. I can make two blocks. Meathead was making me walk like two miles a day. I usually did it slowly. The foam shoes I am wearing that sort of resemble tennis shoes without any promise of durability.  They are not fit for this city's sidewalks. I step around a broken glass bottle and a pile of something that could be human feces. A pair of younger looking people run past before stopping and turning back to look at me. One meets me on the sidewalk. "Give me your credits you *Smellfungus!*" The person... I am loosely using that generalization, shouts at me. This androgynous dwarf that easily could have been a Jim Henson creation points a finger in my face and repeats itself.

"Are you really using a 18th century fictional character as an insult reference?" I ask, trying to think of something I can say with enough sarcastic humor to defuse the situation. The creature grabs my crotch with one hand and jabs a finger in my chest with the other while squeezing my junk. Its ears are pointed and its face grimy enough I can neither discern a gender or age. "Your credits, fart factory. Now!"

The pain of my balls being squeezed like a juiceless orange prohibit me from laughing, but laugh at this insane scene, I want to. The second... thing comes over and starts rubbing its hands all over my body. "It got nuttin, Betty. Nuttin at all. It just Boring."

"How you got nuttin?" The ball squeezer releases me and steps back. "How come you so fuckin Boring, Man? You got nuttin." It grabs the collar of the hospital scrubs and pulls me close to its face. "We ought to kill it and sell the innards, Betty. That's what we ought to do. The kidneys are worth sumthin' …Gotta be!" Now I am terrified. This situation has taken a dramatic turn for the worse. The scene is hilarious if I am not the one smelling the thing's foul odor and if it's not me the subject of whatever mutilation is being contemplated. Motion from my right catches my eye as an arm reaches in with a silver device. Electrical sounds erupt from the device and suddenly I am released and the thing grabbing me is on the ground. The other... creature, I guess? It takes off running. I look at the human attached to the end of the arm. Millie.

"My hero." I croak. "They wanted my innards... whatever that means in today's world."
"       Welcome to the USA. Home of the free to do this sort of thing. Land of... well, there *is* lots of land." Millie says. "Let's go see the things you won't find on the internet."

We start walking down the street. "What is that thing you have?"

"Old fashion taser. I am glad it worked. I'm never sure if the charge is full or not. I hate guns, although I should probably get one. I am surprised that the street people accosting you weren't armed. Usually they are." Millie says. As if on cue, gun fire erupts ahead of us. I want to throw myself on the ground. Millie pulls me forward. "We are just about there. I saw the traffic backup and figured that the Taxi would kick you out."

"So that is normal? Taxi's ejecting customers in the middle of the ride?"

"The companies that own the transporter taxis don't want their assets at risk. Civil unrest is monitored. The taxi company knew that Microsoft Medical wasn't paying to take you anywhere else, so out you went." Millie points ahead. "That's our place."

"It looks like an old Walmart." I observe.

"Good eye. It probably is. The old box stores don't exist anymore. Everything is online. The government bought these stores... or more likely the government had investors develop the stores into housing. It won't be nice; I can assure you." Millie explains as we walk across a crowded parking lot. She points at a clearly older green transporter. "That one is mine, by the way." There is a bumper sticker on the back that says *PEACE Through Unconventional Means*. We walk under a sign that says *Honorable Representative Nancy Pelosi Public Housing, Convalescence and Retirement Center* and go inside. A robot wearing a dress sits at a long desk. "Name and Room Number."

Millie pushes me forward. "I am... New. I am new here. I don't know my room number." I stutter.

The Robot responds with a bored tone. "Name?"

"Justin Thyme."

"You are new. Welcome to the *Honorable Representative Nancy Pelosi Public Housing, Convalescence and Retirement Center.*"

"Thanks?" I reply.

"You are in single room." The Robot answers. A card is placed on the desk. "Unit 21234." The head of the Robot turns to Millie. "Name and Room Number."

"I am with him." Millie says.

"Unit 21234 is a single room. Occupied by Justin Thyme, Single Occupant. Name?"

"She is just a visitor." I say. "Helping me."

"Is visitor Food Delivery, Relative, Government Approved Personal Assistant or Other?" The Robot asks.

"I am a prostitute." Millie says, stepping forward. She turns back to me and whispers, "I am not really, but it is legal now and identities are not usually collected."

"Frequent visitors need to be registered." The Robot says. "Name?"

"My hooker's name is Penelope Puddingsnatch." I say. Millie gives me a *Whatthefuck?* look.

"Penelope Puddingsnatch registered as a frequent visitor. Does Visitor Puddingsnatch need an access card?"

I beam at Millie. "Why yes... yes, she does. Ms. Puddingsnatch does need her own access card." A card is placed on the counter. I pick it up triumphantly and hand it to Millie.

We are interrupted by a woman and four children that burst through the doors. "Cottonwood Family. Room 12674!" The woman yells as she runs past the desk. "Fanny, Danny, Patty and Elf!" She glares at me as she hustles past. "Got the runs. Gotta go!"

"Cottonwood." The Robot says. "Fanny. Danny. Patty. Elf. Clear for entry."

"Name and Room Number?" The Robot says after typing on its screen. I look at Millie. She shrugs. "Justin Thyme and Penelope Puddingsnatch. Room 21234."

"Clear for entry." The Robot says.

"I guess we know how that works, now." I mumble. We follow signs to a flight of stairs and walk up them. Room 21234 is on the second floor of three. I wave my card in front of the reader and the steel door pops open. Millie and I step inside. The door closes with a whoosh behind us A light comes on automatically.

Millie had told me to prepare for sparse. I had steeled myself for a barren apartment in a mediocre neighborhood. I had not prepared myself for what I see before us. To say that jail cells are nicer accommodations than my government issued apartment may be a slight to jail cells in comparison. A twin sized bed made from a stainless-steel tray is bolted to the wall just inside the entry door. Despite it being a single room, a second twin bed constructed in the same fashion is bolted perpendicular to and above and across the lower bunk. On the other side of the room from the lower bunk is a small stainless-steel counter, maybe two feet wide. It appears to have some sort of electric glass hot plate imbedded in the middle of it. I open the only door in the place, a stainless-steel affair to the smallest water closet I have ever seen. I'm going to have to fold myself into a pretzel to use the facilities. "No Shower or Sink." I observe.

Millie steps into the bathroom. She points at the ceiling. "It's an all-in-one thing. The shower is up there. The sink folds out of the wall above the toilet."

"Hygienic place." I say. "I'd compare this to a jail cell, but jail cells have windows."

"In a jail cell, you have to use the toilet in the middle of the room." Millie answers with a knowing tone.

"Serious?" I ask, looking down at her.

She nods. "Guards use to walk the floor looking for us taking a dump. It was mortifying."

"They don't use Robots for prison guards?"

Millie shakes her head. "Not back then and probably not now in Texas. A Robot probably can't be programmed to be as sadistic as Texas prison guards are."

Millie gestures at the bunks. "This is great. I thought I might be sleeping on the floor. We can go down to my transport and get my blankets."

"What makes you think that I would have let you sleep on the floor?" It's not stainless steel. It appears to me some sort of textured surface, same as the walls. Concrete of some sort.

Millie pats the side of my face. "And they say chivalry is dead." She points at the door. "Let's go before it gets dark. I think it's best to be inside at night in this neighborhood."

We exit the little cubby dwelling and walk down the stairs. I may be upright and walking, but taking stairs, especially down in a precarious activity for me. I concentrate on getting one foot in front of the other as we navigate the metal grated declining staircase. "Shouldn't there be an elevator in here? ADA and all?"

"That went away a few years ago. I am sure the courts got rid of the requirement." Millie sighs. "They would have accommodated you on the first floor if you would have said something.

We get to the ground floor and walk outside. Some sort of melee is happening out in the road. "They have a delivery truck on its side." Millie says. She points. "Probably a gang. The delivery trucks are all self-driving with Robotic delivery components. The gangs stop the truck by standing in the road. Then the truck is tipped on its side and looted."

"Holy shit." I exclaim, looking at the crowd of people who seem to be celebrating around the fallen truck. "Does someone call the cops?"

"I'm sure... just as I am sure they will not come. Not in this neighborhood. Maybe drones, but by the time drones get here, all that will be over.  The truck will be empty." Millie opens her transporter. The blankets are all folded on the floor in the back of the vehicle. Millie hands me the blankets and she picks up a box.

"This looks like it might be as comfortable as that jail cell up there." I say.

Millie grimaces. "Maybe. But it scares the hell out of me to sleep in it... even in the hospital parking garage. People aren't very nice these days." "How much for the broad?" A voice calls out. Two men are walking towards us. One has a beard down to the center of his chest. The other has tattoos all over his bald head. I want to make a smart-ass comment, but fear is keeping those little voices in my head from letting my mouth do much more than breath heavy.

"Stay away..." Millie says. "We have the virus."

The men stop walking. Millie motions at me. "Look at him. It's killing him... I'm next, I am afraid. You don't want what we got. It's a killer."

"Fucks dis!" The bald man says. He's close enough that I see he hadn't had a lifetime of good dental care. "Let's go Cooter. Got to stay clear of that virus shit!"

"Virus?" I whisper as we walk into the Walmart turned my new apartment building.

"People are so fucking dumb now; they don't know what to be afraid of. Twenty-two years after Covid, you say *Virus* and people run." She sniggers. "It helps that *you* look a little like a scarecrow that lost its battle with the crows."

"Name and Room number." The dress wearing Robot says at the desk.

I look at Millie with a twisted smile. "Go ahead. You go first."

"      I had no idea that you would be such an asshole." Millie says softly. She leans over the desk and whispers in faux seductive voice. "Penelope Puddingsnatch. Room 21234."

"Penelope Puddingsnatch, Frequent Visitor. Room 21234. Clear for Entry." The Robot says loudly.

An old man leaning on a walker on the other side of the desk straightens up. "Hey, Puddingsnatch... you can visit me if you want." Millie flips him off.

I start laughing. It feels good, even if it is coming at the expense of my only friend. "Justin Thyme. Room 21234." I look over at the old man. "Puddingsnatch here is all mine old man... you just leave her alone."

"Justin Thyme. Room 21234. Clear for Entry." The Robot says.

The man waves at me dismissively. We walk up the stairs. I figure if I do the stairs four or five times a day, by this time next month, I will be twice as strong... which isn't saying much.

We get in the apartment, and I put the blankets on the bed. Millie opens the box. "I have a present for you."

"I like presents." I look over her shoulder at the open box. She pulls out a pair of pants, a shirt and some underwear that is new in a package. "I got them at the Salvation Army store. They didn't have shoes, but we will keep looking."

I almost cry. After sucking in a deep breath, I hug Millie. "Thank you, Millie."

"It's just used clothes, Justin." Millie says into my chest. "And thank you for letting me stay with you."

"Anything for my Puddingsnatch." I crack.

Millie pushes off from me. She's laughing too. "Puddingsnatch... I don't know how you came up with that name so quickly. It must have been a pet name for one of your tramp girlfriends... What rhymes with Puddingsnatch? Speaking of pudding, that reminds me. I brought some food. Hospital grub, but it will work for tonight." She holds up two chocolate soymilk puddings.
We make the beds and sit on the lower one to eat our pudding and two cold veggie dogs. "Tomorrow is going to be a better day, Puddingsnatch." I exclaim, using my finger to scrape out the last of my chocolate pudding. Millie leans against me and sighs. "It will have to be *Romeo Lionheart*. A better day is what tomorrow will have to be."

I snuggle in closer to her. It feels nice. Not romantic necessarily, but comfortable. "*Romeo Lionheart?* Is that the best you can do, Puddingsnatch?"

"I'll keep trying." Millie says with a sigh.

Chapter 21
More Kismet. Don't call me Liz. Loving some eggplant.
Someplace in the United States America.
Home of the Free(ish) Land of the Brave(ish)

Anne Margret waves at Fred and he and Conrad Peterson get out of their driverless taxi transport near the front door of Lettuce Eat, a slow casual restaurant chain specializing in (mostly) animal free dishes. Anne Margret had picked the place in deference to her mother who not only could not stand eating meat, but also disliked watching people consume meat and absolutely abhorred the body order of people who ate meat.

"Mother is inside. She already has a table. Come on!" Anne Margret says.

"Umm, Conrad, this is Anne Margret. Just so you know." Fred mumbles nervously.

"He knows who I am Freddy!" Anne Margret seems to skip through the restaurant.

Conrad chuckles behind his son as they make their way through the relatively crowded establishment. "I think she is sweet on you, son."

"Stop it dad. We are just friends." Fred grumbles. "Like I am friends with Bob."

Conrad shakes his head. "Whatever you say, son. If I were picking though... I'd take the girl."

They arrive at the table where Elizabeth Wilma Eaton sits, iron rod back straight in her chair. She stands. "I presume you are Mr. Peterson." She extends her hand stiffly. "I am Anne Margret's mother, Elizabeth Eaton."

Conrad smiles at the woman and takes her hand. "It is nice to meet you, Liz. I have been looking forward to this dinner."

Anne Margret's eyes go wide. Her mother hates being called Liz. She waits for the icy glare to emit from her mother's eyes followed by what would surely be a cold atmosphere blanketing the table for the entirety of the meal and probably for all eternity. She sees her mother's eyes narrow. Conrad keeps a hold of the woman's hand for an uncomfortably long time.

"I see where Anne Margret gets her beauty from. It is truly a joy to be here with you, celebrating our children." Conrad says smoothly before releasing Elizabeth's hand. "Thank you for including us."

Anne Margret sees her mother soften. A faint smile crosses the woman's face. She feels relief when her mother replies, "I have been looking forward to meeting you Mr. Peterson."

"Conrad. Please call me Conrad." Conrad gestures for Fred and Anne Margret to be seated. He moves around Elizabeth Eaton and pulls her chair out for her. After assisting her in sitting, Conrad takes the open chair to her right.

A robot server comes to the table. After an introduction, the robot reminds the table that tooth care is an important part of good overall health. Flyers for a local dentist office are produced and put on the table. The Robot finishes the advertisement by adding, "Your meal receipt today gets you ten percent off of diamond installation on any tooth."
"Diamond installation?" Fred mumbles. He looks at the flyer. A shirtless man with six pack abs grins from the paper. Little stones glitter from his teeth. "Look at that. Diamonds on the fronts of his teeth."

"That's why you saw on that picture, huh?" Anne Margret whispers with a hopeful tone. "Just the diamonds? On his teeth?"

Fred looks at her with a confused expression.

"Thank you. Please bring us all still bottled water." Elizabeth Eaton demands. "And send back a human waiter."

The robot bows its head. "I am sorry. There are no human waiters available at this establishment. For the trouble of receiving service from me, Lettuce Eat will deduct ten percent from your bill. I will return with your drinks." With what can only be described as a dejected expression, the robot turns and leaves the table.

"Easy way to save ten percent, Liz." Conrad beams. "You must know that there are no human waiters here... or about anywhere else for that matter."

Elizabeth smirks and says proudly. "Of course. I am old enough to remember when the whole *RaaS* - Robots as a Service thing started. The original programming has never been changed. It has always been ten percent off if you demand a human waiter."

Anne Margret rolls her eyes. "Mom. We don't need to be so cheap tonight."

Conrad waves dismissively with a big grin. "It's a great tip, Anne Margret. I had never thought that the robot bios might not be reprogrammed."

"It works every time." Elizabeth Eaton replies. She puts her hand on his with a genuine smile. "And please, call me Elizabeth. It's the only name I know."

"Of course!" Conrad exclaims. "My apologies for assuming a nickname!" He leans into her. "I go by Carlos sometimes, but we aren't there yet."

Anne Margret sucks in an audible breath. She looks at Freddy whose eyes are as wide as the bread plate sitting in front of him. Elizabeth Eaton's face reddens, and she giggles.

"Oh, that's... Awful." She stutters with a laugh. "Carlos." She giggles again and tightens her grip on the man's hand.

"Anne Margret and I are going..." Fred's voice trails off as he stands up. "... to, umm."

"Wash our hands." Anne Margret jumps up. "And maybe our ears. And eyes." She grabs Fred by the shoulder. "Let's go Freddy!"

When they are out of earshot, Fred turns to her, red-faced. "I am sorry Anne Margret. I should have warned you. Conrad... he... usually likes older women. I am surprised, well... Your mom isn't that old and umm..."

Anne Margret giggles, cutting him off. The giggles turn to laughter. "Freddy, I have never seen my mom... flushed like that! And he called her Liz! I thought she might take me and leave the restaurant when he called her Liz!" She straightens, Fred sees that her eyes are watering from laughing. "I think your dad is sweet on my mom. Maybe not. Either way, it's harmless. Let it go, Freddy."

Fred nods slightly. "You aren't mad?"

Anne Margret frowns with a shrug. "Why would I be mad?"

Fred shakes his head. "I don't know. Girl empowerment? Women are supposed to be in control today?"

Anne Margret slugs him in the shoulder hard enough to make him take a step backwards. "You goof. Girls like romance. Since the government took any control we might have had over our bodies, Romance has died a sad and lonely death. Your dad was flirting with my mom. It's sweet! Although, *holy shitballs!* I really did think that she might get up and leave when he called her Liz. She *hates* being called Liz!" She points at a case filled with vegetables. "We are having eggplant tonight. Let's go pick one out."

What makes you think that I want eggplant?" Fred hurries to catch up with her.

"Because you are going to be romantic and share a meal with me, and tonight we are having eggplant." Anne Margret answers definitively.

Chapter 22
America gets Foreign Humanitarian Aid.
Human Doctors. An Awakening.
French Navy Vessel Liberte' Gulf of Mexico.
Just outside of the territorial zone of the United States of America.


After docking at a boat that looks like a large cruise ship, Kitty was taken from the speedboat on a gurney by two orderlies. The woman in the boat patted Yoda on his shoulder and told him to follow the pair and his wife.

Yoda ran after the orderlies who moved quickly into an elevator. They spoke to each other in a language Yoda could not understand. How he wished for a communication device like the characters had in some of the Star Wars series. He looks dumbly at the pair as they speak to each other. "Do you guys know American?" He asks. They both look at him dumbly.

The elevator stops and announces the floor as 'five'. Yoda follows the gurney down the hall and into a room filled with bright lights and a surgical bed. Kitty's sleeping body is transferred from the gurney to the bed. A tall man is followed into the room by an equally tall woman. Both are very blond. The man immediately checks on Kitty's vitals. The woman stands by Yoda.

"You must be Katherine's husband, Yoda?" She asks.

"I am Yoda." Yoda says. He has no recollection of ever seeing a male human doctor working on a female patient.

"I am Doctor Astrid Berg. That is Dr. Liam Bloom. We are obstetricians here on the Liberte'." The tall woman says to Yoda in accented English.
Yoda points at Dr. Liam Bloom. "Should he be touching her?"

Dr. Berg chuckles. "I can assure you that Dr. Bloom is quite qualified. He is one of the premier obstetricians in the world. Your wife is in good hands."

"But he is not a... Robot?" Yoda says slowly. "How can he be as good as a Robot?"

Dr. Bloom comes over to the pair. "She is still out from the morphine. How much did she get?"

"The needle was this big." Yoda holds thumb and forefinger four inches apart.

Dr. Bloom gives Dr. Berg a questioning look. Berg wears a bemused smile. "Dr. Bloom, this is the patient's husband. His name is Yoda."

"Is that short for something?" Dr. Bloom asks Yoda. He has the same accent as Dr. Berg.

"You should not make fun of people's height. Yoda may have been short, but he is very powerful." Yoda answers. "My name is Yoda Storm Trooper Katz Williams. I took Kitty's last name."

"She probably didn't want to be called Kitty Katz." Dr. Berg says with a suppressed laugh.

Yoda's eyes get big. "Never call her Kitty Katz. She hates that!" "You Americans get more and more special all the time!" Dr. Bloom says with a sarcastic tone that is unrecognizable by Yoda.

"Thank you!" Yoda says. "When will Kitty be better?"

Dr. Bloom shakes his head. "She has had too much morphine for us to work on her now. I'd like to talk to her before we do the procedure." He frowns and pauses before continuing. "Maybe late tomorrow or early the next day we can deliver the baby. We will keep her comfortable."

Dr. Berg gently takes Yoda by the elbow. "Katherine is going to stay in this room for a while. Let me show you to a resting room. You can watch the telly or take a nap. Katherine will be right here. You can come see her anytime you wish."

Yoda nods. He pulls away from the Doctor and goes to his wife. He leans down close to Kitty's ear and announces loudly, "I am going to the resting room. I will come back and see you soon!"

"My goodness." Dr. Berg says.

"I think he might have woken the dead baby." Dr. Bloom mutters.

Yoda spins around excitedly. "You think we can wake the baby up if we yell? I *told* Kitty the baby might just be sleeping!"

"Good Lord, they have actually figured out how to make them even dumber in America." Dr. Bloom says.

Dr. Berg gestures at Yoda. "Come on big boy. Let's find you a telly to watch."

"What's a telly? Is that some sort of little animal?" Yoda asks as he is led from the room. "I guess that would be ok, but I would prefer a monitor."

Dr. Bloom walks over to Kitty's sleeping form. He puts his arm on her shoulder and speaks softly. "We will get you taken care of Mrs. Williams. I'm sorry you had to come this far to get help."

Dr. Berg leads Yoda to a small room with a sofa and a recliner. On the wall is a medium sized monitor. The doctor points at it. "That won't work with your communicator. You need to use the remote on the table there." She points at a black wand on the side table next to the sofa. "Have you used one?"

Yoda shakes his head. The doctor hands it to him and shows him the power button and how to make the channels change. Then she leaves the room.

After sitting down in the recliner, Yoda turns the monitor. "Maybe there is a new *I Got Off on That!* on." The screen powers on. There is a blond woman delivering the news. The headline under the woman says *Iranian Government elects new president.* Yoda turns the volume up.

*The nation of Iran has held its second set of Democratic elections since the German Peace accords of 2034. Malakeh Hooshang was elected leader of the Persian government, marking the first female leader in Iranian history. Iran has had several initiatives over the past decade to provide equality for women. Iran is considered a model for the developing world in providing opportunities for women...* The screen changes, An American Flag appears above the news anchor's head. *The United States of America suffered a setback in a United Nations hearing held in Madrid today. The country, in decline for the past twenty years was kicked out of powerful 'Group of Seven' due to its waning power as a world economy and its draconian protectionist tariff policy. When asked for an official response, The Secretary of State sent a five second video of him doing raspberry noises with his lips.* The American flag stays on the screen. The headline at the bottom changes. 'Virus Outbreak Shuts Down State of Florida.' *Staying in the United States, a virus of unknown origin has dramatically affected residents of Florida. The virus, thought to have originated from poorly stored food at the American amusement park, MouseLand is related to the norovirus strains that closed schools across the Dallas, Texas area last year. World Health Officials estimate that more than one hundred people have perished because of the virus. Poor hygiene, inadequate health care for the poor and middle-class populations combined with poor food quality continue to negatively affect citizens of the United States of America...* Yoda talks at the newscaster. "There are viruses in the United States? Is this Old Fake News?" *On the monitor, the news anchor smiles. "Now a look at sports, Tackle Football World Championships wrap up this week. An offshoot of the old National Football League from the United States, the Tackle Football World Championship will feature the China Tigers vs. Scotland Kilts. The Kilts will be going for its 8th world championship in the last twelve years. The Kilt's coach, the American football legend, Sir Thomas Brady has been the coach for all of those championships. He has declared that he will retire after this season..." The news anchor smiles, "But that's also what he said each of the last three years, so we will see. The Kilts have their work cut out for them. The*

*China Tigers are favored by two touchdowns and are led by former American star player Travis Kelce. As viewers know, Kelce is married to the famed Australian Movie Producer, Taylor Swift.*

"They have real tackle football in places?" Yoda exclaims. He uses the channel selector to change the station. A video called "World History" is playing. Yoda watches the screen intently as an old man named Ken Burns introduces the video from his studio someplace in France. For the next seven hours, Yoda doesn't move from the recliner.

Chapter 23
Sookie needs help. It's all on film. Jesus had big feet?
Good Residence
Someplace in the United States America
Home of the Free(ish).. Land of the Brave(ish)..


"Hellllp!" Fred hears a woman's voice call from the inside of Bob's house. He waits patiently by the screen door for Bob to come and open it. "Hello? Help!" The voice calls out again. Fred activates his telecom and asks it to call Bob.

"Yo, Freddy."

"You home, dude? I am at your door." Fred says. "Your proximity meter is not on."

"NahNah... I am over at Geely's house... we are umm..." Bob's voice trails off.

"Yeah... I don't want to know." Fred says quickly as another muffled call for help comes from inside the house. "Listen... I think your mom needs something. Let me call you back."

"Call me later. Much... Much, Much later..." Bob clicks off before Fred can end the call.

After opening the door, Fred calls out, "Mrs. Good? It's Fred? Fred Petersen. Do you need help?"

"Oh, thank God!" Sookie Moonbeam Magi Good calls out. "Please come up to our bedroom, Freddy... I am so happy it is you here!"

A pit forms in Fred's gut. "Is Mr. Good here?"

"Heaven's no. If he was, I wouldn't be in this mess!" Mrs. Good answers. "Hurry please! I gotta go pee!"

"Good grief." Fred mutters to himself. He walks up the stairs hesitantly. Moving down the hall, he gets to the bedroom. Mrs. Good is on the bed, spread eagle and totally naked except a pair of blue stars covering her nipples. A golden crucifix is lodged between her legs. Fred looks away, he can feel the heat of his skin rising as his face turns red. "Umm... Mrs. Good... What? What do you... need?" the teen stammers.

"I got it all tangled up in there. My savior's feet... they must be caught up in the folds of my foo foo. I need you to help pull it out of me." The woman says with a voice indicating that the brass toes of Christ the Savior may be causing more pain than pleasure.

"I... I don't think I can do that, Mrs. Good." Fred says, purposefully not turning his head towards the woman.

"You can. You just need to get a couple of fingers up in there good and move the skin around. It's all I need, please, Freddy?"

Fred shakes his head. "Can't you do it?"

"Noooo... I tried. It's wedged in there at a bad angle. I was trying to make sure the camera would catch the entirety of the body of Christ as I was doing it... I slipped and I am afraid if I move its gonna tear my foo foo in half." The woman lets out a sob. "Please Freddy? Can you please help me?"
Camera? Fred thinks to himself before remembering the ridiculous reason Bob's mother was doing this stunt in the first place. He wants to look for video apparatus, mostly to turn it off, but doesn't want to see Bob's naked mother spread out with a brass cross sticking out of her... *foo foo*. "I think I need to call my dad. He's a doctor. He will know what to do." Fred says. Without waiting for an answer, he asks his communicator to call Conrad Peterson.

"Just tell him to hurry!" Mrs. Good calls out from the bed. Fred steps into the hallway. He toggles his telecom to connect to his father. It goes immediately to voicemail. A tone indicates that he has an incoming call. Without taking time to let the communicator tell him who the call is from, he answers, expecting it to be Conrad.

"Freddy? Are you watching Bob masturbate?"

Anne Margret. The proximity monitor. She knows where I am. "Well... No." Fred answers, thinking about Bob's mom who was doing something very much like masturbation. "Ok, well... I'll be right over. Tell your buddy to put his pants back on." Before Fred can tell Anne that she doesn't want to come over to Bob's house right now, the call ends. A second later the telecom announces an incoming call from Conrad Peterson.

"Dad!" Fred answers in an excited voice. "I need your help!"

"Sure, kiddo." Conrad's voice is measured and even. "What's going on that you can't handle?"

Fred takes a deep breath. "Bob's mom. She... she has a medical issue. Can you come over?"

"Should you call an ambulance?" Conrad asks. "If the Good's don't have insurance, I am sure that church of theirs will pick up the tab."

"Umm... I do not think Mrs. Good wants an ambulance or anything. She... She asked me to help. I can't do it." Fred stutters as he tries to explain the situation without saying exactly what the situation is.
Conrad is silent. "Ok. I will come check things out, but it will be my call if we are going to call a medical transporter or not."

"I think... you can help her." The doorbell rings.

"Is that your dad?" Fred hears Mrs. Good call from the bedroom.

"No. But he is on the way." Fred calls into the bedroom. The telecom rings. It's Anne Margret. "Hello?" He answers.

"I am at the front door. Does the doorbell work?" Anne Margret asks with an impatient tone indicating that she had been pressing a button without result and was really expecting Fred to be at the door waiting for her.

"I will be right down." Fred says.

"Who is at the door Fred?" Mrs. Good's voice sounds pained. "I really gotta go pee."

"It's Anne Margret Eaton. A friend of mine and Bob's. From school." Fred answers.

"Bring her up. Maybe she will help me!" Mrs. Good pleads.

"I really don't think that is a good idea." Fred answers. Without waiting for a response, he takes the stairs two at a time to the front door. "Anne." He greets the girl who grins at him.

"What's going on here. You look flustered Freddy." Anne Margret pats him on the cheek.

Fred shakes his head. "Umm... Mrs. Good... Bob's mom has gotten herself kind of caught up in something."

"Fred, bring her up to me!" Mrs. Good calls out from the upstairs bedroom.

Anne Margret looks at Fred. "What is going on here?" She walks past him and starts up the stairs.

Fred looks at the ground red faced. "You won't be able to unsee what is up there." Anne Margret shakes her head and runs up the stairs. "My dad is on his way." He calls up after her.

Anne Margret walks into the bedroom. She intakes a sharp breath at the scene on the bed. Fred leaves the front door open and slowly trudges up the stairs.

"Sweetheart. Jesus's feet are all caught up in my foo foo. Can you reach in and untangle me?" Mrs. Good asks. She sees the girl's eyes go wide.

"Oh, *hell* no." Anne Margret says, covering her mouth to stop from laughing. "What in the world are you doing?"

"Trying to get myself on *I Got Off On That.*" Mrs. Good answers with a groan. "Reverend Savenutts says the big data metrics on the program suggests that sex with a religious relic might get picked."

Anne Margret finds the small hi-def camera mounted on the wall. She forces a smile on her face. "Well, if you don't get on the show for this... I am not sure what might get you on!"

"I know, right?" Mrs. Good groans. "We will have to edit it down for length."

"Freddy says his dad is on the way. He's a doctor... of some sort. He will help you. I am sure." Anne Margret looks around. The room looks to her like burglars had ransacked the place looking for something very small. Clothing litters the floor. Dresser drawers are pulled half open. Various sex toys lay on the bedside tables. She notes large lights in the corners of the room. They are currently dimmed. "You guys must film a lot in here!" She comments.

"*The husband should fulfill his wife's sexual needs, and the wife should fulfill her husband's need*". Mrs. Good shifts uncomfortably. "That's first Corinthians. Chapter seven. Verse three." She turns her head and looks at Anne Margret. "Are you a religious person, Anne Margret?"

"I like Buddhism. I guess I am sort of a *go for it if you want to*, kind of girl." Anne Margret shifts uncomfortably. "Let me go see if Freddy has heard from his dad." She turns and walks into the hallway. A nervous looking Fred stands against the wall. Anne Margret pushes him backwards to Bob's bedroom. Posters of mostly naked women cover the walls. Fred feels momentarily embarrassed. Anne Margret points at a framed caricature of the forty fifth president of the United States of America with laser beams coming from his eyes. "You think he whacks off to that one too?" She shakes her head. "You were right. I am not going to be able to unsee the last ten minutes of my life. Ever!" She starts giggling bending forward and pulling herself into Fred's shoulder to muffle the laughter. "I can't believe she wanted me to dig the cross out of her.... her... What did she call it?"

"Foo Foo." Fred says with a straight face. The doorbell rings. "My dad is here. Control yourself for a moment."

"*That* is *not* going to be easy." Anne Margret whispers loudly still giggling.

Fred runs down the stairs. He lets his father in. "She is upstairs in the bedroom." Anne Margret appears at the top of the stairwell. "Hello Mr. Peterson."

"Conrad." Fred's dad starts up the stairs. "You can call me Conrad."

"Not according to my mother." Anne Margret answers. Conrad Peterson walks past her and into the bedroom. Fred and Anne follow.
"Jumping Jesus!" Conrad exclaims.

"He's inside her, actually. She literally has the *Son of God* inside of her." Anne Margret offers from the hallway.

"Do not take my Lord's name in vain!" Mrs. Good admonishes. Conrad frowns. "Says the woman with a crucifix shoved halfway up her vagina.

"Foo Foo, please. Call it a Foo Foo. Vagina, seems so..."

Anne Margret appears in the doorway. "Medical?" She offers.

Conrad does his best to observe what the actual problem is. "I assume you are not able to just pull it out?"

Mrs. Good lets out an exasperated sigh. "No. I cannot just pull it out. Jesus's feet are all tangled up in the folds of my foo foo. I gotta go pee. Please, hurry."

"There isn't great light in here." Conrad mumbles.
"Tell her to turn on the spotlights." Anne Margret suggests.

"Tell me what's going on." Fred says from the hallway, uncomfortably standing behind Anne Margret. "Unless I don't want to know. Which, maybe I don't. I am going to wait downstairs."

Sensing Fred's discomfort, Anne Margret grabs his arm and pulls him into the room from the hallway. "Watch the show, Freddy. It's what she wants anyway."

"That's probably true enough." Sookie Good says. Fred sees a smile cross the woman's face as she speaks. She groans when she shifts on the bed. "The remote for the lights is on the bedside stand."

Conrad picks up a pink vibrator off the stand. "These *Barbie* brand vibrators are cheap and unreliable. Hasbro should have stuck with kid's toys. I will have Fred bring you over some of the PPP models. You will like them a lot better."

"Really, Dad?" Fred whines.

Anne Margret slugs him. "Don't ruin this for me." She whispers as the spotlights mounted in the corners of the room illuminate, flooding the bedroom with theater quality light.

"There is some light on the subject." Conrad bends close to inspect Mrs. Good's crotch. "Looks like the intrusion is entangled fifteen to seventeen centimeters in. He pats the woman reassuring on the hand. "You say there are feet on the figure?"

"Big ones." Mrs. Good groans. "We picked the one that had the biggest feet cause, well, you know, big feet mean a big..."
Conrad interrupts her "Ok, Mrs. Good. I am going to lube up my hand and try to reach up and free the crucifix. You may feel some discomfort." Conrad says with his best bedside doctor voice.

"I bet she feels more than just discomfort." Anne Margret says with a snarky tone as she reaches down and grabs Fred's hand with a tight squeeze, both to keep him in the room and because she wants to hold his hand.

"My name is Sookie. We should probably be on a first name basis. You know, since you are going elbow deep in my foo foo." The woman groans.

Fred groans too.

Conrad expertly maneuvers his fingers into place and slides them inside of Sookie Moonbeam Magi Good. "Water Lubricant. Probably not a great choice with a brass... device. Fred will bring some of our proprietary lube. It's a molecular graphite-based product... never wears out or absorbs. I have it in chocolate and pineapple flavor."

"Oh, God." Fred says in a groan. Anne Margret squeezes his hand tighter.

"I've just about got it. I can feel the feet. You are right, they are big feet. Squeeze your Kegel muscles together."

Sookie Good squeezes her eyes shut tight. Anne Margret sees a look of euphoria cross the woman's face. A shot of liquid streams from the woman's *foo foo*, hitting the end of the bed and soaking the sheets. Conrad gently pulls the brass crucifix from the orifice and hands it to the woman who is breathing heavily. She takes it and holds it tight against her bare breast. "Thank you, Jesus. Thank you."

"You know, that show, *I Got Off On That...*" Conrad hooks a thumb at the camera apparatus. "It's no good for my business. Sex toys are prohibited... or just won't be considered." He points at the crucifix. "Also, you should not ever be sticking things like that in your body, Mrs. Good. And if you do, use a good lube. Your Lord's feet might not have gotten caught up in your... *foo foo*, if you had used a good lubricant."

Anne Margret looks at Fred whose facial color can only be described as blotchy candy cane. "Freddy, we can tell Bob that his mother squirts!" She whispers to him loudly. Like an interactive Rorschach display, the red blotches on Fred's face shift.

"You are *so cute* when you get embarrassed." Anne Margret whispers to Fred.

"Perfectly natural. The liquid is just urine... plain old pee." Conrad turns and says. He steps back. "Do you have any pain, Mrs. Good?"

"That's pee huh? I really thought it was something else." The nude woman smiles in the direction of the camera. "No... No. I feel wonderful now. Thank you doctor. Please leave your number… you know, if I need to call on you again."

Conrad smiles and nods knowingly. "Just call Freddy. He always knows how to get a hold of me." He looks at the two teens. "I need to wash up and get going. I have another meeting to get to. The Sultan of Brunei is in town and wants to partner with us for a model of his… umm, *Johnson* to be sold to the women of Brunei." He looks back down at Sookie Moonbeam Magi Good. "Fred will drop off a goodie bag for you tomorrow, Sookie."
"I will take one of the Sultan's toys you are going to make him. Can he autograph it?" Sookie coos, making no attempt to cover her naked body from view of the three people in the room.

Conrad shakes his head. "I am afraid you would have to move to Brunei to get one of those." He points to a framed photograph of the forty fifth and forty seventh president of the United States, displayed on the top of a wooden dresser. "I can send you over a model based on his. It's shaped like a little toadstool."

Sookie's eyes go wide. "Really?" She exclaims. "That would be sooo NOT boring!"

"Good Lord." Anne Margret mutters as she turns to leave the room. "Freddy, I am going downstairs before I upchuck."

"I'm going to see my dad out, Mrs. Good!" Fred quickly adds. "Come on, Conrad." Fred pulls his father out of the room.

"Son, that woman is ready to go. She would be happy to take you right now. Probably you and Anne Margret." Conrad whispers loudly as they descend the stairs. "Just turn the cameras off. She is a good age for you."
"Gross dad." Fred's whole body involuntarily shivers. "Gross to the power of ten million. Just gross."

"I wasn't so good at math, Fred." Conrad chides. "How gross is that?"

"What's gross?" Anne Margret asks from the bottom of the stairs. Conrad giggles as he walks past her to the front door.

Fred rolls his eyes and hikes a thumb back up the stairs. Anne Margret laughs, covering her mouth. "Oh! Well, Mrs. Good is not *that* gross. I mean, if you could look past, she being your best friend's mother and you know, the age thing." She slugs Fred in the arm a little harder than necessary. "You would be into that, right Freddy? If she was not Bob's mom and you know, like 20 years or so younger?"

"Hey now, that's ageism." Conrad protests. He opens the front door, saving his son from having to answer Anne Margret's rather probing question.

"People should not hook up with other people twice their age Mr. Peterson." Anne Margret sniffs.

Conrad laughs. "Get back to me on that when you reach fifty, Anne Margret." He points at his son. "Get a convention bag from my office and give it to Sookie Good. Make sure it is one of the bags with the brand displayed. Maybe she will put it in one her stupid videos. Throw in one of the little gold boxes that has the confederate flag embossed with the numbers 45 and 47."

"Is it really toadstool shaped?" Anne Margret asks. "Why do you even have those? That guy has been dead for like a hundred years. Surely nobody is buying them still."

Conrad laughs. "We made it for the Daughter's of the Confederacy a few years ago. Based on a photograph no less... I am told it was from a self-portrait the man himself took... and yeah, it really looks like a toadstool." Conrad grins at her. "You want one, Anne Margret? Fred, get Anne Margret a Trumper too."

Fred looks at the ground, shaking his head.

"Gross, Mr. Peterson. Just Gross." Anne Margret snaps. She jabs Fred in the shoulder. "You are *not* to get me one of those!"
"Gross. I am hearing that a lot today." Conrad turns back as he steps outside. "Have a good night kids! Don't do anything I wouldn't do!"

"That knocks out anyone under the age of eighty." Freddy mutters with a sarcastic tone.

Anne Margret smacks his shoulder. "Hey… I think your dad is doing my mom. She's not eighty. Yet."

Chapter 24
Another Visit with the Cow and the Grasshopper.
A directive. Dreams.
Public Housing, Someplace in America.
Land of the Free(ish). Home of the Brave (ish).


*After several long hours of entertaining each other with tales from our youth... well, my youth and her life, Millie fell asleep on my shoulder. You think that whatever is happening to you in the moment is a big deal. Trust me on this... It is not. There are very few big deals in life. Only a bunch of very insignificant actions accompanied by some cataclysmic, life changing occurrences. As it turns out, Millie cannot ever have children of her own. She had some health issues that maybe made her infertile. She wanted children, it just wasn't in the cards dealt by the invisible force directing all of our lives. I, of course made a stupid decision to render myself sterile. Did I want kids? I wanted pussy and I wanted it with no strings attached. Children, as it is well known, isn't a string but a goddamn chain attached to a lifetime of giving a shit. In my twenty ninth year, I couldn't conceive of a future instance where I would be happy to have helped produced a life that I needed to care for all the time. What did the cow say? All of you? Until time takes you. That's what the responsibility of children is. I wasn't ready for it and quite frankly, none of the women I was banging were either. In fact, I would go so far to say, that when I was in sack with a woman, the combined emotional IQ under the sheets was less than the cost of a pack of gum. That includes the threesomes I was in. Millie's ex-husband sounds like a sanctimonious piece of shit. I can't remember what I read the name of his church is. Doesn't matter. Apparently, the man was more than quick to sue for divorce and her assets when she was charged with whatever the fuck the state of Texas charged her with. Millie is pretty sure that her husband was the one that turned her into the Texas Rangers that arrested her. The ex was heavy into religion and a big supporter of the Orange Jesus back in the day. When I think of religion, I always think of the assholes. If I am being honest, I am a little jealous that anyone can have such absolute faith in anything. I think a lot of nonbelievers are that way. Not Atheists. Atheists are comfortable with what they believe. When I got turned into a heavy metal sandwich, side of Nike Tennis Shoes and green peas... I didn't believe in shit. Now I must believe in a talking cow with a pet grasshopper and their friend the sarcastic, earring wearing bear. It's not nearly as comfortable as I perceive believing in a benevolent God might be.*

*After we both woke up in the middle of the night with pains in our necks and backs, Millie climbed into her bunk and went back to sleep. Every time we move, the motion detector that controls the lights turns every light in the place on. Millie can sleep that way, but I can't for some reason. I must have gotten use to darkness after twenty years of it. I use the compact bathroom. Taking a piss feels incredibly good. You really have no idea how underrated solo urination is until you don't do it for a few decades. I finish my business and as I do when I am holding my dick in my hand, vaguely wonder if the little fellow will ever return to its full working condition. I crawl in bed and close my eyes. The lights click off and I feel myself falling into the abyss of sleep world.*

*I don't dream these days. I am not sure if I ever did... although the experts say that everyone dreams. Maybe the dead don't have the ability to dream. I can't be surprised anymore to see the reverent Reverend Moo and her pet grasshopper, even though I have seen the talking bovine and the giant bear only twice. When she comes walking into the darkness of my sleeping mind, I am not surprised, shocked or scared.*

*"Reverend Moo." I acknowledge her presence as she walks up some unseen path in my subconscious. The grasshopper has its place on her back.*

*"Justin Thyme." The cow chews her cud. She doesn't seem to be in a hurry and neither am I.*

*"Is my time up? I don't feel like it is. Where is the bear?" I say these things quickly like my brain has processed the situation but hasn't let the rest of me know what is going on.*

*I realize suddenly that I am not nervous. If I am going, I am going. I will be very disappointed to leave Millie. Sad even. However, if one thing has become abundantly clear to me, it is this... When it's time for any of us to go, it's time to go. If there are options offered, consider them; but understand, eventually there will come a time when there is not going to be any option to stay or go.*

*"Do not worry, Justin. Your time again is just beginning. You have found the chosen Mildred and that is a very good thing. Mildred is a very, very good soul. Protect her with all your might." The cow says slowly and in between chews. "Bruno will not be joining us today. There is celebration for Todd Healy I think."*

*"Who is he?" I ask.*

*"Mr. Healy gave the world the Three Stooges, Red Skeleton and Bob Hope. He had a tragic heart attack after he was indecent with a mobster's wife. Mr. Healy was not such a good soul. Status must be obtained for entry to be processed. It takes some souls more time than others. Mr. Healy died in..." The grasshopper comes forward and whispers in the cow's ear. "1937. He passed away due to injuries suffered after a heart attack in 1937."*

*"1937?" I exclaim. "That's over a hundred years ago!"*

*"Mmm. Yes. That is correct." The cow chews slowly. "Like was said, It takes some more time than others."*

*"How much time will it take me?" It occurs to me that the cow might be here to tell me something about Millie. That's why the damned bear, Bruno isn't here. "Listen, Millie is good. She... I think she has done enough here. Don't put her through more pain. What is Bruno doing to her?" I rattle. I must be in a dream state and not dead because even though I am talking to the cow... this Reverend Moo that I associate with being some sort of gatekeeper to a heaven I am not sure exists, I feel bad... I mean really, bad... just thinking about the possibility of something happening to Millie or her leaving me, even if it might be for a greater good. It feels like one of those bad dreams that you have as a kid where some illogical and remote fear almost paralyses you and one of those voices that you apparently only hear as a child or when coming out of a coma speaks to you and tells you to wake the fuck up.*

*The cow's head swings side to side. "You have no time to think about inevitable losses, Justin Thyme. Such things are fruitless and without purpose anywise. You must act now. I would not have come to you out of order if not but strictly necessary."*

*"Out of order?" I ask. "What does that mean?"*

*"You must go to your friend Willem. He needs you and Millie and time is of great importance. It is urgent you go at once. Gather your friends, Justin. You are both the greatest and the least among them. You must lead." The cow's eyes blink slowly.*

*"I must go to my friend Willem. He needs me and Millie. Time is important. Gather my friends? What friends? What if they won't come when I call? How can I be both the greatest and the least of anything? Lead who?"* The cow turns and walks away. I repeat myself to the blackness. *"I must go to my friend Willem. He needs me and Millie. Time is important. What friends do I have? What if they won't come when I call? How can I be both the greatest and the least of anything? Lead who?"*

"Justin!" I feel someone shaking my shoulder. "Justin! Wake up!" I open my eyes. The room is bright. Millie is standing over me. She has her hands on my head and shoulder. Her face expresses worry.

"You must have had a bad dream." She says softly. "You were almost yelling in your sleep, repeating the same thing over and over."

"Did the cow come to you?" I can feel that my eyes are open wide. I'm sure it looks disconcerting. I suddenly become aware that I am drenched in sweat like I just broke a dengue fever. Above me, Millie shakes her head slowly. She kisses my forehead. Her lips feel cool, and the effort calms me. "What did the cow say?"

"Moo." I try to make it sound like I want to joke. Clearly any comedic timing I might have had at one time has dissipated with my abilities to walk at a normal speed and achieve an erection. Millie frowns. I sigh and say, "I need to go see Willem Williams. Did you see the bear?"

Millie shakes her head. "No dancing bears. No grasshoppers. No cattle. Nothing like that tonight. She crawls onto the skinny bunk with me and snuggles under my arm, laying her head on my shoulder. "We will look Willem up in the morning and contact him." She snuggles closer. *"Moo? That was a terrible joke."*

I pull her close to my drenched body and sigh. I feel my heart rate slowing. Millie's breath becomes rhythmic. She is asleep. "I love you, Mildred." I say right before the lights click off. I drift off to sleep and I dream of my youth.

*I am back in high school. It's my senior year and our football team is in the State Championship game. We have just broken the huddle after taking our final timeout. The game is played in a big college stadium that is only like a quarter full, but I can hear the crowd screaming. I look at the clock. There are only four seconds left in the game and we are down by five points. The ball is on the opponent's forty-yard line. The coach gave us the play on the sideline. I know I am supposed to be nervous. I am not. None of us are. Hank Thyme, my cousin and the offensive center walks with me to the line. Conrad Peterson, our all-state quarterback comes up behind him. There is a grin on his face. Marmalade Julius has scored three touchdowns in this game already. He lines up at running back behind Conrad. Willem Williams has lined up as a tight end on the other side of the line. His next movements are key to the success of the play, something our coach calls the 'fumblerooski'. It is a variation of the same sort of play designed by the football geniuses years ago. The play is illegal in college, but not in our high school league. The ball is snapped, and I am about to become an unlikely star. Willem Williams runs down the line and comes up behind me at my tackle position. He picks up the defensive lineman that was about to try and come across the line through me. I have to hesitate for a split second. I can feel Conrad's movements as he steps back and fakes a handoff so well to Marmalade that the local television station covering the game never takes the camera off the future professional running back. I turn and pick up the ball that Hank Thyme and Conrad Peterson has carefully 'fumbled' right behind Hank's size thirteen feet. For a big guy who plays on the line, I am fast, but I don't put on any speed until I am clear of the guard and the tackle on the left side. There is no one between me and the goal line. I cradle the ball and run to the end zone. Touchdown. The play works just like Coach drew it up. The first guy that meets me in the end zone is Marmalade Julius. Willem not only took out the defensive linemen, but he also blew up the outside linebacker too. If Marmalade had gotten the hand off, he would have scored. I hand him the ball and say, "I think this is yours." He grins, drops the ball and grabs me in a hug. I see one of the cheerleaders, a blond girl, blow me a kiss. I can't remember her name, but I know I bang that cheerleader and her best friend in the back of her parent's minivan later that night.*

(Pro hint: Don't give your daughter a minivan to drive.)

*Wendy Smith who will become Wendy Williams is out on the field in her cheerleading outfit. She has jumped up in Willem's arms. They are making out in the same end zone I had run into for the win.*

*Unlike a lot of people who were good at high school sports, I never really thought much of that night after it happened. It was just something I did. Football is a game. I saw it as entertainment for me and my friends. I guess it was entertainment for the people watching too. For most the summer following graduation, people would come up and want to talk about that play like they had something to do with it. I played along with most of them. Who am I to point out that fans of a sports team have almost nothing to do with its success... or failure on the field? Then I went away to college and never had to talk about playing high school football again. I hadn't really thought about that final play that came to me in my dream for almost thirty years, but that play... it was the last time the six of us... Marmalade Julius, Hank Thyme, Conrad Peterson, Willem and Wendy Williams and me were all together in one place. These are the five people that I guess I would have to call friends from my past. It never occurred to me until this very moment after this silly dream where I remembered the past... but until Millie, I never have gotten that close to anyone else.*

Chapter 25
Stand back, I don't know how this is going to work!
Lube is nice.
Geely's house. Someplace in America.
Land of the Free(ish). Home of the Brave(ish).


T. Bob Good squeezes his eyes shut and grimaces.

"Does that feel good?" Geely asks him as she strokes his cock.

"No." Bob says abruptly as he tries to sit up. Geely pushes him down and strokes faster, causing Bob to yelp and pull away. "No, it does not. You are doing it wrong!"

Geely's chubby face wrinkles into a frown. "I did it like you told me to!"

"You go too fast. And spiting in your hand isn't making it slide so well. We need to use lube. Or hand cream. Something besides spit on your hand!" Bob looks down at himself. He is chaffed and sore. It had taken a few agonizing days after the last session with Geely for him to heal so he touch himself. He sighs. "Can we use the lube?" He asks hopefully.

"No." Geely pouts. "It feels gross on my hands. My brothers say that all they use is spit and it works just fine on them."

Bob wants to roll his eyes, but he knows that will piss the always temperamental Geely off. "I'll watch you masturbate." He offers.

"I want to make you... you know, squirt it out." Geely points at him. "And we watched me last time. I didn't squirt it out."
"Maybe you are doing it wrong?" Bob offers. Geely picks up her mom's Malcom Vibrator and throws it at him... and not in a fun way. The rubberized mechanical instrument hits Bob in the center of the forehead. "Ow!" He says, rubbing his head.

"Lay down and let me rub you!" Geely growls. "I want to see you squirt!"

"I think it's called cum." Bob feels a bump forming on his forehead. Geely pushes him onto his back. "Maybe you could take your shirt off or something. That would help me... you know, see your boobs."

"No." Geely says sharply.

"Come on, Geely. I got naked for you. All you show me is your foo foo and you don't really show it to me. I just see your legs and butt, sort of." Bob whines in a way only he can.

"Call it, my pussy." Geely says. "I can't show you, my top."

"Why? Are your boobs funny sized? Cause, I don't care. Even if one has an ugly mole, I am ok. Boobs are boobs. I like boobs." Bob rattles. "Maybe even if both boobs have moles unless they are the big scary ones with hair. My mom had one of those once. Reverend Savenutts prayed on it, and it fell off. The mole, not the boob. That would be awful if someone's boob fell off!"

"If I show you, can I rub you until you squirt?" Geely asks.

Bob hesitates. He nods. "Yeah. If you use the lotion at least."

"Ick." Geely makes a face.
Bob points at his chafed member. "It hurts with spit, Geely. Spit doesn't work. Tell your brothers that lotion is so much better." He points at the lube he had taken from his parent's bedroom. "And that works even better."

Geely seems to consider Bob's words. "Ok. But you have to squirt!" She takes off her bra by reaching under her shirt and pulling it out of an arm hole. Then she lifts the t-shirt over her head. Her belly is bigger than her boobs. Bob frowns.

"What?" She asks, her face turning red.

"I think your boobs were bigger with your shirt on." Bob says.

Geely rolls her eyes. "I have to wear a padded bra to make them bigger. My mom has little boobs too. My brother says it's because we don't get laid enough." She reaches out and grabs the bottle of lotion, exposing her back to Bob.

"Whoa!" Bob exclaims. "Let me see your back!"

"No." Geely says sharply. She squeezes the bottle of moisturizer. A blob of white creamy lotion falls into her hand. "You shouldn't see my back."

"I want to! Please, Geely? Please let me see your back!" Bob whines.
Geely sighs. "It was a mistake at the tattoo place my mom took me to. She had a coupon for this place, and it was cheap... but they got me confused with someone else."

Geely's family goes to the same church as Bob's family. Bob got his cross tattoo on his twelfth birthday. "What did you get?"
Geely rolls her eyes. "It was supposed to be the *Christians in Pursuit of the Scoundrel Pontius Pilate* tattoo... you know... like you have! What *everyone* gets, but I got this." She rolls over clumsily. On her back is a *thing* with the head of a horned goat and the body of a woman. The drawing is done with incredible detail and the boobs are extra-large on the lithe creature inked on Geely's rather broad back. The hands of the creature each hold an upside-down neon pink cross. Across the top of the drawing is the word *Hail* and the bottom says *Baphomet*.

"*What is that?*" Bob asks. He is staring intently at the breasts on the creature.

"It's the tattoo that you get at the *Sanctuary of Satan's Sinners*." Geely says morosely. "Reverend Savenutts made me stand in front of him and the elders totally naked and they tried to pray it away for hours. It's still there."

"It's a really good tattoo!" Bob says. He wants to touch the boobs.

Without warning, Geely turns and slaps him on the cheek. "You don't say that! It's an awful mark of the devil and I must get rid of it, or I will burn in the fires of hell with the sinners at that church for sure." Bob rubs his face. Being with Geely is really painful today.

"Now lay down and look at my boobs and make your thingy squirt for me!" Geely demands.

Thinking quickly, Bob answers, "Ok... but... I have this weird thing. If you sit on me, sometimes it goes quicker."

Geely looks confused. "How will I see it squirt then?"

Bob shrugs. "Look at it, I suppose. You can sit backwards on me..."
Geely shrugs. "Ok, I guess. You better squirt quickly. Mom will be home soon, and she doesn't like it when anyone sees that devil woman goat thing on my back." She stands and settles down on Bob's middle, roughly grabbing his already erect member with her lotion filled hand.

Bob concentrates on the tattooed creature covering Geely's back, staring intently on the inked knockers on the goat woman and imagining, as only he can, about touching them. In less time than it takes to fry a sunny side up egg Bob feels himself start to ejaculate.

"Ick! Ick! It got in my face Bob! It got in my face... oh gross." Geely cries as she rolls off him. "It got in my face Bob! Why did you do that?"
"I guess you did it extra good, Geely." Bob replies meekly as he tries to get one last look at the goat lady on her back.

Chapter 26
We are lawyers now! You are not gay, are you?
Eaton House Someplace in America.
Land of the Free(ish). Home of the Brave(ish).


Anne Margret's communicator announces that Fred Peterson is near her house. Quickly, she slips out of the sweatshirt she has on, removes her bra and stretches a thin white t-shirt over her bare skin. After removing her sweatpants and panties, she pulls on a short skirt she had found in her mother's closet. "Today is the day, Freddy." She says to the empty room. Her communicator announces that Fred A. Peterson is at the door. She pulls a button up shirt over the shear t-shirt and bounces down the stairs. "Hi, Freddy!" She says with a bubbly tone.

"Anne Margret! Are you ready to see if we are…." Fred looks down at the short skirt. "Lawyers…? That's a nice, um… outfit Anne."
*Anne Margret and Fred had taken on completing the six-week law school that was anything but rigorous. They had each taken the timed final/bar exam the night before. The auto-graded results would soon be announced via the law school's internal messenger service.*

Anne Margret puts on what she thinks is her best seductive smile. Fred squints at her. "Are you feeling ok, Anne Margret?"

She shakes her head and grabs his hand, pulling him into the house. "I have snacks set up. The results will be in soon." The pair goes into the kitchen. A laptop computer is on the countertop. Around it are plates of carrots and celery. A bottle of bubbly apple juice is in an ice bucket near two champagne flutes. "You went all out!" Fred exclaims.

Anne Margret gives him a big toothy grin before realizing he is referring to the damn food. "I sure did, Freddy." She pats him on the ass, leaving her hand in place a bit longer than necessary. "Think we passed the bar?"

Fred nods. "I think that we could have both passed that test the day before we started the classes."

They sit down near the computer. Fred takes a carrot stick and munches on it. Anne Margret tentatively chews on a celery stick. Fred looks at Anne and smiles. "Anne Margret, you look like you are up to something."
Anne Margret puts the carrot stick down and leans forward. "Do you like my skirt, Freddy?"

He looks down at the dark plaid skirt that ends several inches above Anne Margret's knees. "Um. Yeah. It's... um... Nice?"

Anne Margret sits back. "Nice?"

Fred points at the clock on the laptop. "Test score time."

Anne Margret rolls her eyes and taps her finger on the biometric reader on the computer. She opens a message from the law school. A bright light flashes followed by a video of fireworks. *You have succeeded at the universal bar exam! Congratulations Anne Margret Eaton! You are a lawyer!* The message scrolls across the screen several times.

"Now let's do you." Anne Margret says, again using what she is hoping is her most seductive tone of voice.

"You aren't coming down with a cold, are you?" Fred asks.

After a long-frustrated sigh, Anne Margret types in Fred's log in identification and passes the computer to him to use his finger to activate the biometric password. A repeat of the success message rolls across the screen. "We are both lawyers." Fred says, turning to Anne Margret. "Want to go into practice together?"

"Something like that." Anne Margret says, leaning back in the chair. "It is sooo warm in here." She lets the button up shirt open and fall down her arms as she arches her back. Fred looks at Anne Margret's bare breasts that are clearly visible through the shear fabric of the thin t-shirt.

He reaches over and pours two glasses of the bubbly apple juice. "We should celebrate. Maybe we should call your mom and my dad."

Anne Margret stares at the ceiling for a long, frustrated moment before responding. "Fred Peterson!" She sits up in the chair, allowing the button up shirt to fall to the floor. "I am *NOT* wearing any underwear. And I cannot *possibly* arch my back, so my tits stick up in the air like that any longer. Is there something wrong with me? Or is there something about you that you need to tell me?"

Fred holds one of the glasses of juice in his hand, his mouth hanging open. "I... No... No! There is nothing wrong with you Anne!"

Anne Margret swishes her long red hair around as she shakes her head. "Ok... Do you have any other mood killing things you would like to say? After we call our parents, should we call Bob and tell him we are lawyers now? Would you like to talk about the growth cycle of oak trees? How about the current state of affairs for people who live on Native American Reservations?"

"You want... *me*... like, *that*? Are you sure?" Fred asks. "Wait... What do you know about the growth cycle of oak trees?"
Anne Margret steps close to Fred. She runs a finger down his well-defined jawline. "I am going to ask you some questions Freddy and I want you to be one hundred and ten percent honest with me, Ok?"

"OK?" Fred says. "But just so you know, I don't know much about trees. Oak or otherwise."

Anne Margret takes a deep breath. "Are you homosexual? Do you think you might like men more than women... you know? Sexually?"
Fred shakes his head. "I am not gay, Anne."

"Cause, it's ok if you are gay. I will go upstairs and put some underwear on, and we can drink apple juice and talk about guys. Are you *sure* you are not gay?"

Fred smiles and shakes his head slowly. "I'm not gay, Anne."

Anne Margret nods. "Ok. Do you think I am attractive? I mean... Do you think you could be sexually attracted to me?"

Fred's eyes narrow. "*Could be?* The answer to that question is *no.*" He pauses, keeping a straight face. He lets a flash of fear crosses Anne Margret's eyes before continuing. "I *have* been attracted... sexually I guess... to you for years, Anne Margret. I think you are smart and beautiful."

"I've made more passes at you then I can remember, and that's just *today!* That's not to say anything about the past year or so!" Anne Margret exclaims. "I'm not wearing a bra, and my nipples could poke your eye out! Did you notice? No!"

Fred takes a deep breath and exhales. He looks into Anne Margret's blue sparkling eyes. "I have no idea how to go about this sort of thing, Anne. All my life I have been around sex. I *literally* live amongst sexuality. There are models of my *mother's vagina* laying all over our house... in multiple skin tones, no less. With hair, without hair. Conrad... Dad... he tells me I need to be with a woman. Preferably an older, *experienced woman.* I get told *that* all the time... but no one has ever told me how to go about talking to someone like you about being in a relationship... And then I read that women just aren't into men. Women apparently don't need men anymore unless you belong to a crazy church like the Good family and that sort of thing just isn't going to be for me. My father's toys are a great substitute for the real thing *apparently*... for men and women, I guess." Fred sighs and shrugs his shoulders. "Let's start over. Sit down." He motions at the chair.

"I'm not sticking my boobs in the air. I think doing that knocked my spine out of alignment."

"Anne, I don't have any idea how any of this works." Fred shakes his head. "I've never done anything sexual."

"Not even masturbate? Honest?"

Fred shakes his head.

"Your dad's toys?"

Fred makes a face. "That's my mom!"

"Yeah, that is awful. Maybe you could have picked the Chinese one or something." Anne Margret cracks.

"I think that model was a one way only thing for me, personally." Fred smiles.
Anne Margret thinks about it for a moment before cracking up. "I get it!" She pokes Fred in the chest. "One way only! That's hilarious!"

Fred hands her a glass of juice. "To us passing the bar and finding new adventures together." Anne Margret takes her glass and clinks it on his. "To us." They drain the champaign flutes.

"So, you have never orgasmed?" Anne Margret says. "Never?"

"I had a wet dream once." Fred says quickly. He refills the glasses.

"Who was in the dream?"

Fred's pale face turns crimson red.

"Gross! It was Bob's mom, wasn't it?" Anne Margret exclaims.

Fred shakes his head violently. "Ick! No! It was..." He hangs his head and shakes it slowly. "It was you, Anne Margret." He looks back up at her stunned face. "I can see your heart beating." Anne looks down. Her left breast is moving in time with her heartbeat under the white t-shirt. "Have you?"

"Have I what?" Anne Margret asks.

"Had an orgasm?"

It's Anne Margret's turn to blush. "Um... maybe. I think so. With my finger. My mom gave me... you know, *toys*. From your dad's company." She chuckles. "Hopefully they aren't modeled off your dad! Anyway, I uh... haven't... you know..."

Fred shakes his head. "I don't know."

"Penetration!" Anne Margret says.

"Aren't we a pair?" Fred drinks his glass of bubbly apple juice.

"I hope so." Anne Margret comes close to him.

"We can start over. I can go outside and ring the doorbell and you can answer the door, and we can do this all over the way that you..." Fred is interrupted by Anne Margret.

"Fred. Shut up." She stands on her tip toes. "Shut up and let me kiss you." They embrace in a long passionate kiss. After breaking away, Anne Margret blushes again. "That's the first time I have kissed anyone like that."
"Me too." Fred says. "Can we do it again?"

"Come with me." Anne Margret grabs his hand and leads him up the stairs to her bedroom. She takes her time unbuttoning his shirt and taking it off him before unbuttoning his pants and pulling them down with his underwear. "Oh, my... the equipment looks like it is working pretty well."

"Never been used. New in the box." Fred cracks as he steps out of the pants that have pooled up around his ankles. "Do we need to worry about... you know? Controlling it? We aren't ready to be parents."

"No need to be concerned. I am on a birth control pill. Mom gets them sent in from Europe. Thank you for asking though. That was sweet of you." Anne Margret pushes him back onto bed and lifts the flimsy t-shirt over her head. "Do you think that we should put on music or something?"

"I like the birds singing outside the window." Fred answers. He reaches out to touch her and she slaps his hand away.

"Me too." In a move she had practiced several times in front of the mirror, she unzips the side of the skirt and lets it drop to the ground. "This is me."

"I love all of it." Fred says softly. "You are so beautiful, Anne Margret." She climbs on top of him and for the next few hours they don't hear a single one of the birds chirping outside Anne Margret's bedroom window. Later, when both are laying exhausted in bed, Anne Margret pats Fred on the chest. "Freddy, I have something to tell you."

"Yes, Anne?"

"I hadn't had an orgasm before. Today was *definitely* the first time for that!"

Chapter 27
A brand-new husband. What's a klaxon?
French Navy Ship Liberte' Gulf of Mexico.
Just outside of the territorial zone of the United States of America.
Home of the Free(ish) Land of the Brave(ish)


Yoda Storm Trooper Williams finishes watching a news update from the British Broadcasting Service. He has learned many things from his hours of watching international documentaries and news programs. *Iraq is building three new chip factories that will have the ability to produce up to thirty percent of the world's supply of high-speed processors. The nation of Turkey is planning to open a series of Movie Studios in an effort to take business from the two juggernauts of the video entertainment business, China and Korea. Russia, led by the Great Grandson of Josef Stalin, American born Piotr Evans Alliluyeva is floundering under a load of international debt, taken on to rebuild the country after the second Russian Civil War, fought between 2032 and 2036. The United States of America, seen as a declining civilization has lost most of the Fortune 500 companies it had in 2030 to countries with favorable working conditions, advantageous tax laws and stable governments. The nation of Spain has declared that all children entering pre-school should start learning two foreign languages and be exposed to computer programing.* Yoda turns off the monitor and walks over to Kitty's room. An IV is hooked up to her arm. He rubs the other bare arm gently. "How are you doing, Kitty?"

His wife opens her eyes slowly. "Yoda. Have you been sleeping?" Yoda shakes his head. "No, I have not gotten to sleep yet. I have been thinking though. Maybe we should look at moving to Europe. Maybe Sweden or Germany... you know, after this is all over. I think those places would be better to raise our family than the USA."

Kitty closes her eyes. Yoda watches her breath in and out. She opens her eyes and looks at him. "Were you watching your shows, Yoda?"
Yoda shakes his head. "No. They have different programing here. I watched something called the BBC and a documentary on the history of the world, but only since World War Two." He frowns and shakes his head. "Our education wasn't very good Kitty. There is a whole world outside of

the United States and I think that the rest of that world is collectively making fun of us and our country."

"What makes you think that?" Kitty turns her drugged body to face her husband. "I don't understand what you are saying. You watched a documentary? A real documentary? About something... real?"

Yoda nods. "Yes. Our government is completed disassociated with its people. The people that have assumed leadership in our government aren't listening to the populous. I never realized it until this moment, everything we do... everything we watch... it's all connected to the profits of some unseen company. Here is the weird thing, everyone in the world seems to know it except Americans. It's like how the people of North Korea were before the reunification of North and South Korea in 2031."

"Disassociated? Populous? Government? North Korea?" Kitty's eyes narrow. "Who are you and what did you do with my husband?"

Yoda chuckles. "It's just me, Kitty." He pulls a blanket up to cover her bare arm. She rolls off her side onto her back.

"Has the doctor been in yet?" Yoda looks at the clock on the wall. "It's only seven in the morning. Maybe one of them will come by at eight or so. I will stay in here with you if you would like me to."

"Seriously. You are acting weird." Kitty says. "Did someone give you a drug of some sort?"
Yoda pats her arm. "It's all good, Kitty. I think that when we get back, we *really* should talk about leaving the United States. Maybe we can take your parents with us. I think they would benefit from moving away. Especially your dad."

Kitty raises her eyebrows. "Maybe the drugs are affecting me, and this is some sort of a strange dream. Pinch me, Yoda."

Yoda rubs her arm again. "I can't pinch you, Kitty. You couldn't pinch me back and what fun would that be for you?"

"Our baby is dead, Yoda. Do you understand that?"

Yoda nods his head. "I do. And I understand now that you are in very poor condition because you couldn't get proper health care at home in Texas." He motions around the room. "This ship... it was an old British hospital ship called the HMS Argus. The French and Swiss government made an agreement to modernize it and take it to the United States to provide free health care to women who could make it to the ship." He winces. "That's an embarrassment, Kitty. The United States of America was once the richest nation in the world and now other countries must send medical aid to help only a few of the fifty percent of our citizens get health care that is no longer available in their home country. The United States once provided this sort of care for third world countries. Now we are receiving it!"

"The United States isn't the richest country in the world?" Kitty asks.
Yoda shakes his head. "We aren't even in the top ten. That's what I am talking about... why don't Americans know?"

Kitty stares straight ahead. A tear forms in the corner of her eye. "I don't understand what has happened to you."

"I guess I just had some time to learn some things." Yoda says.
*"It's only been like eight hours, Yoda!"* Kitty exclaims.

Yoda shrugs with a smile. "No one ever gave me that sort of information before. I think my brain is sort of like a sponge. It sucks up what it is given."

Dr. Astrid Berg and Dr. Liam Bloom walks into the room. "Hello, Katherine and Yoda. It is pleasant to see you both this morning." Dr. Berg says as she checks on Kitty's vitals. "I hope that you both had a restful night."

"Did you give my husband some sort of drug?" Kitty asks. "He seems different. Maybe it is the drugs I am on?"

Dr. Berg looks at Yoda with an appraising smile. "He looks like the same handsome man that I put in the waiting room in front of the telly, last night, Katherine. We certainly didn't give him anything special. What do you think is different about him?"

Kitty chortles. "Well, he seems a lot smarter this morning for one and he is being kind and considerate with me, which is different for sure and... Where did this ship come from?"

Dr. Bloom comes to the other side of the bed. "This is an old British Hospital ship. I can't remember what it was called before the French bought it."

"The HMS Argus." Yoda offers. "And I believe the Swiss and the French bought it together."

"That's it!" Dr. Bloom exclaims. "And yes, of course, our home country, Switzerland was one of the investors in the ship. But the French got to name it, and they drive it, which is good because we Swiss have no real Navy!" He pats Kitty on the arm. "Most of Europe feels like it owes the United States a debt of gratitude. We hope our assistance in these terrible matters allows America to find its footing and hit a reset button... if such a thing is possible."

"This is something." Kitty says. "I cannot believe it!"

"The Liberte' has been operating for several years now, Katherine." Dr. Berg says. "It's real, I assure you!"

Kitty shakes her head and weakly waves her hand dismissively. "I can believe that this ship was sent to the USA by the Swiss and the French. I can't believe my husband knows anything more than what happened on last night's episode of *Shit Happens*."

Both doctors smile patronizingly. Dr. Berg picks up an electronic tablet. "We are going to take you into the delivery room at 9:30. We will deliver the baby by cesarean section. Do you know what that is?"

Both Kitty and Yoda nod somberly. Kitty points up. "No, he does not know what that is." She points at Yoda. "How would you know what cesarean delivery is?"

"I read about it in the waiting room Kitty. A C-Section is a commonly used procedure to deliver babies, especially in at risk situations." Yoda answers. He rubs his wife's arm. "I like learning things."

"This is so new. I'm not sure how I am going to deal with having a husband that can communicate in complete sentences." Kitty shakes her head. "Are you sure you haven't drugged him? Is this going to wear off?"

Dr. Bloom motions at Yoda. "Yoda is welcome to be in the delivery room." He grimaces and shakes his head. "These procedures can involve a lot of blood and may be disturbing to some people."

"I will be in the room for the birth of our child." Yoda says with a resolute tone.

"I think I am going to cry." Kitty whimpers. "I love you Yoda and I am..."

She is cut off by loud klaxons ringing through the ship.

Chapter 28
Whip cream tastes good. Wendy Williams reaches out.
Conrad Petersen Home
Someplace in the United States of America.
Home of the Free(ish) Land of the Brave(ish)


Anne Margret and Fred Peterson walk in the open front door of Conrad and Fred's house. Voices can be heard from inside the house.

"Oh, that is *sooo* very good, Conrad." Elizabeth Eaton says.
Conrad laughs. "You like it, huh. Ever had it like that?"

Anne Margret puts her hand up to stop Fred. 'I think they are doing it!' She mouths.

'What?' Fred mouths back. 'I can't understand you!'

Anne Margret holds his arm and puts her finger to her lips as she drags him closer to where her mother and Conrad are talking.

"I've never done it like this Conrad! You are so naughty!" Elizabeth Eaton exclaims. "Do it again!"

"Open up wide!" Conrad says. A noise is heard.

"Oh, my God, I can't believe I've never done this." Anne Margret's mother exclaims before adding, "Let me do you!" The noise is heard again. "Oops! I'm gonna lick that off!" She says giggling.

Fred frowns and steps around the corner, dragging Anne Margret with him. "Hi, Dad!"

Elizabeth Eaton is frozen, her tongue out, a few inches from Conrad's bare chest. In her hand is a can of whipped cream. A large blob of the white confection is hanging from Conrad's bare chest.

"Mom! Are you eating dairy?" Anne Margret exclaims.

"Hey kids!" Conrad says. He uses his fingers to wipe the cream from his chest. He offers it to Elizabeth who reflexively licks it from his fingers, her face beet red.

"Anne Margret, you look positively radiant!" Conrad says. He winks at his son. "Lizzy and I were just having a snack before we take a dip in the pool." He points at the can. "It's coconut milk. No cow juice involved."

Elizabeth Eaton straightens up. "I... um. I was just..."

"Having fun?" Anne Margret smiles at her mother. "I'm glad you were having fun... *Lizzy*." She hugs Fred's waist. "I think it's adorable. It's adorable. Right, Freddy?"

Fred nods. "Of course. *Adorable* is a good... safe... word to use."

"I think I might be a red as Fred is." Elizabeth Eaton picks up the can of whipped coconut cream and sprays some in her mouth. "It's so good!" She smiles at her daughter. "What have you two been doing?" She asks with her mouth full.

Anne Margret smiles and takes the can. "We are both lawyers. I guess we were celebrating!" She squirts some of the whip cream on a finger and licks it off. "This *is* pretty good!"

*"Hello, Wendy! What's up?" Conrad has taken a call on his communicator.* He steps away from the group. Fred watches Elizabeth Eaton's eyes track his father possessively.

"It's his friend Willem's wife, Wendy." Fred explains quickly. "The all went to high school together."

"Open up!" Anne Margret points the can at Fred's mouth. He opens as wide as he can, sure that she is probably going to spray the cream all over him. A bit lands in his mouth.

"You like that, Freddy?" Anne Margret asks in a sultry tone.

He blushes and swallows the foam. "You... um, know your mom is still sitting there, right?"

Elizabeth Eaton laughs. "Anne Margret tells me *everything*, Fred."

Conrad comes back in the room. He is smiling "That was Wendy Williams. She is married to an old friend of mine." He grabs Elizabeth's hand. "We are going to their house tomorrow. Another friend of ours... Justin Thyme... was in a coma most of the last twenty years." Conrad shakes his head as if correcting some misperception he had. "Amazingly, Justin came out of the coma, and he is coming to the Williams' house for a visit!"

Elizabeth's eyes are bright and wide. "That sounds like fun." She takes the can from Anne Margret and sprays a heart on Conrad's chest. "I sort of like this girlfriend stuff!"
"And I think I like this side of my mother I have never seen before!" Anne Margret exclaims.

Chapter 29
The Texas Militia finds its Captain. Torpedoes away!
Gulf of Mexico
Outside of the Territorial Waters of the United States of America
Land of the Free(ish) Home of the Brave(ish)


*Texas Militia Major Richard Lecher had separated from the United States Department of the Navy in 2028 at the age of forty-five as a Commander. Over the course of his twenty-five years in the United States Navy, Commander Lecher had lorded over a variety of ships. His last command was technically of the USSN Ohio, a nuclear submarine that was commissioned two years before Richard Lecher fell from his mother's vagina in Ding Dong, Texas. Technically, because Commander Richard Lecher was stripped of his rank and unceremoniously kicked out of the Navy with the highly unsatisfactory rating of* dishonorably discharged *after being caught in the conning tower of the Ohio with two naked women, neither of which was his wife Drizella, smoking a substance that was later identified to be synthetic cannabinoids. He had never actually commanded the Ohio for more than three or four days of sea trials.*

*Drizella, understanding completely that her husband was a philandering, dope smoking military wash out of the highest order who would undoubtable do it all over again if given the chance, left his ass and filed for divorce before the court martial was over; quickly upgrading, hooking up with a recently divorced, up and coming Captain who everyone said would be a Rear Admiral soon.*

*Richard Lecher, born in the rural village of Ding Dong near Killeen, Texas went home. First, he went to work on an oil drilling platform in the Gulf of Mexico. After falling out of the transport helicopter because he was to stoned to jump out properly, the drilling company sent him home. There he tried his hand at selling life insurance. That was a bust too. One night, ten shots of "DJT's Orange Bourbon" into the evening, ('Merica Made, 'Merican drank, Orange Bourbon makes 'Merica Great!) he overheard two men talking at the pool table about buying a submarine. Lecher stumbled over to the men and asked where in the hell one might buy a submarine. The men explained that they were officers in the recently, officially recognized Orderly and Regulated Texas*

Militia and they were putting together a fund to buy a diesel submarine from the nation of India.

"Got someone to pilot the goddamn thing?" Lecher asked in a slurred voice.

The men looked at each other. "We kind of figured that we would figure it out when we got it. Can't be too much different than driving any other boat."

"You drive your boat blindfolded?" Lecher asks, poking one of the men in the chest.

"No, of course not. Why would you ask that?" One of the men asks, picking up his pool cue in preparation for the bar fight with the obnoxious drunk standing before him.
"Cause'. That's what it's like to pilot a submarine... And... You pilot a submarine! You don't drive it any more than you would drive an airplane! You can't see shit. There ain't no windows. You gots to drive by feel. The sonar techs will help ya, but mostly... it's just yer guts." Lecher stands back and points drunkenly in the general direction of the two men. "Ya all know what da crush depth is on a Kalvari class u-boat?"

"How did you know we were looking at a Kalvari Submarine?" One of the men asked. "You ain't with the government, are you?"

Lecher smiles. "Use to be. They taught me how to drive lots of boats, cluding' submarines." He pokes the man in the chest again. "Let me tell you somethin'..." Lecher lets out a long "DJT's Orange Bourbon" scented belch. "Submarines ain't nothing to fuck with if ya ain't got the experience of piloting one. The Indian's are the only country selling subs. They got themselves a bunch of Nuke boats now. They don't need them stinky diesels. That one you all are looking at is the last of the bunch." He pats the man on the shoulder with a grin. "Ya all best know the crush depth before you go diving... that's all I'm telling you."

The men look at each other and back at the drunk. "Where do we get that info? Is it on the door like tire pressure on a transporter?"

Lecher laughs. "Ya don't. That information is classified." He turns and stumbles back towards his seat at the bar.

*"Can we buy the information, old man?" One of the men calls out with a sly tone.*

*Lecher turns and gives the men the thousand yard stare of a man so hammered that he can hardly stand. "Anything can be bought gents, including me."*

*That fateful meeting in a shitty bar in Houston, Texas is how Disgraced Former Navy Commander Richard Lecher became Major Richard Lecher, Regulated Texas Militia. After the group won the Indian Submarine with the highest bid, Lecher and ten other guys (who had never spent a night at sea, much less on a submarine under the sea) flew to the Island of Madagascar (No extradition treaty with the United States of America) and took possession of their new Kalvari class Attack Submarine. Lecher christened the boat with a bottle of Texas made vodka, renaming the sub, the 'Davy Crockett' after the legendary slave owning mercenary who had surrendered at the Alamo and was executed by Santa Ana's officers.*

*It took Major Lecher almost a month to train his crew of ten militia men to work the boat. He was comfortable that Tinker and Wade, the two Diesel Mechanics he brought along could keep the generators, batteries and engines going. He was less enthralled with the men that said they had sonar experience. One was a retired weatherman and recent divorcee named Fick who wanted nothing more than to try and bang local Madagascan women every night and every day. He had some rudimentary knowledge of the concept of sonar but no practical experience with either sonar or navigation. The other fellow was a twenty-seven-year-old lanky Texan named Sweat whose uncle was also in the Militia. The kid had served in the Navy as a Sonar Technician on a destroyer. Lecher was pretty sure that the boy had sucked more dick than he had eaten ice cream and that was no goddamn good. The Militia Major would have sent the boy home if he had any faith in the navigation and sonar skills of the pussy hound weather man Fick, which he certainly did not. Two of the men, Swallows and Schitz were assigned to the kitchen and janitorial duty and the remaining four, Bang, Ball, Dodge and Pickle were supposed electronics and weapons experts that would start the process of rebuilding the disabled Exocet anti-ship missile systems.*

*It took the motley crew of sailors nearly three months to get back into North American waters after the weatherman turned submarine navigator kept the 'Davy Crockett' on a southerly course for about three days too long. Someplace south of the*

*Thule Islands in Argentina, Major Lecher surfaced the U-Boat, collected his bearings and corrected course. They rode the Gulf Stream past the southern side of Cuba into the Gulf of Mexico where a refueling ship owned by the oil magnate Alistair Whitaker Rutherford loaded the 'Davy Crockett' with a fresh tank of Diesel fuel and a full freezer of food. By now, the weapons crew had retrofitted three of the previously disabled Exocet anti-ship missiles with GPS equipment sourced from old Apple iPhone 22 cases ('XiiXii... Bigger than Ever' was the slogan Apple used to promote the phone. The '22' would be the last iPhones sold. Internal telecommunication units became the must have accessory for the public). Major Lecher started patrolling the gulf coast of the United States on the lookout for migrant ships (migration from Central and South America had largely stopped by 2035 due to the relative unattractive living conditions in the United States.) and rumored 'Abortion Ships' where foreign enemies would rip the unborn from their mother's wombs even into the ninth month of pregnancy.*

"Yo, Texas Militia Davy Crocket, this is Speedy Bob on the William Travis, you there?"

Major Richard Lecher opens his microphone. "This is the Davy Crocket, William Travis. What do you want?" Sometimes they just called to tell him that it was sunny out. Lecher looks at his watch. It is seven thirty in the morning.

"I think we got one of dem' hospital ships in our sights. You copy?"
"You think or you know? We can't go round' sinking some rich dude's yacht. Shit. Rich dudes with yachts finance the Militia!"

"Well, weese followed dis little speed boat that did a pickup on Holly Beach. Intel came from the surveillance drones. The drones had two civilians on the beach, one is listed by *One Health* in Texas as prego... we thinks this is one them boats we keep hearing 'bout. This one is called something faggy French. Liberty... but it's spelled wrong." Speedy Bob says.

"Affirmative." Lecher responds. He opens the communication system for the submarine. "Bang, Pickle! Ready the torpedoes! This is not a drill, Pickle! Sailor Tinker! Sailor Tinker! We need power, now! Sailer Sweat!

I need Sailer Sweat and Fick with me in the Conn! Ball! Wake up Sweat! Swallows and Schitz, put a hold on breakfast, we got us a boat to sink!"

"Is the Liberty under way?" Lecher yells into the microphone.

"Nah... It's not in da way, I mean, pretty wide-open ocean out here. We can just go around the damn thing if we want to. The Sam Houston is on the other side of the Liberty'. We'd have to miss him." Speedy Bob answers.
Lecher closes his eyes and shakes his head. "Willam Travis! Is the goddamn target moving?"

"Negative! It sittin' still in the water, Davy Crockett."

"I need the coordinates of the boat." Lecher says.

"It's here. In front of me!" Speedy Bob replies.
Lecher growls into the microphone. "Goddamn you fucking amateurs! I need the longitude and latitude of the baby killing ship. 'In front of me' is not coordinates unless you are slow dancing with a woman at the Hop and Slop!"

"Oh! You need the Longitudy and Latitudy numerals? Shit. I don't think... Hang with me!" Speedy Bob says. He comes back a few minutes later "25° 46' 15" N / 92° 18' 34" W."

"That's the coordinates of the baby killing boat, William Travis? Are you sure?" Lecher asks.

"That's a big 10-4 good buddy!" Comes the answer.

"Ready a Torpedo, Pickle! On my mark, coordinates, 25° 46' 15" North and 92° 18' 34" West."

"Torpedo locked and loaded sir. This is Ball. Pickle is taking a shit." Comes a muffled reply.

"Where is Pickle taking Schitz?" Lecher asks incredulously.

"I assume the john... I mean head, sir." Ball answers. "He's taking..." The microphone crackles. "shits in the head."

"In the head?" Lecher asks, confused. "Jesus."

"I'm here, Sailer Sweat announces. What do I need to do?"

Lecher shakes his head. "I always assumed that if someone on this boat was going to be dancing the chocolate cha-cha, it would be you, Sweat. I need our bearing to be straight at the Liberte'. We can't miss!" Lecher slides the written coordinates over to Sweat. "Where the fuck is Fich?"

"Fich and Schitz told me that they need to clean the head by the mess, sir."

"Jesus. There is three of them involved?" Lecher mutters. "You got this Sailer Sweat? I need to know that you and Ball are behind me. Can I trust you?"

Sweat nods. "We got you all covered up, Major Lecher. We got you covered!" He sits down and maneuvers the submarine exactly at the coordinates that the Major had given him. "On target sir!"

"Tinker! Give me some speed! I need speed Tinker! Ball! I need Ball!"

"Yeah?" Sailer Ball answers.

"      Is that goddamn fish warming up in the tube?" Lecher yells the question with excitement.

"Umm... The torpedo is in the tube and the coordinates are set." Ball says. "Is that what you mean by *fish?*

"Are we on, Sweat?"

"Yes... Yes. Headed straight at the target." Sweat answers.

"Fire away!" Lecher calls out. In his twenty-five years in the Navy, he had never once gotten to yell, Fire away! It felt good! It made him feel alive!
"Fire in the hole!" Ball calls out.
"Fire in the hole." Sweat repeats.

"Torpedo away!" Ball calls out.

"Torpedo away!" Sweat repeats.

"You know I can hear Ball, Sweat, right?" Lecher asks.

"Umm... Davy Crockett? Davy Crockett?" A panicked Speedy Bob says on the microphone. "Are you there?"

"Davy Crocket to William Travis. Go Ahead." Lecher Says.

"I... Uh, I think that water missile thingy might be coming right at us!"

"I sent it to coordinates you provided...." Lecher looks at Swift. "You got us pointed at those coordinates, right Sailor?"

Swift nods. "Yes. Did William Travis give them to you?"

Lecher realizes what has happened and shakes his head with a look of disgust. "You me gave *your* goddamn coordinates, William Travis!"

"That's what you asked for!" Speedy Bob cries. "What should we do?"

"I'd get off that vessel you are on ASAP! There is an anti-ship missile coming straight at you!" Lecher sets the microphone down. "Ball! Ball!"

"This is Pickle! Ball is in the head, takin' a shit!"

"You guys have been out here to goddamn long, apparently!" Lecher yells. "Prepare another torpedo!"

"Preparing another torpedo! Torpedo in the hole!"

"Sam Houston, Sam Houston, this is Davy Crockett. Over."

"Sam Houston, Go Ahead, Davy Crockett."

"I need coordinates for that baby killing ship. Can you give me coordinates?" Lecher asks.

"Oh, *fuck no* we will not be doing that! You just cut the William Travis in half. I think I see Speedy Bob out there bobbing up and down like buoy. Coordinates are a big *no fuckin' way*, Davy Crockett."

Lecher looks down at Sweat. "Sweat, take us to periscope depth. I'll get the fucking coordinates myself."

"We can do that?" Sweat exclaims. "I thought you were trying to be stealthy! Why didn't we just go up and takes us a looksee? These morons are on fishing boats. They don't even know what coordinates are!"

"I thought we was a goddamn military!" Lecher exclaims. "Men in the goddamn Army know what longitude and latitude are! Sailers fucking better know for sure what coordinates are when yer out on the water!"

The sub starts to rise. Lecher shoves the periscope up. The first thing that he sees is the William Travis on fire. "Dumbasses." Lecher moves the controls and finds the Sam Houston sitting five hundred yards off the Liberte'. "I got your baby killing asses now!" He writes the coordinates on piece of paper and returns to the conn.

After yelling out the coordinates to Pickle, he turns to Sweat. "Are we ready?"

"Affirmative Sir!" Sweat says energetically. "I just need to get the boat turned..."

"Fire the Torpedo!" Lecher yells.

"Fire Torpedo!" Pickle confirms followed by, "Torpedo Away!"
"Um, Sir?" Sweat says.

"What is it Sailer Sweat?"

"I... Um, I still needed to move the..."

"Davy Crocket, this is the Sam Houston. What in the hell are you shooting at? I think that torpedo is going to.... Oh, *Sweet Jesus*... You sunk Speedy Bob! All that's left is his swim trunks floating in the water!"
Sweat sighs. "The submarine. I needed to move the submarine to the new coordinates."

Lecher leans down and growls at Sweat. "Goddamnit! You said *Affirmative!* I need you and Ball and Pickle to quit fuckin' about and do your fuckin' jobs."

"Moving the sub now. Major Lecher."

"Prepare a torpedo!"

"It's our last one!" Cries out Pickle.

"We do not have any more iPhones!" Says Ball.
"Ready the goddamn Torpedo!" Lecher yells. "Fire on my order."

"Boat is on the coordinates you provided, sir."

"Fire torpedo!" Lecher yells.

"Firing Torpedo!" Ball calls out.

"Torpedo away!" Pickle and Ball say in unison.

"Torpedo is away, sir." Sweat says.

"Is it really, Sweat?" Lecher asks sarcastically as he stumbles over to the periscope and pushes it up. He can see the anti-ship missile moving through the water directly at the Liberte'. "Sink that bastard. Sink that fucking baby killing boat!" Lecher growls. The missile shifts direction slightly but appears on target for the stern of the ship. Lecher holds his breath until he sees it hit in the rear eighth of the hospital ship. "We got it! We got the bastards! Whooo Wee! We sank them baby killin' bastards!"

"Sam Houston to Davy Crockett. You hit the target. We will start collecting the passengers for transport to the mainland."

"Just line em' up and shoot em' all dead!" Lecher shouts into the microphone.

"What do you think we are, Davy Crockett, savages? We have to be humane!" Comes the reply from the Sam Houston.

Chapter 30
There is a hole in the ship, dear Kitty, dear Kitty.
There is a hole in the ship.
Hospital Ship Liberte' Gulf of Mexico
Outside of the Territorial Waters of the United States of America
Land of the Free(ish) Home of the Brave(ish)


"You need to get Kitty down to the third deck. We will evacuate from there!" Dr. Bloom says to Yoda. "Use that wheelchair and get moving." The doctor puts three preloaded syringes of morphine in Yoda's hand. "Keep these on you. Give them to her as she needs them for the cramps."

Yoda stuffs the syringes in his pocket. He helps his wife out of the hospital bed and into the wheelchair.

"Are we going to be ok, Yoda?" Kitty asks.

Yoda looks around the room before exiting, He grabs some blankets off the bed. After looking into his wife's panicked eyes, he does something that he had never done in their relationship. *He lies to her.* "Yes, Kitty. We are going to be fine. It is all going to be ok."

He wheels her to the elevator. The flashing lights tell him the machinery is not operating. Quickly he finds the exit stair well and picks Kitty out of the chair and hoists her and the blankets into his arms. There are other people in the stair well, nurses, patients. Some pregnant. Some not. Men hold their wives or girlfriends close. Holding Kitty with his right arm, Yoda helps a single, pregnant woman down the stairs. "It hurts so bad." She cries. "I just want it to be over!"
Yoda doesn't say anything to the girl. They get to the third floor. An orderly is helping people into a bright orange boat. Yoda looks at the back of the vessel. There is no motor.

The Liberte', a hole blown in its hull, starts to list more. People scream. Yoda nestles his face down near Kitty's ear. "Kitty, I love you more

than anything in the world." He takes the syringes out of his pocket and runs his hand up his beautiful wife's pregnant body to her armpit. "There are three morphine syringes here. Keep them hidden. You put them in your arm. Use all the drug in each syringe and only use it when the pain is really bad."
Her eyes find his and he has to bite his cheek to keep from crying. "I am going to put you in this boat. I am not getting in. I promise I will come find you. Don't be scared, ok, Kitty?"

Kitty nods dumbly. "I love you Yoda."

Yoda hands his wife to an orderly and then turns and helps the young woman he had helped down the stairs into the lifeboat. After seeing her and a husband and wife into the orange vessel, he turns and runs down the stairs to the first floor of the Liberte'. The electric speed boat is gone. Water has filled the bottom foot of the first floor. Yoda wades through it and without thinking, dives into the ocean.

Chapter 31
Tension. What are we?
Williams Residence.
Someplace in the United States of America
Land of the Free(ish) Home of the Brave(ish)


*Millie's transporter pulls up the long circular driveway of the Williams house. By up, I mean that we must have to climb a few hundred feet up a hill to get to a flight of stairs that lead into the house. I watch the battery deplete another five percent just going up the first part of the driveway. Whoever thought relying on only a battery to power mobility was a good idea, is a moron. I have no idea what I was thinking about when I bought that goddamn Tesla. Probably pussy. Was it a sex symbol to have a Tesla in 2021? Maybe? The latest iPhone, an Apple Watch and a fucking Tesla S. That's how Big Dog Justin Thyme rolled... Until I didn't.*

"Suing companies pays well." I say into the silence of the transporter. Millie has been quiet almost the whole trip. The auto pilot doesn't work on her buggy... or it never had it, I have no idea. Anyway, she seems mad. I could not even get her to play *I spy*. She had been a big help in calling the William's law office. Whoever Millie had talked to had relayed the message to Wendy Williams who called Millie back. Soon a plan was set. Wendy would call Conrad, Hank and Marmalade. We would all meet at the Williams's house.

"Suing people has always paid well." Millie mutters.

I shift in my seat. "You doing ok?" The transporter stops in the middle of the hill. Millie turns to me. I am hoping that she has stopped the transporter, and we haven't run out of battery. The hill is steep, and I still really don't walk long distances well.

"How are you going to introduce me to your friends?" She asks. There is no smile. In fact, I think her lips have both disappeared.

My sarcastic smart-ass demeanor probably never exposed itself during opportune times *before* my near permanent dirt nap. No reason for things to be any different now. I put on the best, broadest smile I can and say, "I am going to introduce you by your one true identity, Penelope Puddingsnatch."

Her eyes narrow. "You are impossible. How are you... That's not... That's not...!" She stutters.

"Yeah. You are right." I sit back in the seat and exhale theatrically. "I have no idea if your snatch is like pudding."

I see the corners of her mouth lift a little as she turns and looks out the front window. "So, I can't tell my buddies I hooked up with Penelope Puddingsnatch, star of the stage, one of the biggest names to appear at only the finest gentleman's clubs?"

"Are your friends blind?" She asks with a tone dripping in so much sarcasm I am instantly jealous and a little turned on at the same time.

"Maybe. I haven't seen them for a while. A lot can happen in twenty years." I answer.

"Yeah. Like one can be arrested and put in prison for a significant part of her life." Millie says, her face flushed.
"Ah... shit." I moan. "Ex con on the lam from her parole officer was my second choice!" I grin. "Can I still say your name is Penelope Puddingsnatch?"

She chuckles. There it is. That great smile. I feel a significant amount of relief just seeing that smile. She pokes me in the ribs. Her face is serious again. "What are we Justin? That's what I mean. What do we tell people we are?"

"I kind of think we are ghosts." I answer. "Socially and in reality." I sigh. "I wouldn't ever embarrass you, Millie. Not on purpose, anyway. And never to make a joke. I plan on introducing you as my friend, Millie... Millie Ratchet. I suppose they can figure things out on their own. I have no idea how this is going to go. These *were* long time ago friends." I stare up at Willem Williams' big house. "Fuck... I mean, none of them have talked to me. It isn't like you even talked to Willem. You talked to his wife, Wendy. You made it sound like she didn't sound exactly excited to hear about me... but..." I sigh. It's not fair to judge things I have no control over. She seemed ok with calling Hank, Marmalade and Conrad and having us all over."

"I was thinking only of me." Millie says. She pats my leg. "I am still interested in what you think we are. And I am sorry for freaking out. You may have noticed... I haven't socialized much over the past twenty years. Except for some fellow prisoners, it's pretty much just been you." "Really?" I ask. "No one?"

"No one." Millie shrugs and continues. "Too much risk. There is a reward to find me and return me back to the jailers in Texas." She gestures at the house through the windshield. "It appears that Willem doesn't need money. I trust you, Justin... Just protect me however you can." She smiles at me. It's a nervous, weak smile. "Thank you for..." Millie closes her eyes and breaths deeply. "Thank you, Justin."
"Millie, you are all I have." I point out the window. "Whatever lies behind the doors of that big house doesn't really matter. I'm not part of that group... or any other group right now and being away twenty years is a long time." I reach over and grab her chin, lifting her face to mine. "I can't think of anyone else I'd like to be a ghost with."

The big smile returns to Millie's face as she starts to speak. "I think that technically, we might be Zombies. Everyone else can see us, right? If we were ghosts, we would be invisible." The transporter starts rolling forward. "Let's go meet your friends and see what the cow was trying to tell you."

"Reverend Moo. The Bovine champion of the nearly dead." I rub my hands together. "It going to be just great, Millie. I can feel it."

"I hope you are right." Millie answers.

*I hope I am right too. Because I feel anything but just great.*

Chapter 32
Meeting the friends. Willem is not well.
Williams house Someplace in America
Home of the Free(ish) Land of the Brave(ish)


"Conrad, come away from the window." Elizabeth Eaton says. "Let your friend come inside before you continue to judge him!"

"They look homeless!" Conrad Peterson exclaims.

Wendy Williams comes over and peaks out the curtains. "She seems pretty old for him. I would've guessed whoever Conrad was with would be my daughter's age."

Father Henry Thyme comes up behind the pair, a glass of scotch in his hand. "Justin isn't looking like a healthy spring chicken... or even healthy, Wendy. Maybe she is what he could find. The boy never was without a woman to poke."

"Neither were you, as I recall." Wendy answers. "I'm not sure how the archdiocese got that collar to fit on your neck without spontaneously combusting."

"Magic. Just like the Lord." Father Thyme replies. He takes a drink of his scotch. "This is a damn fine whiskey. It is a shame that Willem can't drink this anymore."

Wendy looks at him and purses her lips. "Humph." She looks back out the window. "The car is finally coming up the drive. It's kind of a heap. I think your cousin Justin has become poor, Hank."

"He's probably coming to ask for a handout from us." Marmalade Julius says from the back of the room. Everyone turns and looks at him. A younger man stands behind him, looking at the floor. "What? I am just saying... boy probably has nothing. Who else is he gonna ask? His parents, dead. We are all he has to ask!"

"You think so?" Conrad says. "Maybe. Hey, they are parking now. Archie is meeting them."

Wendy looks out the window. Justin Thyme is struggling to get out of the car. "Oh, my. She does look old! Justin really does looks like a corpse!" Marmalade, Conrad and Hank all come to the window and look out.
Out in the driveway, a robot named Archie walks over to Millie's transporter. He is programed to identify the female in the car and open the door for her. Neither of the passengers are equipped with any sort of communication device. He is unable to determine the gender of either passenger. After few minutes of processing, he opens the passenger door. "Hello, *Guest*. Welcome to the Williams residence. Are they expecting you?"

"Yes, I believe they are." Justin answers. "What is your name?"

"My name is Archie. I am pleased to be of service to you... *Guest.*"

The Robot walks to the other side of the transporter, but Millie is already out. "Hello.... *Guest*. Welcome to the Williams house. I will park your transporter if you give me permission."

"The auto drive does not work." Millie says.
Archie the Robot stands still as it processes. Millie walks around it and over to Justin.

"Nervous?" She asks.

"Yeah. You?"

"Scared spit-less, actually." Millie says as she steadies Justin up a small flight of stairs and then another longer flight of stairs. They push a button near the door and wait. Another Robot opens the door. "Welcome to the Williams house. I am Edith. Are the Williams expecting you?"

Justin nods. "Millie Ratchet and Justin Thyme for Wendy and Willem Williams."

"Checking guest list." Blue and green lights are flashing on top of Edith the Robot's head. "You are on the guest list, Justin Thyme and Millie Retched."

"It's Ratchet." I say.

"I am sorry, Mr. Williams is under the weather today, but Wendy is accepting visitors. Please follow me."

"Millie Retched. That's me." Millie says under her breath. She waits for Justin to start moving and walks at his slow gait.

"Did the Robot say that Willem is sick today?" I ask quietly as I shake my head, trying hard to concentrate on walking like a normal human being.

"Yeah. That's what it said." Millie whispers. She grabs my arm. I think it may be more to steady herself than me.

"Justin Thyme!" I look up. A large, bearded man wearing all back with a Roman collar has appeared. He takes two big steps at me and stands in front of me. Hank and I were always about the same size, height and weight. I am probably just as tall as my cousin if I straighten up, but he is easily two times my weight. "You look like a goddamn scarecrow, cousin! I am Hank, Justin's cousin". He says to Millie.

She smiles at him. "Nice to meet you."

Conrad Peterson comes into the room, followed by Wendy Williams. "Hank! Let them in! Come into the front room." Wendy exclaims. "Edith, get Justin and his friend in here!" Everyone turns and follows Wendy. We follow Edith the Robot into a great room... at least I assume it is the great room... it is the size of a basketball court. Marmalade Julius stands in the middle of the room smiling. Conrad puts his arm around an older blond woman. Hank stands next to Wendy. They are all smiling at us.

"I... Um...." I take a deep breath in. I wasn't at all prepared for this to be as emotional as it turns out to be. Uncontrolled tears start pouring from my eyes. I sob and wipe the back of my hand across my face. "I... I am sorry. I... am just so happy to see all of you."

Millie pulls me into her. "It's ok, Justin." She whispers.

"This... this angel next to me is Millie. She is..." I shake my head. "She is so important to me. Please, welcome her, I wouldn't be here without her."

"Hello Millie." Wendy comes forward and touches my arm before girl hugging Millie. "Let's sit down."

"Where is Willem?" I ask.

Wendy smiles. I *feel* what her smile is saying. Willem isn't well and if he is here, he doesn't want to be seen.

"Willem has been under the weather for a while. Let's talk about you, shall we?" Wendy guides me and Millie to a settee. I settle down in the thing. It feels ridiculously comfortable like it was made for my boney ass. Millie sits down beside me.

Conrad leads the woman next to him over and motions for Marmalade to come closer. The younger man standing behind Marmalade hangs back. Hank pulls up two big wing back chairs, one for him and one for Wendy.

"So, Justin..." Conrad says with his patented big toothy grin. "What's it like to wake up from a twenty-year nap?"

Millie pats my leg and whispers, "It's going to be ok, Justin. I'm fine... I'm fine with *most* of these people."

*My people. I straighten up and look at each person. I am with my people. I guess?*

*Wait.  Did Millie just say, 'Most' of these people?*

Chapter 33
Is that a shark? Rescue at sea.
Gulf of Mexico Outside the Territorial waters of the United States of
America Land of the Free(ish) Home of the Brave(ish)


Yoda Storm Trooper Willams hangs on to a big piece of a fiberglass boat hull. Someone had painted 'William Travis' on the fiberglass with a brush. Yoda makes mental note to look up the name *William Travis* when he is able.

The water had been mercifully calm. After diving out of the flooded hospital ship, he had swum for twenty minutes. When he had stopped, the hospital ship was still listing to its starboard side and the orange lifeboats were all in a line. Another boat was taking people off the first lifeboat. Yoda could see men with long guns standing on the bow of the boat. Soon a second and third boat pulled up and took people off the second and third lifeboat. He watched to see if he could make out Kitty but didn't.

The floating fiberglass had come along at a good time. Yoda was getting tired of treading water. He climbed up and laid on it with his legs still in the ocean. The sun was high in the sky when he had stopped swimming. Now it was in the northern sky. Yoda wondered if anyone was still on the Liberte. The little boats that had come stayed clear of the ship that appeared to have stopped sinking. Yoda looked across the water, wondering if the little boats or a shark would find him first.

"I didn't think this through, did I?" He questions out loud to himself. "Now I have to figure out how to save Kitty and the others *and* I have to figure out how to get to shore." He sighs and tries to make himself comfortable on the sliver of the torpedoed *William Travis* currently serving as his personal flotation device. One by one, the little boats start to depart, Yoda watches the direction that they go and deduces that the direction is north, or northwest. After a few more hours, the sun dips behind the horizon and the sky turns orange. Yoda tries his communicator. There is no signal. Somewhere in the recesses of his mind, he remembers that there is an emergency setting on the internal communication devices. "I NEED HELP!" He says loudly.

*Emergency beacon activated. Help will arrive shortly* He hears the female voice from the device announce in his ear. *Please try and stay calm*

"Ok, just hurry." Yoda says. He watches the water and hopes it doesn't storm. "I think I should have slept too. I am really tired. It was a mistake to watch so much on the monitor." He sighs, "But I learned a lot." He is fighting sleep when motion in the water catches his attention. A tell-tale triangle shaped fin pokes up in the water and disappears. "Shark!" Yoda shouts. He kicks the piece of fiberglass around looking for the fin to reappear again, which it does, closer now. Yoda quickly searches his memory for a movie he had seen where a shark was involved. *Megalodon VIII Return of the Shark* comes to mind. "No. Too big. This isn't a megalodon and I don't have a nuclear warhead to kill it." He shakes his head at the memory. "That was such a stupid movie. I know that now." He kicks his feet some more. The fin pops back up. "*Rambo, Ocean's End*" Yoda shouts. "Rambo kicks the shark, and it dies. I don't want you to die, Mr. Shark. I just want you to go away!" Yoda shouts at the water. "I will kick you though!" The fin pops back up. Yoda watches it wearily. The animal swims by the fiberglass and Yoda yells louder than he had yelled at the alligator. A bright light crosses him and the fiberglass hull and disappears. Yoda yells again at the shark. He sees the fin swim off away from him and the floating fiberglass.

"Yesterday you scared off a giant alligator and today a little bull shark." A female voice that sounds like the voice that tells people to mind a gap in London says from behind him. "What are the odds?"

Yoda kicks and turns the fiberglass shard. He looks up at the boat lady holding on to the helm of the electric speed boat. "Pretty good, I suppose... if you are where there are both alligators and sharks." He answers from the water.

The Boat Lady nods solemnly. "Well, you want to stay in the water and see how you do against other sharks, or do you want a ride?"

"I really don't know anything about sharks. I think that one really may be going to get his friends. I will get in the boat." Yoda lets go of the piece of fiberglass and swims towards the speedboat. "Do you know who *William Travis* is?"

"Anti-Tax settler in Texas when Mexico owned Texas. He was the commander of the Alamo when it was overrun by Santa Anna's troops." The Boat Lady says with a flat tone.

"When was that?" Yoda asks as he finds purchase on the rear deck of the speed boat.

"Over two hundred years ago. 1835." The woman responds.

"Are you an American?" Yoda asks.

The woman shakes her head. "British. Of a sort."

"How do you know about something that happened in America two hundred years ago? I don't know what happened in America two hundred years ago and I am an American!" Yoda says as he stands in the boat and takes his shirt off, wringing it out over the side."

The woman looks at his muscular form with curiosity. "It is important to study history... know what went wrong, what went right. We do that so mistakes don't get made twice."

"Does that work?" Yoda asks. He puts the damp shirt back on.

"Sometimes." The boat lady points at the seat. "There are blankets under the seats. Make yourself comfortable."

"Where did they take my wife?" Yoda asks. "We need to go there."

"Your wife is being taken to a detention center in Galveston, Texas. We are going to Monkey Island." The boat lady puts the electric boat in gear. "There is help for you in Louisiana."

"My name is Yoda. Yoda Storm Trooper Katz Williams. What is your name?"

The boat lady shakes her head. "My name isn't important. But you can call me Esther."

Chapter 34
It's been a long time.  We aren't all that close.
Willem is really in bad shape. A surprise phone call.
Williams house Someplace in America
Home of the Free(ish). Land of the Brave(ish).

*Hours of conversation have caught me up to the fact that over the past twenty years, I unsurprisingly missed out on a lot. I wonder during the conversation how I would have fit into these people's lives. When I went to medical school, I sort of lost contact with all of them. My immediate concerns were pussy, working on people's feet and more pussy. Anything I did was directly related to those three things.*

*Millie has been great. She is holding my hand and listening intently to what is being said. No one has asked her many questions yet, which is good. I am feeling strong enough now to protect her with my wits alone, if needed. I am sensing that everyone is in a happy mood. For whatever reason, I feel really connected to all the people in the room. Maybe because, other than my parents who are dead, these are the people in my life that I had a human connection of some sort with.*

*I start things off with humor I still am not sure is working.*

"So, I got a vasectomy and ended up in a coma for over twenty years." I shrug. "It was dark. There wasn't a lot going on and then I woke up with the night nurse riding me like a rented mule."

Everyone laughs, which is good. Conrad points at Millie with a grin. "Are you the night nurse?"
Millie flashes that awesome smile and shakes her head.

"It was a woman named Joyfull. As in Joy. Full." I answer. "She had the most amazing tattoos on her boobs. One of a former president and the other of a Supreme Court justice."

There are knowing nods. These specific tattoos seem to be mainstream. Or at least mainstream enough that people know about it. "So, what was up with that? Is that what's happening in hospitals these days? Little patient benefits?" I ask.

"Sounds like he was being raped." The older woman sitting next to Conrad says.

I chuckle. "Believe it or not... that's what I told the woman. She said something about women not being able to rape men."

Millie pats my leg and explains that Joyfull had a reputation in the hospital for trying to get pregnant from incapacitated men.

The woman sitting next to Conrad nods knowingly. "Ah... another victim of the proud choices our government has made."

"It was pretty surreal." I say. "She had those weird tattoos. Plus, there was a swastika under her chin. I thought I was being raped by a Nazi." The group all seems to look at Marmalade who doesn't respond to the attention. I get the vibe that something is very off between Marmalade Julius and the rest of the room.

I change the subject to one I really want to talk about. "So, what have you all been doing?"

*Conrad was the first to open up. He talked about his family first. He lost his first wife, Norma Leah in a rock-climbing accident. He told me it wasn't important how he met Norma Leah, but she gave him a terrific son, Fredrick. I am a little jealous about that. I realize now how stupid I was to decide that I needed to get a vasectomy at such a young age. I guess it's too late for me to have kids anyway. He talks about Elizabeth, his girlfriend. They can't keep their hands off each other. Millie whispers in my ear that Conrad and Elizabeth obviously haven't been together long... Elizabeth talks about her daughter, Anne and how she is good friends with Conrad's son Fredrick. Elizabeth and Conrad smile at each other a lot. Conrad tells us about how he parlayed his medical school education and his mechanical engineering interests into an incredible business, PPP which I guess is the world's largest producer of adult stimulation devices, a term that makes my cousin Hank bellow with laughter.*

*Hank goes next. I sit forward, because I really want to hear about how Hank Thyme, a monster of a man child who started having sex with women ten years older than him when we were in the ninth grade made his way into priesthood. Hank starts talking and he clearly has perfected a gift for gab. Repeating everything he said would take days. I try and summarize it in my head while looking at Hank. He had a football scholarship to a mid-major Catholic School, which I knew. He got hurt... knee, apparently. Maybe I knew that. Maybe not. He finished college early. Now my knowledge of Hank is dimming. Everything is new. Went into business working on Wall Street. Lasted a little over a year. Didn't like the stress or the people he worked with. Went back to the football school for a master's degree. Met some girl and was going to get married. She is super-duper Catholic. (I knew Hank wasn't Catholic.) Hank becomes Catholic and at the requirement of the future Mrs. Hank Thyme, starts marriage counseling with the priests at the college. Goes to marriage counseling for a whole year, which seems pretty crazy. At some point, the priest asks Hank what he wants. Hank tells the guy that he doesn't want to get married to the sweet Catholic girl or any girl, he wants to be a priest. The engagement is called off. Hank goes to theology school and gets a master's in psychology. He gets his collar and a vocation. Now Hank gets to ask young people what they want in life although, as he points out... the flock is shrinking and there aren't a lot of young people getting married. Apparently, there was this older couple that came in after losing their spouses to the inevitable that wanted to be married, and Hank talked them out of it. I am not sure why Hank told us this story.*

"Why did you talk them out of it?" Millie asks.

"Well, that's a long story." Hank answers with a wink. "Another time, maybe."

I feel my eyes involuntarily narrow. Cousin Hank isn't gelling the whole story together right. It doesn't feel sinister... just not *honest*. Everything was the *truth* right up until that last, totally unnecessary bit about the older couple he talked out of a marriage. Conrad could always be a little slick, but everything he told me felt straight. I am wondering what this new clairvoyance is that I am feeling when I notice Marmalade.

Marmalade Julius has been up walking around almost the whole time we have been in the great room. One could almost say that the man is pacing. The young guy he is with sort of sits in the shadows, if shadows can be found in the ornate space we are in. "Marmalade, how about you. What's been up with you?"

Marmalade Julius comes around the couch. "Well, you know I played some ball in the league back when there was real football. Got hurt like Hammerin' Hank Thyme over there. Knee. Couple of times. I always liked music you know...so I stated rapping. My pro contacts helped me out there. Got two top ten records out of the deal. That paid a lot more than my NFL contracts did. Got a nice house here... another in LA. A bunch of transporters... Livin' the dream Justin... Livin' the dream.

I am not surprised by the brevity of Marmalade's story. He was never the most verbose guy. He has left a lot of pertinent information out and I am catching on to a sadness to Marmalade Julius that I can't put my finger on.
"What are your songs about?" Millie asks.

Marmalade blushes. "Aww, now it's probably nuthin' you want hear about Ms. Millie."

Conrad laughs. "His raps are mostly about fucking. Very... descriptive fucking."

"Such language." His girlfriend, Elizabeth says. "We should come up with another word."

Conrad rubs her legs. "We can work on a better word for fucking later, Lizzy." He says softly to her with a smile. To the group he says, "Good thing Juice's music came out in the late 20's. No one is listening to that kinda stuff today."

Marmalade smiles. "Conrad is right. *Sex* is mostly what my music was all about. And yeah... thank you Lord for giving me the opportunity when you did! No one today is listening to rap music. Not like that anyway."

"Well, I would like to hear it sometime!" Millie says looking at me. The tone of her voice seems off.

Something isn't right. I turn and find the young man. "Is that your son, Marmalade?" I know damn well that the boy is not Marmalade Julius's son. For one, he looks like he is Thai or Burmese. Also, he's probably about thirty-five years old, which would have made Marmalade like a seventeen-year-old father, which he wasn't.

Wendy laughs nervously. Conrad smiles. Only Cousin Hank and the two other women wear a straight face. Millie and Elizabeth have never met Marmalade prior to this, and Hank obviously has an opinion.
Marmalade looks surprised. "Oh... no... that is not my son. He is my friend Paal. Paal Tan. His name is spelled P..A..A..L.. but he pronounces it, Paul. Like the Apostle. In the Bible."

Strange reference for Marmalade to make. I look behind me at him. "Paal, it is a pleasure to meet you. Please, come join us."

I smile at Marmalade. "We are glad to have him here, Juice." Paal pulls his chair up to the settee that Millie and I are seated on. Marmalade slowly comes and stands beside Paal for a moment before finding another chair over by Wendy.

"Thank you, it is nice to meet you, Justin. Juice... Marmalade told me a lot about you... your time playing football together." Paal says with accented English. "And Wendy. Your house is amazing."

I look over at Wendy. "It's your turn. What have you and Willem been doing over the past twenty years besides making a ton of money and a beautiful daughter?

Wendy looks... Stern? Severe? She inhales deeply. The tension in the room has increased back to what it was when Millie and I walked in. I sneak a look at Hank and Conrad who both are looking away. Something is wrong. Very, very wrong.

"Where is Willem?" I ask with as direct of a tone as I can muster.

Wendy licks her lips. As I remember that little action was a nervous tic when we were in high school. She takes another deep breath. "We both got law degrees, as you know. Michigan. My Katherine went there as well. Met her husband there... as a matter of fact. Things were... great. Just great for us in the beginning. When Kitty was, oh... I don't know eight or nine years old, Willem started losing strength in his legs. He'd get really tired. Sometimes he'd stay in bed for days."

Everyone else in the room is silent... and looking the other way. They know this story, and apparently it is not a good one.

"Willem? In bed for days?" I shake my head. "That's... not Willem." *The guy was a go getter. He worked a nearly full-time job, went to high school and got straight A's and was an all-conference tight end on the football team. Also, he dated Wendy which I always kind of thought was a full-time job on its own. I often had wondered if the guy ever napped, much less stayed in bed all day.*

Wendy shakes her head sadly. "It was not *my Willem*. Willem never took naps... and he never stopped moving!" She sighs. I can see that Wendy is holding back tears. "About ten years ago we started seeing specialists. Willem was diagnosed with ALS. He is in a wheelchair now. Needs a ventilator to help him breathe. When he talks, he talks with assistance of a Robot. It works ok. Sort of one of those computer things like that one scientist had."

"Stephen Hawking." Millie says.

I look at Conrad who is staring intently at me. "What is the prognosis on this condition? You know... today."

There is silence in the room. Conrad shakes his head slowly.

I had been told by Reverend Moo to come and help Willem. The conversational bovine had been very specific about that. I am here now. The friend group is all together. I was medically trained as a podiatrist. I doubt such a thing is even a profession anymore. Robots probably do a better job, and they won't be tempted to masturbate themselves off on some woman's feet. (No, not me... but sadly, I knew of doctors who had.) *I am not the specialist that Willem needs. Millie is an obstetrician. Unless Willem has grown a working womb, she is not the specialist that Willem needs.*

*What are we here for?*

I clear my throat. "Its... It has been over twenty years. Surely medicine has gotten better for ALS patients."

Conrad shakes his head. "The opposite as a matter of fact." He looks down at the wool carpet like it may hold some forbidden secret, which... it's deep enough pile. It could. "When abortion was banned, a lot of the material that was being used for research on diseases like multiple sclerosis, ALS... Cancers... well, all of that research went away. The Europeans are still doing some research using fetal tissue, as are the Chinese. A lot of the funding though is for cancer and the technology is not available here because much of it came from the use of fetal tissues."

Elizabeth Eaton puts her finger in the air. "And don't forget, if medication or treatment was the product of fetal tissue parts or came about because of research using fetal tissue parts... the product or the treatment is flat illegal in the United States now."

I nod slowly. The room is silent. I struggle to my feet. Millie stands up with me. I look at Wendy. "Take me to him."

Wendy shakes her head. "Justin... Willem doesn't like people to see him..."

I shake *my* head. "It wasn't a request, Wendy. I know that you and Willem came to see me in the hospital on a very regular basis up until ten years ago. You think I wanted anyone to see me in the condition that I was in?" I stop and breathe. "Take me to him. I need to see Willem."

Wendy rolls her eyes in resignation. She motions at the others in the room. "Only Justin goes in. I don't want to stress Willem out." She points in my direction. "Follow me."

I stand, slowly. "I need Millie with me, Wendy."

Wendy doesn't respond. I motion at Millie to follow me. She rises. I look over at Conrad. He stares at me vacantly. Dr. Conrad Peterson knows the score. I do too and unbeknownst to anyone else, so does Millie. ALS is an awful, debilitating disease that quickly steals the body and slowly rots the mind. There aren't going to be any last second comebacks here. The best Willem and Wendy could hope for is an easy time. I don't need to see Willem to assess his medical condition. Clearly the Williams' can afford whatever care they want. I think I need to go see Willem to try and ascertain why I was sent here by Reverend Moo.

We walk down a long hallway. Wendy is quiet. I know this is killing her. If I were a whole, undamaged human being, it would be killing me too. My lack of any visible outpouring of emotion might be because I may have already died a couple of times.

She gets to a door that is across from what appears to be a master suite. She puts her hand on the knob and looks at me. "Willem really felt bad when we stopped going to see you. He thought you would lose hope. Now, here you are." She looks at me sadly. "And... here he is.  Sort of without hope." The door swings open.

Even in my emotionally stunted state, seeing Willem Williams's withered body slumped in a life sustaining chair is tough. Millie rubs my back. I muster up some courage and walk over to the chair, grabbing Willem's hand. "Willem. It's me, Justin. Justin Thyme. How are you?"

*Look, to hear me ask, it might have seemed like a dumb question. Willem Williams is being eaten by an invisible monster. He has lost everything... except his mind. When all you have is your thoughts, you have good days and bad days, and you are acutely aware of every single thought that you might have. Even people in the shittiest of situations deserve to have other people ask them the most mundane of questions.*

Willem does something with his pinky finger on his left hand. A Robot in the corner rises and walks over to us. "I am Jimmy. I am Mr. Williams' personal assistant. I provide many services to Mr. Williams including interpersonal communications. The Robot appears to look at Willem. It turns to me and Millie. "Hello Justin. I am very happy to see you, friend. You have gotten old!" The robot points at Millie. "Did you bring your mother with you?"

"Willem!" Wendy says sharply from behind us.

I look at Millie who has a bemused look on her face. "It's good Wendy. This is the Willem I know." I look back down at my friend. I may as well talk to him like I would have twenty-one years ago. "Well, at least I don't look like a black snowman that is melting in a chair, so I think I am doing just slightly better than you." I grab his hand. "I am sorry to see you like this, Willem."

Jimmy the Robot shakes its head. "I came to see you when I was still walking, and you looked a lot worse than you do now. You owed me. Glad you got your ass out of bed to come see me before I'm gone. *Melting black snowman.* Now, that is some funny shit." The Robot laughs mechanically before pointing at Millie. "Now, introduce me to this attractive woman you brought with you."
I look at Millie who continues to wear a faint smile. I look down at Willem. "Willem, this is Penelope Puddingsnatch."

There is quiet in the room. Then the Robot starts laughing. "That's funny Justin, you are making me laugh today. What is her name, really?"

Millie steps forward and crouches down to Willem. She is wearing that million-dollar smile. "Willem, it is a pleasure to meet you. My name really is Penelope Puddingsnatch." She touches his arm.

I see Willem William's body move a little. He's laughing, I think. As if on cue, Jimmy the Robot laughs mechanically in an animated fashion.

I step over. "Willem, Puddingsnatch here is really a beautiful, intelligent woman named Millie Ratchet. She has been taking care of me since I woke up from my nap. She is very, very important to me."

"So... is her snatch really like pudding?" Jimmy the Robot asks. I look Willem's face. It appears to have a little smirk on it. Wendy mutters a few words of protest colored by some very descriptive curse words.

I look at the robot. "Robots can't whisper, can they?"

Jimmy the Robot shakes its head from side to side.

"Millie and I are just friends Willem." I answer.

The robot scoffs. "You would have to be dead not to be hitting that, Justin!"

I smile. "Willem, you have no idea." I look down at him in his chair with a sad expression and squeeze his arm. "Or I suppose you do... don't you?"

"Conrad's toys get us through, Justin. Jimmy and I watch." Jimmy the Robot answers for Willem. It points at Millie. "Serious. Get on that, buddy! As I recall, smart and intelligent women were not descriptions we used to describe your dates back in the old days. You have turned over a new leaf! Hell, boy... You should change your name to Lazarus... since you seem to have been raised from the dead. It looks to me like you got a good gal in your orbit. Better reel her in and figure out how to keep her happy... and you know what I mean!" The robot grunts twice while thrusting its hips.

"Willem!" Wendy exclaims. I look over. Wendy Williams is blushing. Her face wrinkles into confusion. "Hang on, I have a call coming in from one of our clients... Weddington? Is that you?"

Chapter 35
Yoda meets the Robot god.
Wendy and Willem get a surprise.
Monkey Island, Louisiana, USA
Land of the Free(ish). Home of the Brave(ish).


Yoda Storm Trooper Katz Williams stands on the bow of the speed boat with a rope in his hand as instructed by Esther who pilots the boat into a slip. In the darkness, Yoda can see some sort of structure on the land behind the dock. A Robot, blackened from the ocean air stands and walks out onto the dock.

*"Nosotras somos de la libertad."* Esther announces.

*"Si!"*. The Robot extends its arms. Hooks end each appendage.

"Throw the rope." Esther instructs Yoda. He complies, tossing the rope on to the Robot's outstretched arms. Quickly the Robot uses the hooks to pull the speedboat in and lash it to the dock.

*"Bienvenidos a la Isla de los Monos."*. The Robot says. *La autoridad ha sido notificada."*

*"Si."* Esther says. *"Lo encontraremos."*

"How do you know that language? What is that language?" Yoda asks. "I only speak American."
Esther smiles. "We call the language you speak, English. I know lots of languages. That one is Spanish. It is what that Robot was programmed to speak. It's important to be able to communicate properly." She points at the structure. "We need to introduce you to Weddington Coffee. He supports what your people sometimes call the resistance."

"That's what Dr. Hole in One called it!" Yoda says. "He was a friendly guy. I don't think Kitty like him much... until he gave her morphine. Then she liked him just fine."

Esther starts walking towards the structure. As they get closer, Yoda sees that it is less a building, and more pieces of scrap wood and metal arranged in a way that looks like a building. Esther pauses as if to think. "Dr. Hole in One. I know that name. He sends many people to us."

"He's not really a doctor." Yoda says.

Esther shakes her head from side to side. "He is not a Doctor. Mr. Hole in One is what Weddington Coffee calls a crusader. He lost his wife in the mid-twenties. The wife was pregnant in Texas. There were problems with the pregnancy. She couldn't get out of the state for treatment. The wife died in a hospital in Killeen, Texas. She needed to get the fetus that had died and become infected out of her body. None of the hospital staff would provide the care she needed. Weddington Coffee says that if the medical people would have helped Dr. Hole In One's wife, they would have been arrested by the authorities."

"That is Kitty's story too." Yoda says sadly, not noticing the mechanical way that Esther is talking to him. "I left her..." He involuntarily sobs. "I left her on that lifeboat. Alone. Now she is in a jail and is still in danger."

Esther stops walking and puts a hand on Yoda's arm. There is a long pause. Yoda looks into the woman's blank eyes. She blinks and responds. "Yoda... You did the right thing. The Texas Militia have taken the people who were not pregnant to a different facility. If you had stayed with your wife, you would not be able to help. You are the only one who jumped off the ship instead of getting in the lifeboat. Because of that, we have a chance to get your Kitty and maybe the others... assistance." She points at the building. "Help is in there." She leads him through the ramshackle structure to a wall. She bends mechanically and types in a code on a silver pad and the wall slides open revealing an ornate interior that reminds Yoda of Kitty's father's office. A solid built gray-haired man in a mechanical wheelchair rolls into the room. Yoda immediately sees that the man has no legs. Esther walks over to him and bends at the waist, kissing the man on the forehead. "Hello, father." She turns to Yoda. "This is my father, Weddington Coffee. Father, this Yoda... Williams?"

Yoda walks over and extends his hand as both of his father's had taught him to do. "I am Yoda Storm Trooper Katz Williams."

Weddington Coffee takes in the image of Yoda standing in front of him. Yoda's clothing is still damp from being in the water and his hair disheveled. Coffee taps on his chin. This person appears awfully familiar. "That's quite a name Mr. Yoda. Nice to meet you." He looks at Esther. "This have something to do with the explosion on the Liberte'?"

"Yoda jumped overboard when they took his wife and the others captive." Esther says. "The Liberte' was hit by a torpedo or some other projectile."

Yoda looks at Esther. Her voice is still the one that sounds like the voice from the London Tube telling people to *Mind the Gap* but it's different. The voice and the woman's movements seem slower, like she has gotten very sleepy.

"The goddamn Texas militia got themselves a submarine. Now they are going around blowing ships out of the water." Coffee shakes his head. "The world is off its goddamn rocker."

Esther motions at Yoda. "Yoda needs help. What should he do?" "Wife still pregnant?" Coffee asks. Both Esther and Weddington Coffee look at Yoda.

He nods. "Yes. The doctors on board said that she would need a cesarean delivery. They were planning to do it when the ship got hit." Coffee nods. "Ok. Texas will plan on keeping her until her due date, which is certain to be on file with the state."

"But... the baby is dead." Yoda says.

Weddington Coffee makes a face. "That won't matter one goddamn bit to those ignorant, all hat, no cattle, rednecks that calls themselves Americans." He shakes his head. "Stupid mother fuckers think that thoughts and prayers are going to make things *all better." All better* is said in a sing song voice as the man pulls out an old-fashioned cellular phone. "Your woman needs help, and she needs it right goddamn now!" He hands the phone to Yoda. "You got people to call?"

Yoda takes the phone and looks at it like it might be a meteorite from outer space. "Sir... I... Um, I don't know how to use one of these."

"Jesus, Mary and Joseph!" The man exclaims, looking at Yoda with wild eyes. "It's a telephone, son!"

"Are any of those three people you mentioned able to help me use it?" Yoda asks. He thinks that maybe man is being sarcastic in asking for three people that clearly are not in the room.

Weddington Coffee's lips twist into an expression of confusion. "Who are you going to call, son?"

"I should call Kitty's father. He has a bad sickness. He lives in a wheelchair, more advanced than yours and he cannot talk, but he is super smart and will know what to do next."

"Do you have his number?" Coffee asks slowly.

"I just ask my communicator to call Willem Williams." Yoda shrugs. "That's all I know how to do..." He motions at the cellular phone. "But I would like to *learn* how to use that thing."

Coffee's eyes narrow. He knows now why Yoda appears to be so familiar. "Your father-in-law is Willem Williams? The attorney Willem Williams?" He manipulates the phone. "And your mother-in-law is Wendy Williams?"

Yoda nods enthusiastically. "Yes! Do you know them?"

Coffee glances over at Esther who is slumped over by a table. "Esther! Go Recharge!"

Esther straightens. Her eyes are red lights that are blinking slowly. "Yes, Father." The voice is slurred. She walks towards a hallway and disappears. Yoda watches in shocked amazement.

"Esther there is one of my creations. A true humanoid robot that moves like a real person and can respond appropriately in ninety five percent of all human interactions." Coffee explains. "Her battery life is around twelve hours. After that ship got hit, I thought maybe I had lost her. I guess that both her programing to survive and the module I built to help others worked in concert with each other."

"You made Esther?" Yoda exclaims. "That is the best Robot I have ever seen!"

"Esther is pretty good. Ariel, Bernice, and Dinah were good workers... but I lost all of them at sea. One thing I have not been able to program is an ability to swim..." Coffee shakes his head. "My girls will all sink like very heavy rocks!"

"Do you need Mr. William's contact information?" Yoda asks.

Weddington Coffee shakes his head. "Nope. Willem and Wendy Williams represented me against the goddamn weapon manufacturer that stole my fucking legs with one of their not so bomb proof trucks. I know your in-laws personally... They are how I got the funds to build all of this!" He motions around the room to illustrate exactly what *all of this* is before pushing some buttons on the phone.

The phone rings a few times before going silent.

"The old network has to transfer to the new network." Coffee explains unnecessarily. Yoda had not heard a handheld telephone ring very many times in his life. He had no idea what he was hearing or what *network* the legless man is talking about.

"Weddington, is that you?" Wendy Williams answers with a surprised tone.

"As I live and breathe, Ms. Williams." Weddington Coffee says into the phone. "Listen, we haven't got time for niceties. I'd like to hear how Willem is doing and maybe shoot the shit with him, but we've a situation down here in Primate Paradise. Seems the sea has puked your son in law up on my sandy shore."

"Oh?" Yoda hears Wendy Williams say with a confused tone. "Is my Kitty with him?"

"Hello, Mrs. Williams." Yoda says. "Kitty has been detained... by the Texas Militia, I guess?"

There is a sharp intake of breath on the phone followed by some rustling. "Willem, you need to hear this!" Wendy's voice says in a panic. Jimmy the Robot speaks. "This is Willem. I am here. Wendy is still here too."
Yoda quickly explains in limited detail Kitty Williams's medical condition. He skips over the alligator incident but tells them about the ship and how there was an explosion. Wendy Williams is heard sobbing over the phone.

"Weddington... describe the man in front of you." Willem directs Jimmy the Robot to ask.

Weddington Coffee quickly describes Yoda's physical characteristics. He could give Willem his son in law's exact dimensions but holds back. "And he is still soaking wet. Dripping a little on the goddamn carpet!" Coffee adds.

"This guy talking doesn't sound at all like our son in law. Our son in law says *umm* a lot and rambles on about things with questionable relevance." Jimmy the Robot says.
"Yes sir, Mr. Williams." Yoda says. "It's really me. I have been learning a lot. Maybe I have improved my communication skills."

"Son, you seem to have gone from *See Spot Run* to quoting Shakespeare." Jimmy the Robot's voice says.

"Why didn't Katherine call us?" Wendy Williams sobs.
"She wanted too, Mrs. Williams. There was no service on the ship... or really when we were driving to the pick-up point." Yoda answers.

"Pretty rural down here, Wendy." Coffee adds. "And that hospital ship usually sits just outside of territorial waters."

"Weddington, what is your advice?" Jimmy the Robot's voice asks. "What should we do next?"

Coffee clears his throat. "Well, I'd take about six guys armed to the teeth with military grade rifles to the holding facility in Galveston and kill every one of the mouth breathing males in the place. Then I would put all the women on a boat and get them the hell out of there. Maybe take them to Paris or Beijing where they can get proper medical care."

There is a long pause. Then Jimmy the Robot's voice answers. "OK. What would you do to *not* start a war in Texas?"

"I'd be sneaky." Coffee answers. "But I don't know exactly how to do that. I believe that your daughter and the others are *technically* under arrest, as stupid as it sounds to be arrested for being pregnant. I am sure there is some sort of kangaroo court arraignment that either has happened or is going to happen. Get some lawyers together to go see her." Coffee looks up at Yoda who appears to be near tears. "I'd take Yoda. He's done a good thing here, Willem. It was quick thinking and brave to leave his wife to the unknown and jump off a sinking ship not knowing if or when he would be fished out of the drink. That militia would have separated them and made this much harder... hell, you might not have known even where your daughter is if not for Yoda here. You should be proud of your son in law and your daughter should be very happy to see him."

"You still have a runway on that island of yours?" Willem asks through Jimmy the Robot.

"I do. Thirty-two hundred feet north to south." Coffee answers. "You are sending your jet?"

"I am. Probably first thing tomorrow morning." Jimmy the Robot says for Willem.

"We need to go right now!" Wendy exclaims.

Jimmy the Robot is heard sighing before Willem gives him some more words. "Dear... We need to plan this. I believe we have the right people to help us out, here at the house, right now.  Vert fortuitous that our old friends are here."

"Keep in touch." Weddington Coffee ends the call with the Williams. He looks up at Yoda. "I have a bedroom for you. Also, I have some dry clothes that will fit you exactly."

Chapter 36
Let's talk about what happened over the past twenty years. Surely, we all
agree?
Williams house Someplace in America
Home of the Free(ish) Land of the Brave(ish)


*Millie and I had gone back out to the... Sitting room? Drawing room? Parlor?
I have no idea what people as wealthy as Willem and Wendy call things. Conrad looks
at me with a raised eyebrow. I shrug as if to say, 'It is what it is.' I sit on one of the
chairs. Since no one is talking, I ask what I know is no simple question.*

"How did things get so fucked up?"

There is silence.

It's Conrad that speaks first.

"The election of 2024." He answers. "It messed everything up.
First, the Orange Jesus wouldn't debate. Then he did... and that was disaster
for the other side. As such, there were really no debates between the
candidates in the primaries and no real debate in the general election. The
results were queered by the media and that's when distrust in the
government really started to expand. It got bad, really quick. After that
election, the citizenry lost interest all together in how things were being run.
Basically, we went from being the powerful USA to being run like a banana
republic in a very short amount of time."

Marmalade Julius claps his hands. "That's bullshit. You liberals
want to blame the Trumpster for everything. He has little to do with where
we are today."

"I hardly think I am liberal, Juice." Conrad says with that bright
white tooth showing grin.

Father Henry Thyme cracks a smile. "If we are looking for a place to put blame, I think you would have to go back to Clinton fucking that intern in the Oval Office and then lying about it. That's when things started to go downhill. Then we went to war in the Middle East for like thirty years."

"He just diddled that girl with his cigar." Conrad cracks. "And then jizzed all over her blue dress. No sex whatsoever!"

"And then President Clinton *lied* to the American people about it. What were you? Like two years old then?" Elizabeth Eaton asks Conrad with a poke in the ribs. I see that she is smiling.

"Na. Six or seven, I think." Conrad smiles. "Old enough to know what was being talked about."

"The Clinton thing may have started the extreme rancor between the parties." Elizabeth Eaton starts. "But the modern issues really started when trust in the government deteriorated after the election in 2020. She points at Marmalade. "I'm not a liberal either, really. If your guy... The Trumpster Fire, would have accepted the results of the election in 2020, we would only have half the problems we have now."

*"My guy?"* Marmalade scoffs. "He wasn't just *my* guy. Seventy-Five Million People voted for the man in the 2020 election.  Probably even more in 2024. What did he do that you find so reprehensible? He only wanted the best for the country... all the country. Not just the rich fuckers. You know... Like *everyone* in this room."

"In 2020, it was just short of seventy-four million people, and he lost the election by over seven million votes to President Biden." Elizabeth says calmly. "Here it is, twenty plus years later and we are still talking about it."

I point at Hank. "Not everyone is wealthy. Father Thyme there took a vow of poverty. And... I am not sure what happened to my wealth or my debt. I suspect they canceled each other out."

Hank shakes his head. "Nah... I'm a straight, mainline priest. Didn't join any of those crazy religious orders where you sleep on a cold rock and drink warm beer. My priest buddies and me... we are alright with money. No vows of poverty."

Marmalade rolls his eyes. "He's just part of the kiddie fucker crew now. That's all."

"Juice!" Paal Tan exclaims.

Hank waves his hand dismissively. "It's ok, Paal. The church didn't exactly handle things right with the sex abuse scandal. It's been almost forty years, and the abuse allegations stick with the church like a glue trap to a mouse." He looks at me. "Just like the mouse, all we can do is piss all over ourselves and wait to die. What are you getting at, Justin?"

I look over at Millie. She has a neutral look on her face. "I go into a coma for twenty years. I remember the acrimony after the election of 2020... the insurrection at the capitol... but we should have gotten over all that. Like Elizabeth said, it's been over twenty years. Instead, it appears the Supreme Court gutted women's rights in a single ruling that may have been technically correct, but the legislative action... or inaction, as it was, after the decision has been devastating. The government isn't offering protections for the people that we once counted on. The EPA is largely gone. Health and Human Services... gutted. The department of education... I am not sure that there even is one. The country seems to have gotten in the habit of electing idiots to the office of president and so far as I can tell, the population is mostly only educated to about a second-grade level." I look around the room and try to smile to lighten the heavy mood I seemed to have unwrapped. "And most disturbing, unless they are using Conrad's toys... people aren't having sex anymore."

"That remark about education may be an insult to second graders everywhere else in the rest of the world." Hank cracks.

Conrad shrugs. "My business does provide products that are useful to people."

"People are having sex." Marmalade Julius protests. "I can assure you..."

Paal shakes his head slowly. I see how Paal looks at Marmalade. These two are more than friends. "What are you thinking Paal?" I ask. "Marmalade is referring to our church, where sex has become part of the Bible study. But... not all kinds of sex are accepted there." Paal answers.

"What church is that?" I ask with genuine curiosity. "If actual sex would have been part of bible study, I would have been significantly more interested in church."

"Christians in Pursuit of the Scoundrel Pontius Pilate." Paal answers. Marmalade scowls at him.  I feel Millie tense beside me.

"How long have you two been together?" I ask. I would swear that the temperature in the room dropped twenty degrees after the words left my mouth.

"About ten years." Paal says with an easy smile. "We are trying to decide what to do about the church, still."

"Juice, did you get the back tattoo?" Hank asks Marmalade. The former NFL running back and rapper freezes before answering. "To be a full and accepted member of the church, you have to."

*Marmalade is lying about something. I am not sure what, because clearly, I don't understand this church thing. The rest of the group seems to harbor a diminished view of Marmalade Julius. Is it because he is gay? This seems unlikely. It's 2042 and outside of the Eaton woman, we all grew up with homosexuality being accepted. It must be Marmalade's involvement with this church.*

Elizabeth Eaton clears her throat. "The issues in the United States didn't start with one thing. It's always been a country that is divided by ideas." She grimaces. "But, after 2020, we no longer talked about the *merit* of any particular set of ideas. We only talked about one or the other side's viewpoint. Politics became a sport with two distinct sides, like that football you all use to play. Even simple policy discussions, like how to handle immigration, became flash points for angry hostilities. Soon, people just stopped talking about the issues. Universal income probably did not help. The United States lost its competitive edge after that was instituted, for sure. We don't innovate anything anymore." She gestures around the room. "No offense to our hosts, but product liability lawyers didn't help things out either... even though I do believe that people need adequate protection from companies that sell things." She looks over at Conrad. "I mean, how would you feel if one of your... devices... ripped someone's body part off?"

Conrad grins. "The Norma did, once. We did get sued. Turns out the guy had tinkered with the device to give a tighter fit. He guessed wrong on the adjustment. Really, really, wrong. Wendy defended PPP in that case."

"Well, the government went downhill when it stopped being in the business of protecting its citizens. *We the people* are the government. *We the people* don't trust the government." Elizabeth sighs. "How can those two statements both be true?"

The conversation is interrupted by Jimmy the Robot pushing Willem Williams into the room. A tearful Wendy Williams follows. "Friends." Jimmy the Robot says for Willem. "I am thankful you are all here."

"Our daughter is in trouble." Wendy sobs.

I look over at Millie who grabs my hand and squeezes it.

*Now we are going to find out why we are here.*

Chapter 37
Robots can have sex and kill people.
Monkey Island, Louisiana USA
Land of the Free(ish) Home of the Brave(ish)


Yoda Storm Trooper Williams is sleeping the sleep of the dead when he subconsciously feels a light hand stroking his naked chest.

"Wakey, wakey." Says a soft feminine voice. "Wanna have some fun?"

"Huh?" Yoda says groggily. "Esther?"

"Esther doesn't do things like what I am going to do to you. *Nothing* does things like what I am going to do to you. *I am special.*" The voice says. The hand goes lower.

"I don't understand..." Yoda reaches for a light. His hand is slapped away. "Ow!" Yoda says. "Who are you?"

"My name is Cozbi." The Robot coos. "I would like to have some fun. Would you like to have some fun?"

"No?" Yoda answers as he tries to scoot away from the Robot.

"Yes! Yes, you do!" The Robot lunges at him. Yoda's raw athleticism allows him to escape. "I *want* to have *fun* with you!" The Robot says in a seductive voice that does not at all match its aggressive actions.
"Weddington!" Yoda yells. "Weddington Coffee!" Yoda yells louder. He pops up and moves quickly away from the Robot to a switch that turns the lamp on the other side of the bed on. Cozbi the Robot is wearing a tiny set of panties and a shear brazier that leaves little to the imagination. "You need to go away!" Yoda says to the Robot. Her face is

beautiful. High cheekbones. Rounded eyes. Pouty lips. Her brown hair frames the features perfectly. "Weddington!" Yoda calls out. He hears commotion from outside his bedroom. Coffee comes into the room on the ground, using his massive arms to move quickly across the floor.

Cozbi the Robot has braced herself on the bed and is reaching towards Yoda's neck threateningly with her right hand when Coffee yells out. "Cozbi, you beautiful bitch! Crash!"

Just as the Robot has lunged forward, grasping Yoda's neck with its manicured nail tipped fingers, it collapses onto the bed.

Coffee comes over to the king-sized bed and hoists himself up on it. "Sorry about that. I forgot to tell her that you were staying with us tonight." "What *is* she?" Yoda asks.

Weddington Coffee shrugs. "She is... a lot of things. At night, she provides security for my place here. Cozbi can cook and clean. She knows how to supervise the lessor Robots. Also, she is my *companion.*"

"Companion?" Yoda asks as he looks at the Robot who looks more like a model or a centerfold than a security guard. "Oh! Companion!" He looks at Coffee wide eyed. "Sex with Robots is illegal!"

*Sex with Robots in the United States and its remaining territories was made illegal by congressional law in 2035 around the same time that contraception was banned completely.*

Coffee looks around with a conspiratorial grin. "Who said anything about sex? I said *companion.* You know why Robot Sex was made illegal? Because once you go circuit board, flesh and blood will be a bore." He rolls Cozbi onto her back. He marvels at the sight. "She is just perfect. She doesn't judge me. She doesn't care that I am missing two legs and more than a few brain cells and she doesn't mind living here on this mosquito and alligator infested island." The breasts are firm and don't move more than just a little jiggle. "Want to touch them? Go ahead!" Coffee gives each breast a hearty squeeze. I am proud of how they came out!" He points at the Robot woman. "And she can kill a man with her bare hands! Which, is what she was about to do to you!"

Yoda looks at the Robot's very human and very attractive body. He had been wondering if Cozbi the Robot was trying to get him to fuck it or kill him. Coffee had confirmed the latter. "Nah... I'm good. How many Robots have you made?"

"Esther and Cozbi are the only two operating bots I have right now. As I say, I lost a few." Coffee says. "Alphabetically, I call them after names in the Bible. Gomer is the next female Robot I am making. Cozbi needs a little competition."

"No male Robots?"

"I have just one. Felix is under development." Coffee quickly changes the subject. "Willem sent a message a few hours ago. The jet will be here at 0600 to pick you up. Then it's off to Galveston for you."

Chapter 38
Now we know. Millie gets outed. Big Prayers. Bigger Plans.
Williams house Someplace in America
Home of the Free(ish) Land of the Brave(ish)


*Through tears, Wendy Williams repeated to us what her son in law, Yoda had told her. The Williams's daughter Katherine, known as Kitty, is pregnant. The baby is dead in utero. Texas makes expectant mothers wait until a delivery date to 'have' the baby. To do otherwise would be considered an abortion. Kitty and her husband tried to get to an offshore French Hospital boat to get proper medical care. (I want so badly to ask the group if they think this a fucking ordinary situation... some other country providing medical care on a ship to American citizens because America won't.) Things sort of go to shit at the end of the conversation when Elizabeth Eaton looks square at Millie and says...*

"It's a damn good thing we have an experienced obstetrician here."

"Ah, that's sweet dear. I haven't practiced for almost twenty years. Also, I mostly did in-vitro work when I was a practicing doctor." Conrad says. "Never delivered any babies outside of a couple at the beginning of residency."

Elizabeth shakes her head and pats his hand. "I am sure you were a good doctor, Conrad. *Now you make sex toys.* And that's a nice story." She points in the direction of me and Millie. "I mean her."

I look at Millie. Her face is sort of the color of a pound and half lobster after the fifteen-minute jacuzzi. I start to protest. "Elizabeth, I am not sure..."
Elizabeth Eaton shakes her head. "I can get us into the facility to see Katherine Williams. I am not sure I can get her out so she can get medical care... but we can bring the medical care to her. We are in the

presence of a brave woman. A genuine American hero. I'd like to introduce all of you to Dr. Mildred Cockburn."

I grab Millie's hand and squeeze tight as I look at the group. "Now might not be the best time…"

"Millie Cockburn is a board-certified obstetrician that spent a portion of her life in a Texas Penitentiary for assisting a woman who desperately needed it, with an abortion. We couldn't ask for better help. It makes me think that there might indeed be a higher power, and *she* is at work here."

Lady, you have no idea. I think to myself.

*"This is why we are here, Justin. It's why we came back."* Millie says in a whisper. She looks at Eaton. "I caught you looking at me Elizabeth. I figured you knew who I was."

"Will you help out, Dr. Cockburn?" Elizabeth asks. "We need to help Wendy and Willem's daughter."

"Justin and I will help." Millie says firmly before glancing at Conrad. "I don't think you should come, Conrad. There will probably be… consequences."

Elizabeth nods at Millie's comment before looking over at the Williamses. "Put Millie Ratchet and Justin Thyme on your payroll. Make them attorneys under your firm. My daughter and Conrad's son, as well. We are going to need all the help we can get."

I shake my head. "I don't understand."
"You can become an attorney in the United States now by two different ways. Take a six week to six-month course of study or study under a licensed lawyer. Most people do the six weeks of course work because it is faster." Elizabeth Eaton makes air quotes. "Willem and Wendy here have *tutored* you two for the last six months. You will go into the facility in Texas as lawyers."

*"We may go in as lawyers, we will come out in handcuffs."* Millie mutters under her breath so only I can hear.

"Fred Peterson and my daughter Anne Margret have both passed their law school examinations and the bar exam, such that it is now. They can do research for us up here and be on call if we need them down there." Elizabeth Eaton stands. "I'd like to take the priest with us." She looks at Hank. "If he is willing to go."

"What would I do?" Hank asks. "I'm particularly good with counseling people not to get married, drinking scotch and diluting the sacramental wine for my own selfish purposes."

Elizabeth Eaton smiles. It's not a happy, gosh, I am glad to know you smile. It's a frightening smile. The kind an owl would make before pouncing on the rabbit. If owls could smile. I even see Conrad flinch when he sees it. "They will never suspect that we are going to deliver that baby in the fashion that we are if a Catholic priest is present."

"The baby is dead, for sure?" Hank asks.

Wendy Williams nods tearfully. "Yoda said so."

"Then I will baptize the baby and give it last rights." Father Henry Thyme says.
"We aren't Catholic." Jimmy the Robot says for Willem. "We aren't anything."

"The baby will be waiting for you in heaven until you make the decision to go the right direction." Hank says with a smile.

Wendy leaves the room. She comes back in with what I guess are a couple of old-fashioned Cellular phones. Edith the Robot follows her with a basket full of clothes. "I figure that Millie and Justin could use some clothes. I grabbed some of Willem's suits for Justin and my stuff for Millie. Edith will do the alterations to make sure that it fits."

"You are giving him my Canali Suits?" Jimmy the Robot exclaims for Willem.

"All you have is Canali suits, Willem! And none of them fit you!" Wendy answers.

"Well, they aren't going to fit Justin's scarecrow like frame either!" Jimmy the Robot exclaims and then laughs. "I have scheduled the jet to take you to pick up Yoda. Then take you to Galveston, Texas. The detainment facility is there." Jimmy the Robot says. "We will get the paperwork in order that shows Millie and Justin as attorneys for Williams and Williams."

"I am already registered as an attorney in Texas. I will call the facility and let them know we are coming." Elizabeth says. "We will do our best to set your daughter free."

Millie walks over to Elizabeth. I follow along slowly.

"Willem, give Justin one of your canes. That boy moves like he's eighty years old." Conrad says.
"I know." Jimmy the Robot says for Willem. "I am jealous of him."

"Ms. Eaton." Millie says in a near whisper. "I need some things. I am guessing that you may have a source for what I want."

"Call me Elizabeth." She says. "Surgical kit?"

Millie nods. "We will want to do a spinal tap. Get me three compounded dosages of Sufentanil and Fentanyl. It comes in a three pack."

"Get two packs." I say. Both women look at me. "We may lose one. Be prepared."

After a slow, confused nod, Millie continues. "And I need some Oxytocin. Two vials, please."

"Make it four." I add.

Elizabeth Eaton commits the list to memory.

"It might be best if the Oxytocin is labeled saline or insulin... something benign. It is probably illegal now in Texas." Millie says, "Unless the kids are using it to get off in the clubs now... maybe we can get it at a convenience store."

Elizabeth Eaton laughs. "Millie, *you* are illegal in Texas. But I get the point."

"What do you need us to do?" Marmalade asks. I am happy to see Paal standing at Juice's side with his hand on his shoulder.

"You were really a big-time rapper?" I ask. "Like you had a following... people who would listen to you if you started talking?" Paal, not Marmalade nods in response, which makes me think they have been a couple for quite a while. "Marmalade has *quite* a following." He says happily.

"I'm not sure how social media works now... but I have sort of figured out that the only news being shown is about achieving orgasm in some fucked up way or doing something stupid. Can you get the word out about this French Hospital Ship?" I look expectantly at Paal. It's Marmalade that answers.

"Things haven't been so good since you went away, Justin." Marmalade frowns. "Maybe Conrad's girl is right... we all got wrapped up in defending stupid ideas... not listening to what others say. Everybody be doing some crazy shit. I guess it's time to come correct, huh?"

"Yeah." I answer. "It's the fourth quarter and it looks to me like we are down by a whole lot, brother. What are we going to do?"

"We should probably think about kicking some ass." Marmalade smiles. The gold caps on his front teeth sparkle. "Let me think of some things we can do to help things. Paal and I got some friends in the information business. We will get the details on that hospital ship and get something going." He walks over to Willem and puts his hand on the stricken man's shoulder. "Come on in, ya' all. Let's say a prayer."

*Prayer? A together prayer? This is not something we would have done in our youth.* I look at Millie and shrug before hesitantly putting my hand on Willem. With the other, I pull Millie close to me. Hank walks over and puts his hand on Marmalade's shoulder. Elizabeth and Conrad come in close. Wendy kneels by her husband's right side. Paal puts himself close to Marmalade's muscular form.

`Marmalade lifts a palm towards the ceiling and closes his eyes before starting to speak. His baritone voice echoes through the room. I swear I can feel that voice in my chest.

*My heavenly Father, Our souls ache as we face this new challenge, and our hearts are heavy with the pain for our loved ones. Some of us feel distant from You. Others are unsure of who You are. And some are struggling to trust in Your goodness and plans for our lives. Lord, we come to You humbly, asking for Your presence to fill our lives. Breathe new life into our hearts, reigniting the embers of hope and faith within us. We need You, God, to be victorious in our hearts so we can experience the fullness of Your love and the strength that comes from trusting You, God. You are our rock and refuge, God. You have called us to be more than conquerors, and today we choose to believe that truth by faith. We declare Your victories, even when we can't see the way forward. Lead us, Lord, through the uncertainty and into Your light, for only You can guide us.Let us rest in You, surrendering the battle of faith in our hearts into Your hands. With You, there is triumph, and we trust You completely. In Jesus' name, Amen.*

"Amen." Says Father Henry Thyme. "Very nice, Juice."

"Amen." Says Willem through Jimmy the Robot. "Thank you, Marmalade."

"What did you say that you did with that church?" I ask. "Christians chasing a Scoundrel..."

Paal turns and corrects me. *"Christians in Pursuit of the Scoundrel Pontius Pilate.* Marmalade was an elder. He was very important! He has his own followers." The Thai man whispers.

*I have no idea what that means.*

The group breaks up. Willem is pushed away by Jimmy. Marmalade and Hank talk about something. Making up new prayers, I suppose... what else do religious people talk about? Elizabeth and Millie talk together. I motion to Paal, and he walks over to me. Conrad comes over. "Thank you Paal for being here. I am really glad you guys are here." He nods in thanks as I pat the man on the shoulder.

Conrad watches him walk off before turning to me. "They are all batshit crazy... that church Pontius Pilate... whatever it is called. I could tell you stories. I would bet Juice can tell us some too."

"We never were believers, Conrad. I was always sort of envious of people who are." I say, looking him in the eyes. "Look... neither Millie nor I should be here. I mean medically, you know. I know that for absolute certain." I shake my head. "I think we are zombies, Conrad. Both of us."

Conrad rubs my shoulder and shakes his head. He looks at me with a little bit of an expression of wonderment. "Dude, I don't know about Millie. But I do know for certain about you, Justin Thyme. I read your charts every time I went to visit you. *You died a very long time ago.*"

Chapter 39
Judge this. Not rosy in Texas
Texas Criminal Justice Hospital Facility Galveston, Texas
Still a part of the United States of America
Home of the Free(ish) Land of the Brave(ish)


"Let's go ladies. High step it!" The male prison guard yells out to the line of eight women trudging slowly down the pale green hallway.

Kitty Williams walks behind the second to last person in line. Her all-white prison uniform is too small. The pants legs end just below her knee. The top, a flimsy long sleeve thing that has the silhouette of a baby screen printed on the front and a bright red letter 'A' screen printed on the back stretches tight over her swollen belly and breasts. When she had been taken off the lifeboat by the Militia men, she had jabbed one of the three needles of morphine in her arm. When the militia boat docked in Galveston, she injected herself with the other two needles. When she came to, she was wearing the Texas Prison uniform given to women accused of trying to abort a pregnancy.

A black wooden night stick comes down in front of her.

A white face bracketed by a dark beard comes within inches of hers. The man's breath smells something awful, and his bottom teeth are blackened. "Yer a purdy one... I think I might want ta get ta now ya better. I ain't had dark meat as fine as you for a long while." The stick taps gently on her left nipple poking through the thin cloth of the prison uniform. The man sniffs in exaggerated fashion. "Maybe get ya showered up first. Ya kinda stink."
Kitty glowers at the man. The morphine is wearing off and she can feel the beginnings of the cramps returning. "Fuck you." Defiant, despite the effects of the morphine and the oncoming cramps, Kitty keeps her eyes trained on the man.

"Yeah... ya know exactly what I wanna do." The jailer lowers the stick. "Hurry ya little ass up, darkie."

The line is led down more corridors to a makeshift courtroom. Three tables are set in the front of the room. Two Texas flags bracket the head table. Three rows of chairs sit behind the tables. The women are told to sit in the chairs. Kitty looks at her fellow inmates. Of the eight in this group, four are sobbing. One stares straight ahead, almost catatonic. Two seem to in some stage of sleep. *And then there is me.* Even in her morphine induced haze, Kitty knows she is at a criminal court arraignment. She hadn't studied much criminal law at Michigan, but everyone had to take a few weeks of the subject.

Two suit wearing men come to the two tables facing the front of the room. They remain standing as a man wearing a long black robe walks into the court room. One of the jailers' shouts. "All Rise!"

Kitty struggles to her feet, along with the four sobbing women. The catatonic woman and two sleeping women stay in their chairs.

"Bailiff, get those women up. I demand respect in this courtroom!" The judge bellows. A cramp passes though Kitty and she doubles over.

"Number 8! Stand up straight!" One of the jailers, apparently also acting as court room bailiff shouts.

*Apparently, I am number 8.* Kitty thinks as she starts the breathing exercises taught to her by Dr. Hole In One. She puts a finger in the air and takes a deep breath, willing the pain to go away.

"That's one credit against you, Number 8!" The jailer yells as he walks to the three unresponsive women.

"They are all out, your honor." Another Jailer comes over and pokes the woman who is staring straight ahead with her eyes open. "This one is awake... She is just... I don't know your honor... she just goofy!"

"I charge them all with contempt!" The judge announces. He bangs on the table with his gavel. *"Contempt!"* He sits down. "This is a serious matter, and the accused will act appropriately.

Kitty turns her head and looks at the woman whose unfocused eyes stare straight ahead. Her fingers have turned a blueish color, and her pale skin has taken on a grayish hue. "You should check for a pulse." She says to the nearest jailer.

"Prisoners do not speak unless spoken to!" The jailer shouts at Kitty. "Number 8 is talking out of turn, your honor."

Kitty shakes her head and tries hard not to think about the wave of pain that is building in her midsection. "Hey! Gray suit on the left side. Are you, our representation?"

The man at the left table turns with a surprised expression. "Yeah. I'm yoose female's defense lawyer."

"Yeah..." Kitty takes a deep breath and closes her eyes, steeling herself for the crescendo of pain. "I... I... Think that Number 6 there is having a medical emergency."

"Are you a doctor?" The lawyer asks.
Kitty starts breathing like Dr. Hole in One had instructed her to. Breathe in. Count to four. Breath out. Count to four. Rest for four. Breath in. Count to four. "No. I am not."

"Keep your uneducated opinions to yourself then. That's my advice." The lawyer says, turning back to the judge.

"Hey, this woman has no pulse." The Jailer says, holding his hand on number 6's throat. "I think she might be dead!"

"I'm still charging her with contempt!" The judge hits the table with his gavel. "Get her and those other two non-competent bitches out of here so we can begin these proceedings!"

Kitty keeps her eyes closed as Robot orderlies come and take the deceased women and the two sleeping women from the room. She concentrates on her breathing and thinks about the happiest things she can remember.

Chapter 40
Debating with the Priest.
The Government would like your sperm.
Someplace in the Air Above the United States of America
Land of the Free(ish) Home of the Brave(ish)


The law firm Williams and Williams has a nice jet. I had never been on a private aircraft. Let alone one with a Robot butler. The three-hour flight to Monkey Island, Louisiana was quite smooth.

Millie sat next to me and reviewed the surgical procedure she would be completing for Katherine Williams on an electronic tablet.

Elizabeth Eaton sat in the front of the plane reviewing her options and talking to her daughter Anne Margret about research that needed to be completed. Based on what I could overhear, the lawyers were preparing for Millie and me to be arrested.

Hank sits across from me. About fifteen minutes into the flight, he leaned over and grabbed my knee. "I want to tell you what I think... so there are no misunderstandings later."

I shrug. "Ok?"

"Abortion is no good, Justin. It is a grave moral and social wrong."

I stare at the floor in thought before responding. I had spent some time doing research so I could have this very conversation. "Always? You don't have room in your heart to make allowances for different situations? Rape? Incest... which is really the same thing as rape? How about cases where the fetus is medically unviable? Cases where continuing the pregnancy may irreparably harm or extinguish the life of the mother?"

"The life of the unborn is no different than the life of a fully formed human. It has the same rights as you and me." Father Henry Thyme starts.

I chuckle. "Hank, I have never been fully formed."

"All human beings are called to respect human life at all stages of life and scientists have agreed, life begins at conception. It is our duty to ensure a society where crimes of violence are; as far as possible, prevented. Abortion is the direct killing of an innocent human being - a violation of the rights of the youngest members of our society. It is not just a matter of personal choice, religious opinion or women's rights, but a basic human right and a social justice issue."

"Is that your position as a Priest and a member of the Catholic Church?" I ask.

Hank nods. His face very serious.

"Do you believe that your right to practice Catholicism is guaranteed as an empirical right, granted to all human beings?" I ask.

Hank nods. "Of course."

"So, you would also agree that you have the right to not be Catholic?" I ask.

The Priest taps on his arm rest. "Sure. I guess that would have to be the case."
"As a citizen of the United States of America, such that it is still today, do you believe that you have the right to express yourself in the fashion you see fit?"

"That is our first amendment right. The most important right, really." Hank answers.

"Yes. Americans have the obligation to determine for themselves what is and what is not a social justice issue." I motion with my hand. "Elizabeth up there may think that feeding starving children is a tremendous social justice issue. You may decide that helping the homeless population is a greater, more important social justice issue." I say.

Hank furrows his brow. I continue.

"You are a Catholic priest. I assume by nature of that fact that you are celibate and not currently participating in procreation."

Hank nods. "Let's assume that."

"Can the government demand that you impregnate Millie here?" I ask. "Let's say that the government decides it is in the best interest of the state, for you to impregnate Millie."

Millie looks up. "Justin, what are you *talking* about?"

I pat her leg. "Don't worry about it. I think I just had an idea."

"I'll alert the media." Millie says, returning her attention to the electronic pad.

"Don't bother. The media seems to have disappeared, years ago." I turn back to Hank. "Father Thyme... you are a healthy male that can still produce sperm, and despite the vows you have taken to the contrary, that sperm can be used to impregnate a woman. Can the government demand that you impregnate my friend Millie, here."

"No one is impregnating me, Justin." Millie growls. "Not happening. Ever. That time has passed. And..." She looks over at Hank with a sharp shake of her head. "No. Not happening."

Hank glares at me. "No. The government could not tell me to do that."

"Why?"

"It's my body. I have made the choice, I suppose, to not procreate."
His face wrinkles. "That's an old argument and one that isn't intellectually
sound. Women don't need to have sex. And neither do men."

I smile. "So far as I can tell, in today's United States of America,
people are not having sex. If that was the point of banning abortion and
birth control, it was a success." I point at his crotch. "It might be
considered an invasive demand to make you impregnate another human
you did not want to impregnate. Sort of an unreasonable seizure of your
*assets*, as it were."

"Let's agree to disagree on that point." Hank says.

"I am prepared to do that on all points, cousin. We are just talking."
I smile. "Do you think that having consensual sex with another person is a
legal issue?" I continue my probing line of questioning. I don't care if Hank
is getting uncomfortable. He started the conversation, after all.
"It can be a legal issue... if such activity results in a pregnancy."
Hank replies.

"But the use of birth control has been sharply controlled. So far as I
know, birth control is illegal now in the United States. How can we both
control access to birth control and abortion and expect women to
participate freely in sexual relations with men?"

"Women shouldn't have sex unless they are prepared to conceive a
child and carry that child to term." Hank says, nodding his head.

"Then you do agree it is the woman's choice to have sex."

"Of course." Hank says.

"If she is forced to have sex through an act of rape or incest, should
she also be forced to conceive a child?"

Hank's brow furrows. "She wouldn't be *forced* to conceive a child because she wasn't *forced* to have sex." He raises his empty scotch glass in the air. The Butler Robot brings another glass of brown liquor to him.

"Let's say that she did not have the choice, Hank." I pat his arm. "Let's say that the woman is raped and instead of going to her doctor, she goes to her grandmother who tells her to eat the root of the wormwood plant. She does and has a miscarriage. Have both women committed a crime?"

Hank sighs. "Under the law, yes... and committing a crime when no one other than the criminal knows that a crime has been committed is still committing a crime... it's a crime even if the person committing the crime doesn't realize the action is illegal. In that example, the grandmother also committed a crime."

"And... it's a mortal sin in the Catholic Church. One the woman would need to confess to obtain absolution?"

"Of course." Hank says. "As I said, Abortion is the direct killing of an innocent human being."

"In this, case, conceived by sin."

"Rape is not a mortal sin." Hank says. "Grave? Yes. Mortal, no."

I shake my head. "Some other time, we can talk about the difference between grave sins and mortal sins. What if the girl is Jewish? She has no obligation then to obtain a confession to avoid a mortal sin, since one would not obviously exist for her, but does she have the obligation to carry a baby conceived by rape to term?" I ask. "What matters in Talmudic Law is the woman's life and health, both physical and mental. In fact, the Old Testament is clear on the matter. Exodus twenty-one, verses twenty-two through twenty-five say that if a man accidentally hits a woman and she dies, the offender must be put to death — *the penalty shall be life for life*. But it also says that if the man accidentally hits the woman and she miscarries, he must pay a fine to her husband. If the fetus were seen as a full human being, the punishment would again be execution, not mere financial compensation."

"Under the current law of the United States of America, she is required to carry the baby to term." Hank shifts uncomfortably in his seat. "When did you become a Jew?" He asks irritably.

I ignore his irritable comment and continue. "So... today, only Catholic and like-minded people have their first amendment rights intact in the United States." I purse my lips. "To answer your question, I became Jewish last night. Just after I became a Lawyer. Jimmy the Robot helped with the circumcision."

"He was already circumcised." Millie says from beside me.

I smile at Hank. "I have been in a coma for the last twenty years. Lots of things have changed. Cars are all electric. Conrad makes dildos and you stopped fucking everything that moves and became a priest. Tell me... with all the changes that have happened, women must be compensated for carrying a child to term... How much does the government compensate women for the use of their wombs for the forty weeks or so they are pregnant?"

"I didn't fuck... *everything* that moved." Hank holds his empty glass up to the Robot. "I mean... I was sexually active back then for sure..."

"When you came to my house, the cat would hide, Hank." I say pointedly. "How much? How much compensation do women get who become pregnant, and are forced to carry a child to term?"

"Easy, Justin." I hear Millie say.  I must sound excited.

Hank shakes his head. "I don't understand what you are asking. Women aren't paid by the government to be pregnant."

"The Third Amendment in the Constitution says that private property shall not be taken for public use without compensation." I pause.

"If a woman is compelled by public law to carry a baby to term, she is giving up her private property to the satisfy the state's desire for her to have the baby. She should be compensated."

"I don't think you are using that constitutional amendment correctly." Hank says. The Robot drops a full glass of scotch off to the Priest.

"Can I take your sperm and give it to Millie?" I ask.

"Let's be clear about this. *I* don't want *his* sperm." Millie says from beside me.

"No." Hank answers my question.

"But I may be able to if you are compensated and it's the law?"

"I suppose so. Maybe?" Hank concedes. "But again, I don't want my sperm used for that purpose."

"You didn't have sex with her Hank, she was just given the sperm that you were required by law to provide."

"Still a big *no*." Millie says.

"I don't know." Hank says. "I think you might be forcing me to give up my property. Isn't that protected by the constitution?  Like you said?"

Satisfied that I got the right answer, I change the direction of my argument. "Let's say that the woman who is raped goes to her doctor. How does that information become public?" I point at the empty glass that had held scotch. "You have had five of those and we haven't been on this plane for more than ninety minutes. Should your alcohol consumption be public knowledge?"

Hank scowls. "No... and this conversation is stressing me out. Shit, you were in a coma for twenty years. I was thinking that I would have my intellectual way with you!"

"So, why should a woman's medical condition be made public record in any situation? Why wouldn't she maintain the same expectations to privacy when it comes to her health as you maintain when it comes to yours?" I ask.

"That's what *Roe vs. Wade* was about, supposably." Hank says. "Privacy. But *Dobbs* changed that."

"Privacy is what the written decision on *Roe* should have been about. But, when Justice Blackmun wrote the decision, he made it about abortion." I reach over and poke Hank. "Justice Alito made the same mistake when he wrote the majority opinion on *Dobbs*. It was framed as a state's rights issue... but the majority opinion is mostly about abortion. The Supreme Court, as it so often has, took a single issue from a complex case and made it the law of the land.

"Well, the court did give the rights to the states in *Dobbs*. Then representatives that were voted into congress made abortion illegal across the whole country. That's the way it should be." Hank says with an authoritative tone indicating to me that he believes in his heart that because the majority of a nine-justice court agreed with whatever his opinion might be, it must be the correct decision.

I nod. "Sure. In a fair, well run and efficient society that has a fully functioning population and political process, you are correct. Issues that are not specifically covered by the constitution should be completely left up to the states or to congressional laws." I wink at Hank. "But here we are... you and I have already deduced that the ban on abortion and, although we haven't talked about it much; birth control, violate constitutional rights. Specifically, the first amendment, third amendment and the fifth amendment... and now let's talk about the fourteenth amendment.

"My cousin Justin, the Jewish *Constitutional* Lawyer." Hank mutters.

"Surprisingly, Justin is doing a pretty good job." Elizabeth Eaton calls out from the front of the plane. "I have been taking notes."

"Privacy." I say.

"Privacy." Hank repeats solemnly.

I smile. *"Griswold v. Connecticut, 1965...* held that the right to privacy included the right for married couples to use contraceptives. In *Griswold,* the court explained that the guarantees in the Bill of Rights have *penumbras,* or somewhat blurred, but still apparently present, extensions, which must be read as creating "zones of privacy", such as the First Amendment right of association, the Third Amendment prohibition against quartering soldiers in a home, the Fourth Amendment right to be secure in one's person, house, documents and such, plus the Fifth Amendment right to not surrender anything to one's detriment, and the Ninth Amendment right to not deny or disparage any right retained by the people."

"How are you going to flog me with this idea?" Hank asks gloomily. "You know, I think you might be taking this lawyer thing too seriously."

"The girl who has become pregnant through rape has an expectation of privacy when she goes to see her doctor. Just like you have an expectation to privacy when you go and see your doctor. You may have some condition where it is important for the doc to know that you occasionally down a half of liter of scotch in one short airplane ride. You have an expectation that the information that you provide to the doctor about your drinking does not become public. Why wouldn't the girl who is pregnant have the same expectation?" I ask.

"Maybe she should?" Hank sips the scotch nervously.

"I don't give a shit how much you drink, Hank." I say with a forced smile. "Here is what I do care about... The fourteenth amendment says, *No State shall make or enforce any law which shall abridge the privileges or immunities of citizens of the United States; nor shall any State deprive any person of life, liberty, or property, without due process of law; nor deny to any person within its jurisdiction the equal protection of the laws.* Hank, *Roe* was a mistake. Not in how it was decided *but in the way the majority decision was written. Dobbs* was a mistake in how it was brought... the case never should have been in front of the court. Conservatives kept pushing it back on the docket until the puppeteers pulling the strings on the Orange Jesus could get it in front of a conservative court. Justice Alito wrote an opinion that could have come from your *Vatican*. If the right issues get back in front of the court in the right context, the laws passed by congress will be invalidated."

"Nor shall any State deprive any person of life." Hank says. His eyes and voice clear, considering how much scotch he has consumed. "You are depriving the unborn of the right to life if you allow abortions!"

I smile gently. I have self-assumed verbal *kill shots* lined up in my mind. "Does the chicken egg in your refrigerator contain a viable chicken, Hank?"

"That egg hasn't been fertilized." Hank says. "So, no."

"What if it had. A little spot of blood is in the yoke. Is it a viable chicken? It's been fertilized."

"Of course not."

"So, we agree that there is a point of viability for a chicken. Can we also agree there is a point of viability for a human fetus?"

"Eventually, we may be able to grow a human in a Petri dish. Hell, maybe we can do it right now." Hank scoffs. "Viability should mean nothing. It's a human after conception. That is the word of God, not man."

"We can probably make a chicken in a petri dish! I'm glad you brought God and his written word into this. The Bible is woefully short on providing any guidance on abortion, don't you think?" I ask.

Hank says nothing. He looks at me blankly. I motion at his unbuttoned Roman Collar. "Christians were quick to invalidate most of the six hundred and thirteen commandments that God sent Moses back with. The books of Genesis, Exodus, Leviticus and Deuteronomy have them, but

Catholics and other Christians largely ignore them. It would not matter on the subject of abortion anyway... abortion doesn't come up in the Old Testament. What does, over and over, is how women should be treated. When the church came up with the New Testament, there was a second chance to show its congregation how God really intended to make himself clear about abortion. Jesus had some strong views of marriage and sex. He considered the Jewish divorce laws too lenient, and Catholics have certainly latched on to that over the years. Jesus was tough on the stone throwers who wanted to kill the adulteress. So far as I know, the Catholic Church has not gone against the word of the gospels and started to support the act of stoning adulteresses... in fact, adultery on its own isn't even a reason for an annulment in the Catholic Church. Catholic women have that going for and against them, I guess... Jesus was willing to heal a Jewish woman who had vaginal bleeding that had lasted twelve years... Hank, the Son of God was no shrinking flower when it came to issues facing women in his day and yet there is nothing recorded that Jesus ever said or taught anything about abortion. Neither did any of the other disparate writers whose words over time became accepted as the New Testament."

"The church has always thought of abortion as a sin." Hank says simply with a shake of his head.

"Listen Hank, I am not anti-Catholic or anti-Christian. A lot of what has happened is just a perversion of history and an assumption of beliefs. In the beginning, Christians had to distinguish themselves from both the Jews they were separating from and the paganism that probably most people wanted to practice. Pagans had orgies. Pagans accepted contraception. Pagans accepted abortion. The church had to be different. At some point, Christians and Catholics decided that sexual pleasure is some sort of evil. But there was moderation, even back then! St. Augustine declared that abortion would *only be a sin* if it was used to conceal fornication or adultery, lending to a reasonable belief that Augustine thought seriously about women's health issues. St. Thomas Aquinas declared that a *fetus first has the soul of a vegetable, then an animal soul and finally, when the body is fully developed, a rational soul.* Women's rights in the eyes of the church sort of went downhill after Aquinas... but even as late as 1917, there were exceptions by the church to allow for an abortion if the woman was young, ignorant or had conceived due to forced sex."

Hank sighs. "Those are all points. *Your* points." The priest shrugs. "But the laws of this land *outlaw* abortion."

"Laws can change." I say.

"You would have to get the right court." Hank says looking into his drink. He shakes his head. "I don't think that should or will happen. The current laws will remain as they are. As they should."
"Well." I sigh. "I guess it makes your job pretty easy."

"What do you mean?"

"People who are believers... *True Believers,* are supposed to act out of *faith.* Today, your parishioners won't have an abortion because it is the *law of the land.* In the past, Catholics might have considered religious teachings before making such a decision." I shrug. "As I see it? Your religion and its lessons are being supplanted by the state. Jesus said *Render unto Caesar the things that are Caesar's, and unto God the things that are God's.* Well, my friend. It was your job to guide your flock, and the government snatched that responsibility away. No wonder people have no use for religions like Catholicism anymore. *Caesar* does a better job. Hell, Hank... at this rate, in twenty more years, the United States of America will have a state religion. Derision will not be allowed. It will be like the Soviet Union, circa 1977." The little Robot comes forward. "We will be landing soon." It says. "I will be happy to refill your drink when we leave Monkey Island for Galveston." Hank hands it the empty glass.

"You got anything else to say that might depress me?" Hank asks. "Yeah." I lean close. "God might be a grasshopper riding on the back of a black and white cow."

"You are an asshole, Justin." Father Henry Thyme says morosely just as Millie; choking back a laugh, elbows me.

"I think God is the bear." She says in a whisper.

Chapter 41
Swoop in and pick the boy up. Those are some nice tits.
Monkey Island, Louisiana USA
Land of the Free(ish) Home of the Brave(ish)

*The plane comes in low. From the window of the small jet, it appears that we are landing in a forest of palm trees and scrub bushes. Millie is a nervous flyer. Just as she had when we took off, she grabs my hand as the wheels touch down on the ground. The plane jerks a bit, and we stop. There is a short taxi, and the little robot announces that we have made a safe landing at our first destination. It occurs to me to ask what it announces if the plane crashes. The Robot invites us to step off the plane and stretch. Hank stands and buttons his priest collar in place. I help Millie up. Elizabeth Eaton gets off the plane first. The four of us walk down the stairs that form when the door is open on the plane. I use my newly acquired cane for balance going down the stairs, which makes things a little easier and faster. A legless man in a wheelchair is pushed around the nose of the plane towards us by a beautiful woman wearing palazzo pants and only a bra for a top. Her hair blows in the breeze. A tall, athletically built man with a dark complexion follows from a considerable distance.*

"Welcome to Monkey Island!" The man in the wheelchair calls out. "My name is Weddington Coffee!" He looks around. "Is Wendy Williams with you all?"

Hank shakes his head. "Based on the situation, it was decided that it might be best to leave her at home."

"Oh." Coffee answers, clearly disappointed. The half-dressed woman walks around the wheelchair and strolls past each of us stopping at Hank. She stares at the crucifix hanging from his neck before raising her eyes to Hank's face. "What is that hanging around your neck?" She asks with a furrowed brow.

"Cozbi!" The man in the wheelchair calls out. "Cozbi, to my side, now!" I look over with a raised eyebrow at Millie who shrugs slightly and shakes her head.

"Is she... a Robot?" Elizabeth Eaton exclaims.

Weddington Coffee beams. "This is Cozbi. She absolutely is a Robot. I made her. Her sister Esther is currently doing patrols out in the gulf."
I see Elizabeth looking up and down at the thing I would have bet money was a real woman. A woman that pre-coma Justin Thyme would definitely have tried to get in the sack, but a real woman none the less.

"You named your Robot... Cozbi... as in Cozbi the concubine of Zimri?" Father Henry Thyme asks.

"That's the one!" Coffee responds enthusiastically. "She is the best I have made so far. Esther is good, but Cozbi does more and better."

"I bet." Hank says under his breath.

"Esther rescued me when I was at sea." The tall good-looking man says as he walks up. I assume this is Katherine Williams's husband and the man we are to pick up. "I didn't realize either one of them were robots." He adds.

*Wendy Williams had told us that her son in law was a good-looking guy. She undersold that fact by a power of about a thousand. She did tell us the man was about as sharp as a bowling ball. I'll reserve judgement. So far, I have learned that he didn't drown when he could have. Score a point or two on the old IQ meter for that.*
Elizabeth Eaton walks close to the Robot named Cozbi. She raises her right hand and pokes the Robot's bare, flat and very toned belly. The Robot swiftly grabs the lawyer's wrist, prompting a high-pitched squeak from the lawyer.

"Cozbi, release." Weddington Coffee calls out from his wheelchair as if telling a pet dog to out down the just retrieved tennis ball. Elizabeth's arm is dropped.

"*Scary bitch.*" I hear Yoda Storm Trooper Williams mutter. Two more points on the IQ meter for the son-in-law, I think to myself.

"That is amazing. I just wanted to see if the skin felt as real as it looked." Elizabeth says to Weddington. "My apologies Cosby."

The Robot's head swings towards Elizabeth. "My name is Cozbi!" It hisses.

Wide eyed, Elizabeth backs up. "Of course. My apologies. I must have heard it wrong."

"We need to get to Galveston." I say as loud as I can. "Weddington, Thank you for letting us use your runway to pick up Mr. Katz-Williams.  It might be best if you let Wendy and Willem know we were here and gone.

"It's not a problem! I owe Willem and Wendy all of this!" Weddington Coffee spins the chair in a circle, motioning with one hand. "Listen, those Texas Militia boys are nothing to fuck with. They got a goddamn submarine and sunk a fucking French Navy vessel. I'm not sure what you are all planning but be careful." He hands a card to Hank. "Padre, that's my contact info. Shit gets deep, call me up. I will send Cozbi over to get you out of the stew!"
"Can she fly?" I ask. Millie gives me a *Are you fucking serious look?*

"What? It *looks* to me like Cozbi does a *lot* of things." I mutter.

Coffee grins. "Not yet... but I am working on personal jet packs for the girls. The Robots may not fly, but I have a Robinson R66 in the hanger ready to go. Modified it myself."

I want badly to know how a man with no legs flies a helicopter, but time is short. "Load up everyone!" I yell as loud as I can. "Thank you, Weddington Coffee for taking care of Yoda."

I usher Yoda, Millie and Hank onto the plane. Elizabeth talks to Coffee for a few minutes before Cozbi pushes him down the runway. I don't know what her seemingly infatuation with the human like Robot is and there are other things at hand we need to get to. "Elizabeth! We need to go!" I call out.

She turns and walks up the steps. The little Robot on board closes the door after I walk onto the plane. I take a brief look at the closed door of the cockpit. There has been no sign of an actual human pilot. I have not asked about this rather disconcerting observation, mostly because I don't want to know... but I figure the plane is like all the transportation like things I have ridden in. It is either self-flying or being piloted by Robots. I wonder when people got so comfortable letting everything be done for them by machines.

Millie leans over to me. She taps on the anatomy book that Elizabeth had procured for her along with requested drugs and surgical supplies. I had studied the appropriate chapters for several hours in the middle of the night before we left for the airport. "You are going to be ok assisting me?" She asks.
I nod with my expired trademark sarcastic grin. "Near as I can tell, it is just like a foot. Cut it open, it bleeds. Inside stitches, outside stitches... the bleeding stops."

Millie gives me a *don't fuck with me look*. "Ever pull a baby out of a foot?"

"No... but to be clear, I didn't get to practice very long before I went Rip Van Winkle for twenty years." I shrug. "The scenario may have come up eventually."

Millie shakes her head and laughs. "You are impossible."

"We have got this, Millie. Basically, I am your surgical nurse. You tell me what you need, and I will jump to it."

"It's going to go fast. It has to." Millie says. I can see that the worry lines on her face have deepened. I know what she's thinking. Honestly, I have been thinking about the same exact thing. Elizabeth Eaton told us what her plan is. I am sure that the two of us may end up being lambs sacrificed at the altar of the state of Texas Justice system.

*You know that feeling you get when you are in a room with someone, and they are stressed out? Millie is blowing that feeling out of her body like a Yellowstone Park geyser. I make a mental note to check and see if Old Faithful is still ejaculating on a regular basis.*

I grab her hand and lean close. "You and I are going to be ok, Puddingsnatch. We have each other." I pat her leg. "How big is your lucky mark?"

"Still the same size. More or less." She whispers. "I check it every day. Silly, huh?"
I shake my head. "We know where we were and why we are here. It's not silly at all." I put my forehead on the back of her neck and kiss it. "When all the luck wears off, Millie, I want to be with you."

Millie's closes her eyes. "Thank you, Justin." She squeezes my hand. "You know we might both be arrested and put in a jail cell, right."

I grin. "If that happens, I will summons all my powers to become like the *Kool Aid Pitcher Man.* I will bust down the walls and break you out of the prison."

"Will you shout, "Oh, Yeah" in that deep baritone voice when you do it?" She asks, laying her head on my shoulder.

*"Ohhhh, Yeah."* I say a bit too loudly. Everyone in the plane including the little robot turns and looks at us. Millie cracks up.

Elizabeth Eaton stands. She gives us a confused look followed by a shake of her head. After motioning for Yoda Williams to move close, she crouches down in the aisle and goes over her plan, again. At the end, she looks at Millie and me. "We will likely have to leave you two behind. I have my daughter Anne and Conrad's son Fredrick working on the paperwork they will file to get you released as soon as possible.

Millie clenches my hand like a young Hulk Hogan crushing a beer can.

"We got it, Elizabeth." I reach over and lightly punch Hank in the shoulder. "You two just get Katherine and Yoda to safety."

Chapter 42
Court is in session.
Texas Criminal Justice Hospital Facility
Galveston, Texas. Still part of the United States of America
Land of the Free(ish) Home of the Brave(ish)


The fifth hearing of the day was a girl who could not have been more than fourteen or fifteen years old. Tearfully, the pregnant girl described to the staring men in the front of the room how an older cousin had forcibly impregnated her. She claimed to be four months pregnant. Katherine Williams continued to watch the proceedings with little interest or enthusiasm. It was clear to her that the Judge and the attorneys are dismissive and dispassionate about any of the women's claims. One of the two sleeping women was brought back into the court room. She was placed back in a chair ahead of Kitty where she almost immediately slumped over.

"Lucky bitch." Katherine mutters to herself.

Just as he had for the previous four defendants, The judge hit his gavel against the table for the fifth time, pronouncing the accused woman guilty of attempting to terminate a pregnancy and declaring that she be held until the birth of the child before being sentenced for the crime. Kitty concentrated on her breathing. The pregnant teen, her belly swollen more than one might expect for only being four months pregnant and her stringy blond hair tied back into a ponytail doubles over as she is led from the defense attorney's table.

"Get her up!" The judge bellows. "Get her up and out of my courtroom. If she's pushing that child out unnaturally, we will tack on time!"
"Pushing the child out unnaturally?" Kitty mutters. "Seriously! What the fuck?"

"You got something to say, number eight?" The judge yells. "It's your turn number eight! Bailiff, get number eight up here!" The jailer comes over and roughly pulls Kitty up from her chair. She is placed beside the public defender, a bored looking man who fidgets with some sort of plastic device.

"Name?" The Judge asks.

Kitty remains silent.

"Name?" The Judge asks again, clearly annoyed.

"Give him your name." The defense attorney looks at his paperwork. "The name registered to her communicator is Katherine Katz Williams. Your honor."

"I know this bitch isn't a mute. She had plenty of smart-ass things to say early on." The judge says. "Do you have control of your client, counselor?"

The attorney nods. "We can do the proceedings sir; it won't make much difference if she talks or not."

"You are being charged with Attempting to Terminate a Pregnancy prior to a medically assigned due date." The judge glares at her. "How do you plead?"

Kitty takes a deep breath. "I am asserting my fifth amendment rights, your honor." She exhales slowly.
"You! You are! You are asserting *what rights?*" The judge's face has turned a shade of red that is commonly associated with cartoon characters. "You are a *pregnant woman!* You don't have any goddamn rights!"

The doors of the courtroom swing open. Kitty and the public defender standing next to her turn at the commotion. A tall blond woman with a severe expression leads a well-dressed woman and a priest into the

courtroom. "I think that the Constitution of the United States of America, of which the state of Texas is still a part of, would strongly disagree with that last statement, your honor." Elizabeth Eaton says loudly. "My name is Elizabeth Eaton, and I am counsel for Katherine Katz Williams."
Kitty turns and pokes the court provided attorney sharply in the shoulder. "I think you have just been replaced."

"Bet me." The lawyer says. "You think this judge is gonna let an aborter like you disrupt his proceedings just because some do-gooders showed up claiming to be your lawyer?"

The judge is looking at Elizabeth Eaton's credentials when the courtroom door swings open again. Yoda Storm Trooper Katz Williams leads a tall older man walking with the aid of a cane though the door. Kitty doesn't recognize the man with the very familiar looking cane, but she certainly recognizes her husband. "Yoda!" She cries out. Involuntary, tears roll down her cheeks. "Yoda!"

# Chapter 43
## The Calvary arrives. Prayers. Delivering the goods.
### Texas Criminal Justice Hospital Facility
### Galveston, Texas. Still part of the United States of America
### Land of the Free(ish) Home of the Brave(ish)

*When we arrived at the jail medical center, a young receptionist was probably a little more helpful than the State of Texas wanted her to be. She looked up where Katherine Katz Williams was in the system and told us that she was scheduled to be arraigned in the hospital facility courtroom. After checking all of us in and giving us visitor badges... something I might have thought would be gone the way of the dodo bird by 2042, she had a Robot escort us to the impromptu courtroom. I had encouraged the group to rush on without me. Even with the cane, I move much slower than everyone else can. Elizabeth had already explained that it would take some time for the judge to review her legal credentials and admit her (and by extension, us) to the court. Yoda proved to be quite a gentleman. He hung back and walked with me as I hobbled along on my borrowed cane. I could tell that he was very nervous with what we are about to embark on. I unsuccessfully tried some jokes. Then I tried sarcasm. It occurred to me about halfway down the hallway that there really is nothing very funny about a dead baby or the situation that he and his wife had found themselves in.*

*When we got to the courtroom and opened the doors, Kitty immediately called out to Yoda. Elizabeth had told Yoda not to run to his wife, but to wait until the group went over to her. The lawyer had correctly assessed that things would happen quite quickly after the judge admitted us into the courtroom. We had a plan 'B' in case the judge didn't admit us... but it wasn't necessary. Plan 'B' wasn't much different than Plan 'A' except in Plan 'A', only me and Millie get arrested.*

*As soon as we walk up to the bench, time both seemed to accelerate and stop all at once.*

"What is the meaning of this!" I hear the judge shout from his makeshift bench. "Who are you people?" I note that the bench is just a folding table. Elizabeth Eaton and Cousin Hank tower over the man.

"My name is Elizabeth Eaton. I am registered to practice law in the state of Texas. This is Millie Ratchet; she is my associate. The man that just came in, is our other associate, Justin Thyme and this big fellow here is Father Henry Thyme. He is providing spiritual guidance." Elizabeth places papers in front of the judge. "That tall good looking young man behind us is Katherine's husband, Yoda."

"The husband probably should have been arrested on that abortion ship; I suspect." The judge mutters as he looks at the papers.

"I think I better see those credentials. This is very unusual, a *pregnant woman* getting counsel other than a public defender." The person representing the State Attorney General's office asks. He rises from his chair on the right side as I walk past.

"Sit down, counselor. It is all on the up and up. This woman represents the defendant, Katherine Katz Williams." The Judge points at the court appointed public defender. "Make room at your table counselor. They got a big crowd."

Elizabeth Eaton turns and gives Millie a plastic smile. "We are on. Let's make things happen."

Millie turns to me and nods. I squeeze between Katherine Williams and the public defender. "Katherine, I am Justin Thyme. Your father sent me and Millie. We are here to help you out." Without asking, I grab her arm and start feeling for a vein. Millie comes over to her other side and starts whispering in Katherine's ear. I know that she is explaining exactly what is about to happen.

"I'd like to say a quick prayer for the court, the accused and this very sensitive situation." Father Henry Thyme announces. "If that is ok with his honor."

The judge furrows his brow. "Of course, Padre. That would be very nice. Quite nice. I often think that God should be more involved in these proceedings."

This is part of the plan. Hank is the distraction we need to get things started.  I hear the priest's baritone voice announce, "Please bow your heads in prayer." I look at the judge who has squeezed his eyes shut and is grasping his hands tightly together on his makeshift bench. The attorney next to me kneels on the floor. *God bless the believers.* I think as I pull a syringe filled with Oxytocin and a rubber tube from Willem William's Canali suit coat pocket. Quickly, like I hadn't missed twenty years or so of medical work, I tie the band around Katherine's arm and find a good vein. After a quick poke, I inject the contents of the syringe into her arm and release the tube. Millie is still whispering in her ear.

I barely hear Hank's prayer, but it sounds nice. If there is a God, Be it the Cow, a Grasshopper, or a big man with a head of white hair and a long white beard, I hope Hammerin' Hank is well connected and whatever he is saying is resonating with this God, whatever form he or she might take.

*Lord Jesus Christ, You came to destroy the works of the devil and to call us into the family of God as His beloved children. You have sent us the Holy Spirit, our Advocate, to lead us into all truth, especially in this time of darkness and confusion. With humility and trust, we turn to You, begging for Your help and guidance.*

*Father, we implore You: send forth Your holy angels—mighty in rank, number, and power—to defend us against the assaults of the evil one. Protect our families, our communities, and our nations. Command Your angels to surround us with heavenly light and strength, driving away all forces of darkness and evil.*

"Say it, Father! Say it!" The judge says loudly. I look over. The man's eyes are still squeezed shut. *God bless the believers.  I think to myself.*

*We invoke the intercession of the Blessed Virgin Mary, Queen of Heaven, and the entire Communion of Saints. Holy Mother, pray for us and carry our petitions to Your Son. May their prayers join ours as we seek forgiveness, healing, and restoration through Christ. Grant healing to all who are wounded, and may hearts be reconciled in Your boundless mercy.*

*Come, Holy Spirit, and pour out Your grace upon all of mankind. Illuminate our hearts with Your light, convicting us of who we are in the eyes of God, beloved yet in need of Your saving grace. Reveal the depth of Your love, Lord, even as You expose the sin that separates us from You. Grant us the courage and humility to surrender our sins in the sacrament of reconciliation, knowing that only You can make us whole. Transform our hearts and conform us to Your image, Lord Jesus.*

"Amen! Amen! Amen!" The lawyer beside me says.

*Through the powerful intercession of Saint Michael the Archangel, we ask You to lift the veil of confusion that blinds so many. Protect us from the lies of the enemy and lead us on the path of righteousness and truth.*

"Save us, oh Lord!" The prosecutor cries out.

*Lord, as we face these trials, we entrust ourselves to Your mercy and care. Strengthen our faith, guide us through the storm, and let Your victory shine through us. We give thanks and praise, offering all glory to the Father, the Son, and the Holy Spirit, now and forever.*

"We are all sinners, Lord. Hear our prayers!" Someone, maybe a jailer/bailiff shouts out.

*Lord, we beg for your guidance and your mercy as we embark on these trying and difficult challenges. In this we give thanks and praise. All Glory be to the Father, and to the Son, and to the Holy Spirit, Amen.*

As if on cue, Katherine Williams lets out a loud yowl as her uterus makes its first contraction.

When you go to doctor school, you learn about all sorts of interesting drugs. Oxytocin is one of them. Sometimes called the *cuddle drug* by medical types, Oxytocin is a hormone that all our bodies produce naturally... although I have been wondering if my body is still up to the task of that particular production.

Oxytocin: not to be confused with the manufactured opiate, Oxycontin, will make a male orgasm feel as the cock has become a nozzle at the end of a fire hose. I have been told that a female orgasm on pharmaceutical Oxytocin starts as a slow burn and ends in dozen lightning bolts all hitting in the same place at the same time.

Oxytocin also encourages lactation and most important as I stand in this Hospital-Courtroom, stimulates the walls of the uterus to contract. I had put enough of the substance in Katherine Williams' arm to cause her an orgasm strong enough to make her not walk for week if she had been engaged in intercourse... I could have started a countdown to reaction from thirty, but I wouldn't have reached fifteen. When Hank ended his prayer with an *Amen*, Katherine Williams was hit with a massive uterine contraction. Her wail echoes though the courtroom, drowning out the judge and lawyers *amens* to officially conclude Father Henry Thymes very excellent and just long enough prayer.

"I think this woman is having a baby!" Elizabeth Eaton exclaims in a way that might have won her an academy award if there still was such a thing in the United States of America. I swear she even lifted her hand to her mouth in disbelief.

"We need to get her to a hospital bed!" I say, adding to the theater of the absurd. I turn to the judge. "Do you have a gurney, sir? We need to get the mother into a delivery room!"

The judge looks downright panicked. "She's what? She's having a baby?"

I look at the judge solemnly. "Yes, Katherine Williams is pregnant. You knew that, right? Isn't that what this is all about?"

Elizabeth Eaton chokes back a laugh.

"This has *never* happened before!" The judge exclaims. "What do *you* need to do?"

"Me?" I exclaim, pointing to myself. "I know exactly what I am here to do. Texas *must* be prepared for this sort of thing. After all, this state is the leader in forcing women to carry babies to term. There *must* be facilities in this place to deliver said babies! *You* need to get us a gurney so we can take Mrs. Williams to the delivery room."

"We don't *have* a *delivery room*! This is a prison!" The judge is sweating now. He looks at the jailers who all wear dumbfounded expressions. "Jailer... get that woman a cart or whatever that lawyer asked for."

One of the men runs from the room. Yoda is on one side of his wife, holding her hand and gently rubbing his other hand through her hair. Millie holds the other and talks silently in Katherine's ear. Elizabeth Eaton turns and faces the judge. "The defendant pleads not guilty, your honor."

"What?" The judge almost screams his response from the bench. Katherine lets out another wail as she has a second contraction. Millie gently removes the pregnant woman's prison pants with a pair of scissors brought along specifically for the task.

The judge stands and points, "Get that woman dressed! She must be decent in here! This is a court of law!"

Elizabeth Eaton gives the judge that *predator sees the prey* look. It gives me the chills and I was dead, once. "Your Honor, this woman is going to deliver the dead child that is inside of her. There is no easy way to say this sir, either help or get the hell out of my sight. My earlier declaration still stands: *The defendant pleads not guilty.*"

"She is dilated, but not nearly enough. C-Section is still the way to go." Millie says softly to me.

The judge hurriedly picks up his wooden gavel and runs from the room. The jailer returns with a gurney that appears to have been made before any of us were born. "Where is the operating room?" I ask.

"Last door on the right." The jailer says hurriedly. He turns and rushes out of the courtroom. Yoda and Hank lift Katherine onto the gurney. There is no one left in the courtroom except us. "We can do it right here." I say.

"Let's hope there is better lighting in whatever this place considers an O.R." Millie says. She points behind her before grabbing the foot of the gurney and starting to push. "Also, there are cameras in here. Katherine, when we get in the operating room, Dr. Thyme and I are going to give you a spinal anesthesia. After that, I am going to make an incision along the lower third of your abdomen and uterus. We will deliver the baby shortly after that."

"Thank God... thank God." Katherine says. She is working hard at regulating her breathing. I see tears coming from the corners of her eyes. "I thought I was going to die with the baby."
"It's all going to be ok, Kitty!" Yoda says forcefully as we move down the hallway. We crash through the swinging door of the operating room. It is a well-lit place, but if we had hoped for supplies, we would have been disappointed. Even more so if we had hoped for a sterile environment. Two Robots come forward. Millie expertly disables each with a verbal command. After inspecting the operating table, Millie rolls her eyes.

"We aren't using that filthy piece of shit. Jesus." She spits out the words.

"I don't think the son of God has been here." Hank answers with somber tone. "What do you need me to do?"

Millie is already helping roll Katherine on to her side. I have pulled out the giant syringes of the compounded anesthesia. I have done spinal taps. I didn't like it. I had been hoping Millie will handle this. She looks at Hank. "You and Yoda, hold Katherine very still." She looks directly at Yoda. "This is important Yoda, do not let Kitty move!"

"Right here, Justin." Millie has taken a permanent marker and put a dot exactly where she wants me to put the injection. "Let's go, we aren't getting any younger."

I take a deep breath and hobble to the edge of the gurney. Med school was over thirty years ago, which would have been the last time I jabbed a needle into a living person's spine. Then I went into Podiatry where the needles and the stakes are substantially smaller. Gently I line the needle up to the mark that is near the small of Katherine's back. I feel a little pressure before the catheter on the needle penetrates the spinal column. I depress the plunger, emptying the contents of the syringe into Katherine's spine.

"Roll her on to her back." Millie orders after I pull the catheter out. She pulls on rubber gloves and pokes at Katherine's swollen belly. "Can you feel that?"

Katherine shakes her head. Faster than I can grab the sponges from Millie's briefcase turned medical bag, an order comes for a sponge. "Let's go Justin!" Millie demands.

I pull on my gloves and sponge up the blood that has come from the first incision. While I hold the skin apart, Millie makes a second quick incision before lifting a still child from Katherine William's midsection.

*That is all there was to that. Katherine Williams had tried her best to receive the medical care she needed. No one would help her receive the proper care in a legal and safe manner until Millie and I came along. The care we provided was relatively safe. It was not legal. I had helped deliver six, maybe seven babies in medical school. The birth of a child is almost always wonderful. This is the first time I had ever been involved with delivering a dead baby. Even in this terrible instance where the baby is still born, I am reminded of the miracle of childbirth. I am fully cognizant that we are doing this procedure in a prison because the mother couldn't get the medical care she deserved and frankly had every right as a human to receive. It also doesn't escape me that a considerable amount of effort and money has been spent to get to this very moment. Most women today in this same situation would not have had the resources to obtain the care just provided to Katherine Williams. Millie and I have been called to do more than help just this one woman. I am sure of it.*

Elizabeth Eaton appears in the operating room. She has a folded bed sheet in her hand that is handed to Millie. After severing the umbilical cord, Millie tearfully swaddles the baby and walks to the head of the bed to Yoda. "Mr. and Mrs. Williams, your beautiful daughter."

Hank says a prayer that I am sure included last rights as Millie hands the baby over to Katherine. I quickly put the umbilical cord in a plastic bag and seal it shut. I know that Willem's disease is far advanced, but maybe a laboratory in Europe can use the unique cells from his stillborn granddaughter's umbilical cord to come up with an effective therapy.

Millie returns to my side. "Let's get Katherine stitched up and get her the hell out of here. This place gives me the creeps. I would have rather done this in the parking lot of that shit hole we are staying in than this... *prison*... in *this* state."

I nod without comment as we get started. Millie does the inside. I stitch up the outside. For whatever reason, doctors love to sew people up and I am no exception. There is something satisfying about closing a wound or incision with a needle and thread. Just as I close the last stitch and wipe the wound clean, the swinging doors of the jailhouse operating room crash open.

"You are all under arrest!" The judge from the courtroom cries out as he rushes forward, three jailers follow him at a small distance. "You have assisted a woman in aborting a pregnancy. That is *illegal* in the great state of Texas!"

Millie looks at me. She has that smile on her face. The one that makes me feel like a million bucks... even here in this dreadful situation. "This is what we were sent back for Justin. We have done our job."

I wink at her. "We ain't done yet, Penelope Puddingsnatch. Not even close."

"Justin, your cane." Hank calls out.

I toss the priest the wooden cane that had been leaning against the gurney. "Use it well, Hammerin' Hank." Hank grabs the stick one handed before violently breaking it in half over his knee. I look at Kitty's husband who is holding the baby close to his chest. He is so lost in his child that I believe he does not notice that we have unwelcome company in our makeshift birthing room. I address him in a loud voice. "Yoda, do what we talked about. Take Kitty and the baby and go with Hank and Elizabeth."

He nods and hands the baby to her mother who tearfully grasps the bundle tightly. Using both arms, he effortless lifts his wife from the gurney and turns to face the judge. "We are leaving now your honor."

"I said you are all under arrest!" The judge screeches. "You have all violated *Texas* laws regarding abortion.

Hank holds the two pieces of the cane across each other in the shape of a cross and starts chanting. *"We come to you God, for refuge. Oh, God for You will shelter us against the attack of these devils. Protect us, Oh Lord, from the craftiness of these enemies, and save us from their evil plots."*

"Your honor, my name is Millie Ratchet. This is Justin Thyme. We were the attending physicians in this operation. The patient needed our services. We performed those services according to the standards and procedures accepted by the Texas Medical Board and the Federal Drug Administration."

"Abortion of *any kind* in this state… indeed, in the entirety of the U.S of A is illegal!" The judge hisses. He stamps his cowboy boot adorned feet. "I will make you *all pay*!

"The patient didn't have an abortion, your honor. She delivered her baby." Millie replies softly. "The baby was deceased in utero. We performed the delivery via Cesarean section."
"The earliest delivery date for this woman isn't for another two months." The judge waves the paper he had been clenching in his hand, around. "It was an *ABORTION* I know! Because I checked!"

The jailers, for whatever reason seem to be afraid of Hank and his praying over the makeshift cross. Or maybe they are just good sensible people who are creeped out by this entire macabre scene. I haven't met a lot of good, sensible people so far in Texas, so I am putting jailer's reticence on *fear of God*.

Hank, Elizabeth and Yoda carrying Katherine and their baby are allowed to leave. I note that the lawyer has taken away all the evidence that might prove that anything in particular had happened in the makeshift operating room.

"We have video evidence of that man..." The judge points at me. "Injecting something into the arm of the accused! In *my* courtroom!" He turns to the jailers. "Arrest these two baby killers! I will have the militia stop the others at the airport!" The judge gives me a look. His eyes are crazy. "That's right! I know how you all planned to escape! Not today, you will not! Not under my watch! I am going to be quite the hero with the Militia when I seize that fancy jet plane you came in on!"

Millie's lets out a long sigh. She holds her hands out and looks over at me. "Our fates our now in the hands of two people... children, none the less, whom we have never met." One of the jailers fastens her hands together with plastic straps.

I hold my wrists out. "Any words of advice? I have never been put in prison."
"Well Randy Romeo, don't drop the soap and don't pick fights with the biggest gal in the joint." Millie says wistfully as she is led through the swinging doors.

"Randy Romeo? You can do better than that, Penelope!" I call out as I am pushed out of the room after her.

"Probably." Millie answers back as she is pushed again. "Looks like I am going to have some time to think about it!" She looks back at me with a wink. "See you ten years or so?"

Chapter 44
Let our people go.
The Supreme Court of Texas, Austin, Texas
Still a place in the United States of America
Home of the Free(ish) Land of the Brave(ish)


Anne Margret looks over at Fred. He is staring intently at an electronic tablet, flipping through pages of prior court cases.
"You are so cute when you are intense." Anne pokes him in the ribs. "Mom says that this will be a piece of cake."

"Has your mother ever eaten a piece of cake?" Fred asks. "Texas law is anything but straightforward. I think our strategy may work... but I am finding other information to make sure we have a plan B... and C."

Anne looks at the limestone wall in front of the wooden bench they have commandeered. "I bet she has eaten cake. Probably off your dad's chest."

Fred closes his eyes and shakes his head. "That's an image I didn't need to think about right now."

"Kinda romantic. We should try it later. You want chocolate or strawberry?"

"Chocolate or Strawberry what?"

"Cake." Anne Margret slugs him in the shoulder. "I want chocolate." She leans towards him and nibbles his ear lobe. "And I *don't* think I want to eat it off your chest."

Fred gasps. "I got it!"

"You know what part of my body I want you to eat chocolate cake from?" Anne Margret whispers with anticipation as she scoots closer to Fred. "Where? I want to hear!"

"I have closed the legal loop." Fred waves the electronic tablet. "In 2021, the Texas Legislature passed HB 1694, thereafter called the *Jessica Sosa Act*. People who are participating in a criminal act cannot be prosecuted under certain circumstances."

"That's only has to do with drug use, Freddy. But Mom does think that we can use the Texas *Good Samaritan* Laws in Mr. Thyme and Ms. Ratchet's defense, if that is even necessary." Anne Margret rubs his back. "We aren't defending them today. We are only getting them released. We just need to ask this Justice Garcia to sign a release order for Justin Thyme and Millie Ratchet. They will probably still have to come back and appear in court to defend themselves."

"The Judge is going to ask on what grounds we are trying to get the accused released." Fred protests.

"Mom says that we are pulling in a favor."

"How can there be favors in the legal system? Either it's the thing to do or it isn't." Fred protests.

Anne Margret shrugs. "Every argument you have come up with has gray areas. I'd say that the only way these two don't spend a significant time behind bars is we pull a favor, or they do a jail break."

The door opens and a tall brunette woman walks out of an office. She is wearing a robe and her first physical response she has when she sees the two sitting is to let out an exasperated sigh. "I was told that you are here to see me. Walk. I need to get into the courtroom. You have about ninety seconds."

The trio sets off down the hallway. Fred starts. There were two lawyers arrested yesterday at the medical facility in the Galveston detention center. They are accused of providing abortion services to a pregnant woman."

The judge purses her lips. "I suspect that being pregnant is still the only condition where a woman might need such services. I wasn't aware that lawyers provided said services. Seems dangerous for all involved."

"Anyway, I have prepared some briefs providing legal reason to releasing the two from confinement." Fred says.

"You think I have time to read your legal briefs?" The Judge asks. Anne rolls her eyes. "Judge Garcia, we didn't introduce ourselves. My verbose friend here is Conrad Petersen. My name is Anne Margret Eaton. My mother is Elizabeth Eaton. She will be representing Justin Thyme and Mildred Ratchet in their criminal defense. We would like to ask you to sign an order to release Ms. Ratchet and Mr. Thyme."

The judge stops. She looks at Anne for a long moment. "I have heard plenty about you over the years, Ms. Eaton. Your mother is very proud of you. Do you have the orders prepared?"
Fred quickly pulls them up on his electronic pad. "They are set to deliver copies to your inbox as well, your honor."

Judge Garcia quickly peruses the document on the tablet before using a finger to electronically sign them. "Young man, you appear to have the makings of a competent enough legal mind that you may at some point touch above average as an attorney." She hands the pad back to him. "Smart lawyers keep the chit chat with judges to a minimum."

"Thank you, your honor." Fred blushes.

"I told him the same thing, Judge Garcia." Anne Margret grabs his hand. "He has a really quick mind. I am sure he will be an *excellent* lawyer. Thank you for this."

The Judge nods curtly. "Terrible laws we have in this country. Maybe your generation will do something about it. Pass my regards on to your mother." Without another word, she walks into the courtroom.

After the door had closed behind the Texas Supreme Court Judge, Anne beams. "We did it, Fred! We did our first legal thing!"

Chapter 45
Nothing is easy.
Jet Center Scholes International Airport Galveston, Texas
Still a place in the United States
Home of the Free(ish) Land of the Brave(ish)


The transporter had dropped the group off at the front door of the Jet Center. Gingerly, Yoda lifted his wife holding their stillborn daughter from the middle row of the autonomous transporter. Hank got out of the front seat and Elizabeth Eaton climbed out from the rear.

"Where are we going?" Yoda asks. "After we board the plane."

"Your father-in-law has made arrangements for medical care in French St. Martin." Elizabeth answers. She sees commotion inside the fence surrounding the private jet terminal. "Father Thyme, did you call Weddington Coffee?"

"As soon as we got in the transporter." The priest answers.

Elizabeth points at the men surrounding the Williams's jet. "That's good. It does appear that we will require his services... though, I am not sure how a legless man and a couple of Robots are going to help us out here."
"You haven't seen that Robot of his in action." Yoda says, shaking his head. "Cozbi."

"So many things in life are about timing." Elizabeth Eaton answers. She points skyward. "I believe Weddington Coffee is inbound."

"I have him on my communicator." Hank reports. "Hello, Mr. Coffee. It looks like you are right on time!"

Weddington's voice emanates from the small speaker installed for conference calls from Hank's body. "Go on out on the tarmac. I am going to drop Cozbi off. She will get you on the plane."

"We are moving that way now." Hank says as the group quickly goes through the lobby of the Jet Center.

Once outside, Elizabeth makes a quick count of the men surrounding the jet. Eight. Only one is in a uniform of any sort. She correctly assesses it to be a grocery store security guard uniform. Most of the men have some sort of military style weapon hanging from their shoulders. "Well, this is going to be interesting." She says as Coffee's black Robinson helicopter comes in low at an angle. The arrival of the new aircraft has taken the attention of the eight poorly trained men from their quarry. The side door of the Robinson opens and the aircraft hovers, twenty feet or so above the tarmac. Cozbi the Robot climbs out on the landing rail of the helicopter and appears to survey the scene below.

"Wow! That is quite an outfit she is wearing." Elizabeth Eaton observes.

Chapter 46
Hard time. The Rock. An idea.
Galveston County Jail Galveston, Texas
Still a place in the United States of America
Land of the Free(ish) Home of the Brave(ish)


My time in prison, as this county jail is the only thing I have ever experienced that is remotely close to prison... has been relatively uneventful. I am in a mass holding cell. I assume that Millie and I will be arraigned together, but who knows. There are about thirty other men in the cell with me. No one has threatened me yet, although one rather large man asked me with a rather aggressive tone if I had brought snacks with me. After I answered with a tentative shake of my head, he returned to his bench looking hungry and frustrated.

"What is he in here for?" The guy, a homeless looking man who I would assume is about my age, says from my right side. I turn and look at the guy. He is a large man. Not fat. Not fit... just large. He has a head full of gray, curly and unruly hair. What truly stands out is that his question is not directed at me by at a gray rock he holds in the palm of his hand. Written on the rock in black permanent marker is the word, *hoover*.
"Are you speaking to... me?" I ask.

The man shakes his head. "No. I was asking Hoover, here." He sighs and slouches lower against the wall. "Hoover didn't give me a good answer though. He does that sometimes. Can't know everything, I suppose."

"The... rock? You were asking the rock?" I ask, trying to get a sense of where this conversation might go.
The man shrugs. "Hoover guides me. I picked him, you know... so I guess I kind of owe it to him to let him guide me."

I shake my head. "What did the rock... *Hoover* say when you asked him what I am in for?"

The man rolls his eyes. "Hoover said you are doing what you are supposed to be doing." He shakes his head. "Hoover talks in riddles and puns sometimes."

"I am accused of performing an abortion." I answer.

The man nods slowly. "Didn't know that was still a thing anymore... Performing abortions."

I shrug and sit back on the bench. "How about you?"

"Homeless." The man answers.

I nod. I thought he was homeless. "I am sorry about that. What are you in for?"

The man wrinkles up his forehead in confusion. "I am in for being homeless. Sitting on the sidewalk with hoover, specifically."

"Oh." I answer. "I didn't know that sitting on a sidewalk was a crime."

"It is in Texas." The man says. "Least, in Galveston." He sighs. "Five hundred dollar fine." He makes a wide motion with his right arm. "That's what most these fellows are here for. Sitting on a sidewalk." There is something old timey about the man and the way he speaks.
The snack searching fat man approaches a fellow who was just put in the room. The man put in the room hisses at him and the fat man backs away.

"That's Mad Alan." My new best friend with a pet rock says.

"The fat guy or the hissing guy?"

"The hissing guy. We call him Mad Alan. I suppose his first name might be Alan." The guy sticks out his hand. "I'm Mitch. Mitch Palmer."

"Mitch, I am Justin." I shake his hand and think about the last time someone offered me their hand to shake. It seems like such a civil, yet wholly unnecessary thing to do.

"We call the fat one, *Fat Dude*. Don't know his real name." Mitch shrugs. "Hoover doesn't know either. I asked him last week." He shifts to make himself more comfortable on the hard bench. "This is my third time here in the last couple of weeks. Don't know why they just don't keep us inside for a while."

"Third time, isn't that expensive?" I exclaim. "That's like fifteen hundred dollars."

"They bill us. My bill with the county is pretty high. Ironic. Even if I wanted a home, I couldn't get one because I owe the county so much. Mitch gives me a funny look like he just remembered my face from somewhere or he has gas. "You from around here, Justin?"

I shake my head in answer before asking, "How did you get to be homeless?"
Mitch flashes a very quick smile. "Same way everyone does. I couldn't live in the home I had anymore."

"That doesn't make any sense." I blurt out. The words come out of my mouth, and I instantly regret them. In a few months, I also will be homeless. Until she met me, Millie was homeless.

Mitch purses his lips and shakes his head. "I am certain being homeless doesn't make sense to you. You haven't been homeless and by the looks of that suit, you are not going to be homeless. Unless you are nuts. If you are even a little bit crazy, the odds of finding oneself homeless increase dramatically."

"It was a stupid thing to say." I mutter, feeling very stupid.

Mad Alan has taken all his clothes off. The men milling around him seem not to care. "I am guessing that is a regular occurrence?" I ask Mitch, whose eyes are closed. He doesn't open them to answer. "Yep. This happens all the time." Mad Alan starts masturbating. The naked guy is really getting into himself when one of the jailers walks up and calls my name. "Justin Thyme! You have been released!"

I stand slowly because that's how I roll. Slowly. The jailer points at Mad Alan and yells at him. "Knock that off, you Boring fag! Touching yourself ought to be illegal... and just cause' it ain't, don't mean you should be doing it here!"

I tap Mitch. He opens his left eye. It looks at me. "Nice talking to you, Mitch. I think I'm out of here."

"Where were you in 2028?" He asks.

"I was in a coma." I answer simply.

Mitch nods and closes his eye. "A coma was a good place to be in 2028. That was the year my refrigerator started talking to me. It kept telling me to get out of my house. Fucking toaster and its bitch friend the speaker system listened to everything I had to say and told *the man* about it... Madness. Absolute madness. Hoover... he should have known this is what things would come to. Anyway, that's why I am currently without home. I needed peace. Couldn't get it at home. I thought I needed the home to do what I am supposed to do. Turns out I was wrong about that, too. I have been wrong about so many things, I have no idea if I will recognize what is right. I know I need to come correct though. I didn't believe it at first. Boy, howdy, I sure do now. I just don't know what *right* is.  I suppose there are lots of people like me… not knowing what right is."

I nod slowly. It doesn't seem the time or the place to try and distill the crazy things the man is saying. "Good to have met you, Mitch."

"You too, Justin. I feel you, man. You exude some power. I think you might be here to change things. Maybe... I don't know. It's like you might have gotten here just in time."

Mitch's eyes are closed. I don't recall telling Mitch my last name. I really want to ask him why he said that last statement. The Jailer calls out my name again. Mad Alan ejaculates. The jailer lets loose a string of expletives aimed at Mad Alan. I pat Mitch the homeless man on the shoulder and turn to the yelling, judgmental jailer.

"I'm Justin Thyme." I say after I shuffle over to the bars of the sliding door to the jail cell.

The jailer waves an electronic device over my body. "You ain't got a communicator for positive identification. You Boring, man?"

"Probably. I am not sure what that word means these days." I answer. "Was Millie Ratchet released as well?"

"That the baby killing cunt you came in here with?" The jailer asks. "Yeah, she released to. She also ain't got a communicator. Yoose both Boring!"

Mad Alan has started masturbating his erect self again. I feel a little jealousy towards the man's ability to recharge so quickly, despite his somewhat apparent... mental health issues.

"Crazy fuckers come in here and whack off. It ought to be illegal. Whacking off!" The jailer rants as we walk out of the jail. "Masturbation ought to be Eee-legal!"

"I will see what I can do to make that happen!" I say with more enthusiasm than I intended. I walk around the corner and into the arms of a smiling Millie.

"      Still an anal virgin?" She asks after the embrace.

"You are assuming my butt cherry was intact *before* I got locked up?" I grin at her.

She hugs me again and sighs contently. "Maybe we can get your rich friends to fly us to Europe or Asia... someplace where we won't have to deal with this craziness anymore."

"There was a guy whacking off in there. Stripped down naked and everything. Gave me an idea. I think I have a plan to make it stop."

"A *guy* whacking off gave you an idea? To do what? Make what stop?" Millie releases me. Her smile has turned upside down.

"The craziness. I think I have the start of a plan to make the craziness stop. I need your help."

"Yo... Justin! Millie!" I hear Marmalade calling to us from public side of the prisoner/public barrier.

"And here... is just the guy to help put my plan into motion!" I announce happily.

*I hear Millie sigh. It sounds more like a sigh of exasperation than a sigh of relief. I don't take the time to figure out what that's all about.*

Chapter 47
Cozbi, on the scene. Texas Militia In Action.
Jet Center Scholes International Airport Galveston, Texas
Still a place in the United States
Home of the Free(ish) Land of the Brave(ish)


From Yoda's arms, Kitty looks up at the woman standing on the landing bar of the helicopter. She wears bright yellow palazzo pants and a coordinating polka dot yellow and white bikini top. "What in the world is that woman doing?" Kitty asks in a loud voice so to be heard over the beating of the helicopter blades. Yoda glances up just in time to see Cozbi jump from the landing bar to the ground.

"Oh, my goodness!" Kitty grasps her dead baby tighter. "Is she hurt?"

"I doubt it." Yoda says warily. "That *she* is a Robot."

Cozbi rips the polka dotted top off and starts doing jumping jacks. "Come on boys. Pull out those cocks! Let's see what you all have got!" The Robot yells in an amplified voice.

Yoda sees the men carrying weapons all look at each other. Only the man wearing some sort of uniform chooses to challenge the topless woman in front of him. He points his military style rifle at Cozbi. "You there! You are interfering with an official Texas Militia activity! You need to get down on the ground and prepare to be arrested!"

The Robinson helicopter takes off.
"Well, big boy." Cozbi coos. "If you'd like to, you can try and put some handcuffs on me." After rubbing its breasts in a seductive manner, the Robot dangles its hands out in front of the uniformed man. "Come on over here and *hook* me up!"

"Think she'll give us all blowjobs, Captain?" One of the men asks. Elizabeth Eaton sees the opportunity and starts to lead the group towards the Williams's jet. One of the armed Militiamen notices the action and runs towards the group with his gun extended. "We are seizing this jet. It is now the property of the Organized and Regulated Texas Militia!"

"Cozbi! You beautiful bitch! Some help here!" Yoda calls out.

"Is there something I need to know about you and that Robot?" Kitty asks with a suspicious tone.

"Yeah." Yoda answers. "She tried to kill me last night."

Cozbi the Robot drops its arms and looks at the uniformed man with a cocked head. "Maybe later, big boy." Like a deer, she springs to her right and in two leaps is between Elizabeth Eaton and the guard pointing a gun at the group.

"Let this group pass." Cozbi orders. "Let them pass to the jet plane."

"Suck my cock, bitch." The militiaman answers. He raises the weapon. "That plane belongs to us now."

"Your desire to seize that plane is a violation of the owner's rights granted to citizens of the United States of America under the fourth amendment of the constitution. I cannot permit you to execute such an egregious violation of any person's constitutional rights. As for your request that I suck your cock, I will be happy to do so. If only you will allow me to remove the appendage from your body, first." Cozbi lunges forward as the assault weapon discharges. She catches the round on the left side of her chest. After grabbing the weapon and pulling it free from the militiaman's grasp she heaves it in the air. Yoda watches the military style rifle fly to the roof of the Jet Center. Then he watches as Cozbi the Robot picks the surprised militiaman up and flings his body in much the same direction. "Rain check on the cock sucking?" Cozbi calls out after the man in a very feminine voice. Her body abruptly stops and her head swivels unnaturally, apparently looking for another victim. The seven remaining militiamen, wary of what they have correctly assessed to be a threat rather than a potential victim are smartly backing away from the plane. The door of the jet opens and unfolds, Yoda, carrying his wife who is still holding their dead baby takes the steps two at a time.

"Are we still going with them?" Hanks asks Elizabeth. "And are we taking the Robot?"

"I will be flying home with Weddington Coffee, thank you." Cozbi answers, her head swiveling like a sentry. "You and the tall older woman named Elizabeth Eaton should get on the aircraft and continue to your destination."

"Thank you, God." Hank says with an exhale as he bounds up the aircraft stairs.

"Thank Weddington Coffee!" Cozbi the Robot calls out. "God has had little to do with the results you see here."

"That's for sure." Elizabeth Eaton steps onto the folding staircase. "Tell Weddington Coffee thank you, Cozbi." She points. "I see your ride coming in to pick you up now."

Cozbi points at the open door of the jet before taking off down the runway at a dead sprint. Elizabeth enters the plane and pushes the button to retract the folding door. The jet starts moving. "Next stop, The island of French St. Martin." Eaton announces to the passengers on board before bending forward to look out the window. Weddington Coffee brings the helicopter down to a spot ten or so feet above the runway. Cozbi the Robot's speed seems to pick up. It takes a single leap, then another and grabs a hold on the landing rail. The chopper starts to rise. Elizabeth watches as the Robot hoists itself onto the landing rail and then into the helicopter.

"Those are some spectacularly well-made tits." The lawyer says in awe to no one in particular and the aircraft owned by Williams and Williams turns south towards the Gulf of Mexico.

Chapter 48
Flying on another Jet Plane.
Marmalade's Church. Business issues.
Somewhere above the State of Texas. Still a place in the United States of
America Land of the Free(ish) Home of the Brave(ish)


"My plane ain't as nice as Willem's." Marmalade hands Millie, me
and Paal bottles of waters. "And I hate Robots constantly doing things for
me. I got Robot pilots because that is all there is... but no Robot stewards.
There are more drinks up there in the front galley. Get them yourself. "

"Are we going back to the Williams' house?" Millie asks.
Marmalade shakes his head. "Nah. We need to pick up Conrad's boy and
his woman's daughter." He points. "They are in Austin. Then we go back
home."

"Austin. Not my favorite place." Millie answers with a sour tone.

"What's this big plan you want to tell me about?" Marmalade eyes
Millie as he addresses me.

"My plan is very dependent on that church you belong to. The one
that makes you get a big back tattoo to join. How powerful is that church...
In the big scheme of things?" I ask. "Christian's chasing some scoundrel."
*"Christians Chasing The Scoundrel Pontius Pilate."*. Marmalade says. "Damn
powerful. Too powerful, truth be told." He taps Millie on the knee. "Ya girl
here knows. She didn't tell ya?"

*The temperature in the aircraft has dropped and I don't think it is from the air
conditioner turning on. I am suddenly aware that I have not been paying attention to
details like I should have been.*

"Leave me out of this." Millie all but growls. She pokes me hard in the ribs. "I don't know what your crazy idea is... but if it involves that *fucking* church, leave me the hell out of it."

"*Fucking* church." Marmalade smiles. "I like that. That's very astute."

"Why did you leave the church, Juice?" I ask, patting Millie on the knee in manner I want to believe can be described as *reassuringly*... The tension I fell under my hand indicates that the action is being received as *patronizing*.
Marmalade gives me a dismissive wave. "In mixed company, Paal likes to say that I left the church. That isn't how it works." Marmalade sits back in his chair and grins. "Think of my current status as *on sabbatical*... I needed a break from those nut jobs. I "can't really *leave* the church. If I want out, I have to *sell* my franchise."

I shake my head. "I don't get it. What do you mean you have to *sell your franchise*. Normally, isn't one in a church or not in a church?"

Marmalade chuckles and leans forward. "You been gone a long time Justin... you know how I make my money?"

I wrinkle my forehead. "Juice Baths? Some sort of gym thing, I guess?"

The former professional football player laughs. He looks over at Paal. "Hear that, Paal... my friend thinks that selling memberships at a Saltwater Bath pays for a jet."

Paal looks up from his computer and smiles before returning to whatever it was, we interrupted him from.

"Paal there... and a very small army that he commands, they keep me relevant in *everything* I want to be in... which is anything that makes bank." Marmalade laughs. "Sometime after my pro career was over and after I had won a Grammy for song writing... I realized that the average

American attention span was only about four minutes long. There better be tits dangling or a cock out to keep an ordinary citizen of the USA engaged for any period of time past that four minutes or you ain't got them. So, I looked into porn. Almost bought a production studio... But there are so many jamokes making porn now... shit, you haven't needed real people to make porn since about 2025. And... after Texas made Porn basically illegal, people got to work harder to access it." He looks at Millie. I look over at Millie. The temperature in the plane has dropped another ten degrees. She is now *glaring* at her knees so hard I think they might turn into jelly.

Marmalade chuckles again. "Millie knows the score, don't you girl? Shit... I didn't realize who you *really* were till Conrad's woman dealt you out."

"I don't want... anything to do with this." Millie growls.

Marmalade leans forward. Millie seems to recoil. "Listen to me, Millie... I know him better than you *ever* did."

*Millie is crying now, and I am suddenly very unhappy about being on this plane and having this conversation. Shit... I just wanted to figure out how to start a movement to ban male masturbation in the United States in an attempt to bring attention to women's rights being violated. Making Millie cry wasn't part of any plan. I kind of thought she would think it was funny. This is not off to a good start at all!*

Marmalade sighs and starts speaking. "I own a regional territory for the *Christians Chasing the Scoundrel Pontius Pilate*. For a long time, I *led* my assigned flock. Showed up on Sundays... did the sermon. Fun and shit at first. I had the church at the same time I was releasing albums. There was more sex at the church than there was from the concerts." Marmalade sits back in his chair and shakes his head. "Whew. The sex. It was like high school, Justin. Sex. *Every Damn Day*. Anyway, after a year or so, all of it got a little old... Even the sex. Maybe especially the sex. I got smart and trained some guys to do the preaching and fucking bit for me." Marmalade's expression softens when he sees the tears flowing from Millie's eyes. "Let me tell you, Justin... that church territory is the most profitable thing I have ever touched. It makes more money in a week than any one of my pro ball contracts did in a year." Marmalade takes a deep breath. He raises his voice. I assume to make sure Millie can hear him. "And I would like nothing more than to see the whole thing get flushed down a toilet."

There is a silence on the plane. Paal overhears Marmalade's comment and looks up with a surprised expression.

One of the robot pilots announces that we will be landing in Austin, Texas soon.

"Millie?" I ask.

She shakes her head. I glare at Marmalade. He wrinkles his nose and shakes his head dismissively before explaining. "Millie's ex-husband... is Rexford Ratchet. He started the whole concept of *Christians in Pursuit of the Scoundrel Pontius Pilate*.

"He did it with my money." Millie says tearfully. "Money the State of Texas allowed him to steal from me after it incarcerated me for doing my goddamn job!"
*Sometimes it is amazing how pieces of a puzzle can come together so quickly.*

The plane lands and starts to taxi. Marmalade stands up. "I will run into the FBO and get the two kids. I think it is best if you two stay on the plane."

I give Juice a patronizing smile. "I am pretty sure we would stay on this plane if it were on fire at this point." Paal gets up and follows Marmalade off the plane.

"Why trade one burning hell for another?" Millie mutters.

As soon as the pair is out of ear shot, I grab Millie's hand and squeeze it. "I am so sorry, Millie. I had no idea."

She shakes her head. "I know... I didn't tell you the whole story. I guess I thought you might figure it out on your own. And... maybe I hoped that you would never figure it out." She looks up at me with teary eyes. "I know who Marmalade is. I looked him up. It's... he is why I didn't even want to go in the Williams's house."

"No good can come in *assuming* that I know anything, Millie. In the future, let's just *assume* that I am not smart enough to figure things like this out on my own." I lean over so I am looking in her eyes. "Millie... Listen to me. *I love you.* I love you more than anything. You are my world. There is nothing else. If I am *actually* living, I live for you and I am pretty sure that we will die together. I think I have a plan to shock the conscious of America back in line with where it should be..."

"You want to pass a law that does what? Makes masturbating illegal?" Millie scoffs. "Like that would *ever* happen."

"Male Masturbation. Doesn't matter if it becomes a law. Might be faster if it doesn't. The point is this: The State of Texas has most of the country following it down legal rabbit holes. If that stupid church of your ex-husband's makes a big deal about masturbation and if *only* Texas passes laws making it illegal for a man to beat his meat, it goes into effect in a bunch of other states." I smile at her. "It only takes one."

"One what?"

"One case to make in front of a court that matters. Banning masturbation is absurd. The same constitutional rights such a law violates are the same ones violated by the ban on abortion and birth control. Getting a masturbation ban done in Texas might be the first domino to fall on a board full of them." I let go of her hand. "What do you think?"

"That *fucking* church." Millie growls. "Justin, you have no idea how bad that church is. No idea at all. It makes me a more than a little sick that we are riding on a plane with someone who is so involved with the place..." Millie shakes her head in frustration.

I don't really want to defend Marmalade. To do so might come off as defending the *Christians in Pursuit of the Scoundrel Pontius Pilate* and I couldn't defend any church, let alone one I suspect is a scam. "Well, to start with, I am pretty sure it isn't really a church. It's a tax shelter." I point at Marmalade's empty seat. "You heard him, He isn't in it because of a religious belief. He's in it for money. He didn't say he has a *church*... he said he has a *territory*. When I met him and Paal together, I thought maybe they were gay partners. They may be... but more, they are *business* partners. And they seem to be caught up in something they can't get out of easily."

She doesn't smile at me. Her eyes soften though. "I thought there was something off too. Your other friends were not exactly welcoming of Marmalade... and none of them seem to be homophobic."

"It's the church. Conrad is too scientifically minded. He has always disliked contrived things. Willem and Wendy are way too pragmatic for religion. Hank is a Catholic priest. The church. I bet that's it. The sense of discomfort stemmed from the collective disapproval of Marmalade's church." I sit back in the jet's cushy chair. "I wonder if we can take the church down at the same time, we bring attention to women's reproductive rights?"

I look over at Millie. She is frowning at me. "Hell, you heard him... Even *Juice* doesn't approve of his church! Millie, I am telling you this will work... walk with me down this path. If it looks sketchy or if you really aren't comfortable with anything, we will abandon the plan." I grab her hand. "It's just you and me, Millie. Our job wasn't done when we delivered Katherine Williams's baby. The cow told me to *Gather your friends and lead them* It told me that *I am both the greatest and the least among them*." I choke back tears. For whatever reason, thinking about that damn cow and its pet grasshopper makes me emotional. "I didn't understand how I can be both the greatest and the least of anything. I think I do now. I am nothing. I am weak. I am barely a man anymore. But I don't have a business where I am a slave to the income I make. I don't have any contrived beliefs that I cling to like a drowning man. Except you, Millie, I have *nothing*. Maybe that makes me more powerful than any of them because knowing what we know... I don't think that you and I can be separated, but I know that we are powerful together." I exhale. Millie stares at my face.

She reaches out with her hand. I see her nails chewed short and the chapped skin on the sides of her fingers. The hand strokes the side of my face gently. "You know what the cow told me, Justin?"

*I think my heart stops.* I shake my head tightly. Millie smiles and leans in and kisses me. Deep. Tongue and everything. It last just a second and forever. I'll say it's my first kiss, because it certainly feels like it. She breaks the embrace and sits back in her seat. The smile isn't fully back. But it's there... sort of like that Mona Lisa smile... It's a happy smile, but if I shift my glance or look away, it might disappear. "The Cow told me that I was to follow you. The Cow said that you will know what to do."

"The cow isn't much of a feminist." I comment.

"The cow is right. I will follow you." Millie closes her eyes. "Just... protect me when you can."

"Can you kiss me like that again?" I ask.

The plane shakes a little as people start boarding. Millie grabs my face and pulls it into hers.

Chapter 49
Bob beats the bishop while a queen makes her move.
The Good Residence. Someplace in the United States America
Home of the Free(ish) Land of the Brave(ish)


"Take it all off!" Geely demands. She has one of those old iPhones in her hand.

"Why?" Bob wrinkles his face up. He looks at the clock sitting on the bedside table. It is almost six. "We need to get to Micky D's. It is all meat night!"

"I need pictures of you." Geely says forcefully. "For my mother!"
"That's weird." Bob says. Subconsciously he holds his t-shirt down. "Why does she want pictures. And don't you have some?"

Geely shakes her head. "No. We don't pay for photo data transfer on our telecom plan." She points at Bob. "Take it all off. I want pictures. Then we can go to eat."

Bob looks at the posters on his wall. He does a long exhale and pulls his t-shirt over his head. "Why does your mom want pictures of me?"

"She wants to see your back. I told her that... you know... we are messing around. She said you have to be in the church, or I can't see you." Geely says. "Take it all off."

"She just needs to see my back." Bob says with a suspicious tone.
"Yeah... but *I* want more." Geely answers with a whine. "I won't show the others to anyone. Promise."

Bob shakes his head. "Take the picture."

"Take it all off." Geely says. "Pleeeeze?" She comes close to him. "I will make you squirt."

"With your mouth?" Bob asks hopefully. Geely had refused to give him a blow job.

"Ick. As If!" Geely makes a motion with her hand. "You can start though."

Bob looks at the clock. It is late. They had to hurry if they were going to get to Mickey D's. He drops his drawers. The little phone in Geely's hand makes some clicking noises. "Take it all off, Bob... Take it off!" Geely says excitedly.

Bob Good sighs and kicks his shoes off and steps out of his pants. Standing naked in the middle of his bedroom, he stands still while Geely walks around him taking photos. "Now make it squirt!" Geely says excitedly.

"Does your mother know *exactly* what we do together?" Bob asks.

Geely shakes her head. "I told her we have sex. I am not having sex with you, Bob." She points at him. "But like you can rub yourself and me. I am even ok with that lube stuff now. You had a good idea there. Use some on you. Now! Make it squirt!"

"We need to go, Geely!" Bob whines.

"Make it squirt!" Geely squeals. "Make it squirt!"

Bob sighs and picks up a tube of *PPP Micro-graphite Personal Lubrication*. Fred's dad had sent some over to his mother. She hadn't wanted to use it because it wasn't her *brand*, but he found it useful. He squirts some into his hand and ignoring Geely and her stupid camera finds his favorite poster, a blond woman with bare supersized breasts. With little interest, he starts rubbing himself. "Maybe you should do this." Bob says. "That would be better, yeah?"

Geely shakes her head. "I am doing *this*. For later."

"Later, what?" Bob asks annoyed. He is having a hard time getting aroused.

"I will look at it later, silly. You know... when I touch myself."

Bob rolls his eyes and focuses on the poster. He feels himself getting hard. He closes his eyes and imagines touching a real woman, one that looks like the blond on the poster, a woman who, unknown to Bob was entirely created by Artificial Intelligence. After a few more strokes, he feels himself cum. After making a little noise, he opens his eyes. Geely is fiddling around with the phone. "That's good, Bob. That's good."

"Can we go to Mickey D's now?" Bob asks. "I'm Mickey D Real Beef, All meat, hungry!"

Geely shakes her head. "No. I gotta go. See you later."

"What? I thought we were going to Mickey D's!" Bob exclaims.

"I am, but I told my friends I would meet them there. If you go, you know, I may see you there."

Bob pulls his shirt on, not knowing if he should be relieved to not spend any more time with Geely whose personality left something to be desired or pissed because she had certainly told him that she wanted to go to Mickey D's for all beef night. That was why she came over, wasn't it? He shakes his head in the t-shirt. Fred is right. Geely is weird.

"Ok." Bob says. "See you."

Geely doesn't reply. She just leaves.

Bob activates his communicator and asks it to call Fred. "Hey, Bob! What's up?"

"All beef night buddy! Want to go to Mickey D's with me? Like the old days?" Bob asks cautiously. Since Anne Margret had come into the picture, Fred hadn't been around much.

"Ah, man... I can't. I'm in a plane coming back from Austin, Texas." Fred answers. "Maybe we can hang out tomorrow."

"Yeah." Bob answers sadly. "I think I will be free... But it won't be All Beef night at Mickey D's!"

"Freddy, tell him we can eat real food!" Bob hears Anne Margret's voice in the background.

"We can eat real food, Bob." Fred says. He giggles at something. "Stop that, Anne Margret. Sorry Bob. I am back."

"It's ok, Fred." Bob says sadly. "Maybe I will see you tomorrow." He ends the call.

After washing up, Bob goes through the empty house. "Mom and Dad must be at church." He says out loud, a pit forming in his stomach. "I sure wish Fred was here." He goes out to the garage and grabs one of the hoverboards. After hopping on it, he starts on the path to Mickey D's. He passes the lines of transporters of hungry people waiting to go into the drive through. After parking his board, he goes inside and puts his order in for two all-beef Big Mac Whoppers, two orders of fries and a Coke. He sits down at the table that he and Fred almost always sit at and morosely eats his first burger.

Laughter to his right catches his attention. He sees Geely sitting with a bunch of kids from school. Two guys and another girl. They are laughing. In Geely's hand is the phone she had used to record him earlier. Bob feels his face flush. One of the boys points over at him, doubling over with laughter. Geely looks over and rolls her eyes.

The pit in Bob's gut gets bigger.  He takes in a deep breath and down at the uneaten food. It no longer looks very good. The emotions in his brain are confusing him.  He doesn't know if he should be angry or distressed.  He tries to call both Fred and Anne Margret's communicators. No answer on either. Tears well up in Bob's eyes. They drop one by one, some running off the fries he won't eat and pooling up on the bright pink plastic table. Bob gets up from the table and finds his hoverboard and goes home.

Chapter 50
Leaving the yellow rose behind.
Introduction to the Bible, Juice style. That Church is Wack!
Marmalade Julius's Private Aircraft
Leaving the airspace over the State of Texas.
Still a place in the United States of America
Land of the Free(ish) Home of the Brave(ish)


*Anne Margret and Fred Peterson got on the plane. They are impressive young people and appear very much in love with each other. Or lust with each other. One of the two. My experience with women up until Millie was something on the other side of lust. In any case, the youthful energy is nice to be around. Millie and I introduce ourselves and thank them both for getting us released so quickly. I point out that neither of us were officially booked into the jail and we were not processed before being released. Anne Margret says that she will tell her mother. I think that our ordeal with the state of Texas and Katherine Williams is largely finished. Marmalade and Paal go over some business things on Paal's computer. Marmalade sits down and I quickly explain my rough idea to save the world... or at least the world that is currently the United States of America.*

Marmalade Julius sits back in the cushy airplane chair. His eyes are squeezed shut and his forehead is wrinkled. He opens his eyes suddenly and sits forward towards me. "Let me get this straight. Your big idea is to *ban* male masturbation. Why not female masturbation?"

I shake my head. "There is no need. Female masturbation doesn't produce or waste anything except woman's pleasure and time. Male masturbation destroys sperm which is the seed that fertilizes the egg."
Marmalade nods his head slowly. The two kids have moved closer. They both seem to be listening intently to the conversation. "What exactly is the point of this ban?"

"It's a constitutional wrong. And that's the point." I answer.

"Why would we do something that we know is a constitutional wrong? How on earth would anyone enforce this?" Marmalade asks.

Anne Margret's face lights up. "The Tattle Tale Laws!"

I nod. "That's right Anne. Because of the Alamo Compact, If Texas were to pass such a law that included provisions where people will be rewarded for ratting out masturbators, enforcement will happen among the citizenry." I nod at Marmalade. "I am proposing this because I think that prohibiting you, or Fred from satisfying yourself with a little self-love is unconstitutional on the same grounds that telling Millie or Anne Margret they can't obtain proper health care is unconstitutional."

"Freddy doesn't masturbate." Anne Margret says with a matter-of-fact voice.

"Anne!" Fred protests.

"There is no way that any government is going to ban male masturbation." Millie says. "Not happening. Not when men are still the lawmakers for the most part."

Marmalade puts his finger in the air and looks back at Paal. "Get over here, Paal." He turns back to Millie. "I think you are wrong about that, Millie. Justin may be on to something here..."

Paal sits in the single seat across from us. "What's up?"

"How many current members of the Texas legislatures are active members of *Christians in Pursuit of the Scoundrel Pontius Pilate?*" Marmalade asks.

Paal types on his keyboard. "Of the thirty-one Texas Senators, fourteen are in the church and of the one hundred and fifty members of the Texas House of Representatives, sixty-five are in the church. Another ten percent or so votes reliably with the Church coalition."

Juice scoffs. "Done. No problem."

"Really?" Millie looks aghast. "You think you could get a law passed... just like that?"

Paal shrugs as Juice sits back in his seat and smiles. "Ms. Millie, the church members vote as a block. And... many more members of the legislative bodies in Texas are members of other churches that have similar stances. All we need in both bodies in fifty one percent of the vote."

"And the Governor of Texas... would sign such a bill?" Millie asks.

Fred is typing on his electronic pad. "Yes. Yes, he will." Fred turns the pad around. "The Governor of Texas votes with the religious block nearly ninety eight percent of the time."

Millie closes her eyes and shakes her head. "This is so messed up."

"I know." I say with a grin. "It is so messed up. That's why it will work." I point at Anne Margret. "Your mom is key to this working. We will need to find a case that fits our purpose and get it in front of the courts. Preferably one that isn't in the state of Texas."

"My dad won't like this." Fred says. "But I think Anne's mother will."

Anne Margret nods in agreement as Marmalade looks over his shoulder at the young, newly minted attorneys. He chuckles a little before answering, "Yeah, man. You are right. Conrad isn't going to like this one little bit."

I shrug my shoulders. "He will get over it."

Fred's eyes are wide. "I don't know about that. PPP sells a lot of Norma models. Using them would be... illegal. Right?"

"Any seed spilt outside of a human vagina." I say with a grin.

"Vagina in a human assigned female at birth." Marmalade clarifies.

"Jesus." Millie exclaims.

"Him too. Jesus isn't going to be exempt." Anne Margret laughs. "I like it."

Marmalade drums his fingers on the armrest. He looks over at Millie and smiles. I wait for him to say something, but nothing comes. Eventually Marmalade turns to Paal. "This is going to play into our hands. Real nice. We can take all the bites from the sacred apple we want and keep the damn apple."

"I think so." Paal says slowly.

"What are you talking about?" I ask.
Marmalade is silent for a full minute. "Here is how the church works... Twelve years ago or so, I bought a franchise from Mr. Rexford Ratchet. Millie's ex-husband.  I got three physical buildings and a territory of like four million potential souls. We took the territory by storm. Building something like this is just good marketing. Things went gangbusters... especially when I was in the pulpit every week. As it turns out, rapping and preaching are very much the same thing. I didn't cotton with the whole message Mr. Ratchet was delivering... so I changed things up." Marmalade shifts his head from side to side... "But see, that was no good for the people on top of the church. I had lowered the tithe and stopped the whole free love bit that Millie's ex enjoys so much. H.Q. was pissed because other congregations were getting wind that some branches of the church didn't charge so much and didn't force you to allow your spouse to fuck the neighbors. H.Q. wanted me to come correct or get out." Marmalade grins. "That was a no go... it is a business, see... An asset! I had *bought* a franchise. They had to *buy* me out if they wanted us out, but we made it too big. Buying me would have bankrupted them. Plus, I am protected by state *franchise* laws. The Church couldn't just make me go away. My territory is way too valuable. Shit... I got like twenty physical churches now and our penetration is the best in the country. Maybe close to twenty percent."

"You have twenty percent of the population in the city going to your church?" Anne Margret asks.

Marmalade shakes his head. "Nah... that would be sick though. I'd have to build more buildings!" He grins. "Church As a Service, girl! I got twenty percent of the population just *sending* me money for the salvation of their souls. They can go to a building if they want... and there is good shit in the buildings. We have coffee shops and restaurants. Twenty-Four Hour gyms. Shit people want... with or without the message... Or they can watch services on a monitor at home. Or, you know, they cannot watch anything at all and just assume the monthly tithe gets them on the good guy list in heaven... which is what most of them do. It doesn't matter to me as the business owner if the church members participate in the Church or not. All we are really interested in is the regular tithe. For that, we give our souls *access* to coffee shops, nice gymnasiums and, if they are interested, to a good, positive message and prayers for their eternal salvation."

"And sex with anyone they want." Millie adds.

Marmalade purses his lips. "Rexford is an asshole. Millie. What he did to you was beyond the pale. It wasn't just anti-Christian. It was anti-human. Your ex-husband is a goddamn sociopath. He is a smart son of a bitch, maybe genius level... but he is ironic. Very ironic."

"You mean iconic." Anne Margret says.

Marmalade shakes his head. "No. I mean ironic. The man leads what is currently, the largest religious group in the United States. It took him and his first elders less than five years to eclipse the entire population of Catholicism in the whole USA. Systematically, he has taken souls from all the organized religions and fundamentalist churches and converted people who had no interest in participating in any organized religion. He did it while plainly exhibiting each of the seven deadly sins... Lust, Gluttony, Greed, Sloth, Wrath, Envy and the mother of them all... Pride. The Reverend Rexford Ratchet may be iconic in his own mind... but his very *being* is quite ironic."

"Gluttony? Rex got fat?" Millie asks with a hopeful tone.

Marmalade scoffs. "Boy weighs four hundred pounds. Gets around on a little electric cart." He points at me. "What I was saying... this little idea of yours fixes a problem for me. We gonna let Rex think it is his idea and he's going to love it. He's going to run to his pals in the Texas legislature and get them to make it a law." Marmalade jumps out of his chair. "*BOOM!* Now it is law in like twenty-five or so other states. He gonna have his congregations liking it at first... cause *Spilt Seed...* It is *Biblical!* There ain't shit in the Bible about abortion or for that matter, this whole political right-wing idea that God helps those who help themselves. But jerking off? God whacked a guy for that. Smited a young guy named Onan right off the face of the rock for spilling his seed on the ground instead of putting it in his dead brother's wife."

"Seriously?" Anne Margret asks with a doubtful tone.

Marmalade nods. "Oh, yeah. This guy named Judah had a couple of sons who were all hard partiers. Old Judah was a bit of a freak himself. The oldest son was named Er. He married a broad named Tamar. God didn't care for Er. Couldn't stand the sight of him. The dude that made the platypus and let it live saw Er in action and said, *no fucking way.* Smite. Er is gone. But Er was Judah's oldest son and rules are rules. God tells Judah to get the next son in line to knock Tamar up so Er would have a son and Judah would have a blood line... That son's name was Onan. Onan liked getting with Tamar, she was a hard partying Canaanite after all... but he didn't want his offspring to be called Er's... which by biblical law, they would have been... so he'd be getting freaky with Tamar and just before the main event, he'd pull out. Jizz all over a rock or some shit. God saw this, cause' God sees everything... and he ain't happy. Boss say you do something, you do it. God tells Onan to quit fucking around and put a bun in Tamar's oven. Onan thinks he being sneaky... one day, he gets Tamar all juiced up... they be going at it, all passionate and shit. She starts making the 'O' face and Onan pulls his dick out and shoots it all over her tits. *BOOM!* God don't waste no time. He smites Onan. Boy probably still had his dick in his hand."

There is silence in the plane. Anne Margret clears her throat. "Um... *That* is in the Bible?"

"Sure is. Genesis 38." Marmalade says.

"What... What happened to Tamar? Was there another son?" Anne Margret asks.

"Oh, boy." I say, rubbing my temples. I know what is coming next because when I was sitting in Microsoft's Medical Center and Slot Machine that never stops paying off for Microsoft, I had read the Bible from cover to cover.

Marmalade laughs. "Old Man Judah wouldn't give up his third son, Shelah to this scheme of God's because... well shit, two are gone for the effort already and he's only got one left to do all the hard work sons are supposed to do and he's lost his wife, so no more sons coming. Tamar was a clever bitch. She knows she ain't worth shit as a human without kids from Judah's bloodline cause' that's how it was back then. She dresses up like a hooker and plops her sexy self down right in Judah's path one night. The old man picks her up with the promise of a goat in payment for services rendered and bangs the shit out of her. He's really thinking he's getting his monies worth out of this whore... she's doing him three, four times. Finally, he can't get it up no more and she asks for the goat she damn well knows he ain't got with him. He says to her, *I owe ya one...* She says, *yeah right, I may have been born at night, but it wasn't last night. Give me your family ring as collateral.* Judah pulls off his ring that has his family seal stamped on it and gives it to her. That's a little like handing over your credit card numbers today. Judah sends a slave with a goat for payment the next day, but no one has seen or even heard of the prostitute being described. Judah is thinking that he got a pretty good night out of a cheap tin ring he can reproduce and thinks nothing more of it. Nine months later, Tamar pops out twins. Quick to avoid the controversy of having bastard children, Tamar dangles Old Man Judah's family seal in front of the town mayor and says *These babies belong to the dude who owns this here ring...* Judah goes into a panic... he's shouting and cursing. God comes to see him and after calming him down, *our heavenly father* tells the old man that shit is cool... but, don't ever be sticking your dick in any of your daughter-in-law's again."

I see Anne look over at Fred who is blushing. Millie is laughing silently.  It's good to see Millie happier.  I turn to Juice.  "That's pretty good, Juice. I understand why people want to hear you preach."

Marmalade spreads his hands wide. "Man, shit *happens* to people. Some version of that same story happens for real in the hood like three times a week. No one needs to feel like they gonna burn in hell because they acted like a human being. Don't be a freak like Er... listen to God when he tells you to do something, and everything will be just fine. Of course... there is also the good news bit in the story about triumphing from the shadows and being fruitful in having children as Tamar choose to."

Millie scrunches up her face. "God kills people in the hood for not knocking their dead brother's wife up?"

"I might have liked to have gone to church if it was explained to me the way you just explained that!" Anne Margret says with a smile.

"But not that church!" Fred says loudly. "Not the *Christians in Pursuit of the Scoundrel Pontius Pilate!*"

Everyone in the plane turns and looks at Fred. "What?" He exclaims in protest. "No offense Mr. Julius. That church is just weird. I have friends that go there."

"Who is the lead Elder in their building? Do you know?" Marmalade asks.

"Reverend Savennutts." Fred answers.

Marmalade nods knowingly. "Yes. Savenutts is a strange dude. He is particularly loyal to the home office. One of the fellows I was told I had to hire in fact."

"How did the whole, have sex with your neighbor's wife thing get started, anyway?" Fred asks.

"Now, son... that rule is only in effect if your neighbor is a fellow *Christian in Pursuit of the Scoundrel Pontius Pilate* and you are both in good standing." Marmalade says with his finger in the air.

"Yes, Marmalade. Do tell! I am quite interested in how my ex-husband justifies promoting the sexual acts he does. Is there a clever bible verse? Was it a direct message from God, burnt into his morning toast?" Millie scoffs. "I am God, and I command you, Rex to fuck your neighbor... *Look! It is written out right there on your toast, Rex! Right above the halo on the Rorschach of the Virgin Mary!*"

Paal laughs. Marmalade chuckles with a nod. "Like I said, Millie. I know old Rex better than you ever did... and I have some things to tell you later. The home office uses a variety of messages from the Bible... let's see..." Marmalade looks at the ceiling of the airplane.

"Galatians 5:22 and 23." Paal says. *"But the fruit of the Spirit is love, joy, peace, forbearance, kindness, goodness, faithfulness, gentleness and self-control. Against such things there is no law."*

Marmalade nods and laughs. "Oh, yes. Rex quotes that one a lot. But, right before that verse, The Apostle Paul admonishes the Galatians to not fall prey to lust."
"Yes, but right after it, Galatians 5:25 instructs, not be ambitious of worldly honor, nor provoke one another to wrath, nor envy each other's happiness." Paal says. "I've heard that one a lot. If your wife is happy boning the neighbor, you should let her and not make her angry by trying to stop her."

Marmalade purses his lips and nods at Paal. "Paal wasn't happy about his wife boning the neighbor."

"She wasn't happy with me trying to stop her either." Paal retorts.

"*Big 'D'*" Marmalade mouths.

"The neighbor had a big... dick?" Anne Margret asks.

Everyone looks at her, causing her face to turn red. "I think he means divorce, Anne." I say.

"The neighbor apparently had a big dick too." Paal says gloomily. "Bigger than mine, anyway."

"Galatians is a letter the Apostle Paul wrote to a group of people living in modern day." I tell Anne. "Paul wrote lots of letters. Mostly recruiting people to Christianity. The Galatians were Celtic Greeks and Jews. So, think big parties where there is lots of food and the main event is always a big orgy. These people were living firmly on the edge of Paganism but were also God curious."

"That's right. Paul was big on recruiting Greeks. Mostly Greeks who were culturally Jewish. Old Paul had a bad circumcision as an adult. His writings reflect that. He writes in several letters that men who followed the word of Christ had no need to get the end of their manhood snipped off." Marmalade nods with a smile. "The Song of Songs are also big with old Rexy, too."

"Chapter one, verse two; *Oh, that you would kiss me with the kisses of your mouth! For your love is better than wine.*" Paal says.

"That's a pretty verse. Poetic. That is the Song of Songs? In the Bible?" Anne asks.

"It's not pretty when a four hundred pound, sixty-year-old man is saying it to a fifteen-year-old girl." Marmalade quips. "Makes your stomach turn, frankly."

I see Millie roll her eyes.

"Ick!" Anne Margret exclaims. "*That* is what happens in that church? How is that possible?"

Marmalade shrugs. "This is one of my problems with my *business venture*. The basic idea is good... provide people with the things they want, for a fee... of course... lifestyle, congregation with like-minded people, a sick gym with awesome saltwater baths." He grasps his hands together. "But the leadership of the organization always wants more. More power. More money. You get those two things by perverting people in one way or another. Rex Ratchet chose sex. The actions his church takes are almost always justified by the Bible. You see, Anne... just about any horrible thing you can think of can be justified by a bible verse. For example, Exodus 21 verses 7-11 permit a father to sell his daughter into sexual slavery."

*"If a man sells his daughter as a servant, she is not to go free as male servants do. If she does not please the master who has selected her for himself, he must let her be redeemed."* Paal recites in a sing song voice. *"This is the word of God."*

"*That* is *not* in the Bible!" Anne Margret exclaims.

Marmalade smiles. "Any terrible thing that you can think of has been accepted at some time in history. That verse absolutely *is* in the Bible. Lots of the Elders in the church use that verse and others like it for justification when they ask a family for access to a newly confirmed daughter."

Marmalade continues to explain. "See, once a person... male or female has reached puberty and gets the tattoo I am sure you are familiar with, they are fair game. I know of girls... and boys... as young as thirteen who have been taken by adults. Not in my churches, so far as I know." Juice nods at Millie. "But the sick fuck who Millie here used to know..." He nods his head. "That's how the church has devolved and it's why I want to break free. *Church as a Service* is really good business for me. It doesn't have to be so freaky, and it will still be a good business."

Millie leans forward and looks at me and Marmalade. "Ok you two... I'll bite. How is *banning male masturbation* going to change this fucked up cult of a church that my ex-husband started *and* help women?"

Marmalade speaks before I do. "It's a really bad idea. Phenomenally bad idea, putting a legal moratorium on spanking the old monkey, Millie.

And that's why it works for both destroying the church and doing what Justin wants."

Millie raises an eyebrow. "Well, spill the sperm. I'm listening."

I clear my throat. "Abortion was made illegal in the United States through both judicial and congressional actions. That makes it harder to challenge in court. The written decision in *Dobbs* made it clear that the actual practice of abortion is not mentioned in the constitution, thus making any law regarding the action either something to be handled by the states or by congress as a whole. Same with birth control. All anyone could talk about was the actual act of abortion and not the sex that comes before it. Now we have no birth control, no abortion and it appears, no sex. So, it is unlikely that any abortion cases are going to come before a court that matters. We get Texas to ban male masturbation, or at least consider it and then constitutional issues can be brought up *regarding masturbation*. The same constitutional issues that are violated with the abortion ban are similar to the issues that will be violated if a state bans male masturbation. Freedom of expression. Freedom of Privacy. Freedom of Liberty. Conservatives in this country have long argued that the constitution doesn't protect any rights to individual privacy. I don't think that most of America... even in the stunted state it appears to be in today... would agree with that. American's have always valued their privacy. *Privacy* is... or was, a hallmark of being an American. The political process in this country broke some time ago, allowing conservatives to abandon the general sense of Classic Liberalism that was the basis for most of the political parties since the beginning of time for the United States of America. When they could, conservatives have passed laws and did things that eroded that idea that we all have liberty, we all have agency. Things can only be set right with good legislation or by the court system overturning these crazy laws."

Marmalade nods. "I haven't always thought along these lines, Millie. Honestly, I was a big supporter of Trump and his policies. I thought that he saw a path forward for this country that others couldn't see. I thought he stood up for the little people... people who had no voice. What I know now is that his alligator mouth combined with goof ball actions and his far-right wing political cronies only provided mental opiates for the little people. His supporters thought that they were gaining rights when in fact, we were losing control over the basic ability to self-determine our own providence. We put him into office because we thought he could change the things that weren't working. As it turns out, he got played... and played hard by crazies he surrounded himself with. These bat shit crazy mother fuckers used his lack of experience to jam the bench with court judges that would do their bidding. We screwed the future for ourselves." His fingers drum the arm rest. "As far as the church goes... Paal here is a master at messaging... getting ideas out into the mainstream and turning those ideas into cash. We can use his talents here, I think."

"It's pretty hard to get a message out in the world today. There are so many avenues that people get information from... where would you even start?" Fred asks.

"Son, in one of our businesses, we sell *virtual* gym memberships. We make money off the idea that you can be fit by paying a monthly fee for a *virtual* gymnasium that no one ever goes to. We get this going... Paal is going to use the absolutely terrible idea of a ban on petting the proverbial penguin to destroy the *Christians in Pursuit of the Scoundrel Pontius Pilate*. As soon as I see that the Church has been degraded in the public view... I will take that opportunity to fire the people I have working for me that are loyalists to Millie's ex-husband and the Church. After that is done, I will step back into the pulpit, rename my church and take control of my congregations with a better, healthier message."

Millie looks at both of us and exhales a long breath. "This is one of the dumbest, most convoluted ideas I have ever heard." She shakes her head, and I see a flash of that great Millie smile. "I don't understand it totally... but I think it might work."

"I think it works. If you can get such a ridiculous law passed." Fred says. "I think my dad will be mad at both of you. But, If the idea is to get the issue in front of the courts, I think the idea works."

Anne Margret raises her eyebrows. "I want to know more about this Song of Songs. I had no idea there was sex stuff in the Bible."

Chapter 51
This is what being is poor is like now.
Stupid Wagers. Bad Proposal.
Government Housing Someplace in America
Land of the Free(ish) Home of the Brave (ish)

Millie parks her transporter and lets out a long sigh. "We haven't slept for a while."

"No. We have not." I agree. Marmalade had taken us back to the Williams's house. Willem and Wendy had already left to go to St. Martin to be with Katherine and Yoda. Edith the Robot said she would make a room up for each of us. Millie declined. I had agreed with her at the time. Now, that decision looks like a bad one.

"We probably should have stayed at the Williams's house." I say, looking at the crowd gathered outside of the old Walmart that is now my temporary residence.

"I don't like owing people anything." Millie says. "Let's try and get inside." She picks up her medical bag from the floor of the transporter.

We get out and walk up to the door. A skinny dirty looking man runs past us. "I hope I am not too late!" He calls out.

"Too late for what?" I ask. Millie shakes her head and shrugs. A heavy-set woman waddles close to us. "What is going on?" I ask, motioning at the crowd.
"It be fight night!" The woman looks at me with distain. "You Boring or somethin'? Tonight always fight night."

The woman picks up her waddle. My body still refuses to move at any acceptable speed beyond a fast shuffle. I should have snagged another one of Willem's canes from his house. It takes us a bit to get closer to the crowd. When we arrive, I hold Millie's hand tight and push and shove my way, old man style, into the mass of people. The group has formed a twenty-foot circle. In the center of the makeshift arena, two white men circle each other. Both are shirtless. Jailhouse tattoos cover their torsos. One is nearly bald, the other has long, dirty looking hair.

"Bet! Bet! Bet!" A woman wearing only a bra and panties comes up to me and Millie. "Place yer bet!"

"What are we betting on?" I ask the woman

"Baldy is ten to one to win. Bet ten. Win one. You bet?" The woman steps close. I can smell that more than most of the people around me, she has not experienced the thrill of bathing lately. "Bet!"

I shake my head. "Not good odds." I respond. Wouldn't have mattered if I thought it was a sure thing. I don't have any money or credits... whatever is being used to wager here.

The woman moves on to a guy in a wheelchair who gives her some paper money. She hands him back a receipt from where, I have no idea. I see two young, maybe teenage girls sitting on the ground next to a disheveled woman. The woman, apparently the mother and wife or partner stares blankly at the ground. The girls watch the fighting with interest. In particular they watch the man with hair. Bald man lands a big punch to the right side of his opponent's chin. The man with hair falls to the ground, causing the crowd to cheer. Panic flashes across one of the girl's faces. She crab walks to the man on the ground and says a few words to him. Encouragement maybe? Tips, like... don't allow yourself to get hit in the head? I'd like to think so. The man struggles to his feet and assumes a drunken fighter's stance. Baldy is prancing around the ring pounding on his chest.

"He must be anticipating a big payday." Millie says with a tired tone.

I look at the girl who had crawled out to give what I assume to be her father encouragement. "I don't think that the bald guy is fighting for money." I say motioning to the trio sitting on the ground. Both girl's faces have a frozen, panicked appearance. The mother continues to stare at the broken pavement as if in a trance.

Baldy circles the man with hair, taunting him with unintelligible words. I can hear what the man is saying... I can't understand any of it. It sounds like gibberish. "Is that a foreign language he is speaking?"

Millie watches the macabre scene. "It is to us. The crowd seems to understand it. Street language, I suppose."

Baldy starts playing up to the crowd, bouncing on his bare feet and waving his hands in the air. The man with hair stupidly drops his arms. Baldy roundhouse punches him in the jaw. The fighter's body absorbs the blow, spinning around before crumpling to the ground. Most of the crowd cheers. Some boo. Apparently ten to one was too big of odds for many to pass up. After pounding on his chest for effect a few more times, Baldy walks over to the woman sitting with the two young girls one of whom is crying and grasping her mother's dirty dress. He steps over the unconscious body of his opponent and grabs the girl, pulling her up by her hair. "Mine! All Mine! I won you!" The mother's stare never leaves the broken pavement as her crying daughter is pulled from her dress.

A lump forms in my throat. That's a strange feeling. I really have not been too emotional since emerging from my long nap. The crowd starts to thin a bit. Another fight won't start for a few more minutes. "Justin, we need to go inside." Millie says softly. "This isn't our fight. At least not today."

"Sex trafficking, 2042." I say in observance of what I had just witnessed. Millie leads me to the door. We pass by the receptionist who repeats both of our names in an extra loud voice. I struggle up the stairs. "Do... Do you think people like Conrad... Elizabeth... do you think they know that stuff like this is happening?"

Millie shakes her head. "Maybe they do. Maybe they don't. I think that civilization lost its collective ability to care about one other a long time ago."

I don't say anything in response. What I had just seen on the street in front of where I am supposed to be living wasn't right. It was barbarian. Something that happened before civilization came to accept that people have basic rights... not something that should be happening at any time in the United States of America. But there wasn't anyone in the crowd that I saw... other than the mother, maybe, who seemed to give a damn about the young girl who was basically snatched from her mother's arms. We get to the apartment, and I open the door. The bright light comes on. Nothing in the place has gotten any worse than it was when we left it. Millie sighs deeply and takes off Wendy Williams's altered pants suit. I carefully take off Willem's Canali suit. Millie, clad only in her bra and those totally unsexy granny panties, crawls up onto the stainless-steel tray that is my bed. I know she will take the bra off when the light goes out. "Can I sleep with you?" She asks.

I nod and crawl up into the small bunk next to her. We stay still and the light goes off. "Millie?" I ask.

"Yes?"

"Would you like to use my last name?" I ask.

Her breathing slows. Then it stops. I wonder if I have made her angry.

"Are you asking me to marry you?" She finally says.

I shake my head. "I... don't know?" I pull her tight. "I just wanted to offer to let you use my last name... when you introduce yourself to people."

I feel her nod. "That's nice Justin." She snuggles closer to me. "You are very kind." I feel her go to sleep on my arm.

"I love you, Millie." I say softly. "Will you marry me?"

*That wasn't so hard, now, was it?*

Chapter 52<br>
Driving. Meet my wife.<br>
Making A New Friend. Information controls the world.<br>
Marmalade Julius's home. Somewhere in the United States of America<br>
Home of the Free(ish) Land of the Brave(ish)

Millie's transporter pulls out of the parking lot of the Honorable Representative Nancy Pelosi Public Housing, Convalescence and Retirement Center. She has been friendly this morning. We are on the way to Juice's house. It is about as far away as Willem's house in the opposite direction.

Horns honk as Millie merges into traffic. I see the bald man from the fight last night strutting down the street. The teenage girl he took from her mother's arm shuffles behind. Her posture and face mirror the defeat and despair I am sure she feels. I know I feel it.

"Didn't need to see that this morning." Millie mutters. She swerves to avoid hitting a man who runs out in front of the transporter. We make turns and get on a highway. Millie turns to me. "I want to ask you something."

I tense up and clench my teeth. She is going to ask about my stupid, fumbling questions I had asked in bed. "Yeah?"

"Do you think you can drive? I hate driving."

I exhale. "Oh."

Millie grins. "What did you think I was going to ask you, Justin?"
I shake my head a little and force a smile on my face. "Um... I don't know? Maybe you want the bottom bunk all to yourself?"

"Nah. I like sleeping next to you. It's comfortable. Makes me feel safer." Millie answers.

"I haven't driven for a while.  The last time really didn't work out so well."

Millie nods. "I know. This thing won't drive itself. If it would, I wouldn't care where I sit. I never did really like driving."

"I loved it." I say quickly. A wave of sadness washes over me. I really did like driving. The freedom. The control. It was awesome. I should have done more of it when I was able to.

"I can try. My reflexes aren't what they use to be."

Millie pulls off the road. "Great. Let's try right now."

"Right now?" I ask with a little trepidation.

She nods. "Get out and come over to this side. I will scoot over."

I open the passenger door and walk around to the driver's door. Once behind the wheel, I try and familiarize myself with the vehicle. "Where is everything?" I ask.

Millie shakes her head. "That's all there is. A wheel. A throttle pedal. A brake."

"No speedometer? No tachometer?"
Millie gives me one of her, *Aren't you precious looks*. "What would this vehicle need a gauge that measures engine RPM for?" She taps on the screen that is showing the map to Marmalade's house. "The speed is at the bottom of the map. These display only in kilometers. It doesn't matter though. The transporter won't break the speed limit."

I look over at her. "Really?"

Millie nods. "Cars haven't broken the speed limit for almost ten years. When they went all electric, the ability of the driver to speed went away."

I shrug and pull out on the highway. An autonomous truck passes, shaking the transporter. "Don't get us killed, Justin." Millie comments. "Think I could actually do that if I tried?"

Millie thinks about it for a moment. "I have wondered the same thing. I don't know."

Driving is not a challenge so far. Hang on to the steering wheel. Throttle appropriately. Brake when needed. Listen to the directions as they are given by the mapping program. "This isn't bad."

"No. It isn't. I rather like sitting on this side of the car." Millie smiles. "Relaxing."

We drive in comfortable silence. The neighborhoods change from nice to not nice and back to nice. We go through some sort of industrial area where there are a lot more trucks. The mapping program takes us onto a single lane road that is covered by trees. "Pretty." Millie says.

I nod. We wind up the lane and turn onto a gravel path. "I wasn't expecting this." I look at the mapping program. It says we are two miles to our destination. I drive up the path slowly. Large trees overhang a stone sign that reads, *Marmalade Juice, Magic in every Sip*. "I think we are here."

"I certainly hope so." Millie grins. "Your friend is quite the promoter."

"I'm hoping so." We pull into a shaded parking lot where there is another transporter parked. "Where do you think we go in?"

"There is an opening in the bushes. I am guessing there." Millie looks around. "I am not sure if this is creepy or awesome."

"Maybe it is both." I answer. We get out of the transporter. I look around for a Robot. None come. We walk through the opening in the bushes. It seems to lead us in a maze. At a juncture of choosing to go left or right, I look at Millie. "What do you think?"

"I think if we split up, I will never see you again." She looks both ways. "Right."

"Right." I say doubtfully. We walk another thirty feet or so to a gate. There is a button in the center of the gate. I push it. A pleasing sounding bell rings.

"You found the gate!" An excited Marmalade announces. "Be right down!"

A few minutes later, Marmalade Juice opens the finished wooded gate and ushers us through. "I thought you might call me when you got lost."
"We wondered around for a moment... but we have no way to call you." I answer. "Millie has a cellular phone... but, I don't have your number.
Marmalade waves at me dismissively. "Where you guys staying, anyway?"

"Honorable Representative Nancy Pelosi Public Housing, Convalescence and Retirement Center". I rattle off.

Marmalade stops. "No, you aren't. That place is a hell hole."

I nod. "We are. And yes. It is."

Marmalade shakes his head. "We got room for you both here. You stay here."

Neither Millie nor I respond. The path opens to a spectacular estate. I see a bright blue pool of water that has a waterfall running it to that seems to come from the roof of the house, a structure that looks like walls of windows joined together in some irregular shape.

"Wow." Millie says. "This is beautiful, Marmalade."

"Thank you, Millie." Juice says proudly. "I designed it myself. Can't wait to show you both around." He takes us on a tour. The house is magazine beautiful with complimentary artwork hanging throughout. "Your friend is definitely gay." Millie whispers in my ear after Marmalade has shown us the indoor koi pond that features a fresco reproduction of the *Birth of Venus* on the ceiling.

We are standing on a balcony in a guest bedroom overlooking the pool and waterfall when a woman walks out on the pool deck. She is about our age, solidly built but by no means fat. Her dark curly hair is peppered with strands of gray. "Vel!" Marmalade shouts happily. "Come on up here. I want you to meet Justin and Millie. They are the couple I told you about!" Millie turns and gives me that million-dollar smile. "Couple. I think I like that."

*Yeah, I felt the butterflies.*

A moment later, the curly haired woman is standing beside us on the balcony. Juice gives her a kiss and squeezes her into his side before making introductions. "This is my partner in life and love, Velvela Garfinkle. Vel, this is Justin and Millie!" The woman greets the two of us with a smile that is almost as infectious as Millie's. "Justin! I have heard so much about you over the years. It is so good to finally meet you!" She looks at Millie. "I've met a lot of famous people in my life, Dr. Cockburn. I have never been in the presence of a modern-day Joan of Arc."

Millie freezes. Her eyes dart to me. I put my arm around her. "It's ok, Millie. I think it is ok." *I really have no idea if it's ok or not...* I try and flush the nervousness from my body that I have been infected with from the fear that Millie is projecting. "Vel, it is nice to meet you." I don't say that Marmalade not only hadn't mentioned having a wife, but he also had me pretty well convinced he might be gay. "It's not safe for Millie... you know... to be Dr. Cockburn."

Velvela's face turns red. Her hands go to her mouth. "Oh!" She looks up at Marmalade. "They don't know?"

Marmalade shakes his head.

Vel grabs Millie's hands and pulls them into her rather ample breasts. "Millie. I live a similar existence to you. Fortunately, I have been able to do it in a bit of paradise and mostly outside of a small prison cell. I... am... the leader of the now underground United States Chapter of Planned Parenthood." She looks at me and back to Millie. "I am so sorry for my insensitive greeting. I guess I assumed that Marmalade would tell you who I was."

Marmalade shakes his head. "Darling, I don't even tell people I am married. Yesterday, we had Paal with us... but we also had Elizabeth Eaton's daughter and Conrad Peterson's son on the plane." He looks at me. "You better get used to this. You are going to start needing to live a life behind bars."

I scrunch up my face. "I don't think I understand... what do you mean, behind bars?"

Marmalade smiles. "When you came here today, there were two gates open for you. You probably didn't notice. My security team was watching. As soon as you came onto the property, the first gate closed. When you went past the stone wall, the second gate closed." He nods his head towards his wife. "This property was built as a safe harbor for Vel. She hasn't left this property to go anyplace local for a few years now. When she leaves, it's by helicopter and then only to a private airport. There isn't an actual bounty for her arrest like there is on Millie... but, there are plenty of people out there who want her not in jail behind bars, but dead."

Vel smiles. She punches me lightly in the shoulder. "It's all good, Justin. Marmalade built me a super nice prison to live in." She winks. "And maybe... *your* crazy ass idea will make it so we can all have dinner out in public again someday!"

"Is Paal... security of some sort?" I ask, the pieces coming together for me, slowly.

Marmalade nods. "Paal started out as my head of security. He showed me early on that he really understands modern communications. Paal was able to identify outside threats to Vel and me... mostly Vel. He is very, very good at monitoring all of the different social media channels and finding new ones when they pop up. We quickly figured out that the tools he built for monitoring the different channels... dark web and all that, could be used to efficiently disseminate information. Now Paal is both my personal security guard, and he helps me get the word out on whatever message we need sent."

I look over at Millie. She has relaxed... a little. I turn back to Juice. "The others... Hank, Conrad... Willem? They don't know? You know, about Vel?"

Marmalade shakes his head. "Honestly, Justin... Willem and I got together only a few times after my pro career ended. Until the church thing, I wasn't flying in the same airspace that Willem and Wendy occupy, if you know what I mean. I saw Conrad once... he came to one of my concerts with an older woman that I suppose might have been his first wife." He shakes his head. "The other day was the first time I had seen Hank since high school. Not one of them know about Vel." Juice shrugs and squeezes his wife in a one-armed hug. "She's the most important thing in my life and I can't share her with many people."

"How long have you two been together?" I ask.

"We met in 2028 at one of Marmalade's concerts. A friend's brother was doing security and got me backstage." Vel looks lovingly at Juice. "We've been together since... married for almost ten years."

"So... you were a groupie." I deadpan.

Millie backhands me in the chest. "Justin. That's not nice!"
I grin. "I think it is kind of cool my friend had groupies!"

Vel laughs. "I *absolutely* am a groupie!" She smiles at Marmalade and strokes his chest. Juice had all these young chippies wearing next to nothing clambering to get in bed with him and he picked the Jewish woman with the big hair wearing palazzo pants to hide her big tokhes!"

"It was probably the V neck sweater that got my attention." Marmalade smiles. "I like big boobs. I cannot lie." His hand rubs the back of Vel's neck affectionately. "The rest of the package turned out to be pretty good too!"

"Well, I think you guys are a very attractive looking couple." Millie says happily.

Marmalade looks at his watch. "Paal is downstairs setting up the launch of your grand ideas, Justin. If you guys want to come watch."

Vel shakes her head. She grabs Millie's hand and holds it. "I have my call in starting soon. I would love it if Millie would sit in!"

"Call in?" Millie asks.

Vel grins. "Planned Parenthood has maintained a hidden network that can be accessed online with a VPN connection and a biometric password. Women... and a few men from around the country are helping secure sources of medicine and birth control. We also provide advice to women in trouble." She squeezes Millie's hand. "There is no video or anything, and I certainly won't introduce you by your real name... but I would be honored if you will sit in on the call with me."

Millie shrugs. "I would like that." She looks over at me. "Are you ok without me?"

I gaze at her. Bits of the sun filter through her hair. She gives me that big Millie smile. My heart flutters.

"I don't think I would ever be ok without you Millie." I grin. "But you won't be far away."

"I'll take good care of her, Justin!" Vel says. The two women walk off, chatting happily with each other.

"That looks like a good connection." I comment, following Marmalade out of the room.

Juice puts a thumb up. "I was hoping that those two would hit it off like that." We go down a long hallway before descending a flight of stairs. Another hallway opens to what can only be described as a control center. Large monitors fill the walls. There are several workstations, but only one is occupied. Paal Tan is hunched over a keyboard, looking at the screen in front of him.

"Paal. We are here." Marmalade announces. He points at the monitors on the wall. "We can keep track of over four hundred million unique users and ten thousand different media outlets at any one time. This system is in operation twenty-four hours a day. We listen and look for keywords. If there is a hit, the system starts monitoring the event."

"That's like... ten percent of the *world's* population." I comment.

"Yeah." Juice agrees. "I would like to get closer to twenty percent."

"You don't have a staff of people doing this?" I ask.

Marmalade shakes his head. "Use to. People are dangerous and they make mistakes. Paal and our small technical staff have utilized Artificial Intelligence to make it so we don't need more than a few people in the circle. Much more secure that way."

I look around at the many monitors. Chat feeds are plainly visible on some of the screens. One screen appears to be live porn. Another shows an angry man shaking his fist in the camera. "Can these people tell you are watching them?"

Marmalade moves his head around. "Most of these are public facing websites, or forums where one can get in with a simple log in." He points at the screen with what I think is showing porn on it. "That feed is from the church. That woman is pulling a train. Four or five guys from the church. We grabbed the feed because we know our parishioners are watching. It wouldn't surprise me if one of our Elders is in the video."

"Why?" I ask.

Marmalade rolls his eyes and shrugs. "Like I said. The church is a profitable venture. Very profitable."

I shake my head. "No, why is that happening."

Marmalade just shrugs in response.

"What happens now? Do you bring in some of your ministers and tell them the idea and let them run with it? It doesn't sound like you are on the best of terms with the head of the church to introduce the idea yourself." I say.
Marmalade laughs. "Oh, heavens no, Justin. If I called my people, there is no way in hell they take the idea forward. That would kill it before it starts." He points at two screens that appear to be documents. The pages are flipping by very quickly. "Paal has created a stream of information and started disseminating it slowly out to the world. In effect, we are seeding the idea in places where we know that it will get traction. I think it's going to take off like a wildfire, to be honest with you."

"Already has." Paal says. "You guys are late. I have been here since oh dark thirty sneaking around in the dark corners of the World Wide Web, leaving my documents of discontent." He types a command on the keyboard. "Monitor twenty-eight." A finger extends, pointing to a larger monitor on the right side of the room. "I created a bot named Holy Harold and gave it instructions to be polite but firm that masturbation is an abomination in the eyes of the Lord. Holy Harold has quoted scripture from Genesis, Leviticus and Deuteronomy. The bot made seven unique posts and answered fourteen questions."

I look at the screen. There are over seven thousand posts about banning male masturbation.

"Here are the statistics..." Paal types on the keyboard as he speaks. "Monitor twenty-nine."

Marmalade points and whistles in amazement. "Look at that. Sixty nine percent of the people participating in the chat support the idea whole heartedly, based on eye movements and how they respond in the chat room. We are estimating that seventeen percent think that any ban on masturbation should also include women. Twenty percent are a hard no against any bans on masturbation. Eight percent of the obviously male participants have propositioned obviously female participants in the chat in some fashion. Female participants are against the idea overall, fifty eight percent to forty two percent. Male participants are in favor of the idea overwhelmingly. Seventy five percent to twenty five percent."

"What!" I exclaim. "That is fucking bananas!"

Marmalade smiles. "Human beings will consistently move against their self-interests if it means that they are accepted by the masses better. Men significantly more so than women... but both genders do it." He motions at Paal. "It helps that when Paal crafted this particular message, he used certain key words that motivate specific responses."

"This is creepy." I say. The woman on the porn screen has disrobed. A naked man is in the room with her. They seem to be negotiating something. "Why would she want that filmed?"

"Proof that she is a participant." Marmalade says in a flat tone. "What else we got, Paal?"

"I have the hook set for Reverends Spirebats and Kookluver." Paal says. "When they become active, I'll put it up on the main screen so you can watch."

"Reverend Spirebats and Reverend Kookluver are two of the more enthusiastic followers of Reverend Rex Ratchet." Marmalade explains. "I had to hire all four of these guys to keep my territory. The others we will target are Savenutts and Wacadingle."

The large screen changes from a chat room where the subject was the merits of killing off poor people to remedy suffering. A logo appears for the *Christians in Pursuit of the Scoundrel Pontius Pilate*. Paal points at the screen. "I sent six separate white papers to the inboxes of Reverends Savenutts, Kookluver, Wacadingle and Spirebats. We will see Savenutts in a moment on the screen. He is in that couple's mediation this morning. Wacadingle is in Texas at a retreat. Four of the white papers are innocuous... random things these guys are used to seeing. One of the papers purports to be from a theologian and the other from a phycologist. Both of those papers talk about the harm masturbation, particularly male masturbation does to the male psychology and society in general. Complete and utter bullshit... but these guys won't know that... or care to know such a thing."

"Couldn't they just track the source backwards?" I ask. "These are smart guys, they will figure out that the papers are fake, right?"

Marmalade smiles. "Paal, I will let you take that one."

Paal turns, his face impassive and neutral. "Confirmation Bias is very powerful, Justin." He blinks a few times, waiting for me to respond. Since I have no idea what he is talking about, I remain silent. Paal spins his chair around and types on the keyboard while explaining what he means. "These four ministers are all in our employment because the head church sent them. Each of them has a unique personality, but they were chosen to come here because of their loyalty to the church, rather than to Marmalade." I see Paal's smile in the reflection on the screen in front of him. "We can attack the qualities of those unique personalities by feeding each person small snippets of information that make them confident in their individual beliefs. This is called *self-serving bias*. Feeding another person's ego in this manner is a very efficient way to control their behavior. We know that their loyalty to the Rex Ratchet and his whims creates opportunity to then feed confirmation bias... in this case, the collective tendency of these men to process any information from certain sources in a singular way that is consistent with their own existing beliefs. When one believes, he will be able to convince others who may not believe as strongly to follow suit. Most of the time, this type of thing is unintentional." Paal sighs. "Most people *naturally* ignore information that is inconsistent with their beliefs. In the same vein, most people are very likely to process and distribute information that supports self-held, or group held beliefs when an issue is deemed highly important or self-relevant."

I shake my head. "Is this evil?"

Marmalade puts his hand on my shoulder. "Evil is a construct of man. *We* collectively determine what is evil and what is not. Immanuel Kant was an eighteenth-century Russian Philosopher. He said it best, *morality is not defined by the consequences of our actions, our emotions, or an external factor. Morality is defined by duties and one's action is moral if it is an act motivated by duty*". Juice points at one of the screens. "These ministers *believe* in their duty, and they trust their *individual morality*, such that it is. In this case, we will take advantage of that *belief* by feeding them ideas congruent with the self-serving ideas that they already hold. Because these men are already motivated to act, they will move on the ideas quickly... both because they have the need to feed their individual egos and because they have a *belief* that they not only need to act on this new information, but they also need to incorporate the ideas into their morality structure."

I shake my head. "I never dreamed I might be talking to you about Russian Philosophers, Marmalade." I point at the screens. "These are educated men. How do they not know that the theologian and philosopher didn't write these white papers?"

Marmalade Julius grins. The gold caps on his teeth glitter. "Paal and I created both the theologian and the philosopher, Justin. The papers are real, because both the theologian and the philosopher are real... at least they are to these guys."

Paal jumps up and motions at the wall of screens. "The hook is set."

I look up at the screen. An email is being composed from Reverend Wacadingle to Reverend Rexford Ratchet.

"I thought he might race to be first." Marmalade comments. "He is down in Texas, and I bet he will try and get an audience with Ratchet."

Sure enough, after Wacadingle referenced verbiage from both the theologian and the philosopher, he asked the Reverend Rexford Ratchet for an in-person meeting. Paal grins as he watches the first result of his labors. He claps his hands together. "Just like I planned."

"This is insane." I say under my breath. "Just insane. And creepy."

"Insanity?" Marmalade chuckles. "No. Insanity is doing something without knowing what the result might be. We know what is going to happen next. Justin... when you see how fast *what happens next* rolls out, it is really going to creep you out."

"This power you have is like a drug, Marmalade. You need to be careful with this." I say. I am not sure where the words come from... that little angry fellow in my brain, I suppose.

Marmalade winces like I have hurt him. "This is necessary, Justin. We must monitor things like we do because no one is doing it for us. There is no media to speak of. No effective watchdogs... what you see here? You asked earlier how the United States got to be the way it is?" He shakes his head. "There is maybe another dozen or so groups in the United States that do things to this level. They all have an agenda. I think we are about the best there is..." He shrugs. "This is how *we* get things done now."

My eyes narrow. "Who is *the we* you speak of?" I ask rhetorically. My eyes sweep the wall of monitors. The woman on the porn feed is fellating a man while another grabs her hips and trusts himself into her. There is a large tattoo of a cross on both the woman's back and the back of the man thrusting into her. It is possibly the most unsexy sex thing I have ever witnessed.

"*We*, is the people, Justin." Marmalade says softly.

I nod silently to Marmalade's comment as my mind races. There are a lot of possibilities available using this technology if Marmalade is willing to do it. Maybe the *drug* of this data manipulation is affecting me.

Marmalade motions dismissively towards the porn screen. "Savenutts must have finished with his couple's mediation... or maybe he is in the middle of it. He puts his hand on my arm. "Let's go see how our girls are doing. We will come back later and check on Paal."

Chapter 53
Bob is in a bad place. His parents, worse.
Good Residence Someplace in the United States of America
Land of the Free(ish) Home of the Brave(ish)


Fred Peterson rings the doorbell again on the Good house. He tries the door. It swings open. Fred calls out, "Hello... Bob?"

The silence of the house answers him. "Bob!" Fred yells with a sharp tone. The proximity meter in his communicator says that Bob is in the house. Fred slowly walks up the stairs to Bob's room. The door is closed. He knocks softly. "Bob? You in there?"

"Yeah." Bob says. The tone of the single word answer gives many clues to Trump Bob Good's current mental state.

"You ok if I come in?" Fred asks.

For a long pause, there is no answer. "Bob?" Fred asks again. "Yeah." Bob answers.

Fred opens the door slowly. "I've been trying to get a hold of you, buddy. Anne Margret and I..." Fred freezes. The room is dark. Bob is laying on the unmade bed in just a pair of boxer shorts. An odor of unwashed human flesh overwhelms Fred's olfactory senses. "Umm... Bob? Are you ok?"

"No." Bob answers. "I am not." A sob follows the words.
"How long have you been laying here?" Fred looks around the cluttered room.

"Don't know." Bob answers.

Fred's telecom alerts him to Anne Margret calling him. He opens the line. "You are at the Good house?" Anne says in his ear. Fred ignores her question. He knows that she can see where he is on her proximity monitor.

"Bob. Why don't we get you up? We can go get some food. When was the last time you ate?" Fred asks. His communication line is open. Anne Margret can hear the conversation he is having with Bob.

"I don't want to." Bob answers. His eyes are open, staring at the ceiling.

"I'm worried about you, buddy. Sit up. Let's talk about what's wrong."

"Everything." Bob answers. "Can't be fixed."

"What can't be fixed?"

"Me."

Fred sighs. "I don't know what to do here."

"Want me to come over?" Anne Margret asks in his ear.

"Yeah." Fred says. "That's a good idea."

"Are you talking to yourself?" Bob mumbles. "Cause' if you have a good idea, I'd love to hear it, Freddy."

"I'll be right over." Anne Margret ends the call.

Fred sits on the foot of the bed. "What's got you down?"

Bob shakes his head and squeezes his eyes shut.

Fred sits in silence on the end of the bed for a few minutes. "Anne and I did a legal thing. Our first one. Down in Texas. We got this couple out of jail."

Bob says nothing.

"It was pretty cool." Fred shrugs. "I mean... mostly, Anne's mom did the work. She has a friend who is a judge down there and she called in a favor."

"I didn't graduate from high school." Bob mumbles.

"What?" Fred exclaims. "All you had to do was send the research paper in."

"Yeah." Bob answers. "I didn't do that."

Fred shrugs. "There is still time."

"And then what?" Bob asks. "I am not smart enough to be a lawyer like you and Anne Margret." He sighs. "I suppose... I can just enter stupid contests like my mom and dad. Collect the living wage like everyone else does."

Fred shakes his head. "Bob, you can do anything you want to."

"That is definitely not true, Freddy."

Fred sits with Bob in silence. He hears the front door open. Light footsteps come up the stairs. Anne Margret knocks softly on the door before opening it.

"Jesus!" She exclaims. "What died in here?"

Fred motions at Bob's prone body. "I was thinking Bob. But when I got here, he was talking. I ruled it out the possibility that he might be dead."

Bob lets his presence be known with a sob.

"Bob!" Anne Margret snaps. "Get up."

"Why?" Bob asks.

"Because I am hungry, and we are going to Mickey D's."

Bob sighs. "I don't want to go anywhere. I especially do not want to go there."

Anne Margret sits on Fred's knee. She slaps Bob's bare skin on his leg. "Did you tell Fred?"

"Tell me what?" Fred asks.

Bob squeezes his eyes shut and shakes his head.

"I made some calls on the way over. Apparently, his girlfriend, Geely took a video of Bobby here beating his man meat." Anne Margret puts her arm around Fred's neck for balance. "She's been showing it to everyone and their dog."

Fred frowns. "Why did you let her do that, Bob?"

"We don't blame victims, Fred." Anne says sharply, smacking Fred in the shoulder. "Bob! Get up and take a shower. Put some clothes on. We *are going* to Mickey D's."

Bob sits up. He swings his feet around and puts them on the floor. "I don't want to see anyone."

"Everybody whacks off, Bob. It's no big deal." Anne Margret says. "Go take a shower."

Bob lets out a long sigh. He gets up and picks out some clean clothes before leaving the room. Fred and Anne hear the shower turn on in the nearby bathroom.

"She is really showing it to everyone?" Fred asks.

Anne nods. "Geely apparently tried to send it to one of the social media channels but got rejected." She kisses Fred on the forehead. "Can we not sit in this room. It smells bad."

Fred nods and pats her bottom. They start walking down the stairs just as an obviously angry Sookie Moonbeam Magi Good storms through the door. Her husband, Cliffhanger follows. "You didn't have to *fuck* all of them, for Christ's sake!" He shouts.

Sookie spins, her index finger in the air. "You do *NOT* use the Lord's name in vain!" She glares at Bob's father. "And... as you might recall, Reverend Savenutts has made it very clear that women are to pleasure their husbands. I am a bride of the church! Those men are my *church husbands* It is my religious obligation to... *pleasure* all of them!"

Fred stops a wide-eyed Anne Margret. He clears his throat. "Umm... Hello... Mr. And Mrs. Good." He unnecessarily points up the stairs. "We were just here seeing Bob. He is taking a quick shower and then we are going to Mickey D's."

"Don't get married, Fred!" Cliff Good shouts. "Especially not to a whore!"

Sookie Moonbeam Magi Good cocks her right hand to her hip and looks back at Anne Margret. "Know what sort of man you are marrying, girl. He needs to be strong enough to handle you!" She points at her husband. "And you! What about you! Weren't you with that Roosevelt woman... the fake blond with the big eyelashes!"

Cliffs face reddens. "She... I..." He shakes his head. "Nothing happened. She didn't want to."

Bob's mother shrugs. "She's no Christian! She is not paying attention to the *doctrine* of the church!" Sookie's head swings from side. "Not my problem! I am a woman in good standing with the *Christians in Pursuit of the Scoundrel Pontius Pilate!*"

"If it ever comes up, remind me that *we* are not going to join *any* church." Anne Margret whispers from behind Fred.

"I don't know about this church anymore, Sookie... or Reverend Savenutts." Cliff says. "I don't think our belonging to it is making us a better couple!"

"It is our eternal salvation we are talking about, Cliffhanger!" Sookie Good snarls. "I am not going to burn in the fires of hell because you don't have the balls to obey the minister when he tells you what we need to do to save our souls!"

"Ah... I hear that the parental units are home." Bob says from the top of the stairs. He pulls a t-shirt on over his bare chest.

Cliff Good gives his son a half wave. "Sookie, we need to talk about this later."

"We can talk about it, right now *Cliffhanger!* I still have the godliness of my holy husbands leaking from me. I want you to tell me why I am so evil." Sookie Moonbeam Magi Good slaps her husband hard on the face. "Tell me Cliff! Tell me why Reverend Savenutts, the leader of our *Church* is wrong!"

Bob pushes past Fred and Anne on the steps. "Yeah... this isn't making things *happier* for me. Let's go guys."

Fred grabs Anne Margret's hand and pulls her down the stairs as he follows Bob. He tries to smile and nod at both of Bob's angry parents, but their attention is on each other.

"That was intense." Anne Margret says once outside. "Bob, do they fight like that, often?"

Bob shrugs. "Yeah? I guess so? It's usually about something stupid at church." He pulls out a hoverboard. Anne and Fred get on theirs.

"You know that is not normal... the things your mom and dad were arguing about. Things like that *cannot* be normal." Anne says as they go down the street.

"They always work it out." Bob's voice is worried. "Think it will be busy at Mickey D's? We can go someplace else... maybe a grocery store or something."

"We are going to Mickey D's." Anne Margret says. "We *need* to go to Mickey D's!"

They cruise down the side streets. It isn't *All Beef* day, so there is no line for the drive through. The trio pulls up and parks the hoverboards. "What do you want, Bob? I will buy." Fred asks.

"You know what I want, baby." Anne Margret sticks her tongue in Fred's ear. "And I will share it with you." She adds in a seductive whisper.

"I'll just have an *Unbelievable Burger*, Freddy." Bob has a smile on his face. "And a couple of orders of fries. Real ones... not that soy shit you get! And a large Coke!"

"You got it buddy!" Fred says. "Grab a table. I will be right back with food!" He goes in and places the order. After a few minutes, a Robot puts the food on the counter. Fred carries it outside.

"Geely, you are a *fucking cunt!*" Fred hears Anne Margret's voice shout. His head spins, looking for her and Bob. Anne Margret is poking her finger into the chest of a cell phone holding Geely. Two large grinning men stand behind the chubby girl who is now waving around the old iPhone she had used to record Bob Good masturbating in a mocking manner. A small crowd is starting to gather behind Geely and her brothers.

"Bitch, *you* don't get to call my sister a *Cunt!*" One of the grinning men says with a menacing tone. He pulls his sister back and takes her place in front of Anne Margret. "Why would you defend that pizza faced freak over there, anyway? You Boring?" Fred immediately sees that the man's fists are clenched. He finds Bob sitting with his head in his hands at an otherwise empty table. After setting the tray of food on the table, Fred looks up just in time to see the right fist from Geely's brother make contact with Anne Margret's left eye.

*Years before, Conrad Peterson had insisted that his son take Taekwondo as learning a martial art was widely thought to teach discipline. Young Fred had mastered the practice in a few years, stopping after obtaining a black belt. Conrad used to joke that Fred, with his easy demeanor and analytical mind, was no more a danger with his Taekwondo than Ghandi would have been with a handgun.*

*Conrad was wrong.*

Anne Margret falls backwards onto one of the tables, Geely's brother, wearing a sick grin, steps towards her fallen form. Quickly, Fred hurdles two tables and kicks low into the man's left knee, dislocating it. As Anne Margret's attacker crumples to the ground, the second brother runs up to Fred, his right arm cocked back. Fred blocks the punch and comes up under the man's chin with a fist, knocking the second attacker out cold.

"Freddy, look out!" Anne cries out just as 100,000 volts from the Mickey Ds security guard's stun gun rocks Fred Peterson's body.

Chapter 54
Planned Parenthood calling. This happened fast. Too Fast.
Marmalade Julius Compound Someplace in the United States of America
Land of the Free(ish). Home of the Brave(ish).

*Juice leads me to Velvela Garfinkle's studio. We stand outside the relatively small room and watch through a window. Millie sits beside Vel. Each of them has a microphone in front of their faces. I see cameras in the room, but the lenses are all covered. Juice reaches over and pushes a button that turns on a speaker.*

"Go ahead caller. You are in the chat with our esteemed doctor and me, Vel Garfinkle." Vel says with a smooth voice.

"She has a great verbal delivery." Marmalade beams. "Vel would make a fantastic preacher!"

The caller sounds nervous. "Yes... umm... Yeah... Thank you for taking my question. I am... umm... pregnant. Like six months... and umm... there is *like* this dark line on my belly and my boyfriend says there be, *like* things wrong with me... he think it means the baby ain't his cause' *like* you know, he and I both white and the line... it's... *like* dark... and I ain't been with no one, you know. Just the boyfriend so if I's pregnant, it be his."

Millie smiles. "Well, congratulations on being pregnant. You sound like you will be a good mother." I see Vel roll her eyes. "That line on your belly is completely natural and has nothing to do with who the father is. The mark is caused by increased estrogen levels. When we get pregnant, estrogen boosts our melanin levels, that's a natural substance that gives our skin pigment. That melanin is what is causing the dark line on your belly. It has come right on time... Dark lines like are called *Linea nigra* and they usually start in the second trimester. You are probably going to get a few more of them."

The caller laughs nervously. "Well, I ain't telling him you called it *that*!"

"Do you live with the father of your child?" Vel asks, ignoring the caller's insinuated innuendo.

"Nah. I live with my sister and her friend. Baby Daddy comes round *like* every week er so. You *know* what he be looking for..." The caller answers.
Vel laughs lightly. "You need to be safe while you are pregnant. You also need to be taking prenatal vitamins. Do you have regular checkups scheduled?"

"Yeah. My sister takes me to CVGreens for the Robot docs every month. They check me over and give me the supply of little pills. Dem da vitamins, I guess." The caller answers.

"Take good care of yourself and that baby!" Vel disconnects the call. "Lots of women with very good questions today. Let's talk with one of our medical professionals who is out in the field. Dr. Freda Holehouse, how are things going for you in your practice?"

"Vel, it's a constant battle against the government and big Pharma. Just the other day, state regulators came in and asked why we didn't have more Robots performing patient checkups. Seems they don't want to pay if a real human doctor checks a pregnant woman out." Freda Holehouse's voice sounds exasperated. "As you know, we are in a rural area and we are in desperate need of some things, I am hoping that the network can help us out."
Vel smiles. "We have people on the line that can help, Dr. Holehouse. What are you looking for?"

"Well, the state says that we can't have Oxytocin in the amounts we have requested. So, that. Also, we are chronically low on Ergometrine... that's not necessarily controlled like the Oxytocin, just hard to get these days. We need some Syphilis test material. Been out of that for like three months. Oh yes, just the dumbest thing in the world, we need Proteinuria dip sticks."

Vel types on a keyboard. "I am going to transfer you over to Shelia Fyndet. She is in China working with our offshore suppliers. She is going to help you get what you need and arrange for transport to a pickup point you choose."

"Thank you, Vel. You and Planned Parenthood are lifesavers." Dr. Freda Holehouse says as Vel transfers the call. She looks out the window and sees me and Marmalade standing near the studio. After waving, she points us out to Millie. I wave at Millie who looks happier than I have ever seen her.

"Our last caller is a woman with a question about sex after delivering a baby. Go ahead, miss." Vel Garfinkle says smoothly into the microphone as she opens the line for the caller.

A baby is crying in the background. We hear the woman breathing. Vel makes a circling motion with her left hand. The baby cries louder. "Caller? You have a question about sex after pregnancy?"

"Oh! I am on! Am I on the air?" The caller's voice asks. "I'm so sorry about the baby crying... she does that all the time. I think she thinks my tits are a twenty-four seven convenience store!"

"For her, they are." Millie says with a laugh. "What is your concern?"
The caller takes a deep breath. "I really hate having sex since I had my daughter. My husband is getting really angry about it, and I need to figure out how to fix me!"

Millie nods.

"How old is your daughter?" Vel asks.

"Almost two weeks." The caller answers.

Millie hits herself in the forehead. "Sister! Your body just went through a bunch of trauma! Clearly you are more than a little distracted by your baby and taking care of her… as you should be!" She shakes her head and gathers her thoughts. "After we have a baby, our hormones levels are bouncing up and down like there is no tomorrow. Breastfeeding makes that even more so! When we are breastfeeding, our estrogen drops to like zero… which means that you got no lube down there, no matter how excited hubby might be about having sex with you… or you with him!" Millie pauses and looks wide eyed at Vel, mouthing. *Two Weeks.*

Vel laughs. "Dear, your husband needs some sense talked into him. He needs to leave you alone for another week at least. Two would be better. And even then, you will still be breastfeeding… so make him go out and buy some good lube when you send him out for diapers."

Millie turns her microphone back on. "Be patient with yourself. You are not going to work the same way down there for a bit. Explain this to your husband and tell him you need his patience while your body heals. If your experience is the same in four or five months, you need to see your doctor."

The woman sighs loudly. "Our church… it is so strict on the wife pleasuring her husband." I almost think I hear the woman whimper. "I really hate oral sex… I guess I will have to do that for him…" She sobs a little. Vel points at the window and jabs a finger in Marmalade's direction. *This is your fault* I read her lips say silently.

Beside me, Marmalade shakes his head and answers her unheard comment out loud while pointing at me. "Yeah… but my boy Justin is going to change the world."

The caller keeps talking. "All I ever see is the Robots at CVGreens. They don't answer sex questions. I have tried."

"Call back into us." Millie says quickly. "Don't ever forget, we are here for you."

Vel looks at Millie in surprise. "Yes. I absolutely hope that Planned Parenthood will always be available here in the United States of America and I hope our esteemed Doctor will co-host with us again!" She pauses. "Thank you for logging into the Planned Parenthood talk." She reads off a few cursory announcements and ends the show. Marmalade opens the door. "Sounds like you two are having fun."

Vel pats Millie's leg. "It's great to have an actual doctor answering the medical questions. Makes it easier on me! I hope you really can do this again, Millie." Vel's upbeat personality is infectious. I see it having a positive effect on Millie.

"Yes!" Millie says. "I really liked this! I'd be happy to do it again."

Vel beams. "Awesome. We do it again in a few weeks!"

Paal taps me on the shoulder. Surprised, I turn. "Mr. Justin... you need to come see what has happened." He says.
Marmalade gives him a curious look. Paal shrugs. "It is a bigger response than I thought possible. We are up over five hundred."
"Five hundred?" I ask.

Marmalade's face wrinkles into a frown. "Seriously? I thought we would see a little bump. Not that... how about nationally?"

Paal smiles. "Our donors are better off than any other franchise outside of Southern California. *They* are only up day over day one hundred."

I shake my head. "I don't understand. Are you talking about donations?"

Marmalade nods. "That's the business, Justin. Tithing... donations. Membership fees." He turns back to Paal. "Let's go see."

The four of us walk back down to Paal's lair in the basement. Five hundred dollars seems a lot for anyone to donate because they want masturbation banned. Paal and Marmalade talk about things I don't understand. Vel and Millie talk happily about the call in session they just had. We walk into the room filed with monitors and I hear Millie suck in a deep breath.

"Millie, welcome to our secret sauce. This is where it all happens." Marmalade looks at the monitor wall. "There it is. How about that. We are up five hundred and twenty-three thousand dollars."

"What!" I exclaim. "A half a million dollars! How is that possible?"

Marmalade chuckles. "Spirebats?"

Paal nods.
"These guys are jerks... but awesome fundraisers. Spirebats has a very prosperous congregation in his building." Juice points at the monitor. "He is responsible for over half the amount. Kookluver and Wacadingal both have twenty percent. Savenutts has ten percent, the balance comes from the rest of the members in my territory."

I feel a little sick. People are giving up their money for my idea that really was just a joke. Seriously? *Banning Male Masturbation... people had to think about it like a joke, right?* I look nervously at Millie. Her face is aghast. I point at the screen. "We... we shouldn't do this. Marmalade, I had no idea... I just wanted people to pay attention to the damage the abortion ban was doing to the country."

Paal smiles. "It's working Justin. Let me show you." He types on his keyboard and points at the screen. "There on Monitor eight. I have a chat room up. The forum is not sanctioned by the church... but it's mostly made up of women from *Christians in Pursuit of the Scoundrel Pontius Pilate*. A lot of the money in our territory has come from the accounts attached to women. Look at the things they are saying." I watch the screen. Paal is sorting the comments. "These messages are what we would view as negative commentary." Paal hits enter and the screen shuffles. "Keep in mind, I am not manipulating this audience at all. What you see is organic reaction to the messaging that they have gotten from the four ministers."

"Holy... shit." Marmalade mutters as the comments start rolling on the screen. "These women are angry."

*Ban my husband whacking off? Hell yes. Serves him right for screwing those sluts and saying it's "God's will". I hope it becomes law and there is a reward for turning him in! This is stupidest thing I have seen yet, but it's great, right? Why should we suffer so much, and men suffer none?*

*Yessssssssss this is the best thing ever! Now the men will know how we feel! I gave a big chunk of change! Make this happen!*

*maybe I can get my husband to move to Canada now? They won't be banning masturbation up there! AND I STILL HAVE RIGHTS!*

*LET'S GO GURLS! WE HAVE TO MAKE THIS HAPPEN! I haven't been this happy since the Orange Jesus kicked the bucket!*

*Oh boy! No more men whacking off? What are we going to do with all this Vaseline? I am in... How much money do we need to give to make this happen!?!?!*

*We can and they can't? I LOVE LOVE LOVE it! $$$$ to the cause. GIVE NOW!*

*When this is law, I am going to get drunk! AND NOT SCREW! And laugh my aaaasssssss offff!*

The comments go on and on. I shake my head. "This... is something."

"You have started a revolution, Justin." Vel says in awe.

"This is so... *wrong*." Millie says in a voice just above a whisper.

"It's going to work." Juice says. He turns to me. "I'm cutting you in, Justin. You get twenty percent."

"Twenty percent?" I ask. "Why?"

"Because you and Millie deserve it!" Marmalade leans over to Paal. "Let me see what is happening at headquarters."

Paal clears the right third of the wall of monitors. The screens go black and come back up. "Rex was taken by surprise with this. I hacked into an emergency meeting with the elders he called. He isn't in support of the idea... but they are." Paal puts another monitor up and points to it. "I helped the push with a little grease."

"You gave them a hundred G's." Marmalade smiles in approval. "Nice."

Paal chuckles. "Yeah... a few of his congregants met their yearly tithing obligations today."

"So, is Rex going for it?" Millie asks.

"Looks like it." Marmalade motions at the wall. "Monitor six."

An email appears on the screen. It is from Reverend Rexford Ratchet and appears to be about five hundred words long. I skip to the bottom paragraph.

*Banning Male Masturbation is simply the right thing to do. Each sperm represents an unborn human being that deserves our upmost protection and respect. As we now know with absolute certainty, God's Bible and man's own science is very clear on the matter: Male masturbation is scientifically wrong and an abomination in the eyes of God. Please join me as we support our governmental leaders in banning this atrocity. Christians in Pursuit of the Scoundrel Pontius Pilate stands in support of a total ban on male masturbation.*

"I see that Rex hasn't learned anything new about biology since he was screwing me." Millie says with a morose tone. "He certainly didn't know much back then. How does someone this ignorant get so much power?"

"Power of the people, dear." Vel puts her arm around Millie. "We have been trying for years to figure out a way to break this ridiculous cycle of bad ideas." She points at me. "Justin may have come up with the idea that does the trick. *Another terrible idea!*"

Millie shakes her head. "Bad ideas to beat back bad ideas cannot be the solution! That is a ridiculous premise!"

Marmalade turns. "You are right Millie. If we had a normal, functioning government with a justice system that wasn't filled with partisan hacks whose certain knowledge of the law is superseded by either their personal beliefs or political leanings, good ideas always beat bad ideas." His voice softens. "We know that fire is bad thing. It is very destructive and can rage out of control, destroying everything in its path... but fire fighters can use the destructive power of explosives to extinguish an out-of-control blaze. The explosion causes a larger, more powerful, but controlled fire that sucks all the oxygen away from the burning blaze. Without oxygen, fire can't burn." He motions at the monitors behind him. "I wasn't sure at first that this silly idea could work. Now I am sure that it will. We are going to suck all the oxygen out of the room and put the fire that's been burning for over fifty years, out."

Millie is quiet. I study her face for clues about what she is thinking. There is no smile, but her eyes are wide. She takes in the monitors, starting and ending with the email from her ex-husband. "Make sure *he* suffocates, first." She says, pointing at the monitor. "And... I want to be there when *he* takes his last breath."

*"Millie, you don't know the half of it, and I am not sure you will want to."* I hear Marmalade mutter under his breath.

Chapter 55
Nice to meet you, officers.
Throwing rocks in glass houses is not productive.
Conrad Peterson House Someplace in the United States of America
Land of the Free(ish) Home of the Brave(ish)


"I have called the police." Elizabeth Eaton says calmly. Anne Margret sits on the couch with a frozen bag of peas pressed on her black eye. Fred sits on the couch in a pair of running shorts. A large bandage covers the spot on his leg where the barbs from the Mickey D's security guard's taser had punctured his skin. Elizabeth rubs his hair. "How are you feeling Fred?"

"Achy." Fred says. "Especially in this leg."  He pats on the spot where he was tased.

"I never want to see that again." Anne Margret says. "It scared the hell out of me, seeing you writhing on the ground like that."

"I'm sorry. I am so, so sorry." Bob Good says from a chair across the room. "I should go."

"Stay here, Bob. It isn't your fault." Fred says.

"It kinda is." Anne Margret offers.

Fred shoots her a look. She flashes an exaggerated smile at him before responding verbally. "But we still love you, Bob."

"What did the police say?" Fred asks.
"They said it would have been better if you had shot the Suckamore boy and killed him rather than break his leg with a kick." Elizabeth Eaton answers. "Apparently there is less paperwork. The boy's name is Toyota. It

is a family that likes their transporters so much they name their kids after them."

"Yeah. The other one is named Grumman." Bob adds. "I'm so sorry."

"Stop saying you are sorry." Anne Margret says. "It's giving me a headache."

"I don't know what else to say." Bob moans.

"Well, Toyota Suckamore has already called the police and wants to file charges against both of you. Additionally, Mickey D's has banned both of you from their properties."

"There is a real loss." Anne Margret says sarcastically to her mother. "Where will I eat now to expedite my certain death?"

"This is no laughing matter, Anne Margret. You could have been seriously injured and a criminal record is no way to start a legal career." Elizabeth replies. "Anyway, the police will be around shortly to collect your statements. I will work behind the scenes to get this squashed. I will make sure that no one really wants to help the Suckamore family out in the county attorney's office."

"That's not really fair, is it?" Anne Margret asks. "I mean... the Suckamore family is poor... and stupid... but they deserve to have their day in court."

Elizabeth Eaton smiles sympathetically. "Oh, dear... you still have some of that liberal sensibility that was so endearing when you were younger." She pats her daughter's shoulder. "As they say, it's a little like baby fat. Such thoughts go away as you age."

"Did you call my dad?" Fred asks. "I tried. He didn't answer."
"I did. The Premier of North Korea is in town to have a model of his cock made into a dildo.  It is all the rage now for dictators to have their dick made into something that can be distributed to the endearing masses. I

updated him. He told me to handle it. He will be home as soon as he can."
The lawyer walks over to Bob. "The police are going to have questions for
you too, young man. Do you want your parents here when the police talk to
you? How old are you?"

"Nineteen." Bob answers. "And a big *no* on my parental units. That
would not be good."

"Are you making a Good joke, Bob?" Anne Margret asks. Fred
chuckles.

"No. I was not." Bob offers a weak smile. "That is pretty funny
though."

The doorbell rings. Elizabeth Eaton looks at the three who make
no indication they are about to go answer the door. "I believe that is the
doorbell. Let me go answer it."

Eaton returns a moment later with a male and female police officer.
Both are wearing full body armor and walk stiffly. The female carries her
helmet under her arm. "Thank you for coming officers. Here are the *victims*
you want to talk to." Elizabeth identifies each of the teens. "I represent all
of them legally in this matter." She points at Bob. "He is nineteen and has
informed me that he doesn't want his parents present."

The female officer nods and steps forward. "We have already
spoken to the..." She pulls out a notebook. "Suckamore boys." She points
at Fred. "I assume you are the attacker?"

"I..." Fred starts.

"Don't answer that, Fred." Elizabeth's voice has taken a very
businesslike tone. "Fred was not the attacker, officer. He was defending
Anne Margret... who is a victim. They are both victims."

The female officer rolls her eyes and sighs. "Of course, counselor.
Poor choice of words on my part. It has been a long day, and believe it or

not, this is the best call we have had." She sets her helmet down. "Tell me your story."

Anne Margret starts. She describes how she approached Geely Suckamore and asked her to stop showing the videos on her phone to people. Anne Margret sighs. "I probably escalated things when I called her a bad name."

"What did you call her?" The police officer asks. She uses her uniform mounted camera to take a photo of Anne Margret's swollen eye.

"I called her a *cunt*." Anne Margret says. "Then her brother hit me. I suppose that was Toyota?"

The female office nods. "That's when you kicked him? This guy named, Toyota?" She asks Fred.
Fred nods. "Yes. Then the other one came at me. I think I hit him in the chin."

"You did. Knocked the one named Grumman out cold, apparently. He has a broken jaw."

The other one has a broken leg." The male officer offers, eliciting a glare from the female officer.

"And then the security officer from the restaurant tased me." Fred says. "Need to see?"

The officers both look at his bandaged leg and shake their heads. The female officer turns to Bob. "What's on the video?"

"Me." Bob says, his face turning red.

"Doing what, exactly?" The female officer asks.

Bob stares at the floor.

"It's not illegal, Bob. Answer the police officer." Fred says. He glances at Elizabeth who nods her approval.

"I was... um... whacking... Um, Masturbating. She said she wanted a video of it." Bob mumbles. "Geely... Geely said she wanted a video of it."

The female officer suppresses a smile. The male officer clears his throat. "What was this Geely doing on the video? Just filming... or doing something else?"

"Just filming... holding the phone camera." Bob says with a sad tone.
"Just filming?" The male officer asks. "You can whack off to someone just filming you?"

"I was probably thinking about boobs." Bob says. "Boobs do it for me." He looks at the floor. "I'm sorry."

"He is not sorry for anything. He did nothing wrong." Elizabeth Eaton says. "Bob is just embarrassed. That is no admission of guilt!"

"Wish I could get off just thinking about boobs." The male officer mumbles. "Takes a lot more than that these days."

The female officer shakes her head and looks at the male officer. "Your problem is because of that illegal porn. I keep telling you... Listen to the government! Stop watching it." She closes the notebook. "Well, I think this case is closed."

Elizabeth Eaton looks at the officers incredulously. "What? Seriously?" She shakes her head. "I mean... that's great. I didn't think there was a case here, but..."

The officer looks at her sympathetically. "Well... we arrested Grumman and Toyota, because they were smoking a bong when we walked up to their house. Said they needed the medical effects of marijuana."
"You arrested them for that?" Fred asks.

"No. We arrested both of them for taking swings at my partner when he suggested they put the crack pipes down. And... they really were crack pipes. We arrest people who smoke crack. It's Wack. Crack is Wack. It really is." She nods at Anne Margret. "Then the girl... Geely." The police officer shakes her head. "She called *me* a *cunt* and screamed at me to get off her porch when I tried to talk to her about the complaint." She points at Anne Margret. "I figure they will charge Toyota with assault for hitting you. You may be required to make a statement for the court."

"I shouldn't have called her that word." Anne Margret says, putting the bag of frozen peas back on her eye.

"It was the third time *today* I had been called a cunt." The female officer smiles tiredly. "You'd be surprised how frequently that particular word gets used in ordinary conversations with me these days." She points at her partner. "Me and *Mr. Can't whack off to boobs* are done here. You all have a nice day. My advice is to stay away from the ugly people." The police make their way to front door as Conrad Peterson comes in. After greeting and saying goodbye to the police officers, he turns to the room. "It's been one hell of a day, and it isn't over. You guys need to see what's happening in Texas." He sits down next to Fred and turns on the monitor that fills one wall of the room. "Want to tell me about yours? It isn't often that I come home to two police officers leaving my house."

Chapter 56
Getting people riled up is profitable. Texas Legislature.
A bad day, indeed.
Marmalade Julius Compound Someplace in the United States of America
Land of the Free(ish) Home of the Brave(ish)

*We have been in Paal's control room all day. Marmalade had snacks brought in. The idea of banning male masturbation has spread like wildfire. By noon, the amount of money collected in Marmalade's territory had exceeded six hundred thousand dollars. Over a million dollars had been given nationwide. In Texas, the minister named Wacadingle met with Reverend Rexford Ratchet. Paal was able to use the video and audio feeds built into Wacadingle's laptop computer. We got to hear and see the meeting. Millie took joy in seeing her obese ex-husband hunched over in his electric cart looking every bit like the angry, old, unhealthy human being that he is. I honestly felt a little sad for the man. He really doesn't seem enthused with the idea, but as Wacadingle points out to him, money is pouring into the church because of it. By two o'clock in the afternoon, Reverend Rex Ratchet gained an audience with the Speaker of the Texas House of Representatives and the Governor of Texas. By Four o'clock in the afternoon, the Texas House of Representatives had prepared emergency legislation to ban Male Masturbation as the continued action of men masturbating is a 'clear and present danger' to future human beings. The bill was tagged with the moniker 'Spilt Seed' by the House. By five o'clock, the Texas Senate received the hastily written bill from the House of Representatives. We watched as the thirty-one members of the Texas senate debated the bill with the Governor of Texas overseeing the proceedings.*

Paal adjusts the volume. The largest monitor... a thing that must be ten feet across has the Texas legislative proceedings on it. A fat man with white hair and a droopy horseshoe shaped mustache steps to the microphone. He clears his throat. There are cheers in the senate as he looks down at the group. A caption at the bottom of the screen identifies the man as Lieutenant Governor McKinley Reagan Autocraty. Marmalade points at the screen. "That guy is an elder in Ratchet's home church."

"So, he has a big cross tattooed on his back?" I ask, my eyes not leaving the screen.

Marmalade shrugs with a nod as Autocraty asks the crowd to be quiet with a hand motion. As soon as the cheering stops, the speaker starts speaking.

"Early today, the House of Representatives met in an emergency session to take up the challenge brought to us by scientists and religious leaders on the grave effects of male masturbation. Not since the state of Alabama passed and upheld laws granting personhood to unfertilized female eggs has there been such a serious attempt to protect life. I for one am *proud as hell* to be a part of this historical process. I know many of you feel the *exact* same way." There are loud cheers from the rest of the senate body. Autocraty grins and waits again for the cheering to die down. "The house has sent us the *Split Seed* bill. It is our duty to consider this very serious bill and reconcile it properly so that it can be signed into law as soon as possible. I have spoken with many of you prior to this session on the contents of the house bill. Although it is not necessary, we will respect tradition, and I will allow a brief amount of time for opponents of the bill to speak before our body votes on the bill." There are boos from senate body. More than one person calls out, *Boring!* Autocraty grins. I want to welcome to the senate, our esteemed governor, the Honorable Paxton Flushsack." There are more cheers. "Governor Flushsack has his deal signing pen ready to go! As soon as we pass the vote on *Spilt Seed*, the governor will sign the bill right here, on the senate floor." The camera pans to Governor Paxton Flushsack, a thin man with a full head of perfectly styled blond hair. There are more cheers. Autocraty shuffles some papers. "I will read the bill in its entirety." There are more boos. Autocraty looks up. "Now, don't you be concerned. Our house colleagues have been considerate! The *Spilt Seed* bill is only about eight hundred words long!"

"Eight hundred words!" I exclaim. "I was never in politics... shit, before this I paid exactly zero attention to the political process... eight hundred words seems like it should be the preamble for a bill."

388

Paal laughs nervously. I think even he is frightened by how quickly this is moving. "Coming out of Texas, eight hundred words is a lot. I wouldn't have been surprised if the whole bill was simply a single sentence; *Male Masturbation is banned.*"

Beside me, Millie shakes her head. "Justin... I never would have thought something like this was possible. How have Americans become so stupid?" I don't answer. On the screen, Autocraty has started reading the Texas House of Representatives bill banning male masturbation. The words scroll on the screen as the man reads with his deep southern accent.

*H. R. 69420*

*AN ACT*

*To prohibit the action from any male human as designated at birth from the actions or fulfillment of actions including but not limited to autoeroticism in where defined male person sexually stimulates themselves or is stimulated by another person of indeterminate sexual orientation in a sexual manner as to achieve orgasm and, or ejaculate semen from the male sexual organ in a useless or wasteful manner.*

*Be it enacted by the Senate and House of Representatives of the State of Texas assembled,*

*SECTION 1. SHORT TITLE. This Act may be cited as the "Prohibiting Split Seed Act". SEC.*

*PROHIBITION ON MALE EJACULATION OF SEMEN UNLESS FOR THE SPECIFIC PURPOSE OF IMPREGNATION A HUMAN FEMALE AS ASSIGNED AT BIRTH.*

(a) *Prohibition On Ejaculation of Semen. Section 6969693 of the Health and Human Services Family Promotion Act is amended by adding at the end the following:*

(b) *"(b) Save the Children by any means necessary because they are our future and the love of our lives. Killing Children is wrong, wrong, wrong. On this we all agree.*

(c)

*"(1) PROHIBITION. Beginning on the date that is 90 days before the date of the enactment of this act, and subject to paragraphs (2) and (3), the following will not be allowed in the State of Texas or any one of the United States that have signed onto the "Alamo Compact".*

*"(A) Assigned Male at Birth Person, Masturbation of Sexual Organs to the point of ejaculation of human sperm."*

*"(1A1) Individual sperm shall hereafter be considered crucial to form human life and as such shall be considered equal to and as important as unfertilized female as assigned at birth, eggs."*

*"(B) Masturbation performed by others of any Assigned Male at Birth Person, Masturbation to the point of ejaculation of human sperm."*

*"(2) WAIVER.*

*"(A) IN GENERAL.—Subject to subparagraphs (B) and (C), the Secretary of Health and Human Services may, in consultation with the applicable law enforcement, county and state, may waive the application of paragraph (1) to authorize the such described ejaculations of male produced semen if such semen is used exclusively for the purposes of fertilizing a human egg produced by a woman of child bearing years provided that the fertilized egg is promptly inserted into said woman of child bearing years.*

*"(i) no alternative viable sperm is available to said woman or "(ii) impregnation by standard means of missionary or 'woman on top' penetration is unlikely due to physical disability or mental hangups over sex acts."*

*(B) LIMITATION ON AMOUNTS OF MASTURBATION(S) NECESSARY TO ACHIEVE SUCH ORGASM TO SATISFY (i) AND (ii). "(i) IN GENERAL. Masturbation should be limited to no more than two minutes solo and three minutes if being performed by a secondary party. Collection of ejaculated sperm must be collected in a vessel(s) satisfactory for delivery to female assigned at birth, female of childbearing age sex organs.*

*(ii) ADMINISTRATION. The (I)Secretary of Health and Human Services and the (II) Department of Justice and the (III) Department of Corrections and the (IV) Department of the Treasury shall*

*"(I) administer such limitations on male masturbation and perform education sessions for the public for no less than ten years following the passage of this bill. Known offenders referred to the Department of Health and Human Services Shall be referred to the Department of Justice for enforcement.*

*"(II) be responsible for enforcing the male masturbation limitations described in clause (i); and"*

*"(III) enforce the masturbation and ejaculation limitations described in clause (i) in a manner that imposes a burden on the accused ejaculators. Such individuals shall not be punished by more than ten years in a State of Texas approved correction facility and, or no less than a $10,000 fine and no more than a $100,000 fine to be paid before sentence is competed. All male individuals accused of or convicted of masturbation without ejaculation into the sex organs of a human female as assigned at birth shall be fitted with a locked male chastity cage until such time that accused individuals are acquitted or convicted individuals are rehabilitated by the Texas Department of Corrections. Such chastity cages must be approved by the Department of Justice prior to use. Rehabilitation shall be left up to the discretion of the justice system who shall consult with religious authorities and mental health practitioners as they make such deliberations.*

*(IV) The Department of the Treasury shall, upon satisfactory proof of assistance in gaining conviction provided by the Department of Justice compensate successful male masturbation accusers the sum of $10,000 under the Texas Bounty Law, created to assist the Great State of Texas in enforcing its honorable and protective laws. This proof may consist of anything found to be accepted for the purposes of conviction of violators of the "Prohibition of Spilt Seed Law" including but not limited to video evidence, photographic imagery, or specimen sample: stored or on soiled clothing or other cloth, paper or absorbent.*

*"(C) TERMINATION. This Bill shall not terminate unless done so in a legal manner by the Congress of Texas or through Justice Department Guidance.*

*Passed the House of Representatives*

Seventy Five percent of the Texas Senate, led by the Texas Governor and Lieutenant Governor stands and cheer after Autocraty finishes reading the bill.

"I think I am going to be sick." Millie exclaims. "What I am seeing is... well, this is fucking scary!"

"It's incredible and scary that the bill is going to pass." I answer. "Anyone can write stupid shit. Scary or not."

On the screen, Autocraty grins. "And now, a few words from our opposition. You have the floor for..." He looks at his watch and waves his hand dismissively. "Five minutes. Do what you want."

Three women and two men make their way to the podium. Their faces are somber. Marmalade and Paal have turned away from the screen and are looking at something on the monitor in front of Paal. Vel comes over and squeezes between Millie and me. "These are the primary opposition to the conservatives in the Texas senate. "The tall black girl is Theresa McCorvey. She is the leader of the group. Lives in Austin. Went to UT Law. The short woman is Michaela Yousafzai. She is relatively conservative on most issues, but not women's health. Her mom is a blond hair blue eyed woman who ran a Planned Parenthood in Texas that was burned to the ground. Mom died in the fire. The dad is from Pakistan. The Latino man is Jose Abellio. Firebrand liberal. Not super effective, but quite vocal. We feed him some soundbites when we think it might help get our message out. The white woman is Angie Davis. Green Party. She's probably up there to make sure the other four continue to vote with her on environmental issues. The white guy is Harvey Winehouse, the only openly gay member in the Texas Congress."

"It doesn't matter what they say, does it?" Millie asks. "I mean... five votes are a drop in the bucket... even if the other twenty percent that votes liberal votes with them."

"In the old days, one of these five would filibuster for days to stop votes. The conservatives changed the rules so that such things couldn't happen. As the old *Washington Post* slogan goes, Democracy dies in darkness... Democracy certainly isn't healthy without debate. The trend has been to eliminate discussion of issues in these state legislative bodies so that the public never really hears both sides of an issue... not that the public pays much attention anymore to politics." Vel explains.

Theresa McCorvey steps to the podium. There are boos from the senate body. I hear racial epitaphs being shouted along with the world *Boring*. "So much for decorum." I mutter.

"Decorum in the political process died more than thirty years ago, Justin." Vel comments.

*Ladies and Gentlemen of the Senate. We stand today in opposition of the Spilt Seed bill currently being considered by this body...*

The boos and shouting pick up. McCorvey continues.

*Banning something as mundane as human masturbation is...*" McCorvey shakes her head and looks at the ceiling, searching for words. Something green flies towards the woman and hits her square in the chest. The liberal Texas Senator barely flinches. She looks down with a sad expression at the wet spot on her jacket and shirt the broken water balloon has caused. She sighs audibly and continues, completely ignoring the water balloon strike. Her actions tell me that such juvenile stunts are commonplace. *"This is craziness, guys. Just craziness. If this becomes law... especially in the manner it is written, we will weaponize a common and healthy stress relieving activity... something that each of us probably does daily!"*

There are boos and calls for the group to get off the stage. The camera pans out. A husky-built man with long reddish hair and a beard to match gets up from his seat and walks to the podium. At first, I think there is going to be a physical confrontation. The senate body is cheering loudly. Paal and Marmalade stop what they are doing and look up at the large monitor. "This can't be good." I observe.

Vel is watching the screen with interest. "Mike McCarthy. Conservative voice. Probably going to run for the United States Senate in a few years."

McCarthy turns his back to the senate body and speaks with the five dissenting members. After a short conversation, he turns back to the body and starts to speak. The Senate body goes quiet. *My fellow senators, we are being asked to consider a bill today that would make masturbation, specifically male masturbation a crime in over half of the United States of America. I want you to consider how you vote on this particular bill very carefully... the ramifications of such a bill... the social effects of such a bill... will be huge. He points out into the audience. We are being asked by our leadership to pass this bill on the very day that it came from the house of representatives with no input from members of the Justice system we will ask to enforce the law that is created or any such input from sociologists or physiologists."*

"I think the word you want there is *Psychologists*, senator." Millie says sarcastically.

"They could use input from both." Vel answers. "I doubt most of these men could accurately identify a clitoris on a medical picture or on a live woman."

*"This bill is going to adversely affect poor people."*. McCarthy puts his hands out in a pleading manner. *"We have a bounty program folks. And everyone has a video camera installed on their body! Senator McCorvey is correct. If this bill passes. We are weaponizing a mundane activity. There will be mayhem across the country! We should not pass this bill."*. McCarthy steps back. The senate floor is quiet. Apparently one of their own telling them something contrary to their bias is ok. The camera pans to Governor Paxton Flushsack. As if he knows the lens is on him, he smirks and puts a thumb in the air.

"The vote is already in. The governor knows he has it." Vel says quietly.

Autocraty steps back to the podium. "Let's put our votes in, folks and pass this bill so our governor can sign the *Prohibiting Split Seed Act* in to law!" The screen changes as the senators start voting. Quickly, the scores start tallying. When it is over the bill passes, ten against, twenty-one for banning male masturbation.

"Justin Thyme, you are a genius!" Marmalade exclaims with a grin. "Now the hard work starts."

*I am not sure I feel like a genius.* I think to myself.

Chapter 57
You knew about this?!?
This is how democracy works.
Conrad Peterson House Someplace in the United States of America
Land of the Free(ish) Home of the Brave(ish)


"This is the thing that Mr. Julius and your friend that was in a coma were talking about!" Fred exclaims as the footage of the floor of the Texas Senate plays on the monitor in the Peterson house.

"What?" Conrad shoots his son a look. "You know about this?"

Anne Margret takes the bag of peas from her eye that has turned the same shade of the frozen legumes she is using for relief. "Oh yeah... he wants to ban whacking off. Mr. Julius said that it could be justified with the Bible. Some dude named Onan that wouldn't knock up his brother's wife, so God killed him. Fucked up story for sure."

"Language, Anne Margret!" Her mother says.

Anne Margret rolls her eyes. "Ow. That hurt."

"Maybe you will learn not to do it.  I hate those eye rolls you do!" Elizabeth Eaton retorts, watching the screen. A bearded male senator named McCarthy has delivered a speech against the bill and the Lieutenant Governor is asking for the vote.

"Marmalade thought that this was a good idea?" Conrad asks crossly. "Goddamn him and his church!"

"I told him that you wouldn't like it." Fred offers.
Anne Margret puts the bag back on her eye. "I don't think Mr. Julius thought that this was a good idea... I think he thought that it was

means to getting rid of some bad ideas. I am not sure he knew how he was going to accomplish the end result."

Conrad gets up from the couch and points at the monitor. "Goddamn it all to hell! It passed! Those stupid motherfuckers in Texas! Fuck! This is going to screw us!"

"To be fair, I am not sure that your friend Marmalade has control over the legislature in Texas." Elizabeth Eaton says calmly. "And there is sure to be legal challenges to the law."

Conrad closes his eyes and shakes his head. "You don't understand *that* church. They are master manipulators. *Christians Chasing the Scoundrel Pontius Pilate* are the primary reason that *birth control* is banned. They are *evil!* Pure evil! They get in the heads of these weak-minded politicians... they pad their pockets and get them to vote the way the church wants them too! I am sure that is what has happened here."

Bob Good stands and walks over to the monitor. "They just banned... whacking off?" He asks with amazement. He points at the monitor that shows senators patting each other on the back. ""*These people* can just do that? That can just happen, without asking anyone else what they think?"

Elizabeth Eaton shakes her head. "Well, yes, Bob. The men and women you see on the screen are elected officials in the state of Texas. They represent the people. The people... are us. *We the people* are who put these men and women in office... so, the thought is that whatever these legislators do is the will of *us people*." She stands and walks over to the teen. "You are of voting age now. All three of you are. Voting is a heavy responsibility. It means you have to pay close attention. We don't have to participate in the political process intimately, but we do have to be knowledgeable about the issues affecting our society and we need to be prepared to discuss those issues with our fellow citizens."

"Like that's happened since I was born." Anne Margret says.

"It hasn't happened since I was born. That's for sure." Conrad adds. "If the people of this state actually had discourse, we wouldn't be part of the Alamo Compact and masturbation would still be legal here.... Along with a bunch of other things." He gets up from the couch. "I am going to go pay Marmalade Julius a visit."

Elizabeth shakes her head. "I don't think that's a good idea. You are angry."

"I am. Yes. I am very angry." Conrad says. "Come with me, counselor. You can be my attorney."

"I can't be your attorney if you commit a crime in my presence." Elizabeth answers. "We would have to let Fred and Anne Margret represent us."

"Don't tell us you are both going to commit a crime." Anne Margret says. "Then we can't represent you either."

"That was like, day one in law school." Fred says.

Elizabeth Eaton shakes her head. "My day one was probably constitutional law. Today we tell aspiring lawyers what they need to do to not go to jail on day one."

"Constitutional law was done in the afternoon of day ten." Anne Margret says. "It was boring."

Elizabeth closes her eyes and purses her lips. "Constitutional law. The legal foundation of our country is taught in a single afternoon class. *And it was boring.* We are doomed." She opens her eyes. "Conrad, I will be happy to go with you to your friend's house with you if you promise to be nice."

"No promises. Let's go." Conrad nods at Fred. "You guys staying here or coming with us?"

"It's been a long day dad; we will just stay here." Fred answers. "Bob is going to spend the night. Things are a little volatile at his house."

Conrad nods in agreement. He points at Anne Margret. "Her bag of frozen peas is about thawed out. There are some vaginal balls in the deep freeze. Get those balls on her eyes."

"I cannot un-hear that, Dad." Fred groans.

"I washed them up. They are fine!" Elizabeth Eaton says.

"And *I* cannot un-hear *that*." Anne Margret sits up. "Please go... before we lose all respect for both of you."

"Are we sure masturbation is illegal now?" Bob asks as Conrad and Elizabeth leave the house, giggling.

Chapter 58
Dinner. New bed to sleep in. Conrad says.
How it was. How it is.
Marmalade Julius Compound Someplace in the United States of America
Land of the Free(ish) Home of the Brave(ish)


I watch as the Robots in the kitchen prepare our dinner. They move smoothly and efficiently. Marmalade and Vel come into the room.

Marmalade asks if I want a drink. I shake my head. "I need to drive us back to the place where we are staying." It doesn't seem natural to say that the place is *home*... because it isn't.

Marmalade frowns. "First of all, we don't drink alcohol here. That shit is terrible for you. Leads to early death and even earlier ugliness. I can have an alcohol-free cocktail made for you."

"Do you have just water? Or fizzy water?" I ask.

Marmalade nods and calls out a command, "Cleavon, two club sodas with lime and one tequila sunrise."

I squint. "I thought you said there was no alcohol."

"Nonalcoholic Tequila. It is not bad... been around since the twenties." Marmalade smiles as he sits down across from me. "Want one?" I shake my head. "No. I'd prefer the club soda."

"You shouldn't go back to the Government Housing, Justin. It's not safe for you and Millie. I have plenty of room here. You can stay as long as you want." Juice leans forward. "It's a long drive and you will be coming back here tomorrow, anyway."

Cleavon the Robot drops off three drinks. Vel comes and sits down beside Marmalade. "Did you tell him he is staying here?"

"I did." Marmalade frowns. "I don't think I sold him on it."

"Millie and I both like to be independent." I mumble.

"What do I like?" Millie comes in behind me and puts her hands on my shoulders. I immediately notice a pleasant, flowery smell.

I look up. Millie has taken a shower. Her radiant face is framed by blow dried hair. Vel must have given her a dress to wear. It clings to her form. She looks... awesome. "I... I, umm." I stutter. "You look terrific, Millie!"

She beams. "Justin has only ever seen me in hospital scrubs or thrift store clothes and never freshly showered with real soap and clean water!" She sits down beside me. "What were you talking about?"

"I was just telling Marmalade that we would go back to our government housing tonight because we like our independence." I answer.

"I bet you would like a good shower, Justin. With clean water. And soap." Vel says laughing. "You will still be independent. We won't *make* you take a bath... or sleep in a comfortable bed."

She has a point, I think. The showers at both the Microsoft Hospital and the government housing had just enough water pressure to get the water out of the shower head and little else. Also, the water at both places smells suspiciously like rotting eggs and if I am being honest, showering where I also shit is disgusting. I look over at Millie. "Your call."

Millie smiles at me but remains silent.

"The government places, hospitals... they use recycled water, Justin. We do too... it is the law. But our process is a lot different." Marmalade gestures around the room. "Please, stay here. It will give me great joy to share my home with you and Millie."

"We have stuff at the government place." I mumble, eliciting an eye roll from Millie.

"It's good, Justin." Millie says. "We can stay here tonight and get our stuff some other time."

"Yeah!" Vel jumps up and rushes around the table to hug Millie. "You are my first guests!"

"How long have you been here?" I exclaim. "We can't possibly be your *first* guests!"

Marmalade shakes his head. "I told you. We have had to be very careful, Justin.  That means no guests."

"Too long!" Vel answers. "Millie! We can take a swim in the morning. We can go for a walk! This is awesome! Thank you, thank you, thank you Justin!" She pecks me on the cheek. Like I had anything to do with the decision to stay or not.
Marmalade takes a call on his communicator. "They are?" He says after listening for a few minutes. "I... don't know. Hang on."

Vel looks at her husband expectantly. "Conrad Peterson and his girlfriend... the lawyer are at the gate." Marmalade says slowly.

"Are you going to let them in?" Vel asks.

Marmalade sighs. "I don't know." There is a hesitancy in his voice. In those three words I can hear fear and doubt. Understanding that I can hear such hidden things in his voice surprises me.

I reach over and put my hand on his. "Conrad has heard about the Spilt Seed law coming out of Texas. He is our friend, Marmalade. We know him. Let's explain it to him."

Marmalade shakes his head. "Conrad is single minded about that business he has. It makes him a lot of money and he doesn't like things that get in his way. I know that, because I am the same way!" Juice looks at me with sad eyes. "Things ain't like it used to be when we were growing up. People don't *discuss* ideas. They *fight* about them." He points at Vel. "I have to protect her above everything else. I cannot... We can't let outsiders in. You and Millie are different. You didn't come here with an agenda."

*But we did.* I think. *It's just an agenda from beyond.* I sit quietly for a second before responding. "Transparency lets light in, Marmalade. Light produces life. Let's explain what you... what *we* are doing. I think Conrad will understand. I have seen Elizabeth Eaton in action. Her motives are good, I believe."

Marmalade looks at me. "I hope you are right." He opens his communicator back up. "Let them in."

"Oh, goody! More guests!" Vel exclaims. "I will have the kitchen make more food! Good food always makes people happy!"

Marmalade goes to greet Conrad and Elizabeth. I grab Millie's hand. "Are you ok?"

"I have a really good feeling about all of this, Justin." She says softly. "I felt really good talking with Vel today and doing that call in... it was super empowering. It felt nice using my knowledge for good... you know, doing the things I was supposed to be doing."

After a few minutes Marmalade returns to the dining room with Conrad and Elizabeth.

"Justin!" Conrad exclaims. "I didn't expect to see you guys here." He nods at Millie. Elizabeth smiles and comes over and embraces her.

"I hope your stay with the Texas penal system was better this time." She says to Millie after breaking the embrace.

"It was certainly shorter." Millie says with a grin. "Prison time might have permanently damaged poor Justin though... he is so sensitive."

I smile. "I got some good ideas out of the experience." I turn to Conrad. "It is good to see you, Conrad. I really appreciated the help that Fredrick and Anne Margret provided getting us out of jail."

Elizabeth Eaton's face lights up. "About that... I have great news... Neither one of you have been charged. That Militia Judge didn't file any charges against you. I am guessing the whole system isn't very organized down there. Unless they have a pregnant woman, they can hold... they aren't interested pursuing charges that might result in spending money to keep people in prison."

"That is great news." Millie says flatly as Vel comes into the room.

Marmalade looks unsure of what to do. Vel looks at me and moves close to her husband.

"Conrad, Elizabeth... This is Marmalade's wife, Velvela Garfinkle." I say.

There is a weird quiet in the room. Conrad looks at Elizabeth. They both look surprised. I know what's going through their minds. They thought Juice was gay and Paal was his partner.

"You are married, Juice?" Conrad asks, the disbelief evident in his voice. "To a woman?"

"Yeah?" Marmalade answers with a curious tone. "Who else would I be married to?"

Elizabeth sticks out her hand to Vel. "Velvela, my name is Elizabeth Eaton. This discordant fellow next to me is Conrad Peterson. He is a friend of your husbands from high school."

Conrad raises his hand. "Hi... I am, um... Conrad Peterson."

"You own PPP! The vibrator manufacturer!" Vel exclaims. "I had a *Malcolm* for a long time!" She pats Marmalade on his chest. "I don't need *that* anymore!"

Conrad nods sheepishly. "Yeah. PPP... that's my business."
"Probably why you are here." I say. "I am guessing, of course."

The Robots start bringing out food which fills the room with some awesome smells. Vel motions to the table. "We were just about to sit down and eat. Join us! We have plenty and if there is something you require, I will have the kitchen make it up." She smiles. "We are vegetarian here... I hope that is alright."

"That is *perfect!*" Elizabeth Eaton says. "We are vegetarians too!" She pokes Conrad who is still very tense in the ribs. "Aren't we, dear?"

Conrad nods silently. I go and sit beside Millie. Marmalade and Conrad stand staring at each other.

"You two going to fight or kiss?" I ask, looking at the two men.

The three women look from me to the pair of men standing like very fit oafs at the edge of the room.

I sigh and shuffle closer to the pair. "Conrad, you have come here because you are not happy about the Texas *Spilt Seed Law* and you think that Marmalade and his church had something to do with it passing."

"I know it absolutely did. I saw that asshole Reverend Rex Ratchet sitting next to the Governor of Texas." Conrad says, not taking his eyes off Marmalade. "And I know that Juice is asshole buddies with that religious zealot, and he probably had influence over the process."

"Maybe some of that is true." I say. "But the idea of putting a ban on male masturbation was mine."

Conrad's neck snaps and he shifts his glare to me. "What! Why? Why would you give a damn? Jesus, Justin! Do you have any idea what this is going to do to my business?"

"When I was in prison, I saw this naked homeless guy whacking off and it did scar me." I say with a straight face. "Millie was right. I am scarred. I can't be held responsible for my actions."

Conrad starts to speak and stops. He opens his mouth again and closes it. Finally, he says. "Justin, you were in a *county jail* for all of maybe three hours. How scarred could you possibly be?"

I smile. "Sit down Conrad. Let's talk about it over dinner."

Vel asks Elizabeth if she wants a drink. She points at the Vel's Non-Alcoholic Tequila Sunrise. "I will take one of those." After talking Millie into one, Vel turns to Conrad. "You want a drink, Conrad? We are no alcohol here."

"I haven't drank booze in twenty years... but man, I think I might need some now." Conrad grumbles. "Just water is fine." He pulls out a chair near Elizabeth and sits down. "OK. Start talking. Tell me what the fuck you two think you are doing supporting this absolutely ridiculous idea of... what did Texas call it? *Prohibiting Spilt Seeds*? How very biblical of you, Marmalade!"
Millie puts some food on my plate. It looks like eggplant and tomato mixed with some sort of grain. I take a bite. The flavors explode in my mouth. I wasn't aware that I could still taste food flavors like this. For twenty years I was fed through a tube. After I woke up, the hospital food was dreck, and it isn't like Millie and I eat much more than soy pudding and whatever else she scrounges up. Taking my time, I take, chew and swallow three more bites before I realize that everyone at the table is looking at me. I look at Marmalade. "Oh, you want me to take this?" I say with my mouth full. "This is really great food!"

Marmalade nods. "Justin, you can explain what we are doing better than anyone."

Reluctantly, I put down my fork. I remind myself not to stab anyone who tries to take the food off my plate. After folding my hands together and considering my words, I start to speak.

"In 2022, shortly after I became the mayonnaise and tomato part of a Tesla and Big Truck sandwich, the Supreme Court of the United States overturned *Roe v Wade* by deciding *Dobbs v Jackson* in favor of the state of Alabama. This was an egregious wrong done to the people of the United States... all the people, not just women." I take a deep breath and continue. "The Court was not wholly wrong in its approach. The constitution is a brief document. From the beginning, it was assumed by the founding fathers that issues not covered in the constitution would be taken up by the states.  Those founding fathers probably assumed that the states would work to the will of the people they represent.  The court in 2022 and the jurists on the court today consider themselves *Originalists* meaning that the constitution should be interrupted as it is written and should bind constitutional actors. *Living Constitutionalists* contend that constitutional law can and should evolve in response to changing circumstances and values."

"It is beyond me how anyone thinks that a document prepared and signed in 1787 can be used in 2040 for the same exact purpose." Vel scoffs.

I note that Elizabeth Eaton, the only real lawyer in the room is listening to me intently. "Therein lies one of our country's problems." I say. "We elect our leaders, and those leaders have the responsibility, from the local level to the state level to the federal level to fill open court positions. The public has done this to themselves by not paying attention to the delta between how *we the people* collectively really feel and who *we the people* are supporting for any political office. Since President Buchanan... our fifteenth president who left office in 1861, the political system has had two parties. The parties have become clubs... ones that rely on total felty to survive financially and maybe it worked for a time, but then it stopped working and when that happened is not important. All that is important is that we can make things better. The issues that most of America is unhappy with can be worked out. Collectively, we can correct the wrongs we have created.

Defeasible court decisions are possible... under the right situations and circumstances.”

“There’s a five-dollar word.” Marmalade comments. “Defeasible.”

“It’s an adjective.” I answer. “It means, subject to or capable of being annulled or made void.”

“I’d like to see some of the more recent stupid decisions annulled and made void.” Elizabeth Eaton scoffs. “It’s getting those right situations and circumstances that is the big challenge.”

“Are we getting to the part where you explain how banning male... and only male... ejaculation into my silicon molds makes a difference?” Conrad asks.

“Yes.” I answer. “Be patient, Conrad. I will get there.”

Elizabeth pats his hand gently. Vel asks the Robot to bring another round of drinks for the table. Under the table, Millie squeezes my leg before leaning into me to whisper in my ear. “I am getting this! I think I am *finally* understanding the path you are on.”

I take a drink of my club soda and keep talking. “Roe was not a bad decision *only* because it was the right outcome. Prior to 1972, things were as they basically were right after *Dobbs*... Laws regarding abortion were left up to the populations in each individual state. The true issue in Roe was this: Jane Roe, a woman named Norma McCorvey wanted an abortion, but she lived in Texas where at the time, abortion was illegal except when necessary to save the mother’s life. Her attorneys filed a lawsuit on her behalf against the local district attorney; Henry Wade, alleging that the Texas laws regarding abortion were unconstitutional. A three-judge court in the Northern District of Texas ruled in favor of McCorvey. Texas appealed the decision to the Supreme Court. In January of 1973, the court ruled seven to three in favor of McCorvey. The argument presented by McCorvey’s attorney was that the Due Process law of the Fourteenth Amendment provides a *fundamental right to privacy* and as such, protects a pregnant woman’s right to an abortion.”

"That's the way it should be." Vel says as the Robot drops off drinks.

I raise my hand in the air with my index finger extended. "There was dissent on the court even among those who favored the decision. Blackmun's written decision reflects those differences. The written decision held that the right to an abortion is not absolute, and the government must balance the people's interest in both protecting the woman's health and prenatal life. Blackmun reconciled the competing interests on the court by announcing a pregnancy trimester timetable to govern all abortion regulations in the United States."

"The Protestant concept of quickening." Vel mutters. "Fucking religion. It will be the death of us all."

"That's for damn sure." Conrad says agreeably.

"What's quickening?" Marmalade asks. "And we are in a house of the Lord. Religion has its place, you two."

I nod at Millie. "You want to answer this? The question on quickening, not the comment on religion." She nods. Even before she starts talking, I take the opportunity to shove food in my mouth.

Millie gathers her thoughts before she starts speaking. "At the creation of the country until the mid-eighteen hundreds... abortion was legal under common law in the entire United States until the woman experienced quickening. *Quickening* was a common use term for when a pregnant woman starts to feel the fetus move inside her. As Vel said, quickening is based on old Protestant Christian beliefs that *personhood* starts when movement of the fetus can be felt by the mother... basically between the fourth and sixth month of the pregnancy. In 1821, Connecticut passed the first state law regulating abortion when they forbid the use of poisons when performing an abortion. It was all downhill from there until Roe. In the middle part of the eighteen hundreds, there was an upsurge in abortions... mostly because there was an expansion of the wealthy class and women came into the medical field. The medical profession came out against the practice... this was both political and misogynistic. Women were starting to work as doctors, albeit doctors who had not gone to medical school because women were not allowed in medical school at the time. The men, most of whom had medical degrees didn't like that women were starting to take business from them. As it turns out, *women like having women doctors*, especially when it comes to OBGYN issues. The practice of abortions was one of the first medical specialties and it was mostly performed by unlicensed people, many times, women. Also... and this is no small thing... It was mostly those well-off people who had abortions or who paid for abortions… the practice of providing abortions paid quite well. By 1883, sixty percent of American states and territories had laws against abortion prior to quickening. By 1900, *every* state had anti-abortion laws. In all states throughout the nineteenth century and early twentieth century, pre-quickening abortions were always considered to be actions without a lawful purpose. This meant that if the mother died during the procedure, the individual performing the abortion was guilty of murder." Millie sighs. "The states wanted to criminalize abortion to preserve the life of fetus, protect the life and fertility of the mother and create a deterrence against future abortions. Judges quickly figured out that arresting women who had an abortion was unproductive as juries would not convict... so they sent law enforcement to interrogate these women and used that evidence to convict the doctor who provided the abortion... something I sadly became well familiar with a century later."

"But the McCorvey woman, she was allowed to have an abortion and Roe changed all of that, right?" Conrad asks. "It's *Dobbs* that messed things up in the modern era."

Vel shakes her head angrily. Happily, I pick my fork up and after encouraging Vel to speak, keep eating. *I can see how one might question how I am able to eat in the middle of such an important and intense discussion, but this food is incredible. Literally the best thing I have had in my mouth in over two decades.*

Vel pushes her chair back angrily. "Norma McCorvey was pregnant in June of 1969, Conrad. The Roe decision was handed down in early 1973. Human women don't *carry* babies for thirty months. She had the child and put it up for adoption. The lawyers that took Roe to the Supreme Court, Sarah Weddington and Linda Coffee were looking for candidates to push the issue up through the legal process. McCorvey was young. The family was low income, white and Protestant all of which made her a good candidate to put before the court. You see, abortion is also a socioeconomic issue. McCorvey knew she couldn't afford to give another child any quality of life. In 1969 there *was* abortion available in some places. Alaska, California, Hawaii, New York, Washington, and Washington, D.C. all allowed abortion, but woman like McCorvey had to be able to travel and then the woman having the abortion would have had to be able to pay cash for the services. There was a woman in Florida named Shirley Wheeler. She was charged with manslaughter in Florida after her doctors reported her illegal abortion to the police. Florida gave her a sentence of a two-year probation. After Roe, Wheeler's conviction was overturned by the Florida Supreme Court. Roe made it so women could have an abortion *if* they could find a provider. Women in most of the south and parts of the Midwest and near west never did have good access to reproductive health care." Vel pauses to sip on her drink. "There were a bunch of other important cases that no one speaks of. For example, *Doe v Bolton*... That decision was handed down on the very same day that *Roe* was. The issue with *Doe* was restrictive laws in Georgia that included the requirement of a physician's approval to obtain an abortion. The same seven to two majority struck that down. The written opinion reiterated the importance of protecting the *right to privacy when considering matters involving marriage, procreation, contraception, family relationships, child rearing, and education.*" Millie speaks up. "And we can't forget two very important cases, *Griswold* and *Casey.*"

"*Casey.* Jesus, *Casey.* The start of the downfall." Vel shakes her head. "Prior to *Dobbs, Griswold* and *Casey* were more important than *Roe.* While *Casey* reaffirmed a woman's right to an abortion, it also gave states more leeway in passing laws restricting abortion... especially after the first trimester. *Griswold*... Estelle Griswold, was the head of Planned Parenthood in Connecticut. She filed suit against the state, in effect asking to be able to provide birth control to *married* couples. The courts found in favor of *Griswold*, largely leaning on privacy rights."

"But those privacy rights are imaginary or something... right?" Conrad asks.

Elizabeth Eaton shakes her head. "Penumbras." She sips on her nonalcoholic Tequila Sunrise. "Privacy rights are not *imaginary*. Both the ninth and fourteenth amendment of the constitution contain our rights of privacy, and they were referenced in the majority ruling on *Griswold*. In 2033 we lost our rights to birth control by *congressional action*.

I clean the last of the food off my plate and look at the dish holding more. Millie senses my desire and puts another scoop on my plate. Steam waifs off the dish. I inhale and enjoy the aroma before I start talking again. "Conrad, starting with the Supreme Court in the State of Alabama in 2024, courts have recognized that the female egg is a human being. Before IVF was banned all together, certain states made egg donors make arrangements to take care of their eggs permanently." I chuckle recalling the humorous article I had read online about how women would take their cryogenically frozen egg *children* on a *vacation* to Europe only to leave the frozen embryos with a research facility or more frequently in a public bathroom. "To make a real, functioning baby, that egg needs sperm. Tell me... Why would it be ok that male ejaculation can be wasted into a Kleenex or one of your... devices when we are *so* very concerned about the female equivalent?"

Conrad wrinkles his face up and shakes his head. "It's two very different things, Justin! Sperm from an adult male is not guaranteed to be good. Temperature, diet, the health of the man all affect the quality of the sperm. Also, men have a seemingly unlimited amount of sperm for nearly all their life and women only produce one... maybe two eggs per month... for only a portion of their lives. Finally, the medical profession has long considered male and female masturbation safe and healthy."

I glance around the table. Marmalade is looking at his hands, which seems appropriate. The three women are looking at Conrad in disbelief, which also seems appropriate.

"Justin didn't ask you for the medical reasons that masturbation should be accepted, dear." Elizabeth Eaton pats her boyfriend's hand. "He asked you why the production of an egg by a human female should not be equated with the production of sperm by a human male."

"This is anti-gay!" Conrad exclaims. "You are criminalizing gay men!"

"Yes. I considered that." I nod. "Those men are unfortunate and innocent victims in my diabolical plans."

Elizabeth nods at my sarcastic comment. "*Lawrence v Texas, 2003* could be at risk because of the *Spilt Seed* law."

"Do you think that the eggs produced by females are actual children, Conrad?" Millie asks.

Conrad shakes his head angrily. "No, of course not. That is a stupid concept. It would be like saying the chicken eggs in your refrigerator are really chickens."

Elizabeth Eaton looks at me and smiles at the recognition of one of the arguments I used with my cousin, Father Henry Thyme.

"Then why..." Millie asks slowly. "Would we consider the second... but equally important part of the creation of a human being any differently?"

Conrad puts his head in his hands and rubs his temples. "It's the laws regarding women's health that need to change! We don't need laws banning male masturbation!"

Elizabeth Eaton clears her throat. "Congress has banned abortion, birth control and IVF by law, Conrad. It was passed in both houses and signed by the President of the United States. It will be nearly impossible to get an abortion, birth control or IVF case before any court, let alone the Supreme Court."

"But male masturbation?" Conrad asks. "What if congress takes it up and makes it illegal across the whole country?"

Vel smiles. "I think I *really* understand now." She points at me. "I thought this stunt was mostly about Marmalade's church business with the side benefit of poking the idiots that outlawed abortion. It isn't. You really think this will bring us together as a country."

I nod silently.

Marmalade sits back in his chair. "How this affects the church is just convenient. Justin led me to it, and we happen to have the tools to make information spread very quickly." He looks over at Conrad. "I didn't set out to harm you or your business, man. It was never like that."

"I know you think that my business is propagating sins or some shit like that." Conrad grumbles. "Your church members aren't going to be my customers. That's for damn sure."

Marmalade laughs. "Conrad, I don't have any problem with self-pleasure and neither does my church. Sure, we would rather people have sex *with other people* because that is what the Lord intends." He smiles gently. "And the people of my church simply can't afford your products Conrad! In most of my buildings, the only income the congregants have is the government living wage. Your products are the Louis Vuitton of the sex toy market!"

Conrad bristles. "We don't sell *toys*. We sell personal satisfaction devices."

Marmalade wrinkles up his nose in response. "*Personal satisfaction devices…* sounds like luxury to me, buddy."

I put a scoop of food in my mouth and chew. The Robot refills everyone's drinks. The group seems to be looking at me.
"What?" I ask with my mouth full.

"How is this going to work, Justin?" Conrad asks. I can tell he still miffed. "And when will male whacking off be legal again?"

"That's redundant. So far as I know, males are the only ones that *whack off*. Females *rub one out*." I say with my mouth full. I chew and swallow my food. "Juice, Vel... this is best food I can remember eating. I mean that." I look over at Millie. "I mean, we eat food... but this is delicious!" I sigh contentedly before answering Conrad's question. "Eventually there is going to be a trial. Some guy is going to get caught by his angry girlfriend or ex-wife flogging the one-eyed snake and she is going to turn him in for the reward money. After that, I am hoping that Elizabeth picks the best one to run with and takes the case to highest court she can."

"What grounds will you use to defend the accused?" Conrad asks. Elizabeth Eaton raises an index finger. "Same things that Blackmun should have emphasized when he wrote the majority opinion on *Roe*. Ninth Amendment and the Fourteenth Amendment."

"Talk to me like I am not an attorney who went to a real law school back when there were such things." Conrad grumbles.

Elizabeth smiles. "The ninth amendment is simple. It says this; *"The enumeration in the Constitution, of certain rights, shall not be construed to deny or disparage others retained by the people"*. James Madison added the ninth amendment. It is documented that he was concerned that future governments might try and limit the people's rights to what was covered by the constitution and nothing else. The ninth amendment clarifies that the constitution is not a comprehensive list of every right of every person in the United States and yet un-defined and unnamed laws are entitled to protection by the law."
"I feel better just hearing her explain it." Millie says softly.

"No kidding!" Vel adds.

The lawyer shakes her head. "The ninth amendment went into the constitution in 1789. Obviously, it hasn't always worked as a defense." She points at me. "Justin reminded me of the power of the fourteenth amendment, maybe our most important amendment after the first amendment as it actually denotes limitations on government intrusions on personal privacy. The amendment was proposed in 1862 and ratified by 1865. To gain admittance back into congress, the states that succeeded from the union had to vote to ratify the fourteenth amendment."

"I think those southern states are still butt hurt about all that." Vel grumbles.

"If you are referring to the results of the civil war in general, yes. The south is still *butt hurt* about *all that.*" Elizabeth answers with an eye roll. "The due process clause of the fourteenth amendment acts as a safeguard from arbitrary denial of life, liberty, or property by the government outside the sanction of law. It is the Due Process Clause's protection of liberty where the Justices found reasons to find for *Griswold* and where Justice Harry Blackmun located the right to privacy in *Roe* in 1973. *Roe* of course, was the decision that disallowed most state and federal abortion restrictions. In *Casey*, *Roe* was upheld but states were given leeway on the laws they could pass. *Dobbs* changed all that, as we know. There are other important uses of the Due Process clause in the fourteenth amendment. In *Lawrence v. Texas (2003)* the court found that a Texas law against same sex intercourse violated the right to privacy. In *Obergefell v. Hodges (2015)* the court ruled that the right to marriage included same-sex couples to wed." I watch her take a sip of her drink and eye each of us in the room. "*Lawrence* is what overturns this case... or..." Elizabeth Eaton shakes her head.
There is silence in the room. Elizabeth Eaton's" or" hangs in the air.

"Or, what?" I ask.

"Any challenge to this *Spilt Seed* foolishness will happen in state court. It really doesn't matter what state brings charges. If one state in the compact is attacked, it's as if all of the states in the Alamo Compact are attacked. There will be a tremendous effort to get the appeal all the way to the Supreme Court in a big hurry."

"So, if a fellow gets caught petting the penguin, he goes to jail. Some broad gets a bounty and the case goes in front of a state court, then the appeals courts, then the Supreme Court. How long will this take?" Conrad asks.

"Might be a guy." I say.

"Huh?" Conrad asks. "What do you mean, it might be a guy?"

I shrug. "It might be a dude that turns the masturbator in. Could be a boon for less than polite members of the gay community."

Conrad shakes his head and stops. "Wait! If gays can have sex and that has already been decided by the Supreme Court, than this Spilt Seed bullshit is just that, legally... bullshit."

Elizabeth Eaton smiles gently. "That's the problem with using *Lawrence v. Texas*. The core issue decided by the court in *Lawrence* was whether or not prohibiting sex between two people of the same sex was legal. If we use *Lawrence*... I am at a loss to see where we might use any *other* case, and if we lose... well, that is likely the end of gay rights." Eaton's head goes from side to side. "But that is how the law works. As John Locke said, *"The end of Law is not to abolish or restrain, but to preserve and enlarge freedom. For in all the states of created beings, capable of laws, where there is no law there is no freedom."* We use the laws to defeat inequities. We just need to make sure we don't create more inequities with our efforts."

"How long before we can get women's health rights restored?" Vel asks.

A heavy silence settles over the room. I look at the ceiling, a habit I had in high school when trying to complete hard math problems in my head. "Twenty years." I answer. "Give or take three or four."

"Twenty years!" Marmalade exclaims. He looks at Elizabeth. "That long?"

She bites her bottom lip and nods. "Justin is probably close. The Texas Supreme Court is likely to uphold this law as it is mostly conservative and thanks to our forty fifth and forty seventh President, mostly religious. It will take one to three years to get a least one *Spilt Seed* case in front of a State Supreme Court. One or two more years to get a case in front of the United States Supreme Court. I am confident *Spilt Seed* will die, so long as

Congress doesn't enact a national law. We must hope that we get enough out of the first case to find elements to challenge the current national laws against abortion and birth control, then we need to hunt down a specific sort of abortion case that has all the elements in it that we want so we can get that case through the courts and eventually in front of the Supreme Court. I would have said fifteen or sixteen years, at least."

"This is hopeless." Conrad says.

"Maybe." I stand up. The cow's voice is in my head. I must lead. Even if I don't want to. "The population of our country is divided. It is not just because of what has happened to women's rights. We let the political process, and our stupid, petty differences get the best of us." I point to both Marmalade and Conrad. "An hour ago, you two were staring at each other like a couple of angry bulls. Once upon a time, you were *friends. Best Friends.* Now?" I do my best to glare at both men. It's not a good glare... I am pretty sure my eyes just look sort of dead. "Now, Conrad has a bias against Marmalade because of the church he belongs to... and Marmalade... How often have you reached out to Hank? Conrad? Willem and Wendy? You became an island. Why?"

"I just didn't give a shit." Marmalade points across the table. "Conrad made it big; you know... biggest sex toy maker in all of 'Merica!"

I shake my head. "Dude? You are living in a mansion with like twelve layers of White House level security. We see you! You were a successful professional football player, a successful musician and now a successful businessman. Why forget about the people you came up with?" I lean on the table with both hands. "You have made yourself an island, just like most of the people in this country. Your island appears to be more than just a little bit hypocritical. You are married to a woman that spends her days trying to assist women with health care that is illegal but necessary while running a franchise of a church that appears to do nothing less than trample on the rights of women every day.

"It's not like that exactly in the church, Justin." Marmalade looks at the table. "Conrad made fun of the church... I guess I just thought, well, if he be against me, I'm against him."

I stare at Juice. Conrad starts to speak, and I wave him silent. "Juice... people get full back tattoos on their bodies to celebrate... announce... individual inclusion into your church. You literally brand your members, principally it appears so sexual partners outside of marriage can be chosen properly because apparently the church not only condones but promotes some sort of polyamorous activity between its members and it does this, unbelievably, in the name of God. The founder of your church, who happens to be the ex-husband of the woman that I love is a four-hundred-pound sloth in an electric cart moving around like a cartoon character trying his best to get busy with teenage girls a quarter his age. Conrad made *fun* of your church?" I throw my hands in the air. "*Juice...* If I was a comedian, I could do a whole damn stand-up routine on the business you shroud as a church! For the love of God, *Jesus ran the money changers out of the temple. You* have made a church into a regular ATM!" The night is going to either end or continue on that note. I watch Juice closely. He stares at the table. The room goes silent. I feel Millie's hand rub the back of my leg. Slowly, a big smile starts to cross Marmalade's face. He looks up and leans across the table. I am suddenly very concerned about what is going to come out of his mouth.

"Millie, I told you that I know that man who used to be your husband better than you ever did. Let me tell you about him now." "Marmalade, maybe this is not the time." I say.

Marmalade looks at Millie and ignores me. "Right after you went away, he started his church. As you suspect, it was your money he used. Six months into the deal, he got caught in a hotel room in Dallas, Texas with three underaged girls and a grocery bag of methamphetamines. Luckily, he happened to have recruited a local assistant district attorney into the church. The charges were dropped. That was before I bought into the business. After I purchased my franchises, Rex Ratchet was invited to the White House by the President of the United States. He was recorded agreeing with the sitting President of the United States that all the Jews should be sent back to Israel because they were doing this country *no damn good.*" He looks at his wife.

Vel nods in agreement. "I saw the recording of the schmuck in that meeting. It was pretty awful. Juice isn't telling the half of it."

"Not as awful as what happened next. The *next* president used that video recording to blackmail Rex into bringing migrants from Brazil into Mississippi as part of a fake *church mission* service. Those people were put into chicken processing plants that the President's family owned. The people from Brazil *had* to live in the processing plant. They were basically treated like slaves. Ten of those people *died* before the group managed to run away from the place. I'd like to say it made the news, but by that time, there was no *real* news. Of course, no charges were filed."

Millie's face is white with anger. I want to make Juice stop. He sees me start to raise my hand. "No! No, Justin. I need to finish so I can make *my* point to Conrad." He leans on the table. "I was five years into this, and my sources tell me that Rex Rexford is banging a girl less than ten years old."

*For some reason, I can no longer react appropriately to this sort of information. I see Millie shaking her head sadly. Conrad and Elizabeth look stunned. Vel has obviously heard this information before. Her head is bowed, and her hands tented in front of her.*

"I found out later that the girl was six. Six. Years. Old." Juice bangs on the table with each word. "That's when shit got serious, real fast. I went scorched earth on the man. I dug up men and women who were abused in his church... either by him or by his minions. You know what happened? Nada. Nothing. Zilch. Rex denied everything. Then one of the women who came forward disappeared. Flat ass vanished. I never have found her, and believe me, I looked. The rest of the people who had a story to tell quickly recanted. No charges were ever filed. After that, I got saddled with four of Rex Ratchet's favorite bastard ministers and was told I couldn't preach anymore." Marmalade stands. "Conrad, the thing you think is a church is a *business* for me. I own a *franchise*. My *business* produces more money than I could ever have dreamed of, and the product really is good for *some* people. For others... not so much... but I intend to fix that. I just hadn't figured out how until this man..." Marmalade looks at me. "This man whose story comes straight from the good book... Justin... *risen from the dead, Justin Thyme,* comes around and he has this crazy ass idea to make whacking off illegal.

Not only might his idea restore some justice for women, but also, I can use it to take down Ratchet. The government won't do it. Not the feds and certainly not Texas. He is too tightly ingrained in the system." Juice stops and takes a drink. "You know who can destroy Ratchet's temple, Conrad? His very own congregations. The people who pay their tithes to belong to the church." The empty glass is pointed at me and Millie. "The Reverend Rex Ratchet is no different than the money changers in the Temple. He takes and then takes some more. Rachet is a thief, taking advantage of the people seeking to worship God with their tithes and sacrifices. Just like you are, Conrad, I am concerned about profit in my businesses, but what I really want is a better church."

I look down. I am relieved to see that color has been restored to Millie's face. I rub her shoulders gently. Juice sits down and calls for another round of drinks. I look over at Conrad. "You good, Conrad?"

Conrad shrugs. "I had no idea that your church is like a fast-food franchise, Marmalade." He pauses. "I... I am not religious. Neither Elizabeth nor I ever have been religious.  I don't understand why people put so much into religion... and I understand even less why there such strident arguments for this religion or that one. To me? It's like me arguing with Justin that my imaginary friend is more powerful than his imaginary friend."

I feel Millie chuckle quietly. *If you only knew, Conrad.* I think to myself. Something Juice had said hit me. *The congregation can change the church.* "It's our government." I blurt out.

Millie looks up. "What?"

"It's our government. The government is us. All of us are *We the people*.". I point at Conrad. "That's why this works. Banning masturbation? *Preposterous!* But... maybe this really is the thing that will wake the population up. Maybe people will start paying better attention to how the government actually works. The United States in 2042 is a long way down from where we were when we were born, but... maybe we can claw it back and maybe this is the thing that brings us all together. *We the people* starts right here, right now with the four of us!"

There is quiet in the room. I think maybe I have gone too far when Elizabeth stands. "Justin is right." She looks down at Conrad. "This may hurt your business for a while, but in the long run, banning male masturbation will help the country by showing people how ridiculous the laws and rules the government has been passing are. We can work towards a happier future. Happy people like sex. People who like sex, buy your products. This will benefit your business, long term." She gestures around the table. "That said... We need to be careful here. You see, there are still two political sides... We only seem to cast stones at the people on the right side of the political spectrum. It is easy to see where things would be so much easier if more consistent and generally less constraining state and federal laws were in place. We all want our Constitution and Bill of Rights to reign supreme. Therein lies the big conundrum. We take this *Spilt Seed* law to court, and let's say that we get it overturned and maybe even get language that says the states have no right to arbitrate any person's right to liberty, however that is defined. Then we need to have some sort of national governance that establishes a central power... which would have the ability to negate all our personal liberties. If that happens, the *progressives* win and of course... such control over our lives is the progressive goal for this nation."

We are all silent. I look over at Elizabeth. "If that happens, you think that the progressives will take charge and go after other things, like the second amendment."

"I could do without all the guns that people seem to have." Vel comments.

"There is a lot of poor people out there who seemed to have been left behind by society." Millie says. "We see it down where we are staying."

Elizabeth nods. "I am just saying, politics in a democracy is a balance. Any one action taken may have effects on a whole bunch of unrelated things. The Robert's Court wasn't necessarily wrong when it decided *Dobbs*. The issue is this, like Blackmun's decision in *Roe*, the *Dobbs* written opinion from Alito was about abortion. The opinion in *Roe* said abortion was legal as making the act illegal would be a violation of the ninth and fourteenth amendment, but the Blackmun court put limitations on abortion by defining a trimester and bringing up the issue of viability. *Casey* furthered that track, opening the path to continued challenges by the states. The opinion in *Dobbs* more or less said that abortion was not included in the constitution and could be legal but left the decision to ban or allow abortion up to the states or Congress. Later, Congress, because of political preference on other unrelated issues swung right, and abortion, along with birth control and IVF became illegal across the nation." Elizabeth sighs. "I am certain that we can defeat this contrived *Spilt Seed* law... but if *We the People* don't start paying attention to how things work, everything will swing the other way and our country is likely to split into parts... weak, ineffective parts that are all individually controlled by a central point of power. I don't think there is anyone at the table that wants national control over our lives. We already have the living wage that makes it, so people don't have to work. The country has lost so much because of that. There is no innovation. There is no manufacturing. The creative class seems to have run off to Europe or China. When was the last time anyone saw a movie that was made in the United States? In the mid 2020's the public thought that the biggest issue was immigration. That's no longer a problem because no one sees the United States of America as the land of opportunity. This country has lost its way for sure... but we can't lose the idea of Democracy completely. If the political spectrum swings all the way to the left, we might." Elizabeth sighs. "If that happens... well, the world will not be better off."

I look at Millie. She is staring at the center of the table. Marmalade is looking at his plate like it might hold the illusive answers to cold fusion. Conrad seems to be staring off in space. Vel smiles at me. "What do you think, Justin? You seem to have been brought back to fight this battle."

"I think that we must tackle one issue at a time. The rights of fifty percent of the population were trampled by the Congress that passed a national ban on abortion and then birth control." I look over at Marmalade. "Juice, you have shown me some of your powers. Think we can use those powers for good? Start informing the population what needs to happen so they can take their country back?"

Marmalade nods slowly. "It takes money." He says with a flat tone. "How much money?" I ask.

"More than I have." Marmalade answers. "But let's see what happens tomorrow. Maybe I will have an idea about how we can mobilize large tracts of the population... maybe speed everything up."

Conrad stands and walks over to Marmalade. "Juice, I am sorry that I have judged you. I don't like what you do with that church. But that's ok. You are my friend, and I want that to remain the case no matter who your imaginary friends are."

Marmalade cracks a smile and stands, grabbing Conrad in a long, tight embrace.

Elizabeth and Conrad leave, turning down Vel's repeated offer of bed for the night. Millie looks at me with tired eyes. "I'm glad we are staying here tonight." I nod silently. Vel leads us to a guest bedroom. I lay on the bed while Millie uses the restroom. The bed is... other worldly. The mattress meets my body like a glove, cocooning me in a warm, soft embrace. Until this moment, I had no real memory of what a true mattress should feel like. The bathroom door opens, and Millie comes out in a robe. She flashes that million dollar smile a few feet from the bed and lets the robe drop from her shoulders. Her naked form intoxicates me.

"So, this is what a woman's body looks like when its well on the way to sixty years old." Millie announces. "Ever seen one before?"

I say the first, sarcastic remark that comes to mind. "Well, there was a cadaver once in medical school. But I didn't have the opportunity to sleep with her."

Millie laughs and crawls into the bed. "That cadaver would have been more fun than I will be tonight."

Instantly, I start worrying about the reaction - or lack thereof - my recently moribund friend hanging between my legs may have towards this nude angel crawling into bed beside me.

Millie pulls back the covers and snuggles close to me. "Is your offer of using your last name still good?"

"Of course." I answer. *There go those nervous butterflies banging around in my gut again.*

Millie sighs and closes her eyes. "Good. I think it's time I no longer go by Ratchet, and I certainly can't go back to my maiden name." In a few moments, she is asleep. I lift the covers and look down at my shriveled member.

"We dodged a bullet, there, little soldier." I say softly.

Chapter 59
The Police are here to talk to you.
What is that thing and how do I put it on?
Good Home Someplace in the United States of America
Land of the Free(ish) Home of the Brave(ish)


Bob Good lays on the floor alone in the dark in his bedroom. He can hear his parent's angry voices resonating up the staircase. The argument had been going on for several days. From what Bob could tell, his father was mad about something his mother had done at the church and his mother was angry that his father was mad. He hears the doorbell ring. Quickly, he checks his proximity locator. Anne Margret and Conrad are together at Anne's house. No one on his contact list shows at his front door. He sighs and switches off the internal device. The doorbell rings again and his parents stop arguing.

He hears the front door open. His father is speaking to someone. Bob can't make out what they are saying. He recognizes his father's heavy footsteps as they ascend the staircase. There is a light knock at the door. "Bob?" his father says softly. "There are some police people here to see you."

Bob groans. "Probably the shit with Geely." He sits up.

"Can I come in?" Cliff Good asks. "What shit with Geely?"

"Yeah come in." Bob answers. He stands. "Geely is just a weird chick, dad."

His father opens the door to the dark room and turns on the overhead light. "Most women are. What are you doing here in the dark?"

"Thinking." Bob answers. "What do the police want?"

"They won't tell me. They say it is a matter they need to talk to you about." Cliff answers. "Did you do something Bob? Something criminal? Is Geely ok?"

"No." Bob shakes his head. "I mean, no, I haven't done anything wrong. Not that I know of, anyway. Geely is Geely. Fred says she is far from *ok*." He walks past his father and down the stairs. The two police officers that had come to Conrad and Fred's house a few days before stand inside the open front door. "Trump Bob Good? You are the guy from the other night." The female officer says with a surprised voice.

"He did say that he was spanking the old monkey on that video. I guess that girl figured out a way to get even with him!" The male officer says.
Bob looks at the pair. "What's up?" His father comes down the stairs and stands beside him.

The female officer clears her throat. "Well... this is awkward. We haven't done this before..." The woman shakes her head. "I can't believe that I get to do it now!" The police officer has a wild look in her eyes, like whatever she is about to do is exciting her. She looks at her the male officer and speaks quickly. "Did you bring the device? We *have* to install the device!"

"Fuck no!" The male officer exclaims. He exhales. "I left it in the transporter. Do you really think we need it? I don't see any reason to use that stupid thing."
The female officer frowns. "Absolutely! It's the best part!" The male officer shakes his head and exits the house, walking slowly to the black and white painted transporter sitting at the curb.

"What is this about?" Cliff Good asks. Bob's mother appears on the other side of Bob.

The female officer's face lights up. "Well, apparently the other day, a law was passed that outlaw's male masturbation." She sighs happily. "We have had a complaint filed about your son, Bob... with video evidence. We must arrest him."

"Masturbation is illegal?" Sookie Moonbeam Good exclaims. "How can that be?"

Bob shakes his head defiantly. "I didn't do that after the law was passed."

The male officer reappears. He has a male chastity belt in his hand. "What is that?" Sookie Moonbeam Good points. "And what in the hell do you intend to do with it?"

The male officer holds up the chastity belt. It is a square cage made from some sort of metal. Small fake diamonds adorn the cage, and the nylon belt attached to it. "It's umm... all we had. This is a new thing. There is no, like serious chastity belts and the law says we must make sure the accused are wearing one... you know, so they can't, umm...."

"Spill any more seed." The female officer finishes the male officer's sentence with a triumphant tone. "Let's do this right...". She pulls out a small notebook and starts reading from it. "Trump Bob Good, you have been accused by an anonymous bounty collector of violating section sixty-nine of the state health and human services criminal code now known as the *Prohibition of Spilt Seed* law, recently accepted into law by our state in accordance with our agreed participation with laws of the state of Texas. In our enforcement of this law, we are going to arrest you, fit you with..." She pauses and holds up the chastity belt dangling from her partner's hand. "This device." She lets go of the diamond studded belt and continues talking, "You will be booked into the county jail and arraigned at the court's convenience." She sighs happily and motions at her partner. "Hook him up."

The male police officer, dangling the chastity belt looks unsure. "You want *me* to put this on him? Oh, hell no."

The female police officer shakes her head. "Let's start with cuffing him. So, the criminal is secured." She says with an exasperated tone.

"Whatever." The male cop looks at Bob apologetically. "Turn around."

"Is this really necessary?" Sookie Good asks with a nervous voice. "Cliff, do something!"

"Officers, can we talk this over? I am not sure I understand this law. Are you sure that it really exists?" Cliff Good asks. "What did you call it? Prohibit Spilt Seeds? That sounds like something from one of the monitor shows!"

"The law exists dad." Bob says. "I saw it get passed in Texas the other day when I was at Fred's house. He turns around. The male cop pulls his wrists back and puts the handcuffs on him.

"Now we need to put the chastity belt on him." The female officer announces.
"Why didn't we let him do that?" The male officer asks with a slow, doubtful tone. "Seems... more *hygienic* to let the perp put his own chastity belt on."

"You can't take my baby away!" Sookie Good yells. She comes over and pulls her handcuffed son by his wrists. "He didn't do anything wrong!"

"Like we never hear that twenty times a day!" The female cop sneers. Pulled off balance, Bob falls to the floor with a thud. "Put the belt on him." The female officer says to the male officer.

"No." The male officer shakes his head hard from side to side. "No fucking way."

"It's the rule." The officer points at Bob. "And I am your supervising officer. I am telling you to put the chastity belt on that man!"

"It's *my* rule that I don't put chastity belts on other men. Or myself, for that matter. Also, I think it is a stupid, Boring rule." The male officer answers.

"We can't just not do things because we think it is Boring or a stupid rule." The female officer argues.

"I'm not sure how he might be able to masturbate with his hands cuffed behind his back. Didn't you *kind of* already put the belt on him?" Cliff Good suggests.

"Cliff!" Sookie Good cries. "It's like you want my baby taken away!"

"I thought Miranda was a stupid rule, so I stopped doing it... and look at us now! No Miranda. People shouldn't do stupid things just because there is a rule!" The male officer exclaims, ignoring Cliff and Sookie Good.

"Umm... I can't get up." Bob says from the floor.

"I want my first collar on this charge to have that thing on. Get that chastity belt on him!" The female officer shouts. "It is the *rule!*"

"If you help me up and take the cuffs off me, I will put it on!" Bob says from the floor.

"No!" Both officers say in unison. The female officer adds, "You are a dangerous criminal, and we do not take the cuffs off of dangerous criminals until we have them secure in a jail cell!"

"I'm dangerous?" Bob asks. "I don't feel dangerous."

"You are a serial masturbator." The female cop says. "An *admitted* serial masturbator. You told us so the other night."

"I did?" Bob asks, his voice muffled by the floor.

"When did you talk to my son?" Sookie Good demands. She turns to her husband. "When did these *pigs* talk to our son?"

"They are actually quite nice people, mom." Bob mumbles from the floor. "At least, they were the other night."

"In the course of another investigation, we obtained information that your son is a serial masturbator. Today, a related party provided video evidence of Trump Bob Good's crimes against... well... the state." The female cop points at Bob. "And now, we are going to be the first police officers in this *state* to protect the lives of *un-conceived* children by arresting a serial masturbator for violating the *Prevention of Spilt Seed* mandate."

"This whole thing really seems like something that would be on *Shit Happens*." Cliff Good says. "Can we talk to a lawyer or something?"

"You can talk to your Jesus, for all I care... Consult with the Flying Spaghetti Monster. Call a damn lawyer!" The female officer grins and points at Bob's father. "Doesn't mean shit to me. All I know is I am arresting this person for a crime! A crime against society this is!"

The male officer shakes his head. "My partner really doesn't like masturbation, apparently." He reaches down and roughly pulls Bob up. "I'm not putting that Boring chastity belt thing on him though. Either let him do it or do it yourself."

"I'm not touching his Boring junk." The female officer comments with an offended tone. "No fucking way." The two police officers stare at each other.

"Give me the damn thing. I will help Bob put it on." Cliff Good reaches for the chastity belt. "Don't worry, son. We will find you a lawyer. I don't know how we will pay for one, but we will find one." The male police officer pulls the chastity belt away from Cliff's reach. "You have to do it right here. The perp must stay in our sight."

"That's right. The perp has to stay right here. I want to see that belt put on him!" The female officer says, continuing her glare at her partner. "And if he makes any attempt to escape, I swear to all that is Boring, I will tase him into next week."

"Oh, God!" Sookie Moonbeam pleads.

"Wish I hadn't heard you say that so much when Reverend Savenutts was plowing you." Cliff mutters.

"Not now Clifford!" Sookie moans. "Our son is being arrested! For being a *serial* masturbator!" She adds tearfully.

Cliff sighs. Using one hand he pulls his son's chin up and looks him in the eyes. "Bob, I am going to pull your pants down and put this stupid belt on you. Just stand still and don't give these guys a reason to tase you."

Bob nods tightly. Tears well up in the corners of his eyes. "Ok.... Ok." He starts breathing heavy.

Cliff pulls down the boy's loose pants, exposing his genitals to the room. "Good choice of pants today, son." He puts a hand out for the belt. The male officer hands it to him.

"Goodness, your boy is well equipped, Mrs. Good." The female officer remarks.

Sookie cranes her neck to look. "Is he? I haven't seen it for ten years or so."

"Mom!" Bob cries out. "Go away!"

Gingerly. Cliff fits the jewel studded cage on Bob and fastens the belt in place. "You guys know this is just a sex toy, right? He can just unhook this belt when his cuffs are off."

"He pulls any Boring shit like that; he will be getting a tasing!" The female officer replies sharply.

Cliff shakes his head and pulls Bob's pants up. The cage forms a square in the pants at the crotch.

"I guess everyone will know what you are in for!" The female officer chides. She pokes her partner in the ribs and looks at Sookie. "Get this perp in the car. You people can probably pick him up at central booking tomorrow."

`Cliff watches as the male officer roughly pushes Bob out the front door of the Good house. As he stumbles down the front walk, Bob turns his head back over his shoulder. "Call Freddy, dad! He will know what to do! He and Anne Margret are lawyers now!"

Chapter 60
Working it out.
Marmalade Julius's House Someplace in America
Land of the Free(ish) Home of the Brave(ish)


"Wakey Wakey." I hear Marmalade's voice in my ear. My eyes open to a dark room. "What?" I ask.

"It's time to go work out." Marmalade whispers. "I can't stand seeing your scarecrow ass like it is. We need to put some meat on those bones."
"It's the middle of the night." I say.

"It's five thirty. The early bird only gets the worms left behind by those who hustle." Marmalade whispers loud enough to make Millie stir. "Get your skinny ass out of bed and let's get hustling!"

"This bed is so nice." I mumble. "Can't we work out later?"

"Nope. Later we gots to change the world. We have time to work out, right now. You can sleep when you are dead."

"That's not funny, Marmalade." I say. Resigned, I swing my legs off the bed and stand up. Marmalade hands me a bag. "What's this?"

"You ain't working out in Willem's old suit. That bag has some shorts, underwear, socks and t-shirt in it. Also, some real shoes. Got to get you wearing real clothes again." Marmalade answers. "Ain't no one else in the house awake. Get dressed in the gym. Let's go."
"What about Millie?" I ask.

"Let her sleep. I laid it on her pretty heavy last night. She needs the rest." Marmalade replies. "Goddamn that Rex Ratchet. He fucked up a beautiful woman there."

"She is still beautiful." I say with a defensive tone.

"I didn't say she ain't beautiful.  I said she was mind-fucked by her ex."  Marmalade huffs.  "Let's get moving."

"What's going on?" Millie asks with a sleepy voice.

I reach over and rub her shoulders. "Marmalade says I need to work out and put some muscles on my bones. You get to stay here and sleep."

"That's good." Millie mumbles. "Go get some muscles. I like muscles."

"Let's go." Juice says from the doorway.

I follow him out. We walk into Marmalade's gym that looks like something any YMCA would be proud to have. He opens a glass refrigerator and pulls out a bottle full of something green. "Drink this." He commands, pulling out a second one and twisting the top off.

"What is it?" I ask.

"Good for you." Juice says after he swallows half of his bottle.

I look at the glass container. There is no label. "Did you make this?"
"It's greens. Leafy greens like collards and chard. Also, there is a carrot in there. Good for you. Drink it." Juice commands.

I shrug and twist the cap off, the first sip is ok. It tastes... green.

"Better to do it fast." Juice says. "Then fill the bottle with water and drink it down."

I chug the green juice down and fill the bottle with water. After downing the water, Juice points to a door. "Locker room. Get in there and get changed. Your tighty-whities concern me."

I roll my eyes and go into the locker room. Like the gym and the rest of Juice's estate, it is marvelous. Dark wood walls are lined with photos of Marmalade playing football. There are pictures of the church buildings along with some pictures of Vel and Juice together. I set the bag of workout clothes on a bench and pull the contents out. The t-shirt has the logo for *Juice's Gyms* on it. I pull it over my head before pulling on a clean pair of underwear and the work out shorts. Everything is a little big, which I guess is to be expected. I see a mirror and pull the shorts down a little. My good luck mark from the grasshopper still seems to be about the same size. I make a mental note to look at Millie's mark later. I pull the shoes on and go back into the gym. Juice is waiting for me by a pair of stationary bicycles. "Ten minutes. Full Speed." He announces.

I get on and start pedaling. "Full speed isn't very fast these days, Juice." I say, breathing a little hard.

"Baby steps, Justin." Juice says. His legs are a blur on the pedals. "So, what was it like?"

I look over at him. "What was what like?"
"Being dead." Marmalade looks over at me. "You were dead, right? Conrad says you were."

I nod slowly. "Yeah. I guess I was."  I have little interest in telling Marmalade anything about the Cow, bear and grasshopper.

Juice looks out the windows of his gym. They are floor to ceiling affairs. The sun is just cracking over the horizon, creating the orange hue that signifies the end of darkness and beginning of a new day. "You and Millie both, you have the same eyes. They ain't right you know, your eyes and hers. They aren't... I don't know how to describe it." He looks over at me. "I mean no offense Justin... but I *know* you. Those ain't your eyes.

Whatever you got in those sockets, man... they are lifeless. Same with your girl, Millie."

"Marmalade..." I want to speak, but at three minutes into this bike ride to nowhere, I am a little out of breath. "We... we both..." I shake my head.

Marmalade seems to pedal faster. "It doesn't matter. Maybe you are still healing, and your eyes will be more lifelike when your body has fully repaired itself." A light beeping is heard. "Five minutes left! Push it hard, Justin!" Juice calls out in an excited tone that I might reserve for buying a guaranteed winning lottery ticket or seeing a real dinosaur. I try speeding up my pace. My legs feel like they have become rubberized. I push harder, and my legs respond. I'd like to think that I am thankful to feel my heart beating in my chest because that would mean that I both have a heart and not, as Juice suspects, that I am dead inside. As it stands, I am not at all thankful right now to feel my heartbeat. Every beat feels like the poor dumb thing is trying to break free of the sack and rib cage holding it in place. I try my best to suck in air and fail. An alarm goes off someplace. My brain is trying hard to keep up with my heart, which is running away like a truck flying down a mountain highway looking for one of those emergencies pull offs that are really just piles of loose sand. Even the little voices that normally speak their sarcastic mind when stressed like this are silent. I tell myself that the pace is ok, but we should stop peddling and continue on to whatever Marmalade has in store next in the workout. I wait for one of those sarcastic mother fuckers in my head to slow the pace down so I can stop and get off the bike. It reminds me of the year I thought jogging was the best thing on earth. I would go out every morning looking for that runners high, except the damn high seem to come longer and longer into the run. I start wondering if there is such a thing as a bike rider high.

"Justin!" Marmalade is beside me. I am still peddling. I look over at him. I don't need a mirror to know that I am wild eyed. Marmalade puts his hand on my wrist. "Justin! *Stop peddling!*"

I tell myself to stop moving my legs. Nothing happens. *Hey!* I scream silently. *Stop the legs!*

*Stop the legs. Start the legs. Pedal faster. Don't Pedal!* A little voice says in my head. *You say so many silly things. You want to stop? Just. Stop...* My whole body locks up, nearly pitching me off the stationary bike.

"Jesus, Justin. You were really moving there!" Marmalade comments. "I thought you just wanted a little extra time on the bike. You've been riding full tilt for like twenty minutes." He looks at me. "You ok, man?"

I nod. My mouth isn't working quite yet. What I want to say is that maybe I need to take the workout thing a bit slower. Juice gives me a curious look. "Can you get off the bike?"

I shake my head tightly. I can't get off the bike. At the moment, I can't do *anything*. My brain is scrambled. I don't even know what to ask myself to do. I look forward, out the marvelous floor to ceiling windows that line the east wall of the massive gym. The sun has broken free across the horizon, painting the sky with beautiful shades of blue, orange and yellow. A faint haze of mist rises from the vegetation and trees surrounding Marmalade's compound. I want to comment on the beauty and ask my friend if he sees what I am seeing. Instead, everything goes black.

Chapter 61
Call a lawyer! Household appliance fun.
Conrad Peterson House
Someplace in America
Land of the Free(ish) Home of the Brave(ish)

Fred Peterson's communicator wakes him. The call identifier tells him that the caller is Clifford Good. Fred shakes his head to clear it. The motion wakes Anne Margret who was sleeping beside him. "What?" Anne Margret mumbles, turning over. "What time is it?"

"It's Bob's dad." Fred mumbles. "Hullo?"

"*Its Bob's dad* is not the time." Anne Margret retorts.

"Hullo?" Fred says again.

"Freddy?" Cliff Good says in his ear. "Are you there? You sound muffled."

"I'm sleeping. Sorry, Mr. Good." Fred sits up. "Is Bob, ok?"

"No. That's why I am calling you. He has been arrested." Cliff Good says.

"You must do something Freddy! You have to go help my baby!" Sookie Moonbeam Good cries in the background.

Fred sits up straighter, more awake now. He activates the speaker phone as he pats Anne Margret on the shoulder. "Wake up, Anne!"

Anne Margret rolls over and opens her eyes. "Did Bob get himself busted for whacking off?"

"Yes! Yes, he did! How did you know?" Sookie Moonbeam Good wails.

"Informed guess." Anne Margret yawns and stretches her arms.

"Where is he?" Fred asks.

"County jail. The cops said something about an arraignment?" Cliff answers. "I don't know what that is."

"An arraignment is a formal reading of the criminal charges in the presence of the defendant. The purpose is to let the accused know what the charges are against them." Fred answers. "In our jurisdiction, Bob will have to plead guilty or not guilty. He needs to plead *Not Guilty*. Does he know that?"

"Noooo!" Bob's mother wails. "My baby knows nothing!"

"I don't think so, Fred. Bob said you are a lawyer now? Or maybe you know a lawyer?" Cliff Good asks.

"I am. Anne Margret and I both are. And Anne's mother is an attorney." Fred answers as he pulls on his underwear and a pair of pants. He picks Anne Margret's panties off the floor and throws them to her. "We are getting dressed. Do you know what time the arraignment is?" He looks at the small clock on his desk. It is a little after seven in the morning.

"I didn't even know what an arraignment was until you told me, Freddy." Cliff chuckles. "Is this something that Bob's mother and I should be at? We don't want to miss anything important."

"Well, it's not a school play. I don't think Bob will care if you are there... but he should have an attorney present." Fred answers. "We will figure out what time the arraignment is and let you know." He ends the call and addresses Anne Margret. "Did my dad and your mom come back here last night?"

"Got me." Anne Margret answers. She triggers her communicator to call her mother. There is no answer. She shrugs her shoulders. Fred tries his father and gets the same result.

"We can go to the courthouse. All we need to do is get Bob to say *Not Guilty* when he is asked what his plea is." Anne Margret says.

Fred nods. The pair goes down the hall to the kitchen.

Sounds coming from the guest bedroom startle both of them. A high pitched *Arf, Arf, Arf* echoes off the high ceilings.

Anne Margret looks at Fred in surprise. "Do you have a pet that I am unaware of?"

Fred shakes his head. The high-pitched barking is accompanied by male grunting. Anne Margret rolls her eyes. "I guess our parental units *are* here." She whispers.

Fred quietly goes to the refrigerator and pulls out some orange juice. Anne Margret takes a seat at the kitchen island. He pours two glasses and puts two pieces of bread in the toaster. He is slicing open an avocado when the both the volume and the tempo of the barking and grunts increase.

"Good lord." Anne Margret whispers with a shake of her head.

"You have never heard this before?" Fred asks quietly.

"I'm not even sure my mother had ever had sex with a man before she met your father. I'm a test tube baby, remember? The sperm that made me came from a turkey baster."

"Actually, IVF happens when the sperm and the egg are cultured. Then the fertilized egg is transferred into the uterus." Fred says.

"Are you mansplaining how I was conceived?" Anne Margret asks with a hard look.

"It's how I was conceived too." Fred replies defensively. "I looked the process up because I was tired of the turkey baster jokes. I don't even know what a turkey baster looks like."

The barking and grunting stops. Elizabeth Eaton's voice is heard. "Let's do it on the *washing machine!*" Giggles follow the suggestion.

Anne Margret eyes go wide, and she covers her mouth. Fred sighs. He opens the pot and pan drawer and takes out a fry pan, dropping from chest height to the tile floor.

"I think the kids are up!" Conrad Peterson exclaims.

More giggles. "I don't care. Put that thing on spin and bend me over, big boy!"

"Please tell me there is an actual washing machine in there." Anne Margret mutters.

"There is." Fred replies. The toaster dings and toast pops up. "Dryer, too. We are flush in household appliances. If that is what gets them off, they have plenty of things to pick from." He takes the toast from the toaster and lays slices of avocado on each one. After sprinkling some salt on each of the slices, he hands one to Anne Margret. The barking and grunting have started back up. "I will make it stop." Fred says in calm voice. He walks over to a small cabinet on the wall and opens it. After a moment of looking at the fuse box, he flips a switch and closes the cabinet.

The barking stops. After a few more grunts, there is silence.

"Thank you." Anne Margret says happily as she takes a drink of orange juice. "I didn't really need to start my day hearing my mother get railed on or by a *household appliance.*"

"There are worse things." Fred says.

Anne Margret chews a bite of the toast thoughtfully. "None are coming to mind at this moment."

A few minutes later, Conrad and Elizabeth come into the kitchen.

"Good morning, Mother. How is *your* morning going?" Anne Margret asks, deliberately not looking at either her mother or Conrad.

"Dad. Ms. Eaton." Fred acknowledges the pair as he takes a bite of his toast.
Conrad walks over to the cabinet that holds the fuse box and opens it. "Will you look at that, Poppet! We blew a fuse!"

"*Poppet?*". Anne Margret exclaims with a tone suggesting disbelief.

"Well, flip it back over and let's get back to it, Maestro!" Elizabeth exclaims. "Let these two finish their breakfast."

"Well, *Poppet*... I think I might lose my breakfast. Before you go back to scarring me for life with your carnal expressions of lust, we have something that we need to talk to you about." Anne Margret says in a much too loud voice.

"Oh?" Elizabeth Eaton pulls her robe tight. "We were *trying* to be quiet."

"Ball gag. I told you. We need to use the ball gag!" Conrad says. "What have you two lovebirds got going on?" He takes the rest of his son's avocado toast and eats it.

"Bob Good was arrested last night. Masturbation." Fred says.

Conrad's face falls. "Ah, shit. I am so sorry, son. Just tell him to bring the ticket over here and Liz can look at it."

Elizabeth Eaton is shaking her head. "When is the arraignment?" She looks back at Conrad. "It's a felony charge, Conrad."

Anne Margret shrugs. "We don't know. We thought we would go over to the courthouse and figure things out. You might want to get dressed and come."

"She wants to do *one* of those things." Conrad kisses her ear. "Meet you back at the laundry mat, Poppet."

"You are so *awful* Maestro." Anne Margret's grinning mother blushes. She looks at her daughter and her expression turns serious. "But Conrad is right. I have things I need to attend to here." Her face breaks into a smile. "The good news for young Mr. Good is that two of his very best friends are attorneys. Go to the court, plead him not guilty and ask that he be released on his own recognizance. I think he has to wear a chastity belt or something. Agree to that, but no money and no time."

"Chastity Belt?" Anne Margret sniggers. "Really, mom?"

"I've got to get back to the... *laundry.* You two will do just fine." Elizabeth Eaton wiggly waves a hand at her daughter and quickly leaves the room.

Anne Margret watches her leave before responding with a sarcastic tone. "Alright, *Poppet.* We will get right on the case!"

Fred is slicing open another avocado. "Conrad ate my toast. You want another one?"

"No. I am going to go wash my eyes and ears out. Do you happen to have a memory erasure device here? I'd like to lose the last fifteen minutes or so."

After putting a piece of bread in the toaster, Fred comes over to Anne Margret and embraces her. "Does this mean you won't bark like a seal for me later?" Anne Margret's hand comes up and grabs his crotch. She pulls him close and squeezes hard.

"No, but I bet I can get you to bellow like a walrus. Unless you wanted to wear that ball gag your dad mentioned." Anne Margret whispers in his ear. "In that case, I have a whole lot of things I want to do to you!"

Chapter 62
Passing out. Another visit to the great beyond.
Breaking rocks and ribs.
Marmalade Julius's House Someplace in America
Land of the Free(ish). Home of the Brave(ish).

*It's dark. And silent.*

*I have no real idea what happened to get me here and I have no idea how long I have been out. I vaguely remember peddling my ass off on a stationary bicycle, stopping and passing out. Maybe I stroked out.*

*I guess my time is up.*

*A small figure starts walking towards me in the distance. It's not the cow and it is definitely not the bear. As it comes closer, I see it is the grasshopper walking like Mr. Peanut... only without the cane or the top hat. I stay silent. I sort of thought this curious little creature may have been the one in charge.*

*It keeps doing a little jumping walk/dance until it gets close. It's no longer small, but very large and soon the once little creature is very close. I can see all the parts of its compound eyes, and, thanks to my sixth-grade biology lessons, I can correctly identify the different sections that make up its head.*

*Justin...* The voice booms in my brain. It is neither male nor female in tone. I don't feel fear, but one of those little voices in my head is openly questioning why the flight part of the flight or fight hormones aren't being released.

*"Yes?".* I answer.

*"You are, so that I can address you."* The grasshopper's little mouth parts aren't moving. But that voice is very clear in my head. I want to make

a smart-ass comment about the grasshopper's speech pattern being very similar to a little green creature from a well-known science fiction movie but quickly decide that this creature may be a God of some sort and may not have appreciation for the same sort of sarcastic humor I do.

*"Yes."* I answer. It seems like an appropriate answer to the nonsensical statement.

The grasshopper stares at me. Maybe my answer wasn't sufficient. It's antennae twitch some and I hear the voice in my head. *"The word rock, bothersome it is. Rock is an inexact and inappropriate word. Significance should be given not to a simple stone when another word appears to lend so much more exactness."*

I think I nod out of politeness. I'm not sure I am nodding, but if I am, it is *surely* out of politeness because what this Grasshopper is saying sounds like gibberish. I now do not believe myself dead because if I was, I am pretty sure the bear handles things with the really and truly deceased. I believe I may have been brought in front of the Grasshopper to receive a message. What that message is; so far, is not clear. I can tell already that it would have been a lot better if Reverend Moo was here to translate.

The grasshopper shakes its head from side to side. *"Easy words do not come in all colors. Say, I think, what you can hear. But hear not you will.".* The Grasshopper seems to ponder its thoughts for a moment. Maybe it is pausing to get the translator in its little head on the right language. I am vaguely aware of a discomfort in my chest. I try and put my hand on the pressure but fail to either feel my chest or for that matter my hand. I must be feeling the heart attack that is either going to kill me or put me back here for an indeterminant amount of time.

*"Your kind gives significance to the Rock."* Eureka! The Grasshopper makes a sentence I understand. I am thinking that it is likely not talking about the muscle-bound movie star who makes movies in China now, but literally the word *Rock.*

*The church was never built on a rock...* The Grasshopper's voice says. *"A thing, the church is not. The church is always a process that was built in the hearts, minds and souls of the people who conceived it regardless of its type or worship.* The insect hops a little from side to side. *And so, it always was and always will be, when hearts and minds and souls have separate but equal ideas, the system divides, like a tree may split a river into two channels. Two channels, only one true path. All paths arrive at the same destination as has always been. This is same as math. One and one make two just as three from five make two. Two paths to same result! Divided systems that achieve the same can be good. Flow. The answer is flow. Divided systems of belief make hearts and minds and souls grow. There is no one way when all is free to flow. Water finds its own path and so shall, hearts and minds and souls. That is the only way. All things must be water. There is no Rock. Only Water. Rocks cannot flow without destructive elements! Only water easily flows. Flows create new. New is life.*

Am I being given a sermon? It's not a bad one, albeit a little hard to decipher at times. The Grasshopper is no Marmalade Julius in its delivery, but it's a pretty good message I suppose. Downright extraordinary coming from an insect.

*Take the Rock. Destroy the Rock. Make the Rock, Water.* The Grasshopper is more animated now. I want to ask how it intends for me to turn a rock into water, but the Grasshopper's voice keeps going without pause in my head. *Splitting a baby worked once to change the direction of hearts, minds and souls. That leader before you was timid and afraid like you but he made decisions that made flow."* It waves a little grasshopper leg dismissively. *"So too, shall your epileptic scheme make flow.* I figure that the little insect is referring to the legend of Solomon's wisdom, the Spilt Seed law and the word *epileptic* means crazy. The Grasshopper seems to shake its head. *You, Justin, are necessary to break the Rocks where you see fit. That is the way. Water should find the easiest path. Be water. Growing and living ideas and things need water. Not rock. Make the rocks into water!*

"You want me to destroy the church?" I ask the Grasshopper. "Marmalade's church or all churches?"

The Grasshopper shakes its head and hops from side to side. *No! The church can be necessary to guide hearts and minds and souls. Not all water can make its own path without help."* The Grasshopper appears to look for its next words. Its little compound eyes light up. *"Frozen water needs guidance to melt and flow as intended in the way!* A little leg points at my eye. *"Big Rocks can become little rocks that are meaningless! Meaningless in size and in life! Break up those rocks that impede flow! That is the proper way. Nothing should stop the proper flows of waters!"*

"Ok." I say. Satisfied that the pressure in my chest is not going to keep me here long, I am thinking more about the words I am hearing. I am not sure how to respond to this sermon-grasshopper rant. *Break rocks. Tear down walls. Increase water flow?* I believe what the little fellow may want is for someone to make people understand that they have the power to control their own destiny. "I think I am on the same page as you." I say slowly. "Do you have suggestion for how I should go about doing this?"

The Grasshopper shakes its head and seems to come even closer to me. *"No. This is not for me to do. I give the world, leaders. I give the world you, Justin! You are not accepting the gifts I have given you in the manner I wish them to be received, you are wasting the gifts. Must love and cherish. You should! Pay attention! You should! I give you gifts, you ignore them!"*
"Gifts?" I ask. I know I am not supposed to be thinking about something gift wrapped and all that. *Gifts* is clearly a metaphysical thing in this case.

*"Little voices I give you! Guidance, I give you! I give you, me. A little of me is always with you! You don't listen to the voices; you don't use the gift!".* The grasshopper hops back and forth in its agitated state. *"You work well with the people. You and the very precious woman! You work so. Much better for both of you so if you put to use with my very useful gift! Pay attention! The gift of mine is a tool for you to use. Use this tool! Be clever! Break the rocks! You should not abide by any Rocks!".*

The Grasshopper points to me. *"You need to go back before they hurt your physical shell. Violent they are. Go back now. You use the gifts! Use them to break the rocks that impede growth!"*

The Grasshopper comes even closer. It seems to grab my face with its front legs, which seems weird, since I am pretty sure my head is significantly larger than the average grasshopper's reach. Weirder is that I am completely understanding every crazy thing the Grasshopper is saying to me. *"Justin, I picked you because you show no fear. Aimless and misguided you have been but fearless. Solomon was a coward. Bold with foolish confidence. He misused his foundational gifts, that boy! Foundation, you have is good! You have the tools. Attention you should give! My bidding you shall do!"* There is a snap and pain erupts across my chest. The Grasshopper is gone. The darkness has been replaced with light filtered by my eyelids.

And just like that, an incredible, sharp pain erupts in my chest. I gasp and open my eyes. A tearful Millie is on her knees beside me. Her fists are together on my chest, and she is counting. A worried looking Marmalade stands behind her. He appears to be praying. "Stop." I say as loudly and firmly as I can.

Millie freezes. She is wearing the robe from Juice's guest bedroom. It's open a little and if I knew that she wasn't just giving me chest compressions to revive what I am sure was my stopped heart and if I wasn't smarting a little from the broken rib, I would make some flirty comment about the perfect breast and nipple I can clearly see.

"I'm back." I say with a cough. It hurts.

Millie collapses on me, crying. She kisses my cheek. "Goddamn you." She whispers in my ear. "If you are planning to leave, you better take me with you!"

"It wasn't planned." I whisper back. "I was just exercising and fell off the bike."

Millie sits up on her knees and looks at me with worried, dark eyes. "You were gone. No pulse." I look over at Marmalade. His eyes are bright. In contrast to Millie's... and I am sure mine, Marmalade's eyes reflect light. Millie's are dark pools. In fact, now that I am paying attention, I notice that Marmalade has a vitality to his being that is clearly not evident with Millie. Don't get me wrong, Millie is the most beautiful and precious thing in my orbit... but there is a clear difference between her *being* and that of Marmalade Julius. I sigh and struggle to sit up. "It was just an episode."

Juice is squatting down on his haunches. The look on his face is a combination of worry and curiosity. I guess the preacher have never seen someone actually resurrected from the dead. "It's all good Juice." I say in as strong of a voice that I can muster.

"I couldn't find a pulse!" Marmalade exclaims. "I thought... Jesus... I thought you were gone, Justin."

"Just had to go see a grasshopper about man." I say dismissively with a smile. A thought occurs to me. It's a broad and complex thought but I know that the thought has a simple beginning and end. I also know the answer to the question that I am about to ask. "Say, Juice, do you have one of those tattoos on your back? The kind the people get in your church?"

Marmalade looks at me with a curious expression. "No. I do not. I always thought that the tattoo is a bunch of hooey. I have a tattoo artist that does a fake for me if I need one... you know, for show."

Millie helps me to my feet. The broken rib really hurts, and I absently wonder if a bone will heal in a person who is sort of dead. I look at Marmalade. I don't think I am controlling my expression. I know the look I am giving him is hard and I am aware my voice has an angry edge to it. "You should stop the tattoo business immediately. The church should not *brand* its members. Making your congregation get tattoos as part of the membership of your church destroys the natural flow that your worshipers should have as part of their spiritual journey. The church should financially assist its members to remove those tattoos. They are an abomination."

Marmalade looks at me stunned. "Yes. Sure, Justin. I agree with you. I'm not sure about the removal part. We can stop telling the congregation they should get the tattoo as soon as we separate from the main church in Texas."

"*You are not listening!*" I growl. "The church has *branded* its congregation. You will stop it. *Now!* And you will pay for those who wish to do so to remove the tattoos." I say to a nodding Marmalade who has wide eyes.

Millie closes her eyes. She grabs my hand and squeezes it. "What else did *he* say?"

I squeeze back and do my best to tell her silently that I will tell her everything later. I look back at Marmalade. "I love Millie, and I would like to marry her, if she is willing. I would like to do it as soon as you *and my cousin Hank* can do the service together. Can you make that happen, Marmalade?"

Marmalade's eyes are still wide open in surprise. "A few minutes ago... you were dead, Justin. Are you feeling ok now?"

"I wasn't dead, Juice. *There is no such thing.* You should know that." I pat him on the shoulder. "I feel fine."

I turn to Millie. She is clearly the best gift I have been given. "I love you, Millie. Will you be my bride?"

Millie's eyes fill. She nods and hugs me tight. "Yes." She says into my chest. "Yes, I would love to marry you, Justin Thyme!"

## Chapter 63
Everyone gets his day in court. No one wants this.
Municipal Court Room Someplace in America
Land of the Free(ish) Home of the Brave(ish)


"All Rise." The bailiff announces the arrival of the judge into the courtroom.

Anne Margret watches as Trump Bob Good is led into the room by a pair of jailers. Beside her, Fred Peterson flips though his electronic pad, reviewing courtroom procedures. Bob is wearing a bright orange and white striped jumpsuit. There is a square outline at his crotch. One of the faux diamonds on the chastity belt has worn through a section of orange stripes. As Bob walks, the fluorescent lights of the courtroom reflect off the glass stone. Bob's head hangs, his chin nearly resting on his chest, his eyes glassy. The sheriff's deputy leads him to the table and stands him next to Anne Margret. She rubs his arm encouragingly.

The judge sits and bangs her gavel. "Court is in Session. Be seated."

Fred takes a moment to look over at the County Attorney who is reading the case for the first time. The man, a middle age bearded fellow reads through the documents with a serious expression. His brow furrows and he looks over at Fred. "Is this for real?" He mouths. Fred, not knowing what the decorum should be between a defense attorney and the prosecutor, shrugs. The prosecuting attorney returns to reading the documents in front of him.

The judge starts laughing. She looks up at the court and sighs before breaking into another fit of laughter.

Fred looks behind him. There is a smattering of people of various types in the courtroom. Mostly family of accused people scheduled for arraignment. He turns back to the laughing judge.

The magistrate shakes her head. "Let's get this started." She points at the defendant's bench. "In the Case of Trump Bob Good, who is appearing for the accused."

Fred, relieved to have a question he had prepared himself to answer stands. "Umm... Anne Margret Eaton and Fred... Fredrick Peterson for the defense, you honor."

"What firm are you with?" The judge asks.

Fred looks down at Anne Margret. She rolls her eyes. "Willams and Williams, your honor." She answers.

"Counselors, approach the bench." The judge orders.

Wide eyed, Fred follows the prosecutor to the Judge. Anne Margret follows the pair. The judge looks at the three of them. "Is this your first case, Peterson?"

Fred nods nervously.

"Mine too." Anne Margret says with a smile.

"Are you Elizabeth Eaton's daughter?" The judge asks.

"Yes, your Honor." Anne replies. "She will be assisting us with the case."

"She is not with Williams and Williams though." The Judge says more than asks. Fred and Anne stay silent. The judge scratches her chin. She leans forward. "Before we go down this particularly dark rabbit hole, I want the three of you to know that I have very little latitude here." She looks at the prosecutor. "All things being equal, I would dismiss this bullshit out of hand because that what judges are supposed to do with bullshit. Unfortunately, our state has decided to ride or die with the craziness that comes out of the State of Texas. Let's get this done as quickly and as painlessly as possible." She points. "Step back."

Fred and Anne take a step back. The prosecutor looks at them curiously before returning to his chair.

"Counselors, *Step back* means go back to your chairs." The judge whispers in a voice that can be clearly heard by anyone in the courtroom.

The prosecutor smirks as the pair returns to their seats by Bob.

The judge lets out a long sigh. "Trump Bob Good, please stand."

Handcuffed, Bob struggles to get out of his chair. The metal chastity cage gets caught on the edge of the table. The prosecuting attorney chortles as the doors of the courtroom open noisily. Fred turns to see Sookie Moonbeam and Clifford Good enter the room.

"You told my parents to come?" Bob cries out to Fred.

"My baby!" Sookie Good cries out theatrically as she rushes to the defense table. "They have you in a terrible prisoner's outfit."
"Umm... Mrs. Good..." Fred tries to stop the woman from coming through the little swinging doors that separate the onlookers in the courtroom from the actual court proceedings.

"Fred, I need to be with my baby!" Bob's mother exclaims while slapping his arm away. Cliff Good hangs back, shaking his head. The judge starts banging her gavel. "Order! Bailiff! We need to control that woman!"

"Sookie! Sit down! Now!" Anne Margret orders in a stern tone that sounds so like her mother, Elizabeth that it startles even her. The bailiff, assessing that Anne Margret might be more of a threat to Sookie than he, returns to his spot.

"I just want to be with *my son*, Bob!" Sookie wails. "This is so unfair! He has done nothing wrong! This is a witch hunt! Just like they did to our hero, Donny J! A *fake news* witch hunt!"

"Yes. That's what we do here in state district court. We hunt witches." The judge says crossly. Mr. Petersen, I assume that person is the accused's mother. Please get control of her or I am going to charge her with contempt of court."

Fred sighs and looks at Cliff with pleading eyes. After hesitating, Cliff grabs his wife's arm and seats her behind Bob. Anne Margret helps Bob stand as Fred addresses the judge. "We are ready to proceed, your honor."

"Uh huh." The judge says doubtfully. "Trump Bob Good, you are charged with violating this state's *Prohibiting Split Seed Law*." The judge shakes her head. "Do you understand the charges against you?"

Bob Good sobs. "No!"

"We understand the charges, your honor." Anne Margret volunteers.

"Yes, well... I need to hear him say it, or else I will be forced to have a competency hearing." The judge says with a tired tone.

"The state would have no objections to a competency hearing, provided the accused remains in custody. We wouldn't want more... innocent sperm... being spilt with a premature release." The prosecuting attorney says with a smirk.

The judge, clearly trying very hard to keep a straight face, points her gavel at the state's attorney. "That will be about enough out of you!" The gavel waves around. "One more remark like that, and I may charge you with contempt!"

The prosecutor nods with a solemn expression. "I will make every attempt to remain the master of my domain, your honor."

The courtroom is silent except for an elderly man laughing in the back row. *"Master of his domain!* I remember that show!"

The judge looks at Anne Margret. "Young lady, you seem to have a grasp on the issue here." The elderly man in the back of the room chortles again. The judges head snaps up. "You, back there! This is a *courtroom!* I expect decorum! What is your name?"

The old man stands. "You *aren't* going to like it, your honor."

The judge glowers at the old man. "What is your name, sir?"

"Mike Oxlong." The man answers, stifling a laugh. There is raucous laughter around the courtroom.
The judge silences the court by banging energetically on her bench with the gavel before angrily addressing the man. "Mr. Oxlong, do you have business here in the court?"

Mike Oxlong shakes his head. "Nah. Saw this case on the docket. First case against someone that I know of! Law against masturbation! Silliness! What have we come to in this country?"

"It is our job to enforce the laws made by the government!" The judge exclaims. "It is a very serious responsibility!"

The man waves his hand. "No offense, your honor, but I can think of about a dozen laws on the books the *state* chooses not to enforce. If you'd like an example, perhaps we can go outside and smoke a joint and talk about it!"

The judge looks at her bailiff. "Get that man out of my courtroom!"

"I'm going! I'm going!" The old man shakes his head as he shuffles from his seat. "I'm just an old man looking for a little entertainment. I mean jeez, this better than the shit on the monitor! Ban on masturbation? What are the stupid politicians going to do next?"

After the courtroom door opens and closes, the Judge looks down at the defense table. "Counselor, did you clean all the cobwebs out of your clients head?"

One chuckle is heard from the courtroom as Anne Margret purses her lips. "Your honor, our client is prepared to answer your questions." The judge nods. "Trump Bob Good. Do you understand the charges against you?"

Bob looks at Fred who nods his head slowly.

Bob looks at the judge and nods his head.

The judge shakes her head. "Let the record reflect that the accused is nodding his head in the affirmative of understanding the charges against him. Let the record also reflect that I am instructing the accused to answer my questions verbally."

"Yes, Judge." Bob says.

"You have been accused of violating the Prohibiting Spilt Seed Law. How do you plead?" The judge asks.

Anne Margret leans over and whispers in Bob's ear.

"Anne Margret says I am not guilty." Bob replies.

There is more laughter in the court. Bob blushes.

Sookie Moonbeam Good stands up and turns to the crowd. "You stop laughing at him! He is just a precious little boy! He has done nothing wrong! You are all just Boring! Boring!"

The judge's gavel hits her bench. "Mama... I gave you fair warning. I charge you with contempt of court!" She turns to the bailiff. "Get her out of here!"

"Mom!" Bob wails as the bailiff pulls Sookie Moonbeam Good from her row and puts handcuffs on her.

Fred puts his head in his hands. Anne Margret rubs his back. "This is a disaster." He whispers.

The judge looks back down at the defense table. "Let's try this one more time. Trump Bob Good! You have been accused of violating the Prohibiting Spilt Seed Law. How do you plead?" The judge points the hammer at Bob. "And... the words must be yours, Mr. Good. Not your lawyer's."

"Not guilty? Judge." Bob mumbles.

The prosecutor stands. "Now that we have that in hand..." He smirks at his innuendo. "The state requests that the accused be held on $100,000 bail." He points at Bob. "This man is clearly a danger to himself and thousands of *unborn* children... although, between you and me, judge... I struggle to figure out where those women might come from."

The judge glowers at the prosecutor. "The accused will be released on bail after posting a $10,000 bond. As per the guidelines accepted by the state, the accused must continue to wear a state approved chastity belt until such time that he is acquitted or has been rehabilitated." She bangs the gavel on the bench twice for effect. "Counselors, a preliminary trial date will be set by the court. Try and get yourselves familiar with the rules of evidence and the general procedures that need to be followed in a courtroom before then." Abruptly, the judge stands. "This court is in recess!"

"Your honor?" Fred asks.

"What?" The judge snaps.

"Can you set Sookie Good free? Getting one Good out of jail is going be hard enough. Two might break the family."

"You got brass balls, son." The judge growls. "No. The boy's mother can post bail too. When I decide what that bail is, I will let you know."

Anne Margret raises her eyebrows. "Bob is in jail and needs to post bail. His mother has been jailed on contempt of court charges, which as I recall from some paragraph in our legal textbook is an act that can be punished at the judge's discretion." She pats Fred on the back. "*Now* it's a disaster. Hope your dad got my mom got off on the washing machine or ironing board so at least some of us had a good day!"

Chapter 64
Hoover's aim is true. Setting Mitch Free. Rescue.
Honorable Representative Nancy Pelosi Public Housing, Convalescence
and Retirement Center.  Someplace in America
Land of the Free(ish) Home of the Brave(ish)


*I am still wearing the workout clothes that Marmalade had given me. The shoes are pretty comfortable. Millie suggested that we go back and gather our things from the public housing unit before it gets to be nighttime. Not wanting to see any more fights over human flesh, I agree.*

*I follow the turn-by-turn directions to the housing unit and tell Millie about my conversation with Mr. Hop, the god like grasshopper. She listens quietly.*

"It seemed pretty riled up about rocks." I sigh and turn onto the road where the Robotaxi had pitched me out the day I was released from the hospital.

"Rocks are a metaphor, obviously." Millie says.

I shrug. "I guess. Or maybe, I am supposed to look for actual rocks. You are probably right. The metaphor thing makes more sense." I wince. The broken rib more than sort of hurts which makes me think I am not all the way dead. "Do you believe in free will?"

Millie shakes her head. "I used to. Now I am not so sure."

"Same. I motion with my hand. "We were picked for this. Willem and Wendy's daughter. Marmalade's church... his communication apparatus. Hank is a priest. You were an abortion doctor that was *jailed* for performing necessary medical procedures on a woman." I inhale and wince again. "My chest hurts."

"Sorry. I thought I was bringing you back to life." Millie smirks. "It's good it hurts though. I sort of look forward to feeling some pain. Makes me think that I might sort of be alive."

"Well, on our wedding night you may feel the pain of disappointment and exasperation if I can't get my equipment working." I reply.

Millie shakes her head. "Nah. I know how to do a spinal tap. You'll just have to lay still."

I laugh. It hurts but still feels good. A familiar looking homeless man leans up against the building next to the parking lot of the old Walmart that is now public housing. "Hey, I know that guy. He was in prison with me!"

Millie's face wrinkles up. "You *weren't* in prison!" She looks over at the man. "Are you sure? Texas is a long way away from here, thankfully."

"It's him." I nod. We park the car in the lot. The broken rib has made moving no less of a challenge. I gingerly get out of the driver's side of the transporter and walk around to the rear. "Let's go talk to him."

"Why?" Millie asks. A big delivery transporter speeds by us. During the day, the trucks seem to move fast. I suppose so crowds of people can't easily stop them and empty whatever is inside.

I shrug and start off towards the brick building Mitch Palmer leans against. "I did hard time with the man!" Millie shakes her head and follows me. As we get closer, I see that Mitch is talking to the rock he had held so tightly in his hand at the county jail in Texas.

"Hey, Mitch. Long time no see!" I say in greeting. Mitch's head turns to me. I notice several things all at once. For one, Mitch Palmer's eyes are the same dark pools that Millie's and mine are. His skin is a strange lifeless color of gray. My brain seems to register that this man has been in

the space between life and death for a very long time. I look at the rock that still says *Hoover* across its face. *The rock.* Mitch Palmer relies on that *rock* for support.
Mitch makes no attempt to stand. He cocks his head and stares at me slowly. "Hoover said I would know people here." He nods hesitantly. "Hello, Justin."

"How did you get here?" I ask.

"Texas said we should go live someplace else. They put us on big transporters.  Like a bus in the old days. The trip stopped here, and they told us to get off." Mitch Palmer shrugs. "I got off and sat down. I am trying to figure out how to get home. Hoover says I need to be patient.  So far it is better in that I have not been arrested for sitting on the sidewalk."

"Where is home?" Millie asks.

Mitch shrugs and looks at the rock, not at Millie. "I don't rightly know, miss. I thought I was there once, but I was told I couldn't stay cause I had things to correct. Things... Well, I don't even know what things anymore. The world as I know it has changed so much for me that I can't remember where I came from or what I was supposed to do. I had instructions. I asked Hoover to remember for me. He tricked me, I think. Hoover was always pretty tricky. People don't know that about Hoover." Mitch Palmer sighs. "I have failed, I suppose." He turns back to me. "You both look so familiar. Justin, have you two been here long?"
"Not as long as you." I look down the street. The bald ogre who beat a man half to death in a circle of onlooker's struts towards us. He holds the end of a long black leash in his hand. I see irregular motion several feet behind him. What was once a vibrant child watching her father anxiously, has become a disheveled and dissonant woman child, struggling to follow the large man who yanks on the leash that is wrapped tight around her neck like she is disobedient puppy. "This ends now." I mutter. I look down at Mitch. "You want to go home?"

Mitch looks at the rock. "Hoover, do we want to go home?"

"The rock is of no use to you anymore, Mitch." I say with an authoritative tone... *or at least it sounds like that to me.*

"What are you doing, Justin?" Millie asks, worry in her voice.

"Give me the rock, Mitch." I order. Hesitantly, Mitch stands. He looks at me with wild eyes. "I cannot give you Hoover. He is my *rock.*"

"You don't need Hoover anymore." I turn Mitch and point. "See that man? He took that young girl from her mother. He has been abusing her. I want you to get rid of him. You can go home then." I don't know where the words come from. Maybe I am talking out of my ass or maybe I am using my *gift.* "Give me the rock, Mitch. You don't need the damn rock. You never did."

Hesitantly, Mitch Palmer hands me Hoover. I take the rock in one hand and hold his gray crepe paper thin skinned hand with the other. Looking in his dead eyes, I say, "Mitch, you will know what to do next." I drop the hand. Mitch nods and turns. The bald man tugs on the leash.
Millie sees the girl stumble and fall to her knees. "Oh! Oh, my goodness! He's dragging her by a leash!" There is a concern in her voice I had not heard before.

Years and years ago, before a two-decade long coma, a massive car accident and a few alcohol-soaked years in medical school, I played a little high school baseball. Catcher. I wasn't bad. I could pick off a runner at all three bases. I found the game of baseball to be about as interesting as watching grass grow, so I didn't last long but I was there long enough to perfect a throwing motion. I look down at Millie. "Go get the girl."

She nods nervously and struts towards the man who is angrily tugging on the leash. The girl struggles to get up and quickly falls again. I shake my head as I rub the rock with the edge of my thumb as I might the seams of a baseball. *The United States has devolved into some sort of dystopian nightmare of a place. No wonder we were sent back.* I think to myself as Millie angrily confronts the man. I see him puff up his chest and square up to Millie.

"Go get him, Mitch. Make this end." I say, knowing that Mitch Palmer who had been wondering this earth for far too long would know exactly what I was asking for. I plant my back foot and cock my right arm back. I glare at the spot between the man's eyes just above the bridge of his nose as I release the rock three quarters of the way through my throw. Mitch Palmer is halfway to the bald man who has raised his fist to Millie when the rock smacks the ogre in the face. I'd like to say that it was a real *David vs Goliath* moment, and my rock fell the giant... but remember, high school me may have been able to knock a man down with a rock like the biblical shepherd. Post Coma, broken rib me was able to get the rock to the target and little more. The strike did make the bald man drop the leash. Millie hurries to the girl and huddles around her protectively just as Mitch Palmer plows into the man and pushes him into the street in front of a speeding delivery transporter. There are several thumps as the heavy, driverless vehicle runs over both men. I see the transporter brake lights go on. The vehicle pauses briefly and then continues on its path. The lifeless bodies of the bald man and Mitch Palmer lay in the middle of the road.

I go to Millie who is consoling the girl. "I need to call Vel." Millie says to me. She pulls out her old-fashioned cell phone.

"You have her number?" I ask dumbly.

"No, dear, I'm just going to start dialing random numbers until I get her." Millie rolls her eyes.

"See, this is what I love about you, you know how to do sarcasm." I look down at the girl. It's not a good sight. The clothing she wears appears to be made from sweatshirt material. What may have once been a white top is gray and yellow. Both the top and the baggy sweatpants are streaked with blood and other unidentifiable stains. Her hair is dirty and matted. The skin on her face and wrists are bruised. I see and feel the pain and fear in her eyes. I extend my hand to her. "It's ok now. You are safe. Millie is going to get you help."

The girl stares at me before recoiling closer to Millie. She starts shaking. "Mama." She shudders. "Mama?"

"We will find her." I say, not really knowing how that might happen. "Is your family staying there?" I point at the old Walmart. The girl nods. "Mama. I want Mama!" The words come out in a cry. Millie's eyes close and open, holding back tears as she says a few words into the phone. I hear her say the words *rape* and *vaginal damage*. The call ends. Millie's dark eyes are filled with tears. "Vel is sending someone."

I nod. Motioning at the leash, I whisper to Millie. "She fears me, rightly so. Hold her so I can take the leash off her neck."
Millie nods and pulls the girl close, stroking her dirty hair and whispering softly near the little girl's head. I gently lift the leash, a heavy affair clearly designed for an animal, from around her head. Her neck is covered in open sores and pus-filled blisters. I hear the girl whimper and see her pull from Millie who tightens her grip.

Three people... I'd like to say they are men, but honestly, I really cannot tell, shuffle across the road towards us. all are wearing something that looks like onesie pajamas for children, complete with padded feet that have worn away with time and abuse. A print of some sort of cartoon character covers the onesies. They stop and look at the dead bodies of Mitch Palmer and the large bald man. One of the people, a bearded elfin looking thing with an angry expression bends at the waist and rifles through dead bald man's pockets. A bunch of papers - money I suppose - is transferred from the clothing on the dead body to bearded elf. I hold the leash in one hand and attempt to look as menacing as possible with my emaciated frame decked out in Marmalade Julius workout wear. After checking Mitch's body for valuables and finding none, the three continue their shuffle towards us.

"We want the girl. Give us." One of the Cartoonish elfin looking people shouts, its voice high pitched, almost a shriek. I shake my head and alternate glaring at each of the people.

"He took her. Now he has no use for her." The bearded one says gruffly, hooking a thumb at the still body in the center of the road. "You give her us. We pay you." The elfin character pulls out a wad of bills, taken from the dead man. "See? Pay!"

The third person, this one more troll like in appearance, with a wild shock of red hair jutting at all angles from his (surely a man?) scalp Looks at Millie and the girl like a starving cartoon dog starring at a steak dinner. The look is complete with bulging eyes that I am sure is due to some undiagnosed thyroid issue. He grabs his crotch and tugs on it. "Oh beans... we got mad *uses* for this meat..." I am unsure if by *meat* he means whatever the flesh between his legs is or the two women he is currently drooling at. "We gots enough to pay the man for both dem?" He asks the bearded one.

"There is no one for sale here. You are not interested in these women." I say calmly, channeling my inner Jedi/grasshopper.

The bearded elf points at the little girl. "That was weaned from her mother by him." There is a vague motion at the dead bald man. "She available now." He glances at Millie and shrugs. Millie gives me a fearful look. I guess her crackling shock stick isn't in her back pocket.

"Do you know this girl's mother?" I ask. "The girl is badly hurt. She needs medical attention. We need to talk to her mother." I see flashes of recognition in the bearded elfin man's face.

The red-haired troll protests in words I don't understand. The high-pitched voice one nods energetically in agreement with whatever is being said.

The bearded one steps forward. In this gang of three, the bearded elf is the leader. He spits on the ground beside Millie. I am hoping this isn't some sort of declaration of territory. "We needs sex. Youse gots pussy. We make deal?" He motions at the girl. "She damaged goods. Not worth much, heh?"

I shake my head. "No deal. Who and where is the girl's mother?"

The bearded man squares his shoulders up. I am in no condition to fight this turd. Even without the broken rib, I move about as well as the rusted tin man. I narrow my eyes. "This is not worth it for you. Better for you to give me the information you know about the girl's parents."

The troll says something in protest again and moves to grab Millie or the girl. Without even thinking about it, I let the leash unroll and snap like a whip against the red headed troll's flat nose. He lets out a howl and backs away.

"How do we find the girl's mother?" I ask with my best menacing but even tone.

The bearded elf kicks at the ground. "Information costs. Whatcha got to trade?"

I hold up the leash. "You can have this if you tell me."

The dwarf like one with the high-pitched voice seems to perk up at the prospect of getting the leash that was once around the young girl's neck. "We know!" He grins exposing several missing teeth. "We knows that answer." After poking the bearded elf. "Tell it so we can take the leash. We gots uses for that leash."

"This is so Boring!" The red headed troll exclaims. "Maybe weese takes the girl and da old woman and da leash!"

I don't even want to think about what other *uses* for the leash these three deplorable things might be considering. I let leash out and smack the red headed troll in the nose again. Winey elf sniggers as the Bearded Elf seems to ponder the deal. "Ok. Gimme the leash."
I shake my head. "One of you stay with us. The others go and get the girl's mother or father. Preferably, both." I hold the leash up. "When they are here, I will give you the leash."

"What if ya don't?" The troll asks, "What if we can't find da girl boring parent?"

"No parents, no leash." I answer. "You get nothing."

The Bearded elf says something unintelligible to the other two. After some high-pitched protesting, the red headed troll and the one with the high-pitched voice run off towards the old Walmart.

"She nuttin' more than a hole to use. Youse shoulds lets me take her. Take da credits and go away." The bearded elf says. Millie looks at me in horror. *What the fuck?* she mouths.

"You will give her father the money you took from the dead man." I say.

"Eyes founds it! It my moneys!" The bearded elf protests. Reflexively, I put my hand on the thing's shoulder. I tower over the creature. My black, dead eyes hold its stare. "You will give the money to the girl's father. I will give you this leash and you will leave with your friends." I feel the flesh under my hand tense and relax. "The money rightfully *belongs* to the father." I add.

I realize from my reading the actual bible during my stay at the Microsoft Hospital that the words I am using have biblical roots. If I am being honest with myself, I am not really choosing what I am saying as much as the words are simply flowing from someplace in my brain and falling out of my mouth. The bearded elf nods tightly. A few minutes later, I see a shock of red hair shuffling along the street leading the girl's mother, her younger daughter and the girl's father. Winey elf follows at some distance, the foot on his onesie flopping as he moves.

Millie stands to one side of the girl but holds her tight by the shoulder. I know what she is doing, there is help on the way and neither of us want the girl and her family to dart off. Not that I think any of these people have an ability to actually dart.

"Wheeze gots thems!" The red headed troll exclaims. "Gives us da leash!" He ogles Millie. "Ands the old woman too!"

Wordlessly, I unspool the leash again and pop the troll on the side of the cheek. It lets out a yowl. "She's not old." I growl. "And you can't have her!"

The mother's face lights up and she shuffles faster to her daughter, embracing her sobbing child into her emaciated body. I see tears streaming down Millie's face. The younger daughter holds tight to her mother's tattered dress. Winey elf and the father come up to us.

"Give the money to her father." I say with a firm tone to the bearded elf.

"Whats!" The red-haired troll exclaims. I let the leash loose and prepare to strike the thing a fourth time. The bearded elf looks at his red headed comrade and shakes his head. He reaches into the pocket of the onesie and fishes out the paper bills, extending them to the father of the children.

I look at the man. The beating he took in the makeshift ring was severe and the wounds were not properly attended to, if at all. I am sure that his left cheekbone is crushed. The swelling around the left eye is immense. Cuts and contusions fill the rest of the canvas of his face irregularly, outlining a broken nose and split lips. He gingerly takes the money from the bearded elf and looks at it in amazement. I do not know if the amount is fifty cents, fifty dollars or fifty thousand dollars, but the man's trembling hands tell me that he thinks it's more the latter than the former. I hand the bearded elf the leash before stepping in front of the father. "This money was taken from the man who you foolishly wagered your daughter on in a fist fight." I put my hand on his chest and guide his focus to the two dead men in the street. He looks closer. I think I see one side of his lips curl a little into a smile. I put a firm hand on his shoulder and refocus his attention on me. His one good eye looks into my eyes with fear. "You should not bet the well-being of your family. You and your wife use this money to take care of these little girls. Do you understand me?"

The man nods quickly and grasps the bills tightly.

"Put that in your pocket and keep it safe." I lean in close and speak softly. "Your daughter is badly hurt. Help has been called for. It is on the way."

The man nods again as a white transporter pulls up. A black woman gets out the passenger side of the vehicle as a large man with dark Arabic complexion exits the driver's side. The three pajama clad misfits seem immediately suspicious of the large man but quite happy with the leash. They waddle off quickly. The woman comes over to Millie. She is maybe our age but like Vel and Marmalade and Wendy Willems looks healthier than us and more... well, *alive.*

"Doctor...." The woman smiles and nods a little in clear respect. This woman clearly knows who Millie is. The man appears to be security. He doesn't approach us or even acknowledge our presence. Instead, he stands guard near the corner of the transporter, surveying the area for threats. I see his eyes land briefly on the two dead bodies before continuing his visual sweep of the rest of the scene. The black woman and Millie confer briefly. The girl and her family are loaded into the transporter. The woman slides the door shut and returns to Millie.

"You are a hero, Dr. Cockburn. It is quite an honor for me to meet you." The woman takes Millie's hands into hers. "An absolute honor. We will take care of the girls and their mother."

"Please have a doctor look at the father. He took quite a beating a few days ago and the wounds have not been attended to." I say in a low voice. The woman nods at me and turns back to Millie. "I am so glad you are helping the movement, Doctor. We need more people like you!"

"We need to move!" The big man says. "Now!" He opens the passenger door on the transporter. A delivery transporter wizzes past, running over the bodies of Mitch Palmer and the bald giant. A crowd has formed on the street near the old Walmart. There is a scream as several people are hit by the speeding transporter. In moments, the delivery vehicle is on its side. I can hear cheers from the crowd. Millie and the woman exchange glances, and the woman gets in her transporter. After getting in the driver's side, the large man turns the vehicle around and it speeds off in the direction they had come from.

I put my arm around Millie. "You did good."

She nods her head tightly as the transporter disappears in the distance. I turn us around and walk towards the old Walmart. A few feet into our journey, I see the rock Mitch Palmer had grasped so tightly in his hand throughout what I assume was his second journey upon the earth. It is broken cleanly in two pieces between the double O's in the word *Hoover*. There is one rock destroyed, I think.

I check us both in with the Robot Receptionist. The old man in the wheelchair nods at me as we move past him. We walk up the stairs in silence and open the door to our room. The bright lights go on, filling the windowless space with harsh light. Millie turns onto me and buries her face in my chest. I feel her sobbing heavily. Gently, I guide her to the lower bunk, and we sit, me holding her tight and her crying into my shoulder. The lights go off and we sit in darkness.

Time passes. Hours maybe. "Justin?" Millie's muffled voice says from my tear-soaked t-shirt.

"Yes?"

"I was wrong. One hundred percent wrong." Millie sobs.

"About what?"

"Pain. I don't want to have to experience pain to feel alive."

Wordlessly, I squeeze her body into mine a little tighter.

## Chapter 65
### Public reactions. Wedding bells.
#### Marmalade Julius's House Someplace in the United States of America
#### Land of the Free(ish) Home of the Brave(ish)

*Millie and I stayed at the Honorable Representative Nancy Pelosi Public Housing, Convalescence and Retirement Center instead of going back to Juice's house. Vel called Millie's old fashioned cell phone at some point to say that the family was safe, and the girl was being cared for. The news seemed to make Millie a little happier.*

*In the morning, we gathered all our things and took them out to the transporter. I didn't mention to the Robot Receptionist that we probably weren't coming back. After all, we may need somewhere to stay before the paid lease is up.*

*I drive to Marmalade's house largely in comfortable silence. Millie reaches over occasionally and touches me, which is nice. We pull into the drive and park the transporter. Millie gets out and hooks the power cord up to the charging port on the vehicle.*

Marmalade greets us in the drive.

"You two got to come check out what's going on with this crazy masturbation ban!" His voice is excited. He points at me. "Justin, it is good to see you upright and ambulatory. Now, hurry. You are really going to want to see this!"

We follow Justin into the room with all the monitors. Vel is standing behind Paal who is typing furiously on his keyboard. Vel gives both me and Millie a hug. Marmalade points at the screens. "This is has taken off. It's really amazing."

I look at the monitors. Numbers fly across the screens. "What am I looking at, Juice?" I ask.

"The whole world is talking about America's ban on masturbation! By *world*, I mean all four corners. Places that have limited internet are making fun of the United States. I must tell you, Justin. We are in awe of how well this has worked."

That sick feeling fills my gut. "I am not sure how this is good, Marmalade." I motion at the screens. "I just wanted people to pay attention."

"Oh, Justin, people *are* paying attention!" Paal turns and says. He points at the screens. "For certain, members of the *Christians in Pursuit of the Scoundrel Pontus Pilate* are supporting the ban - blindly, our data shows. Hell, if Rexford Ratchet said everyone with red hair needed to drink poisoned orange drink, there would be blind, broad support for the idea." Paal types on his keyboard. "It is the opinions coming from other places that is interesting. The idea of banning male masturbation is being roundly rejected by a large majority... eighty eight percent... of the population not affiliated with a religion. That is both male and female, regardless of race."

Marmalade's hand squeezes my shoulder. "He isn't telling you the best part... that population is openly saying that banning male masturbation is the same as eliminating women's choice when it comes to health care. *And they don't like it.*"

I nod slowly. "My idea *is* working."
Paal makes a motion in the air. "Check this out... even people who are publicly *pro-life* are questioning if the government should have such an impact on private matters. Look at the comments on monitor three."

I hear Millie reading the comments aloud softly as my eyes search for monitor three.

*My husband and I are pro-lifers. Have been since the Donald was president! This is too far. Maybe all of it... the bans on abortion and bans on IVF... were too much.*

*Banning Male Masturbation seems a bit much, don't ya think?*

*I thought banning abortion was a sensible thing to do, after all, babies need a voice, right? I didn't think that letting the government have that sort of control over my life would be so terrible. That was before this crazy spilt seed law.*

*Ugh! Another step towards the United States government controlling absolutely everything! I need to move to China! At least they started allowing more freedoms after their revolution in 35'!*

*Spilt Seed law, huh? We are really using the Bible to make laws now? My son was pretty sassy to me last week and I have a lot of debt. Can I sell my son to my creditors as is described in 2 Kings? How about my wife? She doesn't put out as much as I would like. Can I sell her too?*

*When I was young, my grandfather told me that being conservative meant keeping your nose out of other people's beeswax. Now it's the fucking conservatives that want to be all up in my beeswax. How does this end?*

*This is it. The bans on IVF and abortion were ok. I mean, we really weren't affected. I never had any need to get an abortion. Now this? My husband and I are fed up. Looking into apartments in France. Our neighbors moved there last year to get away from this nonsense!*

"Holy shit." Millie says.

Vel nods. "It's incredible. These are people who support... or use to support the restrictions on women's health care. Paal hasn't shown you the vitriol coming from the known pro-choice groups."

"We don't need to go there. We knew those people would be saying, *I told you so*.". Paal remarks. "For the most part, the pro-choice groups are mixing in that message with some anatomically impossible suggestions for Rexford Ratchet and the governor of Texas."

"What do you think we should do next, Justin?" Marmalade asks.

"Me?" I exclaim. I point at the wall of screens "You are asking me what to do next? You guys are the master of the message!"

Marmalade nods. "Yep. That we are. What message would you like to send? So far you have been on point."

I look at the screens and sigh. "A few miles from here there are destitute people who have no idea that there *is* a ban on masturbation... or for that matter that the concept of health care should be something that everyone has equal access to."

The room is silent for a while. It's Paal that speaks first. "You were gone a long time, Justin. After about 2030 the social structure *really* broke down. The right decided that poor people could just go to the churches if they wanted help and if they didn't want to be religious, they didn't deserve help."

Marmalade nods. "It started with education, believe it or not. The right pushed and passed vouchers... claiming that public education was too *woke*. Picking winners and losers by where they went to primary school became another way to discriminate against people... and it really solidified division in the United States."

"The left didn't help." Vel speaks up. "The push for inclusion and diversity was misguided. What started as an effort to give more minority groups equal access turned into an effort by a whole lot of fringe groups claiming minority status." She clears her throat. "At one time, most parents wanted a high value education for their children. Now they are afraid that their children might be taught something they disagree with. Thirty years ago, we could have some discourse about what is good and bad, now... well, now it's bad if you aren't on my team and it's your idea. There is no such thing as critical thought anymore."

I point at the screens. "Vel, that's not true. I see plenty of evidence that there is still critical thought. It may be uneducated critical thought, but it's critical thought nonetheless."

"Historically, getting the population educated on specific issues has not been easy or productive." Vel mutters. She points at the monitors. "The people who are critical of banning male masturbation are unlikely to act... Just like the people in Germany during the 1930's, we have become a people willing to accept whatever is being fed us."

I shake my head. "Democracy... Government like the United States had was always a battle of grand ideas. Some had merit, some did not. We the people were supposed to be the final check on the government and the two political parties." I walk close to Marmalade. "Feed some new ideas to the masses. First, float the idea of a ban on tubal litigation and vasectomies. At the same time, introduce the idea of a new civil rights law that encompasses health care, specifically highlighting rules that keep *all* personal health care initiatives private."

"Wind them up and give them options to go forward. I like it." Marmalade grins. "Maybe put a few more dollars in the church's coffers."

"Don't forget to set some of it aside for tattoo removal." I pat his shoulder. "Did you call Hank?"

Marmalade nods. "I gave him my address. He said he would be by later to talk with you."

"I need a ring." I say quietly.

Marmalade nods in agreement. He gives me a big grin; the light reflects off the gold caps on his teeth. "Hank and I got that handled already, bro."

Chapter 66
A better day in court. Less than brief.
Not Guilty, Guilty. Your name is, *what?*
Municipal Court Room, Someplace in America
Land of the Free(ish) Home of the Brave(ish)


"All Rise." The robot bailiff announces to the courtroom. "Court is in session."

Fred Peterson stands and watches nervously as Bob Good is led into the courtroom. He looks thinner than before, and his eyes shadowed by dark circles. It had been financially impossible for the Good family to post bail set for either Sookie or Bob. Sookie was finally released by the judge. Bob was left to sit in his cell.

"Looks like Bob lost the fight." Anne Margret says to Fred under her breath. She leans over to her mother and whispers in her ear. The judge walks into the courtroom and sits down, striking the bench with her hammer. "Court is in session. Sit down."

Fred looks around the courtroom. There aren't as many people in the seats as there had been at the first hearing. Fred had asked Cliff and Bob's mother to stay away. A fresh face girl sitting in the middle of the prosecution side of the courtroom catches his eye. She is typing quickly on an electronic pad. The prosecutor slouches in his seat, clearly bored with the process.

After a few minutes of reading, the Judge looks up. "Ms. Eaton, nice of you to join us today. Based on all the correctly used legalese, I would assume that you wrote this motion and not one of your less experienced partners?"

Fred feels his face turn red.

Elizabeth Eaton stands. "Good morning, Judge. Yes, I prepared the motion to dismiss the charges against Trump Bob Good on grounds that the arrest is invalid on the basis of *Harris v the United States of America (1947)*. Clearly Mr. Good's fourth amendment rights were violated in the..."

The judge interrupts the lawyer. "Counselor. I have already done your job for you. *Harris* won't work here. The state will object, correctly, that Mr. Good's statements to law enforcement are evidence admissible under state law. The video that was taken is admissible because *both* parties knew it was being taken... and really, only one party needed to know under state law as we have adopted the *one-party consent law* that Texas put in effect in 2011. I'd like to say that you could use a defense that relies on elements from *State v Brewer: 1973* but again, Mr. Good *willingly* told the police what happened." The judge seems to sigh in resignation. "I am not sure what other elements that you can present to the court in this case. Believe me, I am all ears if you have something else to offer."

Fred looks over at the prosecutor who is wearing a smug look. He looks back at the judge. Her face is sad.

Elizabeth Eaton looks at the table. "It's just wrong your honor. These charges are just wrong."

The judge nods her head. "Clearly. That said, my hands are tied counselor. Your client will have to stand trial."

Fred stands. "Your honor, may I address the court?"
The judge glares at him and shakes her head slowly. "I am not sure I am up for the entertainment today, Mr. Peterson. Have your comments been cleared though Ms. Eaton?"

"No, your honor. They have not."

The judge looks at Elizabeth Eaton expectantly. She shakes her head slightly in response. "Let him speak. Freddy is pretty sharp. Maybe he has a good idea."

"I object." The prosecuting attorney announces from his chair.

"Overruled." The judge snaps. "Just because things are going your way, doesn't mean that I like this case." She points to Fred. "Make it quick, Mr. Peterson."

"*Lawrence v Texas: 2003* concerned the arrest of two men who were involved in homosexual activity. The elements of the case that were considered by the Supreme Court were first, whether the criminal convictions under the Texas law criminalizing sexual intimacy by same sex couples but not identical behavior by heterosexual couples violates the Fourteenth Amendment guarantee of equal protection. Second, the court considered whether the petitioner's criminal conviction for adult consensual intimacy in their home violated vital interests in liberty and privacy protected by the Due Process Clause of the Fourteenth Amendment. Third, the court had to consider whether *Bowers v Hardwick: 1986* should be overruled. The court, of course found for Lawrence and overturned Bowers." Fred swallows hard. He feels his hands getting sweaty.

"I love you, Freddy. Go get it." Anne Margret whispers from beside him.

"You are comparing Mr. Good to the parties in Lawrence?" The judge asks.

Fred nods. "I am. Mr. Good was in the privacy in his home when he was recorded. He was involved in an act that is done by people of all genders... *in all parts of the world.*"

There is silence in the courtroom. Fred looks around. Most of the court room is looking at the Judge. Bob Good is looking at his feet. The woman with the electronic pad continues to type furiously on it as Fred speaks. Elizabeth Eaton stares stoically at the judge who drums her fingers on the bench.

"Can I say something in response?" The prosecutor asks.

"No." The judge answers with a curt tone. She looks down at Fred from her perch. "You do understand in today's legal climate, that challenging a landmark case like *Lawrence* may result in gay rights being rolled back, right?"

Fred squeezes his sweaty palms together and takes a deep breath. "Your honor, I *do* realize that. The decision in *Lawrence* was the correct social decision, but it may not have been the correct *legal* decision. Justice Sandra Day O'Connor, in her concurrence with the majority wrote that she supported *Lawrence*, but not because sexuality was something protected under the constitution, but because if Lawrence stood, it would violate the equal protection clause because it criminalized male-male but not male-female sodomy. O'Conner didn't think the case should be about sexual acts. Instead, she thought it should be about equal protection. If the decision for the majority had been written that way in *Lawrence*, the Spilt Seed laws would be null by default!"

"So, you think that the *Spilt Seed Law* violates the equal protection clause?" The judge says absently. She strokes her chin. "I think that Texas wrote the law specifically, so it did not violate the equal protection clause. It outlaws *male* masturbation because each ejaculation could result in a human life."

"You are getting me so wet Freddy. I am *so* going to introduce you to female, male sodomy later tonight!" Anne Margret whispers in Fred's ear.

"With all due respect your honor, each *human female egg* represents a potential human life. Are we going to outlaw *menstruation* next?" Fred asks as he puts his hand in the air and adds, "Of course not." He shakes his head and continues. "Do you know that the entirety of the European Union allows abortion? The entirety of the European Union recognizes gay rights. No European country has laws against masturbation, and they won't."

"This is not the European Union, Mr. Peterson." The judge replies tersely.

"Yes, well that may be true, but it is not without precedence that we look across the Atlantic to find guidance for legal foundation. In *Lawerence* the majority opinion referenced *Dudgeon v United Kingdom: 1981.* *Dudgeon was a case out of Northern Ireland where a gay activist named Jeff Dudgeon was interrogated by police about his sex life. After being charged with the crime of sodomy, he files complaint with the European Commission on Human Rights. They found for him on the basis that criminalization of homosexual acts between consenting adults was a violation of Article 8 of the European Convention on Human Rights which says, *everyone has the right to respect for his private and family life, his home and his correspondence. There shall be no interference by a public authority with the exercise of this right except such as is in accordance with the law and is necessary in a democratic society ... for the protection of health or morals*

The prosecutor jumps up. "This is ridiculous your honor. If you want to discuss archaic European Laws with this high school kid and his dopey friends, do it on your own time. I have things to do!"

The judge looks at the attorney cooly. Calmly, she picks up her hammer and taps it on the wooden bench. "I charge you with contempt, counselor. Bailiff, remove the prosecutor from my courtroom."

Elizabeth Eaton smirks and chokes back a laugh. She leans into Fred. "I'm not sure where you are going with this, but my advice is to get there quickly." They stand quietly as the prosecutor is led out of the courtroom.

The judge looks down at Fred. "We aren't in the European Union. There is no article eight here. I don't agree with the Spilt Seed law, but it is the law."

"Yes, your honor, and Mr. Trump Bob Good is guilty of violating the law as it is written. Just like Mr. Lawrence and Mr. Dudgeon were both guilty of sodomy. Just like thousands of women are guilty of violating federal law because they took steps to illegally obtain birth control. Because there is a law doesn't necessarily make it right. That's why we have courts! My opinion and frankly your opinion on Mr. Good's actions is not relevant to Mr. Good's human condition. Maybe you have a deeply held belief that masturbation is terrible and a waste of human life. You have every right in the world to broadcast that belief... but the constitution is clear; you don't have the right to force other people to conform to your beliefs."

"I have no opinion on masturbation, Mr. Peterson. My job here is to preside over the proceedings of the trial and maintain an orderly court." The judge answers quickly as she picks up her hammer.

Fred shakes his head and taps on the table in front of him.
"Careful Fred." Elizabeth Eaton cautions.

"Your honor, the way I see it, the evidence being used against Mr. Good is improper. It was gathered before the law went into effect. It was collected in Mr. Good's private home. The Spilt Seed law is a violation of Mr. Good's right to equal protection, no matter what laws the state Government of Texas has passed. In general, Mr. Good's right to privacy has been trampled on in this case." Fred points at Bob. "Mr. Good doesn't belong in court fighting a ridiculous charge your honor. He should be at home studying to graduate from high school and preparing to get on with his life."

An audible whimper is heard from Bob.

The judge shakes her head. "The prosecutor isn't going to like this... I am dismissing the charges against your client." She picks up the hammer and starts to bring it down on the wooden bench.

"Wait!" Elizabeth Eaton cries out. "I object"

"You what?" Anne Margret exclaims. "Did you hit your head doing *laundry*, mom?"

"What are you asking for counselor? I was about to set your client free. Most defense lawyers are damn happy about such things." The judge exclaims, the hammer comically held in the air.

Elizabeth Eaton sighs and pats Fred on the shoulder. "Fred has given me a lot to think about in his rather long monologue." She nudges him. "We will be talking later about keeping things *brief* when addressing the court." She turns back to the judge. "He is right your honor. We need to start correcting things in this country and maybe it starts with our client, Trump Bob Good." She shakes her head and mutters, "*All this bullshit started with a Trump. It may as well end with one.*" She regains her poise. "You honor, I respectfully ask that you find Mr. Good guilty, today. Release him on his own recognizance pending sentencing which I would like you to do sooner rather than later. We are going to appeal this case."

The Judge rolls her eyes. "You went to a real law school, right counselor? You understand that we really aren't to the part of the process yet where I can pronounce your client *guilty*. You can put in a motion to change your client's plea to *guilty* or I can *dismiss* the case."

"Umm, I am ok with the case being dismissed!" Bob whispers loudly from his seat.

Anne Margret reaches over and pats his handcuffed arm. "I think you are going to be a poster child in my mom's landmark case. It will be Good vs whatever that douchebag county attorney's name is."

"I don't want to be a Landmark case! I just want to be me!" Bob whines.

Elizabeth Eaton clears her throat. "Please excuse my lack of clarity in my less than professional mutterings. Your honor, there aren't a lot of rules being followed anymore. Let's schedule a trial date. You will find Bob guilty, and we can negotiate sentencing." She motions at the empty prosecutor's chair. "I am sure that he won't complain about the victory. The state may object to about my appeals on the matter."

The judge shakes her head. "Whatever. Get with the Clerk of the Court to get this ridiculous case on the docket. Let the record reflect that I am releasing the defendant into the custody of his attorneys." She points the hammer at Elizabeth Eaton. "I wish you the best of luck, Ms. Eaton. I truly hope you can use this case to make things right, as you say. It would certainly be nice if all of us regained autonomy over our own bodies."

The sound of the hammer hitting the wood echoes around the courtroom as the judge stands and makes an announcement. "Court is dismissed. I can't take anymore today."

The girl with the electronic pad comes over to Fred. Her dark hair frames a pretty *girl next door* face. "Mr. Peterson, can I get a few comments from you and... umm... your client?"

"Who are you?" Anne Margret asks defensively as she steps between Fred and the woman.

"My name is Likmi Delores PuLese. I am a reporter for the Beijing Times. I am covering important legal proceedings in the United States. We are very interested in how this *Spilt Seed* law is going to play out. So far as I know, your client is the first to be found guilty under the law."

"What did she say her name was?" Bob Good asks in a very loud whisper.

"Is that your real name?" Anne Margret asks the reporter with a frown. The reporter just stares at Bob Good.

"Your organization owns the New York Times and the Washington Post now, right?" Elizabeth Eaton asks.

"We also own the Houston Chronicle, Chicago Tribune, the Wall Street Journal and the Los Angeles Times." Fred notes that the woman doesn't smile. In fact, she shows little facial expression of any kind. "Readership in the United States isn't very high... but the ex-pats living around the world are very keen to hear what is going on in their old country and cities." She pats the older attorney on the arm in a mechanical, forced way. "Don't worry. I'm not writing a hit piece. Most of the world is quite horrified to hear about what is currently happening in the United States. I think my coverage may help you and others put pressure on your political leaders. Your government is very reliant these days on aid from the rest of the world."

Elizabeth Eaton gives the girl a patronizing smile. "We will give you an interview. I will send you my contact information and we can speak at my office."

"Thank you, counselor." She looks back at Bob and winks at him. The action looks as natural as a parrot walking a dog down the street. "I really want to talk to Bob Good though... Can I talk to *him* at your office?"

"*She* wants to talk to *me?*" Bob says slowly. He shuffles closer to the woman. "Are you real? Or a Chinese droid of some sort?"

Likmi Delores PuLese steps close to Bob. "I am real. I watched you today. All through the hearing. You and I are very much alike, Mr. Good." The reporter snorts through her nose in laughter. "I like to touch myself too!"

Elizabeth Eaton rolls her eyes. "I'll see what I can do, Ms. PuLese. We like to protect our clients from unnecessary public exposure at Eaton, Peterson and Eaton." I am sure we can make an exception in this case.

"Hey! Am I the first Eaton or the third partner in this firm?" Anne Margret questions with an indigent tone.

Chapter 67
The Priest has arrived. Moral Quandary. A plan is hatched.
Marmalade Julius's House
Someplace in the United States of America
Land of the Free(ish) Home of the Brave(ish)


We are watching the monitors as Paal feeds information and disinformation to the world. The reactions are so quick, I think that the best thing we could do to help the world would be to get rid of the internet completely. Apparently, all anyone does is sit around and look at whatever social media is popular.

Marmalade gets a message that Hank Thyme has arrived. This is it. Millie and I are finally getting married! The thought gives me little butterflies in my stomach. Juice goes to get Hank. I point at one of the monitors. "What is happening with that Monitor. Some of the messages seem downright sane."

Paal looks at it. He nods. "That board is made up of a group of government workers in Washington DC. Many of them are quite old now... they were educated in American Ivy League schools before such things became irrelevant. These people keep the country running... at least the best that they can." Paal sighs. "Most of them are well beyond retirement age, but they know that there is no one that will replace them." After a few keystrokes, the information appears on the large screen. He points, "We know a lot of these people. They are regular people. Some are church goers. Some are not. They are all intellectuals, which means that they probably don't have much of a life outside of work."

"There is really no one who wants to replace them when they are gone. It used to be that government jobs were in high demand. People used the experience to go on to bigger things." I comment.

Paal shakes his head sadly. "Not anymore. The vacated positions will just be eliminated. The *swamp* has been drained. No one thought to figure out what happened in the swamp before they drained it. That is part of why everything is so messed up." He turns in his chair to me. "That was the Trumpeter's biggest error - or his greatest accomplishment depending on how you look at it, I guess. He didn't have a government in either of his terms. There are so many positions that must be filled in the United States Government by each presidential administration. Trump filled very few of them. When Biden was elected, he had a government. The jobs were filled... but then the election of 2024 happened. Now each presidency is one Tea Pot Dome Scandal after another. Only no one thinks it's a scandal. The public just thinks that it is the government acting like the government acts. The public no longer understands that the people are supposed to be the government."

Marmalade comes back into the room. Hank follows behind, his towering figure is slouched, and his bearded face looks long. "What are you guys looking at?" Marmalade points at the big screen. "Don't mess to much with those people, they are the only thing keeping everything running, poor as it may be."

Paal shrugs. "I was just telling Justin about the stalwarts that remain in the government."

"Saints, those people are." Marmalade says. He motions unnecessarily at Hank. "Hank is here."

I had been studying my cousin. I can *feel* that he is troubled. "What's going on Hank?"

"I brought the ring for you." He holds out a box. "I can't marry you though... it's against the rules. Has to be in a Catholic Church. And you know, the people getting married must be Catholic."

I wave dismissively, "Details that don't matter, cousin." I open the box. The ring is beautiful. Some of the stones look familiar to me in how they are set. "Where did you guys get this?"

Hank brightens a little. "It was made with your mother's and our grandmother's rings. I helped design it... And... I... well, I guess I won't have a use for it."

I nod. I know what is bothering Hank now. "Were you originally going to use this ring, Hank?"

He nods. "I had a jeweler take my mother's ring parts out and put your mom's ring parts in."

I see. "Tell me about your day Hank. You seem conflicted."

Hank looks up at Marmalade and Paal. Juice comes over and embraces him. "It's ok man. You are here with friends. What's going on?"

Hank pulls a chair out and sits down in it. He is quiet for a few minutes before speaking. "I realized the other day that my bicycle was missing. Another priest noticed I wasn't riding it anymore and asked me what happened to it. I told him that my heart was heavy, because I thought that someone in my parish had stolen my bicycle. My priest buddy who has his own parish says to me "Hank, that is terrible! Then he says, "This is how you should get it back. On Sunday, give a fire and brimstone speech about the Ten Commandments. When you get to *Thou shalt not steal*, really get serious. Maybe the thief will feel guilty and return your bike." Well, Sunday comes, and I do the sermon. I'm really going strong on *thou shalt not kill*. I finish that one up and then I remember exactly where I left my bicycle."

The room is silent. I shake my head and let a long sigh. Paal whispers to Marmalade. "Was that a joke? I don't get it."

"Do you have a bicycle, Hank?" I ask.

"Nope. Haven't had one since I was in high school." Hank answers.

I nod slowly. I pull a chair up and sit down beside Hank. "It's the woman that you counseled not to marry someone."

Hank nods.

"This is the same woman that you were going to marry, before you decided to not only convert to Catholicism but also to become a Catholic Priest." My grasshopper supplied clairvoyance is amazing.

Hank nods and chokes back a sob.

"Did she marry the new guy?"

Hank shakes his head. "No. They broke up. Because of me, I suppose."

"Oh! I get it now! The next commandment is *Thou shall not commit adultery!*" Paal exclaims. "That's a pretty funny joke!"

"How long have you been a Priest, Hank?" I ask.

"About twelve years." Hank answers. He wipes his eyes with the sleeve of his black jacket.

"How long have you been in love with this woman?" I ask.

"About twenty years." Hank answers.

I nod. "Are you a eunuch, Hank?"

He shakes his head angrily. "No, of course not. Why would you ask that?"

"Matthew nineteen, verse twelve... "For there are some eunuchs, which were so born from their mother's womb; and there are some eunuchs, which were made eunuchs of men; and there be eunuchs, which have made themselves eunuchs for the sake of the kingdom of heaven.

That verse is the justification that Pope Gregory used to make men who wanted to be priests *escape the clutches of a wife*." I pat his knee. "Hank, you were not born a eunuch. You have not become a eunuch. At one time in your life, you literally, not figuratively would fuck any woman with a heartbeat who appeared the least bit interested. You are telling us that you have perfectly natural feelings for another human being, and you have engaged in a perfectly natural activity with her, that we assume she agreed to be a part of. You are a good person, Hank. The church's law is man made. It is not the law of nature or any God."

"What do you think I should do?" Hank asks.

"I think you should take half of our grandmother's ring from that thing you made for me and put it with your mother's ring and marry the woman. Sounds like she has been waiting for you for a while." I answer.

"I could not be a priest then." Hank answers. "At least not a Catholic one."

"What do you like about the priesthood?" I ask.

"I like helping people. I like giving guidance. I enjoy the history of religion, and I like talking about it." Hank sighs. "But I know you are right, Justin."

I point at Marmalade. "I am not Juice's hiring manager, but I am pretty sure that he has some job openings coming up. Maybe you can land a spot at one of his churches. I am pretty sure that Julius Jesus 2.0 is going to focus on helping people, giving guidance and understanding history."

Hank shakes his head and laughs. "I'm not sure I can get the back tattoo. Or tolerate some of the other... activities."

I smile. "It's no longer necessary. Like Paul told the gentiles, no body mutilation is needed to join the band. Neither is porking the occasional random congregant."

Hank stares at me. "You are something Justin. When did you learn so much about the Bible and when did Juice start letting you make decisions for his church?"

Marmalade laughs. "Justin has introduced me to some new ideas Hank. He certainly has set my mind straight on the way my church ought to be run and how my congregants should be treated by my staff and other members of the church."

"I spent an inordinate amount of time in a hospital room with only robots to talk to and a bible to read, Hank. I read the thing from cover to cover and then went back and reread certain passages. Several times." I answer.

"I talked to you when you were in the hospital!" Millie walks up behind me and slugs me in the shoulder before laughing. "But I bet there were days when the robots were better company!"

"Never!" I say, standing. "I was wondering when you two were coming back. The priest is here. We can get married."

Vel comes in behind her. "Today? You two are tying the knot today?" She throws her hands in the air. "I was planning a whole ceremony. It was going to be down by the pool, a full dinner... dancing... I was going to build a chuppah and everything!"

"What's a chuppah?" Hank asks.

"Psalms nineteen, verse five. It's the chamber I am supposed to wait for Millie in when she comes out of her closet." I answer.

Vel frowns. "Or it's a pretty little canopy made of sticks and leaves that the wedding ceremony is consecrated in." She punches me in the other shoulder. "Vel Finkelstein, chapter one, verse one. Wedding days are supposed to be special!"

When the laughter dies down, I put on my best serious face, which like my sarcasm carries little effectiveness, except I look like a corpse. "Seriously. I have a ring, albeit one that will be getting some modifications. We can get married right here, right now. There is not one but two ministers." I smile at Vel and add, "And an awesome maid of honor."

Millie looks flushed and... excited. "We are getting married today?"

"Yes." I answer. I look at Marmalade. "Right, Juice?"

"Whatever you say, Justin. Just make sure you don't go rushing into anything." Marmalade answers.

I shrug and look at my fiancé. "There. See, now we have had marriage counseling."

Paal comes up beside Marmalade. "I hate to interrupt the ceremonial planning of what cannot possibly be a shotgun wedding... but Justin's ideas are working quite well Marmalade. There is quite a bit of derision in the *Christians in Pursuit of the Scoundrel Pontius Pilate*. We need to make a run on the foundation of the church quickly while people are still paying attention."

Vel's face wrinkles up in confusion. "What do you mean there is derision? It's been like two days. How is that possible?"

"It's possible because all anyone does anymore is stare at a screen and wait for it to tell them how to think." Hank answers. "Conrad called me to tell me about this Spilt Seed thing. I can't believe it is working like it is."

I nod. "Ok, this is what I think should happen. Millie and I get married here today. This Sunday, we go to the church headquarters where Rex is preaching." I point at Paal. "Start chumming the water with the wrongs that the Reverend Rex Ratchet and the church has committed over the years. We go into the church, and you can take over the technical aspects of the sanctuary. Then I will deliver a sermon."

"You?" Marmalade exclaims. "Why would you deliver the sermon?"

I wink at him. "They aren't going to like my sermon, Juice. You will come in and say some catchy phrase, kicking Rex Ratchet off his own stage and then you will deliver the message that starts the process of bringing the church together. The way you want it to be."

There is a brief silence before Millie speaks. "I want in on this. I want Rex to see that I am helping take him down."

"Yes." I say simply.

"I want to go too." Vel says.

"No. I am sorry Vel. You cannot go." I reply. I look at Marmalade. "It is not safe for any of us. Paal must go because he controls the tech. Marmalade will be ok because he is an Elder in the church and that has to count for something. Outsiders will be in danger. Only Millie and I will go with Paal and Juice."

"I like it." Marmalade says.

"I don't think I like it." Vel says with a frown. "Why can't we fuck with these people from a distance?"

"They need a leader. They need to see the leader." I answer, motioning at Juice. "Marmalade is the leader."

"And what will *you* preaching to them do, besides get *you* maybe killed?" Vel asks sourly.

I smile gently. "Sometimes that is enough, Vel." I spread my arms wide and smile. "Now let's have a wedding!"

Paal, Hank, Marmalade and I go up by the pool. Vel and Millie disappear someplace. I hand the ring to Paal. "You are the best man, Paal. Do me good."

"Yes sir, Justin!" Paal answers enthusiastically.

"We should have thrown you a bachelor party." Marmalade comments.

"I had one for twenty some years. There were lots of strippers and everything. It ended on the ass end of a big truck." I quip as the door opens. Millie steps through it dressed in a white dress. Her hair is up. Her face radiant, except the slightly dead looking eyes. She looks absolutely stunning. "I am speechless." I say as I lean forward and kiss her on the forehead.
Millie and I spend the next ten minutes staring into each other's eyes as Hank and Juice take turns trying to outdo each other with *niceties ministers say at weddings...* I am sure most of it was meaningful and appropriate, but honestly? Whatever they said meant nothing to either Millie or me. Paal handed me the ring. I put it on Millie's finger.

I finally hear Hank say, *You may kiss the bride,* and I did.

The next few hours were a blur. There was lots of food. There were neat little nonalcoholic drinks and Vel made sure that there was dancing. It was fun.

It was fun because I was with Millie.

Juice and Vel talked Hank into spending the night instead of driving back to town. Millie and I retire to our guest bedroom.

I sit down on the bed and my wife comes to me. She puts her hands on my shoulder. "What is going to happen in Texas at that church."

"We are probably going to die." I answer.

Millie nods. There isn't a trace of emotion in her eyes. "Does Marmalade know that?"

I nod. "He knows it is a risk."

"You think being a martyr is what is best?" Millie asks. Her voice is sincere. I can tell that she isn't asking out of doubt.

"I think we have done here what we were asked to do." I answer slowly. "If we die, we die together. I think I like that ending to my story the best." I poke her in the belly. "How about you?"

Millie sighs and looks into my eyes. "Were we supposed to do more as a married couple?" She shrugs. "So many married people do significantly less than what we have already done." She traces the lines of my jaw. "Take your pants off."

I smile. "That's what we should be talking about." I stand and drop my drawers.

"Turn Around." Millie commands. I do and she bends a little to look at my legs. "Yeah... Just like mine."
I straighten up and she turns her back to me. "Unzip me."

Excitement builds in my brain as I feel myself getting hard. *The equipment appears to be back online!* I run my hands over the curves of Millie's body. I find the zipper on the back of the dress and pull it down slowly. "Shall we consummate our marriage?"

"I want to show you something." The dress drops to the floor, revealing a totally nude Millie.

"I might not have lasted the through the whole eating and dancing part of the wedding if I knew you were commando under that dress!" I comment.

"Look at my spot." She points to her leg. I look down. The tobacco stain placed upon her by the Grasshopper is just about gone. Only a little tiny freckle remains where it once was.

"Mine the same size?"

Millie nods.

"I guess our time really is about up." *I don't feel sad really, which is weird, I guess.*

"I love you dearly and deeply Justin Thyme. If we have the next three hours or three centuries together, I am happy." Millie reaches around my neck and pulls her naked body close to me. "*Now* we need to consummate our marriage."

And we did. Several times.

Chapter 68
Kismet. Keys to happiness.
Elizabeth Eaton's house Someplace in America
Land of the Free(ish) Home of the Brave(ish)


Anne Margret puts a seaweed chip in her mouth. "I have never seen him like this."

"No kidding." Fred answers. He watches as Bob Good laughs again at some joke Likmi Delores PuLese fails, again, to tell without snorting in laughter halfway through. "I am not sure what is funnier, watching her try and tell the jokes or watching Bob react."

"It's like they are meant for each other." Anne Margret snuggles close to Fred. "Like us."

"I don't see her slugging him in the shoulder or slapping his face." Fred deadpans. "How can we be sure that it's love?"

"My mother gave me a pegging belt. If you are good, I will use lube." Anne Margret whispers.

Elizabeth Eaton comes into the room. "I am guessing that our roles have changed from legal counsel to matchmaker."

"It's kind of cute." Her daughter says.

"Traditional media doesn't mean much anymore to public opinion... especially one based in China. Just make sure she doesn't publish something that creates problems for us." Elizabeth says. "Did she ask any questions at all?"

"She asked when we thought the issue would be taken up by the Supreme Court." Fred answers. "Then she started snorting and telling Bob inappropriate jokes, to which he responded with more inappropriate jokes."

"Kismet." Elizabeth Eaton says sarcastically. "Ms. PuLese? Bob? Can you come over here?" She turns to Anne Margret. "I just can't bring myself to say her full name like she does... Every time she introduces herself."

Bob helps Likmi up and they come to the kitchen bar. "Yes, Mrs. Eaton?" The woman says.

"It's Ms. Eaton. I was wondering if we needed to supply you with any more information about Mr. Good's case?" The lawyer flashes her best *don't waste my time smile*.

Likmi waves her hand dismissively. "I filed the story last night. It's already published in six dailies. The New York Times will have a weekend special on it." She reaches up and squeezes Bob Good's cheek. "I wish I had included pictures of this one without prison orange on so people can see how *cute* he is!"

"I think I may throw up a little in my mouth." Anne Margret says to Fred.

"You already published? I thought we might have some editorial control!" Elizabeth Eaton exclaims. "That was our deal!"

Likmi smiles, her eyes wild. "Nah, Nah... you don't need to be worried Liz. I told you I would keep it positive. *I like masturbation!*" She picks her electronic pad off a chair and types a few things, snorting in laughter as she does. "I came here to meet Bob Good... He is so cute, and I just felt a pull to get myself here. I don't cover little stories like this normally." She points at Elizabeth Eaton. "The story we posted is in your in box."

"What do you do?" Fred asks. "I thought you were a reporter."

"What do I *do*? Well, I am hoping, Bob!" Likmi snorts in laughter. The snorts intensify and soon she is doubled over, laughing. "But first you have to get that cage off him. We absolutely cannot be doing the horizontal mambo with a monkey cage between us!"

"Yep. Definitely a little vomit on the back of the tongue on that one." Anne Margret says out loud.

Likmi snorts and laughs again. "You are so funny, little Eaton!"

"Little Eaton." Fred giggles. "Now that's cute."

"There is definitely no lubrication in your future Fred A. Peterson!" Anne Margret growls.

Bob Good snorts in laughter and pokes his friend. "No lube? What are two getting up to?" He snorts again. "Now you have me doing it, Likmi!"

Likmi Delores PuLese stands on her tip toes and licks Bob's face.

"What was that for?" Bob asks, surprised.

"You said Lick Me!" Likmi yells with a snort and laughter.
In response Bob roars with laughter.
Elizabeth Eaton puts her electronic pad down. "That is quite a story. You captured what Fred, and the judge said quite well, Ms. PuLese. You are quite a talented writer. What is your normal job?"

"Well, my father *owns* the Beijing Times. I usually just manage all the English language news outlets." Likmi says. "I decided that I would be the one to cover this story! I really wanted to meet Bobby!"

"When will you go back to China?" Anne Margret asks with only a little bit of an annoyed tone.

"Oh, we live in Paris. I only go to Beijing when I want Dim Sum or good noodles." Likmi taps the electronic pad. "You know, everything can be done now on a computer, but good noodles still have to be made by hand!"

"You... you just go to Beijing, China... for dinner?" Elizabeth Eaton asks slowly.

Likmi breaks into a fit snorts and laughter. "No! Silly, Dim Sum is a breakfast, brunch kind of meal. It isn't served at night!" Her face turns serious. "Listen, for reals, Mrs. Eaton. I need to know... can you get this cage off Bob? I need some good lovin' if you know what I mean!"

Elizabeth Eaton sighs loudly. "It's *Ms.* Eaton. And no, I cannot take that cage off Bob. He is required by law to wear it."

"I can." Fred says as he dials up his father.

Anne Margret and Elizabeth Eaton glare at him. "Fred! He must wear the cage! Hopefully he can get it taken off when he is sentenced!" Anne Margret exclaims.
Fred shrugs. "I have seen it. It isn't a PPP cage. But I am sure the key is some novelty thing." Conrad answers and Fred explains the situation. Likmi and Bob exchange several dirty jokes complete with snorts and laughter.

Fifteen minutes later, Conrad appears with a set of keys. He hands the keys to Fred who looks at them dumbly. "What am I supposed to do with these?"

"There are two locks on that model. It might take two people to release them." Conrad says. "Bob is going to need help."

"Are you with Liz? You are such a cute couple!" Likmi says with a snort.

"Oh, hell no." Fred says. "Removing that cage would definitely be a violation of the attorney client relationship. He tosses the keys to Likmi. "Good luck Likmi. I hope things turn out like you want."

The girl's eyes grow big, and she grabs Bob's arm with a snort. "Where is a bathroom? Or a bedroom? We need a room! Now!"

Wordlessly, Anne Margret points down the hall.

"That's the way to the laundry room, Anne." Elizabeth Eaton says.

"What else happens in a laundry room besides sex, *Liz?*" Anne Margret answers with a snarky tone. Speaking of laundry... don't you two have something to do, someplace else?

"Well, I guess it's going to have to be at my house... Looks like your laundry room is going to be busy for a while!" Conrad comments.
Anne Margret gently bangs her head on the faux granite counter. "No... No... I simply cannot un-hear these things."

Elizabeth and Conrad leave. Anne Margret and Fred look at each other as a rhythmic, metallic thumping echoes through the walls.

"I think maybe we should try the washing machine sex. It seems to work out well for people." Fred says just as Bob Good emerges from the hallway wearing only a dirty towel from Anne Margret's bathroom wrapped around his waist.

"I am officially no longer a virgin!" Bob declares triumphantly. "What do you think about that, Freddy?"

"I think that's great, Bob." Fred says with a forced smile.

"Bob." Anne Margret says with a sour tone. "You can keep that towel. Take it home with you... think of it as a memento of this extraordinary event."

"You got it Anne Margret!" Bob says as he rushes back down the hallway.

Chapter 69
RickRolled. A children's play.
Sermon in the Lion's den. Shots are fired.
Christians in Pursuit of the Scoundrel Pontius Pilate
Dallas, Texas, still a place in the United States of America
Land of the Free(ish). Home of the Brave(ish).


*I did not know how this story was going to end for me when I came out of my coma being ridden by Calamity Joyfull like she was late for a very important date. If I am honest with myself, I lived my life before the accident as a disappointing underachiever who was a whore when it came to women. In my re-born life, I see more. Much more. I am more aware of the human condition as it is. I have met a great woman and married her. These are all big deals things for me, but very insignificant things in the big picture. As I said in the beginning, this story was never about me.*

"The plane will be landing in Dallas soon." Paal announces.

I look over at Millie. She is wearing a very conservative blue dress that highlights her eyes, which a still a dull pool of dark blue. *"I love you."* I mouth. Mille smiles and squeezes my hand as the wheels of Marmalade's plane touch the ground.

"I have a transporter scheduled to meet us on the tarmac and take us to the church." Paal says.

Marmalade has been silent for the entirety of the flight. His eyes look sad. I know he really understands what the likely outcome of the day is. "Juice today is a wonderful day, and it is only going to get better. We have been given all the authority in heaven and on earth we need. Before people can change, they must know that they need to. We are doing good work here. There may be disappointments, but the most important thing is the mission. Right now, our mission is to take down the Demigod Rex

Ratchet. When that is done, you can remake the church the way you want to and hopefully we neuter the political influence the church has over the government."

"These aren't good people Justin." Juice says tightly. "It sounds so terrible to say that about people who are members of my own church. I am really worried about what will happen inside the church. They are a well-armed group of people."

"Maybe we can get them to shoot Rex." Millie suggests.

"Rex is not who I am worried about them shooting." Marmalade points at me. "Will you two please wear bulletproof vests? I brought them along." He unbuttons his shirt. "Look, I am wearing one!"

I shake my head. My thoughts are completely clear on this. Millie and I are going into the church as we are. I give Juice a lopsided grin. "It won't fit under this awesome suit you got for me."

"I don't want an ugly Kevlar vest covering up this beautiful dress!" Millie exclaims with a smile. Marmalade just shakes his head sadly.

The plane taxis to a stop. We walk down the airstairs and get into the self-piloted transporter. The ride through Dallas is silent. We pull into the parking lot of what appears to be a conglomerate of shiny buildings that reflect a mural of bright blue sky and the sun off mirrored windows.

"Welcome to the house that Rex built." Marmalade mutters. I can hear the jealousy in his voice. The transporter pulls up to a set of large wooden doors that looks wholly out of place on the ultra-modern looking building.

"Showtime." Paal announces. He climbs out of the transporter door when it opens. Millie gets out.

I stop Marmalade. "Listen, no matter what happens in there, you follow the plan. Millie and I will be ok, no matter what." Marmalade nods tightly and gets out ahead me. He walks up to Millie and gives her a tight embrace.

I motion for Millie wait after I climb from the Transporter. "Are you OK with this? If you say stop, we stop and go back. You and I both know we probably aren't making the return trip to Marmalade's house."

Millie stares into my eyes. Even half alive and half dead, she is the most beautiful thing I have ever seen. "Justin, we have something to do here, and I intend to do it. It's time that Rex Ratchet falls." She looks at the buildings. "All of this needs to fall with him. I am sure of it." Without further comment, she takes my hand and follows Marmalade and Paal through the wooden doors.

We are greeted inside the door by a white, well-built blond-haired man who is wearing a pair of board shorts and a bright blue t-shirt that says, *Ain't nothing free but Jesus.* An assault rifle dangles from his left shoulder. The words on the t-shirt circle a crucifix. "Hello Comrades. Do you join us for services today?" He eyes Marmalade suspiciously.

"We are from a church up north." Juice says. "Just dropping in to get our message for the week."
"All comrades are welcome. Even the northerners. Let's keep making 'Merica great!" The man says with a plastic smile. "You know how things work at *Christians in Pursuit of the Scoundrel Pontius Pilate.* Pretty standard here."

Juice nods and leads us past the man. A large fountain takes up much of the foyer outside the main sanctuary of the church. There are three crosses in the fountain and red liquid flows from the ends of each cross back into the blood red pool. A plaque at the edge of the fountain reads, *Fountain is powered by the menstrual blood of the congregation's virgins.*

"Can't get this over with fast enough." Millie mutters.

We are ushered though another set of double doors into the sanctuary by a woman wearing a bikini top, her church tattoo plainly visible and a man wearing a pair of shorts and yellow t-shirt that says simply, *Cuck for brides of Jesus* They seat us in the middle of the congregation at the end of a row.

There is a man in a white rob on the stage at the front of the church sanitary reading scriptures. I listen for a moment. *...heaven standing open and there before me was a white horse, whose rider is called Faithful and True. With justice he judges and makes war. His eyes are like blazing fire, and on his head are many crowns. He has a name written on him that no one knows but he himself*

Revelations 19:11. *Strangely appropriate verse to be read today,* I think to myself. The scripture reader motions to the giant video screen nearest to him. There are four in the giant sanctuary, just like Paal said there would be. "And now, we will sing *Are you washed in the blood of the lamb.* An AI generated Rick Astley comes on the screen and starts singing the hymn. The congregation stands and sings along.

"I never could have predicted that we would be Rickrolled at your ex-husband's church." I say, leaning into Millie and giving her a little elbow. We both crack up. Marmalade looks over at us with an annoyed expression. "Be serious, you two!" He whispers loudly enough to be heard.

"This is such a creepy song!" Millie says into my ear as AI Rick Astley asks us if *our garments are white as snow.* The song ends and the congregation sits down. I get my first look at the Reverend Rex Ratchet. He sits on an electric scooter, clothed from head to toe in white. He has on a white pointed hat and long white robe reminiscent of those worn by the Klu Klux Klan. His swollen feet are encased by the straps of a pair of white sandals. The man's cheeks and neck are puffy and red. He motions at a young blond woman who is also wearing a long white robe. She stands and announces to the congregation that the children's youth group, *Newborn Individuals Getting God Enlightenment Readings* will perform a reenactment of the last days of Pontius Pilate. She smiles a big bright white smile and adds, "Something we all hope and pray for!"

I lean over and get Marmalade's attention. *"Newborn Individuals Getting God Enlightenment Readings?"* I ask in a whisper. "Seriously?"

Juice shrugs. "They thought it would make the word less offensive."

"They were *very* wrong." I say solemnly.

"I doubt that is what they were really trying to do. Rex is racist as fuck." Millie says in a low growl. "I'm not sure you noticed, but Marmalade and Paal are the only people in the room with any melanin in their skin."

A dozen or so costumed children flock to the stage. The blond youth leader gives them direction. Some of the children are dressed as Roman Soldiers. Four of the boys are dressed in tattered robes tied at the waist with rope. A blond girl, no more than ten years old wears a white bikini top and a long white skirt. She starts the production with an announcement. *"I am Procla, the wife of Pontius Pilate! I forsake my husband and ask to be taken as a bride of Jesus!"*

A small boy dressed in a black robe, presumably playing the part of Pontius Pilate, darts onto the scene and hides behind one of the podiums. The four boys dressed in tattered robes come up to the girl. One steps forward. *"We are disciples of Jesus. We welcome you as a bride of Christ!"*. All four of the boys come and hug the girl and start kissing her cheeks. There is laughter in the crowd.

"Are we watching some macabre version of child porn?" Millie whispers.

The boy in black darts back and forth across the stage.

*You boys should catch my husband and cut his head off so I can be with ya'all!"* The girl playing Procla cries out. *Look, there he is!"* She points at the boy in black just as he darts again.

*"You! Roman Soldier!"*. One of the disciples calls out. *"Help us catch Pontius Pilate!"*

A chase around the sanctuary begins with the children dressed as Roman Soldiers and the four disciples follow the boy in black. The girl stands on the stage and shouts directions. Finally, the boy in black is caught and hauled to the stage by the child sized Roman Soldiers.

*Pontius Pilate! You killed our Jesus! What do you have to say for yourself?"*. One of the disciples shouts loudly.

*"Jesus was nothing but an unruly Jew!* The boy dressed in black cries out. *"I don't know what you and my wife think was so special about him!"*

*"He is the son of God! The Messiah! The Redeemer! That's what was special about him!"*. Another disciple says. *"Roman soldier! Give me your sword!"*

"The children are putting on a murder play. Unbelievable." Paal says in loud whisper.

I watch silently. Two of the Roman Soldiers take swords from their belts and hand the plastic weapons to the disciples. *"Do what you will, follows of Jesus the Nazarene!"*

*"Hold him down!"*. One of the two disciples with swords cries out. *We will cut off the bastard's head!"*. The boy playing Pontius Pilate is held down and both the sword wielding boys bring their weapons down on Pontius Pilate's neck. Theatrical blood bags pop and blood squirts onto the costumes of the Roman Soldiers and the white bikini top on the girl. She leans over and spits on the back of the boy dressed in black. *"Thank you, boys, for saving me from a life of eternal damnation! I am a bride of Jesus now!"*

The Roman Soldiers drag the body of Pontius Pilate to the side of the stage and the boys dressed as disciples gather around the girl and appear to feel her up while kissing her cheeks. The play ends with all the children including the now dead Pontius Pilate coming to the stage and taking a bow. The congregation claps wildly.

"Well, *that happened.*" I whisper to Millie.

"This is worse than I thought." Millie answers. "Thankfully, we probably won't be around to listen to what ever sermon Rex has cooked up."

Reverend Rex Ratchet struggles to get out of his electric cart. He makes his way to the center of the stage. After settling the congregation down, he thanks the youth leader. The man is clearly laboring to stand. Breathing seems to be a real challenge for him as he starts to speak. *"Christians in Pursuit of the Scoundrel Pontius Pilate* are anointed with holy oil. When we do this, we are making a physical effort to open ourselves to the spiritual truth that we are God's, and we are committing ourselves wholly into the care of the *Rock* that is the church. Please approach the alter in an orderly manner for this week's anointment."

*Rock*, I think. There's that word again. We are about in the middle of the sanctuary, so I get to watch as Ratchet performs the act of anointing people with oil. Most of the men get a finger dot or a quick swipe with a thumb across the forehead. The women get significantly more anointing as the Reverend rubs their faces, touching their lips and neck. Marmalade is right. Ratchet sizes up what women he wants with his *church* rituals. A pregnant woman with brown hair approaches the minister. Her bright pink t-shirt dress is pulled tight over her swollen belly. She doesn't look at the man as he erotically rubs oil on her cheek and neck. When he leans forward to whisper in her ear, she pulls away and quickly walks off. Our row is next. I glance over at Paal. "Ready?"

He nods with a smile. A small, old fashioned smart phone is in his hand. He starts accessing the church's private network. Millie steps out into the aisle and starts walking, head held down towards her ex-husband. In her hand is a small can of red spray paint, concealed until now in the folds of her dress. I walk behind her, taking as long of strides as I can to keep up. Millie keeps her head down. There are two people in front of her, a man and his wife. The man gets a quick dot of oil on his forehead. The woman gets Ratchet's thumb and forefinger on her ear lobe and few words softly spoken. The lights in the sanctuary start to dim and a video starts to play on the screens.
Millie lifts her head up. I see recognition immediately in Rex Ratchet's eyes. His mouth forms a circle, and he shuffles backwards like he is witness to a

ghost, which in many respects, he very much is. "Rex Ratchet, you are a bastard. This ends now and I am happy to be a part of your undoing!" Millie growls loud enough for the first few of rows of congregants to hear her words. The can of spray-paint comes up and in two quick swipes of Millie's hand, a bright red, large, upside-down cross is painted on the white fabric covering Rex's ample front. Thanks to Paal's crackerjack technical skills, the screens at every *Christians in Pursuit of the Scoundrel Pontius Pilate* around the country are playing the same thing; A list of the congregants who had filed complaints about Ratchet and the church's leaders are filling the screens along with details of the complaints. Dates of criminal inquires and descriptions of what the inquiries were will follow. I see that Millie is holding Rex Ratchet in a death stare. I genuinely think the man may stroke out. I turn around and face the congregation, most of whom are still trying to figure out what is going on. Paal turns the microphone attached to my suit on.

*Ladies and Gentlemen, my name is Justin Thyme. I am from a time long past. In that time people were generally more decent human beings and the United States of America was a far better place. This beautiful woman with me is my wife, Millie Thyme. We are here today with a message. I am going to tell you how you have been acting and then I am going to tell you how you should be acting.*

"Who is this boring fucker? What happened to Reverend Rexford?" I hear a male voice call out. I glance over my shoulder. Reverend Rex Rexford is sitting on one of the stairs of the church's stage holding his head in his hands. I turn back to the audience, most of whom are staring and pointing at the screens.

*I used to be one of you. I only cared about myself. I did not care about people who I saw as less than me. I did not care about my neighbor in the least. I lied a lot. I took advantage of women. I wasn't a very good man, and I was not a good person. I thought it was how I would get ahead... I thought it was best to only care about what made me feel good, what made me more money, what got me more things.*

I see that a few people close to where I stand are looking at me. I point at one of the men.

*"You have a tattoo on your back. Why is that?"*

"It is to show my allegiance to the church... to God. My tattoo is in honor of God." The man answers. He has an angry look on his face. I feel Millie squeeze close behind me.

*"You like most others in this congregation have the same tattoo. You all believe in the Bible, yes?"*

The man and the woman standing beside him nod energetically. "The Bible is law!" The woman yells out.

*"The laws you refer to are mostly in Leviticus and Deuteronomy. Leviticus nineteen, verse twenty-eight says, "You shall not make gashes in your flesh for the dead or incise any marks on yourselves."*

The whole of the congregation has stopped looking at the screens on the wall listing the misdeeds of the *Church of Christians in Pursuit of the Scoundrel Pontius Pilate* and are now looking at me. I smile. I still look like a corpse, albeit a corpse in a suit. I am sure my appearance is off putting to some of these people. My words more so.

*That's in the Bible that few of you have chosen to read. What else have you allowed people like the Reverend Rex Ratchet to lead you astray on?".* I walk forward a step or two. Millie follows close behind.
*There is all sort of stuff that happens under the umbrella of this church that is just wrong. Earlier I heard your minister say that this church is a Rock. That is not true. This church, any church is composed of one thing and one thing only... it's congregation. You are the church. The church is you. If the Church is bad, you are bad. If the church is good, you are good. Ladies and gentlemen, this church has been bad for a long time. It's time for you change that."*

"Fuck this boring asshole. Someone end him!" A voice in the back calls out. I know I only have a few moments longer to talk.

*"Just recently, this church and the state of Texas put a ban on masturbation. Specifically male masturbation. Men, they made it illegal in this state for you to touch*

*yourself for purpose of self-gratification. A human act has been outlawed. Why? Because the Church said it should be. Just like many churches have said that a woman should not be able to make choices about her own body."*

"What is that on Reverend Ratchet?" A woman close by asks.

I have turned slightly. I see that Ratchet has stood up. Millie did a good job. The upside down cross, a sign of the devil, runs from just below his double chin to just above where I assume his crotch is. I hear Ratchet trying to talk into his microphone. Paal has it shut off. Now he is screaming. I hear him call out, *"Kill the infidels."* and point at us. I shake my head and continue.

*"You need to start asking more questions about what your government does and why it does it. You are all good people. Good people who have been led down the wrong path…"*

A gunshot rings out. I wait for pain and feel none. Am I too dead to feel pain? The congregation gasps. I turn around. Behind me, I hear Millie whisper, *"Holy shit."*

Reverend Rex Ratchet's obese body is on the ground. He is struggling to get up. The red upside down cross has been covered by a dark, widening pool of blood. The pregnant brunette in the pink t-shirt dress stands over his struggling body. In her right hand is a shiny revolver. I don't know shit about guns, but it looks like a big one.

"This bastard did this to me!" She screams, her left hand is on her belly and the right is shaking, but still pointing the gun at the struggling minister. "He put this baby in me. I was a goddamn virgin! Fuck you, *Reverend* Ratchet!" The gun goes off again. Ratchet's body jerks and goes still. *So much for Marmalade getting to dispatch Reverend Ratchet with a cool opening line.* I think to myself.

I turn back to the congregation. *"You have all been made to do awful things. It is time to change. It is time to love your neighbor as you love yourself. That doesn't mean sleeping with other people's wives or husbands. It means caring for one another and working toward shared objectives! Long ago the people of this country forgot that the government of the United States of America is of the People. It's the first line of the Constitution... WE THE PEOPLE!"*

Another shot rings out. You know how in old movies, someone gets shot and says, *I didn't feel it?* That is complete bullshit. I felt it. Millie did too because whatever the ammunition was that hit me went through my body and hit her. She lets out a cry that hurt me a whole lot more than the bullet going through me. I feel her wrap her arms around my middle as Marmalade starts walking up the far side of the Sanctuary towards the stage. A second shot rings out. The bullet hits me in the left shoulder.

*"You are literally shooting the messenger!* I exclaim in a much weaker voice. *We cannot keep silencing people we don't agree with. There are not just two sides to any discussion. Sometimes we must meet in the middle. Do not judge or you will be judged!"*

I hear a third shot and feel the round go through my chest. Millie jerks. She exhales a rattled breath against my neck before saying, *"Justin, I love you."*

Mille and I crumple to the ground. Darkness consumes us. The last words I hear Reverend Marmalade Julius say in his booming, powerful voice are *'Congregation, in this time of tragedy and confusion, please join me in prayer.'*

Chapter 70
Old school chums. My ego is hungry.
Conrad Peterson House Someplace in America
Land of the Free(ish) Home of the Brave(ish)


"I need to take this call." Elizabeth Eaton exclaims as she dismounts Conrad and lays down, naked beside him on the bed.

"Should I just wait here or finish myself, Poppet?" Conrad asks, grasping himself.

The attorney shakes her head with her finger to her lips as she answers the call turning the speaker phone on. "Elizabeth Eaton... Is this really *My Corn Hole is Butt Hurt?*"

"Liz; you cunt, law school was almost a half century ago. Do we need to keep with the incredibly hurtful nicknames?" May Cornwall Bhutthert, Chief Justice of the United States Supreme Court says with an arrogant tone.

"Apparently, yes.  Yes, we do." Elizabeth Eaton answers. "I'll just stick with Butt Hurt."

"Did I catch you preparing a legal brief to sue some poor corporation into oblivion or were you sharpening your pencils to figure out how much it might be worth to take Mickey D's to court over the actual length of their French fries versus what you see on the posters?" Bhutthert asks.

"Actually, I was just fucking my boyfriend. Your call was coitus interruptus. What do you want, *Butt Hurt?*"

Conrad sits up in the bed and looks at Elizabeth with amazement.

May Cornwall Bhutthert laughs. "Liz, it is so good to hear your voice. Sometimes I miss law school and the fun our gang had together."

"And then you remember that you are Chief Justice of the United States Supreme Court and the overwhelming responsibility to look for cases that will bring enough publicity to feed your oversized ego consumes the rest of your day." Eaton sighs. "Seriously, I was just about to cum. My man has a big dick, and he is hard as a rock. I'd like to get back to riding him like a Kentucky Derby jockey before I shift back to finding more billable hours in my passion for protecting the public from immoral actions of corporations. This is not a social call. What do you want?"

"Don't give me that made up *getting laid* shit, Liz, you couldn't get laid in a prison full of men doing life for rape." May Cornwall Bhutthert laughs at her crudeness. "You couldn't get laid by the dog with a jar full of peanut butter and a raw steak."

Conrad chokes back laughter as his eyes go wide.

"At least I didn't get full back tattoo of a certain Supreme Court Justice hoping that she would let me eat her out under her robe when she was sitting on the bench!" Elizabeth Eaton shoots back.

"Yeah, that didn't work out like I wanted. I mean, I've eaten so much pussy that my picture is on a *wanted poster at the humane society*, but I never got lip to lip with that bitch's lady bits! I got the back tattoo removed. *That hurt like hell*, but it was hard to go to the nude beaches in Europe with her pretty smiling face plastered across my back." Bhutthert says with a concessionary tone. "Seriously, now that we have the jocularity out of the way... I hear you have a case."
"I have lots of cases, Butt Hurt. You will need to be more specific." Elizabeth Eaton growls.

"Come on now, you know I need to *feed my oversized ego*. The masturbator. The kid you told the judge to find guilty so you can appeal the case." Bhutthert says. "You are planning an appeal, right?"

Elizabeth Eaton sits up. "Trump Bob Good. Violated the Texas Spilt Seed law that took effect in our state because of the Alamo Compact."

"Yeah, yeah... the masturbator. Perfect first name, God rest President Donald J's very small soul." Bhutthert pauses. That's the one. When do you think you will appeal and how quickly do you think you can get the case to a federal appeals court?"

"Years, probably. It isn't like the justice system moves with any speed these days. Why? You want to find for the state and make a landmark out of this?" Elizabeth Eaton asks suspiciously.

"Oh no! Quite the opposite in fact." May Cornwall Bhutthert exclaims. "You see, I have been noticing that my Q score is suffering. People just don't care what I have to say about deciding in favor of some chemical company dumping polychlorinated biphenyls into a river or justifying partisan congressional oversight of a presidential cabinet department. People are pissed off Liz! They have been so pissed off that most of them can't remember why they are pissed off! I figure the time is right to shake shit up, and your case may be the one to do it."

"I feel like I am going to need a shower after this conversation." Elizabeth Eaton sighs. "Are you telling me that your court is going to find in favor of Good?"
"If you really are raw dogging your man, and I know you wouldn't be breaking federal law by using a condom, Liz, you will need a shower anyway!" Bhutthert cackles again at her own crassness. "Tell me about this young man and the case. Is he a good-looking attractive sort that is going to make women swoon?"

Elizabeth gently slaps Conrad's hand away from caressing her right breast. "Bob Good is a teenager. Swoon?" Eaton chuckles. "I doubt it, but as they say, there is a horse for every rider. He comes from a low-income middle America family who can't afford this nonsense. I would guess he is on the spectrum of autism, but I am not a doctor. My daughter tells me that he whacks off constantly. He had a girlfriend who apparently wanted to end things with him in the poorest way possible, so she recorded him masturbating and shared the video with everyone she knows. Accuser turned him in after the Texas Spilt Seed law passed, I assume for the money and of course there was some extracurricular drama involved. Cops picked him up. He went to court. Here we are." Elizabeth pauses. "May, this guy is a bit of a mess... but no more so and in some respects, much less than the rest of the public that have been utterly fucked with the laws that have passed or reversed in the past few decades. Seriously, what is your angle here? You have not really been a champion of any idea giving the public legitimate autonomy over themselves."

"Is your daughter polishing the masturbating kid's meat whistle?" Bhutthert asks.

Eaton laughs. "No. *Absolutely not.* Her... boyfriend is good friends with this kid. A blessing for Bob Good. He'd still be in jail without the help."

May Cornwall Bhutthert makes a noise that sounds like she might be blowing her nose. Or honking the horn on an antique car. "Ok...Ok... I am going to call the local judge. You know she was a few years behind us at law school? I'll get the boy sentenced. Something light weight. No time. Maybe make him wear that cuck cage those boys in Texas came up with." Bhutthert laughs. "What sort of sick shit are those fuckers into anyway? Wish I was a fly on the wall during *that* committee meeting! Get the paperwork filed right away in Federal court. I will take it from there. We need to be careful with your arguments. I don't want *Lawrence* reversed and I don't want to give the right-wing fucks more of a runway to add things to the Spilt Seed law before it can get tossed in the trash can of legal errors."

Elizabeth Eaton shakes her head. "This is a wholly inappropriate conversation, May." She sighs and adds, "You know where I am taking this case, right? I want to reverse all the shit *you* did to Abortion."

"Liz, you sweet little cunt. *Of course,* I know what you are doing. I mean, it's nice and all that you are representing this poor, autistic, hand fucker but anyone with a law degree or a brain in their head can see that you taking this case can't just be about helping men Lone Ranger without

Tonto! You know, Liz... the courts were absolute heroes when we limited personal freedoms! The right loved, loved, loved thinking they owned some *conservative justices*! We got jet plane rides to exotic locations. Stays in the nicest places *anywhere*. Shit, Lizzo, I had a harem of young men and women I could pick from whenever I wanted after I upheld the bans on abortion. It was *wonderful!*"

"What has changed?" Eaton asks suspiciously.

"I ain't so famous and in the news anymore. I'm a little bored and I want some camera time." Bhutthert says. After we get rid of the self-lovin' ban, we use the precedent in a new case and I reverse *Dobbs* and re-legalize a woman's right to choose, I'll be so goddamn popular that I could run for president! And maybe I will!" Bhutthert laughs. "No need to read between the lines. I am running for President of the United Fucking States. And I will win! You know, Liz. I plan on putting you on my short list for AG. What do you think about that?"
"I think I am happy being an attorney out here in Middle America." Elizabeth Eaton says softly. "But thank you."

"Still the same old Liz Eaton. Can't be bought, bribed or compromised!" Bhutthert honks her nose again. "I think I caught a cold in Ibiza during a gang bang."

"Call a pop star. That could be a song." Elizabeth Eaton says sourly.

The Supreme Court Justice sucks in a breath. "Liz, you *cunt*, that is an *excellent* idea! I always wanted to be a singer! Maybe I can win one of the Eurovision awards! Do they give them to 'Mericans anymore?" Bhutthert sniffles. "Anyway, get the appeals paperwork going. Let's get this *Jackin' the Beanstalk* case moving and May Cornwall Bhutthert back in the news!" The line goes dead.

"I am speechless." Conrad says. "First, you *know* the Chief Justice of the United States Supreme Court. Second, this *personality of yours* that you have been hiding is something to behold!"

Elizabeth Eaton stares at the ceiling. "Yes. Went to law school with her. No, I didn't sleep with her. Yes, I can be bawdy when I am provoked. Please don't tell my daughter."

Conrad raises his eyebrows. "Provoked? You... called the Chief Justice of the United States Supreme Court, *Butt Hurt*. You... intimated that she wanted to perform a sex act on another court justice..." His voice trails off. "I am not sure that Anne Margret would believe me if I did tell her!"

"Bhutthert admitted as much as you may recall." Elizabeth says. "May Cornwall Bhutthert is... Well, you heard what she is. She has not changed one little bit since law school. I happen to think that she obtained the nickname Butt Hurt long before law school, but certainly we *all* called her that more than a time or two. I think she wears the moniker with pride." After turning on to her side, Elizabeth props herself up on one arm. "We are going to take the Good case to the Supreme Court. This is what I want; of course, I... I just thought... well, hell. I didn't know if I would live long enough to see it get to the Supreme Court! I may not like how it's going to happen... but it's going to happen!"

Conrad strokes the side of her face gently. "I am proud for you, Poppet." He reaches over with the other hand and caresses her bare breast. "Now, why don't you work on polishing my meat whistle while I get lip to lip with your lady bits and then maybe we can finish what we started here."

"You learned those colloquialisms from that call, didn't you?" Eaton asks.

"Absolutely." Conrad answers with a laugh.

Chapter 71
An audience with the gods.
Darkness

*I feel like sighing. It's dark. There is no grasshopper. No cow. No bear. I can't sigh any more than I can rub my eyes or hold my hands up in front of my face. Been here. Done this. I think to myself.* Now I wait. A day, a year, a millennium. I won't know the difference. I guess there is comfort in that.

*"Are we dead now?"* Millie's Voice!

*"You are here?"* I ask with what I think is excitement.

*"Where is here, Justin?"* Millie asks.

*"Same place it always has been, I suppose. Nowhere. Somewhere. Anywhere. I am happy that you are in this place with me."*

There is silence. This isn't like Millie and I are sitting on a porch in rocking chairs waiting to hear our fate from the gods of the universe. I can't turn and look at her any more than I can walk away from this and into some other reality. I need to have faith that she is near me and hasn't been sucked off into the ethers of the afterlife. The silence continues for longer than I would feel comfortable with, if I could feel anything at all. Millie finally breaks her silence.

*"Sorry. I was coming to grips with the fact that this is actually the end... which is weird since I was so willing to do myself in not too long ago. I am happy you are here with me, Justin. I just am not sure yet if I am happy to be here. Something feels different from the first time.".* Millie's voice is flat. If this was a movie, reviewers would call Millie's voice *disembodied.*

*"You can feel something? I feel nothing at all."* I answer. *"But that is how it was for me the other times too."*

*"No. I can't really feel anything. We are certainly dead now, right? We were shot multiple times.* Millie answers.

*"I guess so. Both of us were dead before too. I am not sure we ever really came back to life."* I answer.

*"I hope we can stay together, Justin. Do you think we can stay together?".* Millie asks with in that weird, disembodied voice. If I could feel, I would think it was creepy, even though I know my voice must sound the exact same way to her.

There is motion in the darkness. It is faint. Like when you have a floater of dust in your eye. *Can you see that?"* I ask. *"The movement in the darkness?"*

*"Yes. Let's see what it is."*

I want to quip that we don't have much of a choice in the matter but don't, knowing that the sarcastic tone would be lost in translation anyway. The creatures seem to move towards me slowly at first and then suddenly, the Bear and the Cow are right next to me. The Grasshopper is perched on top of the Cow.

*"We are pleased to see you Justin and Millie. You have both done so well."* The cow says in her mooing voice.

The bear looks somber and stays silent. I note that he still has the big diamond earring in his left ear.

Mr. Grasshopper rises on to his hind legs and spreads his four forward legs and feet wide. *"Yes. Well, you have done, Justin and Millie."* It appears that the Grasshopper is smiling and nodding. *"Well, indeed! Plant seeds you did! Seeds make plants. Plants break rocks. Plants feed the people. Eat, People cannot, stones. Pleased I am!"*

*"Are we done now? What happens next? I ask. Can we stay together? Here? Wherever here is?"*

*"Feelings? I would like to know of your thoughts?"* The Grasshopper asks in its funny speech pattern. *"Think, do you. Motions and actions moved the rocks that impeded progress?"*

*"Does he always talk like this?"* Millie asks.

*"I think they can hear you."* I say to Millie. *"I don't believe we have the power to whisper anymore."*

The grasshopper appears to chuckle. I even see a little smile on Bruno's bear snout. The Grasshopper dances a little on the back of the cow. *"Language I have, all from time eternal from all peoples."* The creature's front four legs spread wide again. *"Jumbled may sound to your minds but true it is in mine!".* One of the little legs' motions away from me. I assume it is pointing at Millie. *"Princess of mine, please tell me. Think, do you and Prince Justin move the rocks that impeded the progress of your people?"*

Millie is silent for a few moments. *"I believe that our deaths may change the minds of some of the members of that church. I think that people are flawed in how they think about their beliefs. We are taught that our individual thoughts and beliefs are empirical, and we should act on them. We are never taught that we need to constantly reevaluate our thoughts and apply new information to how we believe and act."*

*"Messiah's, you think you are?".* The grasshopper challenges Millie.

*"No. I don't think that. Our deaths will be forgotten in short order, I am sure. But our actions and the results that followed may allow others... like our friend Marmalade, to create a pathway for people to accept thoughts and actions contrary to their own.".* Millie answers. *"It appears that one of the congregations eliminated my ex-husband Rex Ratchet from doing more harm."*

*"Oh? Murder you think is good?"* The grasshopper jumps up and down on the back of the cow.

Millie's response comes quickly. *"Humans since the dawn of time have killed one another. Sometimes it is justified and sometimes it is not. Rexford Ratchet victimized people after he gained the power to do so. He didn't have to act the way he did, he choose to act the way he did... both towards me and towards the people of his congregation. If he simply would have been a minister and a businessperson like Marmalade, he would still be alive. The girl in the church who shot him said that Rex impregnated her. I am guessing against her will, which we might have called rape only a few decades ago. I suppose the justification for his murder is ultimately up to you?"*

*"Fine answer you have said, Princess Millie."*. The grasshopper turns solemn. *"Rexford Ratchet current waits in the Valley of Wailing where impossible, escape is as it should be. A plan we have for Rexford Ratchet. You are correct Millie. Lives are reflected at all points in existence. We here see to the mirrors.* The Grasshopper seems to turn its attention to me. *Prince Justin, what say you? Is your agreement that you did what objectives you were sent to attend to?"*

I think I am shaking my head. Realizing that maybe the three Gods or whatever they are, in front of me maybe can't see my head shake or infer my silent answer, I say.  *"No. I am sure that I did not do everything that I could."*

The grasshopper seems to grin again. *"Fine answer, another that is, Prince Justin...* It hops up and down and I perceive that its face comes close to mine. *"We do what we can when we can and how we can.*

*"We do the can can... can?"*. I can't help myself. The bear shakes its head. The cow seems to laugh a little.  I see the bear mouths the word, *"Smartass."*

The Grasshopper points a leg at me. *Princess Millie, Prince Justin... Decide I have your fates, temporary they are."*

I want to look at Millie, grab her hand, squeeze it and tell her everything is going to be ok. That isn't possible, of course. Instead, I speak up.  *"Millie and I would like to remain together. If that is an option. Please."*.

The bear chuckles. *That can't be a good sign,* I think.

*"Life is long and through it you both had individual dreams of life happenings that humans have.".* The Grasshopper hops off the cow. Like it had the night the thing told me to break up rocks, it walks close to my vision like Mr. Peanut. *I wish I could gift this little guy a top hat.* The Grasshopper appears to stroke its chin with one of its little legs. This seems to go on for more than a comfortable amount of time. If I could feel discomfort, I'd be feeling it now.

*"Princess Millie, babies you have brought into the world, many?"* The Grasshopper says slowly.

*"Yes.".* Millie answers in her flat disembodied voice.
*"Gift, I would like to grant to you and Prince Justin of a child to be born of you."* The Grasshopper continues to speak slowly.

There is silence. I am trying to figure out what the Grasshopper is trying to say. We are pretty dead at this point; I think and neither of us is either able to produce children or of the correct age to produce children.

*"That is a nice gesture."* Millie says. *"I cannot bear children and Justin cannot... impregnate anyone. I mean... you know, his tool... it works well enough. REALLY WELL, I MEAN! It just, you know... shoots blanks."*

The cow chuckles. I see the bear smile as it shifts its weight from one foot to the other.

The Grasshopper turns to me. *"Prince Justin, believe in me, do you?"*

*"Of course."* I answer without thought.

The Grasshopper turns back to where I assume Millie is. *"Princess Millie, believe in me, do you?"*

Millie's voice answers quickly. *"Yes. I do."*

The Grasshopper turns back to me and winks before addressing Millie further. *"Princess of mine, If I tell you that you shall have a child, you shall have a child.".*

I really want to hold Millie's hand now.

The Grasshopper turns back to me. *"Yours this child shall be, Prince Justin. Care for this child you must, care for Princess Millie you must. Responsibility you understand this is?"*
*"With all respect, we are both lay dead on the floor of a church in Texas. We are both old in terms of reproductive humans and neither of us was able to produce a child when we died. How will this happen?"* I ask.

The cow moos out a series of laughter. Bruno the bear seems to dance a little before it says in its deep voice. *"We haven't done this in so long, I can't wait."*

The Grasshopper leans forward into my face. *"Prince Justin, Princess Millie, you are going to rise from the dead.".* Four of its arms spread wide and I *feel* it touch me. The sensation is electric... in a good way! All at once my brain seems to experience optimism, happiness, hope and what can only be explained as unbridled joy.

*"Oh, Boy! Oh Boy!".* The Bear steps forward. *Tell me when, Boss! I love watching the resurrections!"*

The Grasshopper steps back. *"Princess Millie and Prince Justin, a long and healthy life you will live on earth. Help those you can, when you can, how you can. Teach your child well and ensure her upbringing is healthy and happy. She who is born to you is going to be a mighty leader.* It steps forward and touches each of us again with two of its legs. *"I like the name Sarah."* The Grasshopper nods to Bruno the Bear.
The bear steps towards us with those two big paws. Just before touching me, it leans forward, it's snout close to my ear. *"I guess your spank bank has to be empty now, eh, meat puppet?"*

I think I might be grinning when I answer the bear, but who the hell knows. *"Or my spank bank is overflowing!  Princess Millie is pretty hot!"*

The bear growls and says, "Still *a smart-ass.".* Things go dark when he hits me with his massive paw.

## Chapter 72
Resurrection. Rickrolled, again.
Christians in Pursuit of the Scoundrel Pontius Pilate, Dallas Texas
Still a place in the United States of America
Land of the Free(ish) Home of the Brave(ish)

I open my eyes. My face is stuck to the carpet with drying sticky black blood that I assume came from some hole in my body. There is apparently a white sheet over my head because I see nothing but white. I hear the Reverend Marmalade Julius praying. I stop and try and listen to what he is saying. It's something responsive with the congregation. *Jesus save us* or some shit like that.

I feel Millie's hand rub my back. "I'm here Justin. Are we under a sheet? Where did they get a sheet?"

"Who are you? What are we doing here?" I ask with a faux panicked voice. The crowd has started singing a rock and roll version of *What a friend we have in Jesus* with AI Rick Astley. We have been Rickrolled once more.

"No... no.... There has been a mistake! You aren't Justin! Who are you? Oh, God." Millie cries out in a panicked voice.

I try my best *Darth Vader* imitation. "Penelope Pudding Snatch; I am Woody Womb Pecker, controller of Puff the Magic Penis Dragon. I am here to pleasure you!"

There is silence behind me. Rick Astley and the congregation start crooning about trials and tribulations. It strikes me that they are singing along while two or three murdered people lie in their midst.

528

Millie pinches my side so hard it hurts! "You are such an asshole, Justin!" Then she giggles. "Woody Womb Pecker! I never would have thought of that one." She laughs again softly. "What do we do next?"

"Stand up, I suppose."

I hear Rick Astley singing about finding a faithful friend to share sorrows with. Seems like a good time to rise from the dead.

Millie and I sit up and slowly stand.

As it turns out... if you really rise from the dead, it really freaks the fuck out of people. In retrospect, maybe I should have tossed the sheet or whatever it was off our bodies before we stood up. I didn't and I am sure the three women and four men that fainted into the aisle thought we were a pair of ghosts. Rick Astley doesn't notice that his show has basically ended as people have started screaming and running for the exit. I glance around and find the man I am pretty sure put the kill round into my chest. I glare hard at him. He may have had a heart attack. I'm not sure. He grabbed his chest and fell to the ground. Let the Bear and the Grasshopper deal with him. I am sure there is plenty of room in the *Valley of Wailing*.

People push past us to leave the church. It occurs to me that all these people are extremely fearful of exactly the sort of thing they spend so much time praying for.

I reach blindly for Millie, turning to look after my hand finds hers. I freeze.
"Holy shit, Millie! Your eyes!"

"What about them?"

Millie's eyes are the brightest most intoxicating color of blue I have ever seen. I instantly promise myself to spend the rest of my life looking into those eyes, "They are beautiful, Millie. You are beautiful!" I kiss her in the forehead and pull her to the stage where Marmalade is standing with his jaw open.

"You!" He points at us. "You were...". His voice drops to a whisper. "You were dead!"

I look at Millie. She smiles at me. I smile back at her before turning to Marmalade and saying in my best creepy voice. "Are you seeing Dead People, Marmalade Julius?" I lean close to his shaking body and narrow my eyes. "Marmalade Julius, I am here to tell you that wicked people may be cast into the Valley of Wailing at any given moment! The wicked deserve this punishment! Divine Justice, whatever one may think that is, will not prevent the wicked from being destroyed at any moment! The wicked suffer under a constant repression of hell on earth! The wicked should think because they are not in the Valley of Wailing yet, they will soon be on their way there! You must Repent Marmalade Julius! Fall to your knees and ask forgiveness of your wrongs or you may be seized from this earth and taken to the Valley of Wailing!"

Reverend Marmalade Julius, tears falling from his eyes falls to his knees and starts praying loudly. People are still screaming and pushing each other to get out of the church. Millie and I look at each other and hug. She stands on her tip toes and kisses my lips. "Your eyes are a great color too!" She motions at the now prostrate Marmalade Julius who is still audibly wailing and praying beside the covered dead body of Rexford Ratchet. "You may have laid it on a little thick."

"Marmalade. Stop it. Stop blubbering and get up." I command.

He sits up and whispers. "I... I... Justin, It's impossible that you are here."

"Ah shit, Juice. You are *supposed* to be a believer." I point at him with a smile. "Yes. And we are alive. All thanks to you and your thoughts and prayers."

"Really?" Marmalade asks, still whispering.

"No.  Thoughts and prayers are complete bullshit.  The answer in actions." I answer flatly. "But, we are ready to go home now."

"The police are coming!" Paal says. "Someone got outside and called emergency services and told them there are ghosts in the church."

"No one reported the three murders that happened here?" I ask incredulously.

"I blocked all the cell signals so Marmalade could finish the service." Paal touches the bullet holes in my suit. "This is something."

"Everything is something." I say with a grin. "Is the plane ready? We need to get out of here before we have to explain something we can't."

Paal nods. "Got it sitting on the tarmac running and waiting for us."

I turn and grab the still grounded Marmalade under the arms and lift him up. Momentarily, I am shocked at my strength. "Let's go Juice."
"You and Millie were dead. Your blood! It is over there on the floor!" Juice cries out.

I nod. "Yep."

Millie and I help Marmalade as Paal leads us out of the church. A woman comes up to us. "You are actors!" She points at Millie and me. "Actors! And agents of the Devil!"

I glance over at Millie. She rolls her eyes. I can tell some serious sarcasm should be employed here.

"Actors or Agents of the Devil? I think you must pick! Would I let you go free if I were an Agent of the Devil? Would I allow myself to be seen if I were an actor? Is Reverend Julius an actor too? Maybe we are all actors, and the world is but a stage! I motion with one arm back at the black blood that covers a significant part of the carpet in the front of the church. "See for yourself, our blood on the carpet in the church. Your people killed us. We rose from the dead and we have returned."

"You lie! I do not believe you!" The woman cries out.

I pull my suit coat away and wave it at the woman. "Put your fingers in the holes the bullets made! See the holes! Stop doubting and believe!"

"Oh, God!" The woman drops to her knees.

I look down and say, "Because you have seen us, you believe. The ones who are truly blessed are those who will not have seen but believe anyway! Maybe you can hang a bullet around your neck now instead of that cross!"

Paal comes and grabs me. "Dude, she already *has* a bullet hanging around her neck on a chain. Stop fucking around with these people. They have *more* ammunition, and they will shoot you *again*!"

We hurry out of the church and into the transporter. Somehow, Paal gets the thing to go around Police roadblocks. We board the plane and get airborne. Marmalade is silent for a long time before he turns to me.

"Justin... Justin... I... This has been such an incredible day. I simply don't know what else can happen today that would surprise me more than what already has!"

I laugh. Paal is asleep, his electronic pad still in his hand. I look over at Millie and raise an eyebrow. She smiles, rubs her belly lightly and nods.

I turn back to Juice and say, "Millie and I are going to have a baby. It's a girl and we are naming it Sarah."

Marmalades looks at me. His eyes seem to lose focus before they roll towards the top of his head. I reach out and gently lower him into a laying position as he passes out.

"You seem to have gotten some strength back." Millie says, squeezing my bicep. "I think I am looking forward to you carrying me across the threshold when we get back!"

"This wasn't much of a honeymoon, was it?" I ask.

"What girl doesn't want to get shot, die and be resurrected on her honeymoon?" Millie grabs my hand. "It was an adventure!"

"I'm hoping we have some of that Grasshopper luck splotched on us somewhere." I answer.

Millie smiles. She leans into my shoulder. "I used the bathroom when we boarded the plane. I have a spot the size of a saucer on my leg. I bet you do too." She sighs contentedly. "We are going to have a baby! We are going to be *parents*, Justin!"

I rub my head on hers. "I know. We are going to be parents. We needed those lucky splotches to be about ten times bigger!"

Chapter 73
Unfinished Business. Now we know.
Gulf of Mexico
Just outside of the territorial waters of the United States of America
Land of the Free(ish) Home of the Brave(ish)


Captain Edward "Eddie" Smith, soon to stand before congress and become Rear Admiral Edward Smith looks over at his wife, Drizella Smith as she stands beside him in the conn of the new Shark Class Submarine USS Mako. They are on a 'Tiger' cruise where Navy servicemen can go on a short (2-3 day) cruise with family, usually in the friendly confines of United States Territorial waters. He is just about to give his wife *control* of the submarine when his communications officer approaches.

After saluting, the communication officer speaks quickly. "Sir, the USS Hagel and the USS Tiger have located a foreign submarine less than one nautical miles southeast of us. She is at minus three hundred and fifty feet bearing north at a speed of five knots an hour. Conjecture from the Hagel is that the vessel is the rogue Kalvari Class submarine the Texas Militia acquired some time back that is suspected of striking the French hospital ship, Liberte'. We have orders to intercept and either sink or surface the ship, sir.

"How much room do we have?" The captain asks his navigator. She double checks her controls and answers. "We are at minus one hundred fifty sir. The floor is minus eleven thousand two hundred sloping south, southwest to minus thirteen thousand four hundred."

"Communications, see if you can contact that Kalvari class. Send some pings and open all the communication lines. I'd rather surface her than sink her." He looks over at his helmsman. "Increase speed to fifteen knots. Bear right to 190 degrees make depth minus 350. Let's close the distance quickly."

"Aye, Aye Captain." Comes the reply. A ping is heard in the small confines of the fast attack submarine as it drops forward and picks up speed through the water.

The communications officer comes back over and punches a few buttons. "I have the Kalvari on the Gertrude, sir. They say the name of their vessel is the 'Davy Crocket'."

"How appropriate. Good thing we are friends with the Indians, and I know that ship fairly well." Captain Smith says. "Kalvari Class Submarine, this is Captain Edward Smith from the USS Mako. You and your crew are in violation of International Law and United States Law. Please surface your vessel and prepare to be boarded."

"Go fuck yourself, Smith!" Says a course voice over the loudspeakers in the conn. Drizella Smith immediately recognizes the voice of her philandering scum bag of an ex-husband. She looks at her current husband with alarm. *It's him!* She mouths.

Captain Smith nods grimly. "Who do I have the pleasure of speaking with?"

"This is Major Richard Lecher of the Organized Texas Militia. We are citizens of the great *nation* state of Texas! We have just as much right to be here as you do, Smith!" There is some commotion like Lecher dropped the microphone on floor. "This is international waters we are in, in case your compasses stopped working, Mako!"

"Well, Major Dick Lecher, we use an inertial navigation system on this ship. Haven't used a compass for decades. Yes, you are just barely in international waters but there happens to be an *international warrant* out for your arrest and the capture of your ship for the attack on the French Naval Vessel Liberte'. Please surface your ship as it is safe to do so and prepare to be boarded." Captain Smith speaks in a calm and direct manner.

"It's *RICHARD* you ass! *MAJOR RICHARD LECHER!* And you can go fuck yerself if ya think I'm putting this ship topside!" Lecher screams into his microphone.

Drizella Smith covers her mouth with a snort. She doubles over, laughing, not realizing what dangers lurk under the sea.

"Major Dick Lecher, you are putting your crew and their safety at risk. Surface your ship and prepare to be boarded." Captain Smith says with a tone bordering on boredom.

"It is *Richard Lecher! Major* Richard Lecher of the Texas Militia. *The Organized and Regulated Texas Militia!* You think you want a piece of me, Smith? Come and get me!" The sound of the microphone being thrown down is heard over the speakers in the conn on the USS Mako followed by Lecher making an order to take the ship down. "Make those pedophile mother fuckers chase us down!" The crew on the Mako hears Lecher cries out.

"Set depth to minus five hundred feet. Mark speed even with the Kalvari class. I doubt he could hit us with whatever armament might still be on that tub... but, listen for doors opening." The Captain points at the speaker that emits random noises. "He left the connection open and the microphone on. Sonar! Keep me up to date on the depth of that Kalvari."

"Do you know how deep he can go?" Drizella asks her husband.

Captain Smith nods. "I know *about* how deep a Kalvari *can safely* go. I doubt if Lecher knows." He looks down at his wife. "This probably isn't going to end well. Do you want to stay and listen or go to my quarters?"

"Stay." Drizella answers with a firm tone.

"Minus Seven Fifty, Sir!" The sonar tech calls out. "Dropping quickly. Minus Eight Ten, twenty, thirty."

"Major Lecher, you are putting your crew and craft at risk. Stop descending immediately! Surface your ship and prepare to be boarded." Captain Smith says into his microphone.

"Minus 1200." The Sonar tech calls out.

"This is going to be ugly." Captain Smith mutters. "Communications, notify the Hagel and the Tiger what is going on. They are going to hear some terrifying sounds."

"Why aren't you following me, Smith? Are you scared?" Lecher's voice comes over the speakers.

"Nah, Major Dick Lecher. We've got over thirty torpedoes on board, each with a range of thirty nautical miles and they all can outrun that tin can you are in. I don't need to chase you. Why don't you surface the ship? Let's talk this over." The captain answers.

"The Texas Militia will yield to no one! I will not surface the 'Davy Crocket' so you and the goddamn *boring* government can steal it! Ya' all can just go fuck yourselves."

"Do you know what happened to Davy Crocket, Lecher? He surrendered at the Alamo and was executed on his knees by Santa Ana."

Lecher opens the microphone and swears into it. "That is a goddamn lie Smith. Fake fucking news! Crockett was a hero. He died fighting off the goddamn Mexicans for the independence of Texas. He was fighting those fucking Mexican rapists! That's what he was doing! You swamp dwelling government boys is always spreading fake news! Boring fake news pedophile fuckers is all any of you are!"

"The Kalvari is at minus seventeen hundred fifty feet and dropping fast, sir."

"Turn the volume down." Captain Smith orders in a soft, resigned voice. "We don't need to hear what's going to happen next in such detail."

"Should I try talking to him?" Drizella asks. "He sounds like he is off his rocker... but maybe he will listen to me? Shouldn't we try and save him from himself?"

Smith grimaces. "I think it is much too late to talk any sense into Major Dick Lecher."

On board the 'Davy Crockett' there is a large explosion as the hydrogen inside the diesel-powered submarine's battery packs explode. A screaming noise created by metal twisting against itself echoes through the entirety of the vessel as the pressure outside of the submarine equalizes with that of the inside. A severe debilitating pain envelopes the whole of Richard Lecher, as he turns and takes one last look at the depth gauge in the center of the control panel of the ancient India built, diesel powered submarine. Nineteen hundred and ten feet. For a very short amount of time, the only living human being on earth that knew the actual crush depth of a Kalvari Class Attack Submarine was Major Dick Lecher of the Organized and Regulated Texas Militia.

Chapter 74
Where this story ends.
Five Years Later Millie and Justin Thyme's house
Someplace in the United States of America
Land of the Free(ish) Home of the Brave(ish)

## You are probably wondering how this all worked out.

*Sarah Grace Thyme was born. She was and is a perfect little girl. She didn't cry at all. Slept through the night, every night. Eats well and is smart as a whip. Millie and I are both closer to one hundred years old than zero years old. Millie came through the pregnancy well. Vel and I delivered Sarah at birthing center in an undisclosed location. Sarah is a little over four now. Millie and I home school her. She is already reading at a high level and doing basic addition and subtraction. Her god parents, Marmalade and Vel adore her. She will have plenty of guidance through her life, I am sure of it. Millie and I purchased a seven-story building a few blocks from the Honorable Representative Nancy Pelosi Public Housing, Convalescence and Retirement Center. We remodeled and live in the top two floors. The first two floors are a public charter school that Marmalade has helped finance. The third floor is a chapter of Marmalade's new church. The fourth and fifth floor is a medical clinic run by Millie and me. We take care of people who live in the neighborhood. Marmalade pays for most of it.*

*My cousin Hank Thyme left the priesthood. He married the same woman he should have married twenty years ago. They are quite happy together. Hank is the lead pastor at the church that is in our building. Hank takes to preaching like a duck to water. His wife is a corporate lawyer. They don't live in the neighborhood, which is ok. Hank is pretty good with the people. I know he probably wants to move on to a wealthier church.*

*Willem and Wendy Williams moved to France with their daughter Katherine Williams and her husband Yoda Storm Trooper Williams. Willem has undergone a series of stem cell therapies in Paris to treat his ALS. The therapy has helped, but it will only slow the progress of the disease. It will not reverse the damages already done to Willem's body. If he had received similar therapies early on in his diagnosis in the United States, the overall prognosis may be better. Wendy is still practicing law. She handles clients from all over the world with her daughter Katherine. Yoda and Katherine buried their daughter on the island of French St. Martin in a funeral performed by (then) Father Henry Thyme. Willem and Wendy have already planned to have themselves interned by their granddaughter. Katherine's ordeal left her unable to have children of her own. She and Yoda made the decision to adopt two children from the United States. Elizabeth Eaton, Marmalade, Vel, Millie and I all helped with the adoption process. Yoda Storm Trooper Williams has made a name for himself as a coach of American Style Football in Europe. Using his connections from the University of Michigan, he got on as an assistant coach With Tom Brady's seven-time World Champion Scotland Kilts. Today, he is the defensive coordinator for the Paris Poodles.*

*Velvela Garfinkel and Marmalade Julius live in the same place and in the same way. It is still not safe for Vel to go out in public. There are just too many people who would like to harm her. Marmalade Julius renamed his church, Lighted Path. He has over three hundred locations across the country now. It took him a while to flush the Rex Ratchet loyalists out of the church, but when he did, the congregation grew thirty percent. As I had told Juice to do, the church pays for the removal of any tattoo associated with the Christians in Pursuit of Pontius Pilate. Both Marmalade and Vel treat Sarah Grace like she is their child.*

*Paal continues to head up Marmalade's security and help him get his message to the right places as to increase the coffers of the Lighted Path church.*

*Conrad Petersen and Elizabeth Eaton had a commitment ceremony in private. So far as I know, only their children were in attendance. Conrad sold PPP to a Chinese company that quickly decreased both the quality and cost of PPP personal massagers. I'm told that vintage Malcom vibrators sell for a lot of money on the secondary market. I never would have guessed that there would be a market for used vibrators. Conrad and Elizabeth have partnered with Weddington Coffee on building life like service Robots. Elizabeth giggles every time she talks about it. I can't figure out what that is all about.*

*Anne Margret Eaton and Fred Petersen got married. They practice law with Anne's mother, Elizabeth. Both Anne and Fred went to Europe for three years to attend a real law school at the insistence of Elizabeth Eaton who could not tolerate either*

*Anne's or Fred's inability to properly introduce evidence into court. After European law school, the Eaton-Peterson couple returned home and so far, has had two sets of twins.*

*Trump Bob Good's parents, Sookie Moonbeam Good and Cliffhanger Good divorced. Fred represented Cliffhanger who happily gave up the house and transporter in exchange for a speedy resolution. Cliffhanger moved to Canada and is now married to a native Quebecer. When Marmalade changed the church from Christians in Pursuit of the Scoundrel Pontius Pilate to Lighted Path Sookie left the church along with many other back tattoo enthusiasts. Her new church, Love Nest continues to encourage inter-congregational sexual intercourse along with complete fealty to the church leadership. She lost the house gained in the divorce when the Church, desperate for assets, convinced her to take an unaffordable loan out on the paid off property in order to fund a new hot tub/baptismal pool for the church sanctuary.*

*T. Bob Good disappeared shortly after his sentencing. Apparently, he was being interviewed by a Reporter for the Beijing Times. Everyone went to lunch and when they came back, both Bob and the reporter were gone. Bob keeps in touch with Cliffhanger and Fred.*

*Chief Supreme Court Justice May Cornwall Bhutthert experienced a massive stroke a short time after contacting Elizabeth Eaton about the Spilt Seed case. She passed away after a few days in hospice. Nearly five years later, her position as Chief Justice of the United States Supreme Court remains empty due to infighting in both parties over who should take her place as Chief Justice. Bhutthert's death ruined Elizabeth Eaton's plans for a speedy and positive resolution to Bob Good's Spilt Seed case.*

*Elizabeth Eaton has taken the appeals process on Bob Good v State of Texas et al. as far as the Federal Appellate Court. At the request of the Federal Attorney General's office, acting under pressure from congress... who now has oversight over all governmental departments, including the justice system... the appeals hearing on the case that could overturn the Texas "Prohibition against Spilt Seed Law" has been suspended indefinitely.*

*The United States Government is in complete disarray. It really has not been right since the 2020 election, an event that continues to be constantly pointed at by American born commentators who now live in other places. I watch my daughter grow up and I think that maybe we should follow the hordes of ex pat Americans who are now living in other countries. There has been a brain drain from the USA to the rest of the world. Then I remember that I... We, are here with a mission, we do what we can when we can and how we can... I am pretty sure the Grasshopper meant that needed to happen right here in the USA, right now.*

*One might think that rising from the dead would make one something of a spectacle. Maybe two thousand or so years ago, although, I doubt such was really the case, even then. Don't believe everything you read. Especially the stuff written when most people alive could neither read nor write. The incident in Texas was mostly buried by the technical expertise of Paal. Occasionally, some earnest person shows up looking for the messiah couple that died and were resurrected on the floor of a church in Texas. We laugh and laugh and tell them that if such a couple existed, they certainly wouldn't live in a slum next to a public housing unit.*

Millie and I are happy people. Our second lives are significantly better than our firsts. As long as we are able, we will listen to and consider the opinions of others, even those we do not agree with. We will continue to help people find their way in this very confusing world to the best of our ability. We will proudly stand up for the rights of anyone who has or is at risk of losing rights. We will actively and patiently explain the history of how the United States of America got to where it is to anyone who will listen.

**We will continue to do what we can, when we can, how we can.**

I encourage anyone who is able, to do the same.

Notes from the Authors
Somewhere in the United States of America
The Land of the Free and the Home of the Brave.

First, thank you for reading our book. We hope *Spilt Seed* was more fun to read than it was to write. What we really hope is that after finishing *Spilt Seed*, readers are inspired to act.

We started this book in late 2022. At some point, one of us gave up and threw the book away. Lots of authors start and end books they are writing that very same way. Most of 2023 went by and after listening to the news one night... who knows what night, most news cycles sound the same these days... we started writing again. Generally, when you write fiction, you like at least a few of your characters. We didn't like any of the characters in this story. Mostly, we probably didn't like the heavy subject we were writing about. Abortion is a conundrum wrapped in an enigma. It is certainly not the best subject to write about with humor.

By the time this is book is published, perhaps before it is read, Abortion of any kind may well be either illegal or on the way to being illegal in the United States of America. Abortion will never be *not* available. The practice of ending a pregnancy has been available for all human existence in some form or another. Most of those forms have not been safe for the women using them. Making something illegal does not make it unavailable. Generally, it just makes it unsafe.

There are very few things that are truly made up from the depths of our imaginations in this book. In some form, (outside of the 'future dated court cases') everything you have read happened in some form or another at some point during the last fifty years. From people proclaiming to be resurrected to the difficulties of finding proper health care in Texas to different cases of abuse in religious organizations... most scenes depicted in *Spilt Seed* happened. (So far as we know, there are no militias with submarines. *Yet.*)

Some readers might think it is incredible that so many of the things in *Spilt Seed* are painted truths. We happen to think it is fucking depressing.

As we wrote, current events kept changing the tone and tense. *We could not write this book fast enough!* There are things that we had in the book as something that happened in the future that had to be taken out. (Thank you, Texas and Alabama for the collective of fucked up views on women's reproductive rights!) Current events in our rapidly changing world kept adding new elements that had to be included in the story.

We are non-partisan and we have tried to be non-partisan in our approach to the story. *We hope that readers from both sides find objections with something we have written. Objections means you are thinking and thinking is very good.* Neither of us are registered to a political party… but we have been in the past. Both of us believe that the far fringes of both parties are in control, and both the Democrats and the Republican parties left mainstream America behind long ago. There is a danger in this that citizens of the United States of America need to pay careful attention to. When the political Left and the Right touch, ideologically, it is not collaboration or bi-partisanship government.

The likely result is totalitarianism. In case you slept through tenth grade history, totalitarianism is probably not a form of government we will be happy living under. For one, a totalitarian government might not allow this book to be published or purchased. *Worse*, the same sort of government could *force* us to read it!

Let us give you an example based on the subject matter in this book, *Abortion*.

Since Ronald Reagan attracted religious fundamentalists to the Republican Party in the late 1970's, the Republican Party has been proudly and recently, loudly, *pro-life*. Prior to this sync with what is now known as the *Religious Right*, neither the Republicans nor the Democrats paid much attention politically to *Abortion*. On the other side, there are members of the far left that believe that the government should control most if not all aspects of our day to day lives. Regarding Abortion, the far left and the far right are touching, ideologically. The far right wants the government to control the choices women have when it comes to their health care. The far left is ok with that, and members of both parties are looking to see what might be next that the government can control.

When we use the government to sharply limit a woman's right to control her own health care, we open the door for the government to control other aspects of our lives as well. Think of the logic this way; *If the Government can tell us that we must have a child, the Government can also tell us that we cannot have a child.*

Politics is a broad term that includes many definitions; including the Oxford Dictionary definition... *'politics is the activities associated with the governance of a country or other area, especially the debate or conflict among individuals or parties having or hoping to achieve power.'.*

The purpose of government - any government - is to protect its people. In the United States, the government is of the people, for the people, by the people. People make up the Political parties that present ideas in an effort to control the government - at least until the next election. When politics becomes more about seizing control - however that appears - and less about protecting the people, the people lose. For reference, see life in countries like China, Russia, and any one of several countries in Latin America. *Abortion* and many other issues that unnecessarily consume the political process are often thought to be moral issues. It is dangerous to conflate the political process with morality. We can safely have and share moral opinions that determine our individual day to day actions. When we try and apply our personal moral opinions to the broader public, we risk creating an overreaching government that alienates its population.

Neither of us know a single person that is *pro-abortion*. We doubt any of our readers, or for that matter any of the talking heads from the wide variety of available "information sources" know anyone who is *pro-abortion*. Readers may be devoutly pro-choice, meaning they believe that all the population has the right to autonomy with limited or no government interference when it comes to health issues. Similarly, we know people who are devoutly pro-life. We absolutely need both opinions and the people that have them in our population. Discourse is important. We don't think it is best for the population if personal limiting viewpoints become law.

In other words, if you are pro-life, good on you. Minister to people. Drive those big billboard trucks around with pictures of aborted fetuses on the side. Feel free to (peacefully and respectfully) talk as many women (who desire such a conversation) as possible out of having an abortion. Just leave those views behind when you fill out an election ballot - be it local, state or federal - instead, pick the best choice to *protect the people* running by using real, correct information gathered from reliable sources.

This book could have just as easily been about education and how the differing opinions from the left and right are negatively affecting how our children are being taught. Both sides have good points and terrible inconsistencies. (Let's be honest... *education* isn't - and should not be - titillating and the cover of the book would not have been nearly as interesting or as fun to create!) As a subject, education is more important than abortion. If our children do not learn critical thinking, do not learn the importance of knowing history, do not learn how to effectively communicate thoughts and ideas... well, the future of the United States of America is bleak. On a side and totally selfish note... We would both like very much it if the cashiers at our favorite shopping locations could properly count change back to us. Good Education. We are a happier and healthier people if everyone gets it!

The glory of the United States of America has always been its people. The constitution starts out," *We the People of the United States, in Order to form a more perfect Union, establish Justice, ensure domestic Tranquility, provide for the common defense, promote the general Welfare, and secure the Blessings of Liberty to ourselves and our Posterity, do ordain and establish this Constitution for the United States of America.*"

We the people... have been through a lot. This country was an experiment when it started. Whether or not we are actually a *democracy* is a question that can be debated. There are claims in 2025 that our *democracy* is at risk. Let us let you in on a secret; *Our form of government, the United States of America, has ALWAYS been at risk!* The concept of democracy means that our government will always be developing. If the government ever becomes static, we will no longer be a democracy! Our strengths - and let no politician try and tell you differently - is that we have always worked towards common goals of advancing the United States as a whole. Has the USA always been perfect and done no wrong? Absolutely not. *We the people* have truly fucked a lot of things up in the past and we are likely to fuck a lot more things up in the future. That's the cost of open dialog in a free state where people are free to act. Are we a failing state, subject to the whims of whatever figure has seized power? We never have been. That can change though. All it takes is for *We the People* to stop paying attention entirely or worse, stop caring.

The United States of America is great.

We have been and can continue to be a place the rest of the world envies.

The United States of America is a place of opportunity.

The United States of America is the Land of the Free and the Home of the Brave.

As a population, we need to continue to commit to working together so that it remains that way.

We encourage readers who are able to look for ways to participate in local government, even if it is just something simple like helping with elections. Encourage people to think critically, always, even when doing so goes against the current of popular thought. Enjoy, and treasure that we are a free people who can manifest destiny.

Understand that *manifesting destiny* means we can fuck things up if we aren't careful.

*Love Freedom while knowing that* **We the People** *are unique in the world!*

Hannah Love and Bhodi Freedom are writers of other stories and under different names. We are incredibly grateful to have readers, critical or celebratory. Books are but one of the symbols of the abundance and freedom that exists in the United States of America. We know that there will be people who find the subject matter in this book objectionable. There may even be groups (it is seldom a single person) who elect to ban this book in some manner. That's fine. No book in our great country is ever truly banned. We would rather the book wasn't burned (*wasteful!*), but if the mood strikes you, the pages are flammable.

We do believe in re-use. If you have purchased a physical copy of this book, we encourage you to share it when you have finished with it. You can leave it at your local coffee shop, in a used bookstore or donate it through your local donation center like Goodwill or the Salvation Army.

**Do what you can, when you can, how you can, to help your fellow human.**

May a Great Grasshopper bless both our great nation and all the rest of the world.

*XOXO*

*Hannah Love and Bhodi Freedom*

Catch you on the flip side…